Sekhmet's Son

By R.L. Hurst

"Sekhmet's Son," by R.L. Hurst. ISBN 978-1-63868-084-0 (softcover); 978-1-63868-085-7 (eBook).

Published 2022 by Virtualbookworm.com Publishing Inc., P.O. Box 9949, College Station, TX 77842, US. ©2022, R.L. Hurst.

Prelude:

Ten years, six months, and twelve days ago …

"ANOTHER HILL. ALWAYS ANOTHER CURSED HILL!

"Peace, love. You're letting yourself get worked up over nothing."

"Nothing? This ain't nothing! We've already spent two months on a supposed milk run. We're completely off the map, and our comm systems don't work, so no one has a clue to where we are, and I know I'm not the only one to notice that we haven't had the chance to wash ourselves properly for two weeks. All this, and here we are, climbing yet another Gods-damned hill!"

"Lionel, whining your ass off isn't getting us home any faster, so man up and roll the Hells out!"

The warrior sighed as he fell into line. It was always thus. Bel would go the route of sweet reason, Bezi would take the drill sergeant role, and between the two of them, Lionel Seckett would get back on focus and get back to being the lion they need when on a mission.

But, by all Seven Hells, what are we doing all the way out here? It was just supposed to be a recon mission! Some strange, unexpected signs of activity on the western outskirts of Tellerman—the largest, most economically advanced country near the western border of Aldemeron, the second largest of the three continents of Lyrodrylle, a mostly watery planet with the three continents and a plethora of islands of varying sizes. There used to be four continents, but Atlantis shook itself to bits and sunk beneath the waves forty thousand years ago.

The recon slowly evolved into an investigation when the four-person unit discovered the bodies, then the devastated homes, then whole villages destroyed. From what they could tell, the bodies looked torn open in some cases, and in other instances carefully incised by the use of a scalpel, or some exceptionally sharp instrument. Organs were missing from the bodies. All the bodies, including infants.

Another team of The Cadre might call in reinforcement. Perhaps a team of heavy hitters to clear the field for the rest. But Lionel and Belinda's unit *was* the cavalry called in for rescue. They were the heavies called in when a mission went balls up. They didn't call for backup. They simply reported what was found, then decided to seek out the perpetrators of such horror and bring them to final justice, as they had done countless times before. As horrific as the scene of a whole community being murdered was, the unit had seen worse in their seventy years in The Nemesene Cadre.

Belinda used her scrying skills and found a trail that led to Mandrake, a small coastal city on the southwest edge of Tellerman. It was a long haul, and they were glad they brought Hal Bergen with them on this op. Taking the place that belonged to Melene, Hal was simply a middle-aged, fit and healthy human. What he lacked in Talent and beyond-human physicality, he made up with his genius in crafting and serving ballistic weaponry, his positive, light-hearted demeanor, and his ability to operate any type of motorized vehicle. They found a transport in the village that fit all four of the team and their gear, and they made their way to Mandrake.

The team was relieved that there was no evidence of mass homicides in the seaport city, pleasantly surprised to run into a squad of retired agents of The Cadre that gave them a place to stay and a hand in the attempt to locate the perps, but disappointed that the trail they followed continued, out into the Liric Sea. Disappointed, but undaunted. Too many were brutally torn from life for the team to hand it off to another unit. Belinda scryed again, the former agents helped Hal find a strong, sturdy sea craft, Lionel bought it, and they went on.

It was two days out from Mandrake when they realized that their comm systems no longer worked. They couldn't find the fault in the gear. Very bad timing, as they were entering waters that had not been explored for nearly a thousand years. Since both Atlantis and the Island of Lemuria's disappearance, there was no reason to travel this far south and west of the Aldemeron continent. They were out of touch, effectively off the map, and resolved to go on into the unknown.

A bad combination, if safety was a major factor in your decision-making.

Another four days of scrying and sailing brought them to a nameless, mountainous crag sitting alone in the middle of the sea. The trail ended there. They disembarked, gathered their gear, and began walking, climbing, seeking the source.

After a day and a half of hard climbing, and rising 2000 yards higher than when they began, the four found themselves on a ledge, looking at a wall of rock, impossible for a 'normal' sapient being to climb.

"I guess we have to backtrack," Lionel sighed.

"No, we don't," Belinda replied worriedly. "According to my spells, this is where the source ends."

Hal felt himself shake, the slightest tremor. "Trap?"

"You do have a habit of stating the obvious, Mr. Bergen," Bezine snorted with warmth to the human who made himself keep pace with the supreme warriors, never complaining, never holding them back. She knew he came along because of the crush he had on her. She couldn't help him with that, she was too happily 'taken' that he really had no hope. But she did feel a great deal of affection for the tough but nurturing human.

"Damn, it's been so cursed long since anyone had the nerve to come after us," Lionel snarled. "Should have felt it!"

"That goes for us all, except Hal, of course," Bezine snickered. "We better st—"

A shot rang out. Bezine's head jerked back violently, and she plummeted off the rise. A second later, the team was surrounded by enemies. Standing on hoverboards before them. Kneeling on constructed shelves over and around them. They came into view as the platoon of Dark Arts Talents lowered the concealing shields. It's hard to detect spells that were already in place before you arrived in a new, unfamiliar space. The trap was as close to perfect as their unit had ever seen. But then, that level of meticulous detail was one of the chief reasons why this particular race of Sapients were so feared amongst all the other societies of Lyrodrylle.

"Dammit!" Belinda snarled. "Elves!"

She got her shield in place around them just before the onslaught of spells, bullets and bombs could reach them. She felt the impacts, but the shields held.

While she was reinforcing her shield spells, Lionel wrapped Hal in a spherical shield, as strong a shield as he'd ever crafted. "I'm sending you down. Find Bezine, get you and her on the boat, and get out of here. Don't worry about an attack, I'll stop 'em!" He didn't wait for a reply from Hal. He simply used his Earth spells to shape a passage through the rock and sent him off.

A few of the hovering elves tried to follow Hal's slowly descending bubble. They were blasted out of existence.

"Forget about the human!" one of the enemies snarled in his cruel, hateful voice. "We have The Secketts! We—"

His rant was cut off by Belinda's shock spear spell slicing him nearly in half. His death ensured that Hal would land safety, since the remaining enemy forces focused all their attention on the two warriors on the ledge. They needed to. Lionel and Belinda were both exemplar Battle Mages, and they had dealt with overwhelming numbers before. So many times before.

But never thirty Beldamai at once. The Dark Arts equivalent to The Light Arts' Battle Mage, a one-on-one attack by a Beldamus or Beldame would be of little contest to either Belinda or Lionel. Thirty of them? With a company of soldiers shooting off their relatively modern weaponry? Much more challenging. They both tried to form their heavy spells, like Thor's Hammer or Meteor Rain, but non-stop bombardment from their enemies did not allow them the time, so they were limited to the mostly single-person attack spells.

But the Secketts wouldn't quit. They couldn't. One more dead enemy was one less that would go after Hal and Bezine. And until they were standing at the funeral pyre, they refused to believe one bullet and a hard trip down the side of a mountain took out their Bezine. So they attacked.

Belinda shattered their shields, Lionel blew their heads off with his large-caliber handguns. They huddled under combined shields when the Dark Talents unleashed an appalling torrent of balefire, then scorched the sky with sun burst spells in response. The Elves using weapons couldn't be protected by the Talents for long, so after ten or so minutes, there were no more bullets to stop. The lesser Dark Art Talents soon followed the gunners into oblivion, leaving the two facing less than a score of The Beldamai. But they took hits. More than a few. Lionel's genetic immunity to magic shielded him and Belinda from most of the attacks, but not all. Lionel's left arm hung uselessly from an ice lance that found its way through the smallest of chinks in his defenses. Belinda was blind in one eye from a blocked Nova blast spell that still seared the retina. Neither could take the time to cast their healing spells—they had to struggle on.

So, they continued battling. Never giving up, never giving in.

But in the end, they lost.

The other fourteen Beldamai sacrificed themselves so that the last one could clamp the Nullifiers on the two. Bereft of access to their Talent, the two slumped to the ground, defeated.

"It took all of our resources to spring this trap on you two," the Beldamus snarled, his beautiful, evil face in a rictus of rage. "If it is any consolation, I am the last of the Ellovysian Beldamai, for now. And those minions you so happily wiped out of existence were of the very few available to us, at least until we've freed our people from The Trickster's Trap, may he be damned forever."

The Elf leaned in closer. "But, I promise you, you two will have such a long time satisfying our curiosity, lending your vaunted Talents to our various experiments. You will have plenty of time to ponder just how useless your efforts have been—all these decades spent trying to stop us, when what we learn from you two will be the foundation of our eventual triumph!"

As the hideous voice faded away, a tear slowly fell from Belinda's undamaged eye.

Maahes. Oh, my son! What will become of my precious one?

Part I

Chapter 1: Whys, Whats and Who
Mama said there'd be days like this...

WELL, MY MOTHER DIDN'T ACTUALLY SAY THAT, if my memory serves. But my aunt does. Often. Of course, she's usually not the one being sent through a brick wall while singing the stinkin' song.

It's weird, the stuff that passes through your head while your body passes through newly created entryways.

"¡Qué Carajo!"

Happily, the cashier of the storefront I just crashed through wasn't along the glide path of my body. Unless he was a lot like me, he'd been about as wrecked as his outer wall and about a third of his inventory. A whole store of hair care products? Really? Lucky I slammed through the fake hair section, I guess. Wiping off all the oils and gels would've sent me way over the edge.

I took my time getting back to my feet. Had to. The immediate impulse was to return serve on the Lycan douche that decided he had to flex on somebody. It would've been personally satisfying, but serving up a walking pile of scat sunny-side-up wasn't a part of the mission profile. So, yeah, let me take my time, get my game face back in place, and focus on the job.

The store clerk considered teeing off on me, but looked at the expression on my face, noted that one of the few items in the store that wasn't wrecked was me, and decided to lay in the cut, at least for the time being. Smart move. Even in the 2020's, most intelligent beings moved cautiously when in the presence of The

Angry Black Man. He wasn't getting paid anywhere enough to deal with that! Instead, he turned his attention to the laughing and loud talk coming from the other side of the wrecked wall.

"Damn, partnah! Did you see that?" howled one of Jackson's hangers-on. "He went BOOM! Right through that whole scraggin' wall!"

The four other members of Jackson Caine's posse were in hysterics, looking like a pack of hyenas instead of the were-cougars and coyotes they were. Laughing that hard, with no idea of the damage I might have taken, made them as jacked up as Jackson in my mind, or else quick to fall in with the program. If your top was as rich and as twisted a Were-Bear as Jackson was, then you fell in line with quickness, or you too might be plowing through a wall. And those limp-tooled turd buckets didn't look like they could handle the pounding.

"Like I was saying, why would you want a wannabe mall cop like that pipsqueak as your bodyguard, Trini?" Jackson snorted when he laughed. And slobbered. Ick.

"I'm startin' to wonder that myself," I heard my Primary mutter while I climbed through the hole. I saw the look on her face, and I felt that much more shamed and enraged.

And it was such a beautiful face. A captivating mix of Eurocentric and Afrocentric features in a nicely oval face, topped off with lips that seemed slightly too large for her face and hazel eyes that flamed with a passion, a drive that was way beyond average. All that sitting on top of a 'Good Lawd!' figure that was short in stature but packed with a delicious mélange of curves and muscles that reflected the perfect 'slim-thick' profile other females have spent thousands in plastic surgery to achieve. Even with the nearly miraculous achievements of Eliondrian medical technology, there was that clearly detectable something about the 'born' that lifted it just that little bit above the 'built'. And Trini was definitely lifted.

At that particular moment, all I saw was a face expressing a mix of confusion and profound disappointment. Disappointment in me? Likely. Oh, well. Off the job within days. Sucks to be me.

It would be a shame, though. Real big shame. The girl had no idea of the size of the target painted on her back.

4

Trinidad Flores. Age 25, of Puerto Rican descent, born and raised in the Bronx. Stage name: Selene. Rising star in the hip-hop culture. Unlike a number of young professionals in the industry, the girl had a set of pipes that could make a zombie wanna get to the dance floor. On stage, she was the real deal.

Off stage? Well…

I could hear the conversation from across the street. They weren't talking that loud, but my senses, like the rest of me, were on a level far beyond what would be considered 'normal', and that would be true on either side of The Veil.

"Seriously, Meg, do we really need this guy with the rest of the team?" Miss Up-and-Coming addressed this rather mean question to her manager, Meg Trasker, a youngish but experienced manager for a number of acts in the music industry. Meg's parent company, Universal Talent Agency, was the big dog in the business of talent management, and Meg was one of their rising stars. There was a reason, and it wasn't her hot looks and warm personality. It had a good bit to do with her nickname (that is, the one her rivals would use in polite society), 'The Pit Bull in Pumps.'

"Lyam comes highly recommended from a more than reliable source." Her tone was calm, unruffled, and frankly, not to be messed with. She pointed to me as I slowly crossed the street to where the crowd was gathered. "If you'll note, Trini, Mr. Seckett is walking, not limping, across the street. He's walking in a controlled manner, not like a hot-headed wild man looking for payback. From what I can see, he's more than tough enough to take a sucker punch from your boyfriend, and he's a professional. I would think that's exactly the kind of person you would want on your security team."

"I guess." Trini kept her frowny face, though. "At least all those muscles are good for something. But, I mean, he's so much younger than the rest of them! At least he looks younger to me."

"I vouch for him," the chief for our team volunteered in his normal gruff tone. The others on our team nodded in agreement. Out of the other four of our five-person security team, Ben Davies was the only one that had the slightest hint of a smile on his face, but he knew more about the capabilities of a child of The Pride than the rest, and he was a wise-guy by nature, so I had no issues.

To be fair, watching me fly across a two-way street and through a brick wall had to look pretty damned funny. But Greg Sykes, our chief, was a hardcore professional, and his team followed his lead.

"He comes from excellent stock, Ms. Flores, and he's highly recommended. I don't carry any lightweights or deadweights on my team."

"I guess," Trini repeated herself as she ran her eyes up and down my physique. Rather acutely, frankly, which was the reason her bear boyfriend decided to assert his dominance. She wasn't the first person, male or female, to check me out like they were looking over the selection at the local meat market. When you're built like me, with the chiseled good looks and chocolate skin tone (My lady's observations, not mine. But I do trust her judgement. Heh.), it comes with the territory. She was one of the few, however, that was eyeballing me while her jealous, domineering Lycan boyfriend was within arm's reach of my face. Hence, the unscheduled flying lesson.

This time, she was putting me through her scanner while there were ten feet and three other members of the security team between me and him. So all he could do was clench his massive hands and growl. Trini cut her eyes at Jackson, shutting him down in mid-growl, and she continued her inspection. Gotta say, her 'Do what I wanna do' attitude was more appealing to me than her face and physique. Good thing I put my 'personal' on lockdown and focused on my 'professional'. She was the client, nothing more, nothing less.

"I mean, he's cut up all nice and tight, all 'Mr. Ebony Universe' and everything," Trini continued, the look in her eye didn't match up with her demeaning commentary. "But he ain't even as tall as Tilsa there! I mean, come on!"

"Mr. Seckett is just a hair under six feet, and that's plenty tall enough in this business, Ms. Flores," Greg rumbled in reply. "As for Ms. Danville, who is also pretty new to the agency and our team, her mother is a native of Jötunheim, which is why she's taller than everyone else on the team."

I kept my snort of amusement internal. For the Chief, two years on the team was 'new'. They didn't seem to know a great deal about Tilsa, except for where she was from, she was hard-working and loyal, and she was toughest HaCK in the whole Blue Star Agency. HaCK was a term I first heard when I auditioned for Blue Star, meaning hard-core-killer. I appreciated the sentiment and adopted it for my own. So, yeah, Tilsa was their top-dog HaCK. Until me.

"Yeah, well, she might be more of a challenge than Stubby there," Jackson snorted again as he eyeballed Tilsa. Both looked to be about the same 6'8" in height, but Tilsa's physique was trimmer, and more tightly sculpted. Tilsa only smiled in response to his provocation. None of the folks on our team were a joke, but Tilsa was a whole other level of monster.

My intro to the team was a full-contact, all-out match with Tilsa. The aim was to simply see how long I could last with her. When it turned out that the real question was how long she could hang with me (about fifteen minutes before she had to tap out—pretty impressive, for someone not of The Pride!), Chief Sykes agreed with his bosses at Blue Star Security, the preeminent private security firm, that Melene Alabato, my aunt, wasn't just blowing smoke up their tailpipes when she told them, "You ain't getting me, I'm not going active on this. But you'll be on your knees in gratitude you get the kid!"

Tilsa wasn't the only test they threw at me. I think they even made up some stuff on the fly to throw at me, and I came up aces. I'm not bragging. Truly. But there's no way they could come up with anything that could top the nineteen years of tender loving Hell I had to endure with Aunt Melene. Smokey the Butthole Bear thinks he's 'all that' because he put me through a brick wall? Please, stop. Melene would've yanked out a section of the damned wall and thrown it at me!

Now, that's the 'Hard Core' I was raised on.

"All this chest-thumping is a waste of time, Trini," Meg huffed. "If we get moving now, we won't be late for your photo shoot, which UTA would appreciate greatly, because they wouldn't have to pony up overtime fees for the first time in a month. And the longer we stand here doing street theater, the more time someone has to slide under these limos and plant bombs."

"That's kinda paranoid, you know?" Flash Dee, Jackson's semi-official hype man, had to toss his two cents in.

"Using paranoia to my advantage bumps Selene here from rising star straight into mega star, loser," Megan snapped, officially done with the drama. "Let's get moving."

"Yo, Jackson, she callin' me a loser!" Flash looked up at his meal ticket. "You gonna handle that, right?"

I could see that the Lycan considered Flash Dee's jab. I could also see that Jackson wasn't a complete idiot, as he noted all five members of Trini's new security team eyeballing him, gleefully waiting for him to make a move.

"She ain't said jack to me," Jackson replied. "Stop whining like a two-dollar trick, fool!"

Megan paused in her stride. "That reminds me." She turned to her assistant. "Karl, go get the necessary info on the store over there. I'll be sending the bill for repairs to you, Jackson. You break it, you buy it, Mr. Caine. Let's hit it!"

Last trump played, we got everyone settled into the two high-end armored transports and Jackson's massive private ride, and we rolled out.

***

"I appreciate your restraint, Lyam," Megan noted as we pulled away from the luxury suites Trini's entourage was currently occupying in Lower Manhattan. "That could've went south real fast. Even more south, that is."

I sighed as I watched the nearly silent vehicles smoothly move along the flat, uncluttered road surfaces found in most of the Manhattan of the 2020s, streets unmarred by potholes and road crews, used by transports that were fueled by electricity, solar, and other forms of clean, emissions-free power. Nearly everything in view was connected directly or peripherally to the massive infusion of technology and trillions spent in recovery, nearly all sent from the other side of The Veil. New York City, like the rest of the U. S. and Earth, needed all the assistance The Pentagram could give after both Earth and Lyrodrylle were nearly wiped out of existence sixty years ago. I don't know what traffic was like before The Sundering. I've watched vintage shows and movies, read the texts, but I couldn't know just how thoroughly annoying it must have been to sit in smogged-out traffic, inured to the bellowing car horns, breathing the polluted air while attempting to make a way around yet another section of torn-up road undergoing continuous, seemingly useless repair. Just another not-so-subtle reminder of just how different life has become for the average human living in these last sixty years.

Yeah, and I'm sure watching the wall of your store being blown apart, and some dude dusting himself off and striding back through the hole wouldn't be considered 'normal' either!

"Bears are possessive and territorial, Ms. Trasker," I replied calmly. I was still pissed, though. "I should have remembered that and made some space when he came out of his car, like the rest of the team did."

"That's a pile of cat-scat, Lyam. Don't look so surprised. I've heard a few people from the Mystic side of The Veil saying that a bunch of times. I like it, and I get to indulge my sweet tooth for swearing without getting all the stares from the prudes, so I'm claiming it. Anyway, I've dealt with Were-bears before. Just about every variety of Weres. Jackson's an immature, overprotective knuckle-dragger. Trini's a sweet-natured soul under all that 'hood rat' act. That's the only reason Jackson's lasted this long. But our girl can't stand anyone hovering over her, trying to boss her, so his days are numbered, trust me on that!

"And remember, your team was contracted for personal security to Trini." Meg's eyes narrowed in intensity. She didn't play when it came to business. "That's hard to do when you're twenty feet away from her. And didn't I tell you to call me Megan, by the way?" Her lips quirked into a smile. They were rather nice lips. "At least, when your chief isn't within hearing?"

"Hell, Megan, with these Numerian comm systems, we ain't sure when he isn't able to hear us!" Ben sniggered before I could respond. I appreciated Ben riding with me, Megan and her assistant Karl as we made our way to Midtown. The others traveled with Trini and her older sister in the other transport. The older man had already keyed into the fact that I was not even close to as calm as I was acting, and had no problem lightening the mood and giving me space to get it together, as a veteran operator ought to do with a rookie. Besides that, Ben's focus was electronics and weapons, so my audition for the team had little to no effect on him. Even with the chief, there was a minimal but real undercurrent of tension. They expected me to be good, since I was personally vouched for by my aunt. They didn't expect me to take out the whole company's best melee fighter, equal the scores of their top sharpshooters, and wreck all comers when it came to bladed combat. Then there was the icing on the cake. Enough icing for more than a few cakes, actually.

As one of the leading companies in the field, Blue Star Security recognized the need to have users of magic on their roster. Potential threats to their clients came in all different forms, from a multitude of angles. Unlike prior to The Sundering, those who lived their lives on Earth were well aware of the presence of Talents, those beings who could tap into the Arcane Energies surrounding all of creation, and wield that energy, or magic (Mana, for some), to do wondrous or horrible deeds. Hence, to be able to offer comprehensive protection to their clients, Blue Star needed to have as many Talents on their roster as they could find, and/or afford. Reliable Talents did not come cheap.

The high price tag of a competent spell-caster was one issue. Another was, for the most part, weaving magic was all they could do well. Ninety percent of the time, a Talent's focus on developing their skills in The Arts made them close to useless with weapons, a liability in unarmed combat, and if you gave a Talent a blade, they just might slice off their own limbs. A security team that included a sorcerer or sorceress on their roster had to surround the Talent with some hardcore warriors that would protect the Talent as well as the client.

Unless, of course, you happened to stumble over one of those ten percenters. Someone who was trained, nearly from birth, to develop all phases of warfare, including The Arcane, and born with the specific genetic advantages to be able to do exactly that.

Someone like me.

"Is this your first assignment in the field, Lyam?"

I blinked away from my focus on observing the traffic, looking for potential threats to our three-vehicle caravan.

"First with Blue Star, Megs," I responded. She smiled a bit more, pleased that I was comfortable with being that familiar with her. "Second in the field." I looked around at the others in the transport. "And you folks can call me Lee, if you want."

"What was the first, Lee?" Ben asked as he continued scanning the streets from his side of the transport. These particular vehicle types were specifically designed with security in mind. The driver's compartment was sealed off, the body of the vehicle and understructure were armored and reinforced, and the passenger section was closed in with armored, tinted Invisi-Steel, another product from Lyrodrylle—or as the folks from Earth like to say, The Mystic Lands. Basically, Invisi-Steel looks like and has the transparency of glass, and can be reinforced to withstand the force of a missile or the shell of a Main Battle Tank, depending on how much you were willing to spend. The vehicle's design allowed us an unobstructed, 360-degree view of everything around us, while all the people outside the transport could see nothing but a 6-wheeled, electrically powered vehicle, sleekly designed like the late-model personal transports that have grown so popular since The Sundering, though a bit higher, longer and wider than their civilian siblings, with an additional pair of tires. I liked how the seating in the transport was wrap-around instead of in rows, and the Invisi-steel tinted so we could see out without anyone outside able to see in. The vehicle was a favorite amongst security firms.

"My first field work was in Lyrodrylle." I answered Ben. "My first time on the other side of The Veil. There was a village on the northeastern border of Dresselor. The folks there weren't too keen on how their latest Head of State was pretty much wrecking their economy, so they didn't pay their taxes. When a necromancer and her company of zombies came to raise Hell, literally, they were left to fend for themselves."

"So, you were sent with a team to deal with the threat?" Karl, Megan's assistant asked.

"Um, no." I shrugged. "Aunt Melene judged it a minor op, so she sent me."

"Alone?" Megan gasped. "Against a Necromancer and her horde?"

"Not so much horde," I shrugged again as I continued watching the streets. "There were only about a hundred or so. The woman was just getting started. Melene came along, but only as an evaluator."

"Evaluator?" That one got Ben to look away from his watch for a few seconds. "She was using a potentially fatal field op as an exam?"

"Ben, you sat in on the prep for this assignment," I responded. "You know who she is. What she is. What I am. And why I'm on this team."

"Yeah," I saw Ben nodding out of the corner of my eye. "It's just, you know, you don't carry yourself like some kinda superhuman Ultimate Warrior-type, y'know? I mean, sure, you look like a linebacker that juiced up on steroids one time too many, and all, but you don't go swannin' around looking for a fight, showing off and all. It's like you try to hide the fact that you could punch a hole into this ride, or swirl your hands around and lift it and throw it somewhere!"

"The Invisi-Steel is reinforced armor grade, Ben," I snickered. "I might be able to dent it up pretty good, though."

"That's all? Well, Hell." my teammate chuckled.

"So, how did you do?" Megan interjected. "The villagers were saved?"

"Yeah, they're fine. Only minor damage to the building structures. Nobody else killed or turned after we got there."

"And the Necromancer?" Karl asked.

I turned my gaze to him, his expression anxious, almost eager. "I took her out," I answered quietly.

My response, and the look on my face, ended that particular line of inquiry.

"So you passed your, exam, Lee?" Megan's tone was more subdued than before.

"Yeah. Aunt pointed out that I needed to control my emotions better, and pay more attention to potential collateral damage, but, yeah, I did her proud. At least, that's what she said."

"And how do you evaluate yourself?" Ben demanded, but in a supportive way.

I thought about it for a moment. "The field's different from the dojo," I answered quietly, remembering how I felt at the end, standing over the smoking remains of what used to be a living, sapient being. "More real. More…permanent."

Ben looked on, holding me in a firm gaze, a gaze full of his own experiences. "Second thoughts?"

I smiled grimly. "Nah, Ben. Just an adjustment in how I think. No doubts. I know who I am, and who I want to be."

"Well," Megan replied firmly. "All the same, I still hope you, your aunt, the D.I.A., and the Nemesenes are wrong, and Trini isn't a potential target in this stinking mess!"

"Me too," I responded fervently. "Me too."

Chapter 2. Why Him?

I hoped we were wrong, but prepared for being right.

MY MIND WENT BACK TO THE MEETING that took place in one of the conference rooms of U.T.A. In attendance was the firm's president, Josef Hellerman; and Len London, his V.P. in charge of Operations; Nestor Dellums, Director of Division of Interspecies Affairs, Northeastern U.S. Sector; Megan, as Trini's manager; and Brian Foster, Chairperson of Blue Star Security. Included in on the conference was myself and my aunt, Melene Alabato, in her role of Deputy, Field Operations, for the Nemesene Cadre. That last bit was a bit of a revelation to me. I knew that my family was involved in The Cadre to some degree, but had no idea to what extent and level. She showed me her badge a few times, but I didn't know what rank it was at the time, and she didn't bother to tell me. To use human mode of rankings, my absent (and please, by the Gods, not dead) parents were the equivalent of naval captains and my aunts, Melene and Bezine (who I also missed madly) were lieutenant commanders. Director Dellums may have had a higher rank than Melene but, in accordance with The Pentagram Accords, agreed to by the United Nations and all the major governments of Earth, if an agent of Command rank within The Cadre is present on a field operations, they immediately take precedent. Period. The humans weren't happy about it, but that requirement was one of the few iron-clad agreements that had to be in place if they were to receive the gargantuan Assistance Package that came with it, the trillions of dollars in grants and access to technological advancements humans couldn't even imagine for another hundred years. The human governments signed on the dotted line. They desperately needed the assistance from The Pentagram to slow the death rates and speed up the recovery from *The Sundering.*

Even with Melene and Director Dellums having worked on joint operations before, he wasn't the least bit happy about Melene flexing on him. I laughed internally as I watched Dellums try to stare down Melene and fail miserably. Very few people were able to. When my Auntie puts her eyes on a person, there's the innate desire to run like every demon imaginable is chasing you.

I've always been fascinated with her, frankly, weird as all Hells' eyes; amber in color, a smaller pupil than most, and light striations radiating from the pupil. When I was younger, I thought all lionesses of Sekhmet's Pride had them, because my other aunt, Bezine, had the same kind of eyes. But no. Blues, greens, browns like mine, and greys—like most beings similar to humans. Only my aunts, and my father, had these unique orbs to see with.

Even weirder? Melene showed me old photos of my father when he was 11 years old. His eyes were brown, like mine.

Even weirderer...wait, that's not a word. Ever-increasing weirdness? Their eyes closely resembled another predator in the animal kingdom.

You guessed it. Lions.

Maybe you didn't guess. But then, why would you? Sorry, back to the eyes.

I asked Melene a few times how the three of them could have similarly strange eyes. She simply smiled and said, "I have no idea, Lee. I wasn't born with them. My eyes used to be green. We've been to a few experts, and they've all agreed. We pretty much have eyes very similar to a predator that hunts in the night, except that we can see the full color spectrum, when lions and the other animals cannot. Something about three cones instead of two or some such thing. But aside from my vision improving dramatically, they've become the most attractive thing about me. Don't you think?"

I was 14 at the time, and my hormones were sending rather strident messages about the tall, curvaceous woman standing before me. But I was wise for my years. "Yes, I agree."

She chuckled. "Such a liar."

So busted.

Looking to the side of my aunt's head instead of at her (can't hang), the Director continued his diatribe. "Frankly, Ms. Alabato, I'm not at all convinced that this newbie should be involved in such a potentially dangerous and highly charged scenario!" He waved a dismissive hand in my direction, treating me in a rather rude manner. "The boy looks like he hasn't even lost his baby teeth yet. How could he possibly be of much use?"

That was when I decided to grow the goatee and mustache I'm rocking to this day. Got real tired of the 'fresh-faced kid' pile.

Dellums continued, casting his gaze around the conference table. "And while we're at it, I'm not entirely convinced that this conspiracy actually exists. I agree that it is tragic that a number of young women in the performance industry have died so suddenly, without any clear explanation of how it could happen, but to connect them all to a murderous agenda? What would be the purpose? And why these particular women? What qualifies them as targets?"

"Jesus Christ!" Megan Trasker stormed heatedly to her feet. "I'm not a supposed operative in any of your groups, and even I can see the obvious links! Mimi Le Clerc was being recognized for her highly unique interpretation of classical music, and no other human being could match her skills on the cello. Himiko Agawa was merging techno and jazz in a way never done before, and the music Alma Chidoze was creating, using nothing but instruments of African ancestry, was creating a goddamned cultural uprising!

"And those are just three examples! Thank God there's only been those three on this side of The Veil, unlike the twenty young men and women that have been taken out across The Mystic Lands in the last ten years. What the hell do you need, Director? A written manifesto and a crystal ball?!"

I had to look away. It wouldn't do to start laughing in such a highly charged atmosphere.

"I don't have a problem accepting the connection, Ms. Alabato," Hellerman's V.P. interjected while Dellums spluttered. "But this thing about—what you called them, Mee-Nads?"

"We believe they call themselves The Maenads," Melene answered in her low, rich tone. "We have not been able to establish a dialogue with any of the current members of the group. They tend to die violently before, during, and immediately after a given attack, so the information we're working with is admittedly sketchy.

"The group was named after the mythic nymphs that were associated with the Greek God Dionysus. They first started their operations thousands of years ago, when they went after Orpheus, a citizen of Lyrodrylle who was on a walkabout through ancient Greece. The premise was that the beauty of his voice and skill on his harp drove them into an ecstatic frenzy, but they were in all likelihood already psychotic and simply used him as an outlet to their collective insanity. They chased him all the way back through The Veil, and he barely survived their attacks."

Melene smiled grimly. "He wouldn't have survived, actually, if The Cadre, with the armed forces of Sekhmet's Pride, hadn't stopped the nutballs cold. Anyway, they go through cycles of dormancy, then sudden outbreaks of frenzy. The deep thinkers in the Cadre are convinced there is a mystical component to be factored in. We wipe them out, all of them, when they show up, but a hundred or so years later, a whole new set of maniacs pop up out of nowhere, with the same agenda, targeting unique, young, emerging talents that have the potential for greatness. There is no agreement amongst the analysts on why the dormancy period has been so greatly reduced these past thirty years."

Melene sighed, leaned back in her chair. "You all need to understand that the Cadre's casefiles have quite a few unsolved cases involving the death of incomparable music talents that died in their twenties or thirties by mysterious causes. Frenzied maniac swarms weren't present, but the circumstances were, highly irregular, at the least. On your side of The Veil, the list of those we still consider unsolved include Wolfgang Mozart, Franz Shubert, George Gershwin and his sudden brain tumor, the blues artist Robert Johnson, jazz trumpeter Clifford Brown, Buddy Holly. The list goes on. They all had in common incomparable talent, original, gifted viewpoints on the future of music in their genre, and seemingly were on the verge of introducing a new, innovative leap forward in music."

My aunt seemed to age before my eyes as she stared into the conference table. "And, of course, they also had in common that they died, way, way too soon. They, and so many others died too soon. Sudden illnesses from out of the blue. Caught in the middle of unscheduled protests that turned violent any without warning, travel accidents, or, they simply disappeared, never to be seen again. Trust me, people, we in the Nemesene Cadre by this time are angered, saddened, but not all that surprised.

"And now, this. The Cadre was slow to catch on to this latest surge, because we're all in the same boat with every other being on either side of The Veil. We lost a lot of field operatives and analysts in *The Sundering*, and lost even more during the recovery process. The populations on both sides of The Veil are steadily increasing again, while the field operatives we have left are finding it difficult to keep pace."

"Wouldn't have been a problem if you people would have kept *your* problems on *your* side of The Veil!" Director Dellums snapped snidely.

"Yes, Nestor," Melene responded serenely. "Then all you would have to deal with was your Doomsday Clock ticking down to midnight, and Earth being wiped out in a nuclear Armageddon!"

"We have no time for this garbage!" Hellerman snapped, his hard, chiseled features turning a darker shade in anger. "We survived the damned *Sundering*, we're all still recovering, nuclear armament is a thing of the past, and I'm worried that one of my clients is about to be murdered for no other reason except she's brilliant!" He pointed one of his long, thick fingers in my direction. "Now please, explain to me why you think this young man might be helpful in this case."

"First, Maahes Seckett," She paused and sighed at my look. "Alright, he prefers going by Lyam. Anyway, 'Lyam' is a highly trained field operative. He has had experience in the field, under my observation, and he performed admirably."

Hmph, all she said to me was, "You did well enough, I suppose." Talk about underselling!

"Second, and this is critical. We are addressing the situation so it should not be an issue in the very near future, but as of this moment, there is a significant shortage of Nemesene field operatives in this part of your planet. We have a few in the pipeline, but none with Lyam's particular skillset, and he is ready for the field now."

"Yes, but—"

"Nestor, I agree with your assessment that he is, basically, a rookie, but the other factor that needs to be considered is that I, you, and the field operatives you have available, are known entities. That is simply a fact. Those that oppose us, even these supposed fanatics, know who I am and would have no problem identifying your people, if they haven't already done so." She smiled slowly. "You *cannot* assume that our enemies are anywhere near as dumb as we want them to be, Nestor, and I'm sure they've been keeping as much of an eye on us as we have on them!"

Dellums leaned back, thinking. "Hmm. A new face. A new hire into Blue Star Security. Misdirection. Okay. It's clearer now. If they begin a dossier on him, he'll be given the same level of scrutiny as those in that sector of activity. Your people are watched, Brian, but not to the degree of agents for the D.I.A. or the Nemesenes."

"Thank God," rumbled the Chairperson. "There's enough paranoia involved in our business. I don't want to lose more sleep thinking about who's watching the watchers!" He nodded to me succinctly, without insult. It was appreciated. "So, what exactly is it about this kid, Ms. Alabato? I've got fine people in my organization. Real Warriors. We've got Talents, too. Ranked 2 people in Sorcery, even a ranked 3 Sorceress."

Melene smiled.

"You've got warriors. And you've got Talents. Tell me, Mr. Foster, do you have any Warriors who are *also* ranked 4 Sorcerers?"

That shut him up. That shut down chatter across the whole room as they all leaned back in their seats—some in shock, one or two in fear.

Dellums cleared his throat roughly. "A Warrior? And a Talent?" He wiped a bit of sweat off his brow. "He's a *Battle Mage*?"

"No," Melene responded firmly. "Not yet. He has achieved far beyond the level of Warrior skills required for the ranking, but he has only just achieved his level 4 Sorcery ranking, according to his Maestra, and he has more development to undergo before he qualifies for his rank 5, and then to qualify for the Battle Mage trials. But he is close. Closer than any I've seen in a while."

Brian Ford leaned forward. "Level 4 ranking? Where's his staff? Aren't all practitioners of the Arts supposed to have a wizard's staff?"

"Yes. They are." Melene looked at me, her predator's eyes glowing slightly, and nodded.

Not much into 'dog and pony', but whatever. I stood up from my chair and held out my left arm, showing the sleeve of the black Duster I wore into the conference room. (I got a few looks when they saw me wearing the long coat instead of a suit, but look, my aunt got me the coat for my nineteenth birthday, it's a hella smokin' coat with a ton of unique features, as comfortable as a set of pajamas, and I *would* go to sleep with it on if I could!) I pulled up the sleeve and displayed the inside of my forearm. The folks could see that there was a long lump in my arm, about an inch wide. Towards the wrist, the 'lump' ended with a black, round knob of wood, about the size of a ball bearing, that glowed with a sense of warmth and well-being. Well, at least to me it did.

"Let's go, Old Man," I thought in my head firmly.

In less than a second, a thick sliver of wood flew from my arm and into my left hand, then the sliver expanded, growing wider and longer until a staff of naturally black coloring, matching my height of 5'11" or so exactly, quietly pulsated in my hand. The embedded gems flashed with greeting. Show-off.

"Well, you don't see *that* sort of thing every day," snorted Chairman Foster. "Even hanging around Talents!"

Ford leaned forward in inspection. I turned my staff to accommodate. He looked specifically at the row of gemstones. At the midpoint of the staff was the first ruby, indicating the Wizard, 1st Degree. Then came the four moonstones indicating 2nd through

5th Degrees, followed by the second ruby of a 1st Degree Sorcerer. This was followed up the shaft by three emeralds.

He looked up at me and slowly nodded in respect. In the Arcane World, you don't get honors you didn't earn. He could only guess what it took to earn a 4th Degree Sorcerer rank. In my case, he wouldn't even be close. Imagine bringing a shot glass of water into The Inferno. You'd start to get a clue.

I hadn't spoken in the conference until then. Some seemed to be caught off guard by my somewhat low tone. *Definitely, some facial hair was in order.*

"A wizard staff can assume whatever shape and size the Talent wants, once they have bonded. A Talent can operate without his or her staff, but there would be a major loss in the amount of reserved Mystic energy and stored memory of spells that could be available. To access this storage, a Talent has to have the staff in physical contact. My aunt and I tinkered with a number of methodologies through which my staff remained available to me while keeping my hands free for weapons and/or unarmed combat. I finally We decided to copy the technique used by a number of cultures in this world, those that pierce then mold their skin for religious or artistic purposes. In my case I built a shunt, or a sheath, into my arm. Being what I am, it was difficult to build an artificial hole into my arm without it healing closed, but I finally convinced my staff to assist in convincing my body to heal around it, instead of over it."

"What do you mean, 'being what I am'?" UTA's president asked, and then his jaw dropped. "Wait a minute! Maahes Seckett? Seckett? Your last name is *Seckett*?"

From the looks around the room, it seemed he wasn't alone in finally connecting the dots.

"Jesus wept!" Brian Foster whispered. "They had a *kid*?!" He looked to Dellums, who wearily nodded his head.

"Yes. Lionel and Belinda Seckett, Battle Mages themselves, God help us, had a son."

"Well, damn!" Foster eyeballed Melene. "You might think this only a temp gig, lady, but I'm warning you now—you're gonna have a hard time gettin' him back from me!"

"Let's table that discussion until *after* this Maenad problem issue is dealt with, Mr. Foster," my aunt replied with a grin.

Chapter 3: What's in a Name?
The photo shoot went well enough.

I GOTTA TELL YOU, I WAS DAMNED GLAD I was there as a bodyguard. With all the shoe-string thick outfits and "Anything Goes!" poses, there's no way I would've been as cool as Jackson was. Then it dawned on me. He never even glanced at the gyrations Trini was going through, not even once. He was standing off to one side, staring at everyone else. Homeboy was staring at everyone who was staring at her. Either in warning, or in recording the ones who were drooling, so he could express his displeasure.

Was he really *that* insecure? What a tool. A rusty, bent tool at that.

He looked in my direction twice. The first time, I noted the slight smirk on his face. The second time his gaze turned in my direction, he saw me staring right into his grill. Again, Jackson proved he had working brain cells, and that he was in touch with his internal instincts. He might not have known who or what I was for sure, but his reaction to my dead gaze assured me that he was now quite aware of how lucky he was to be on this side of the ground. He blinked, pulled his eyes away from me and displayed his 'Lurking Menace' routine elsewhere.

None of them, Trini, and her entourage, Jackson and his posse, none of them knew me as anything more than a muscle-bound black man, dressed in all in black, and quietly taking in the territory. Jackson's family was pretty high in the 'wealthy' zone, and his father was one of the chief supporters to Clarence Ramsey, The Duke of Walminster in the massive Duchy of Teralon in Lyrodrylle and First Alpha of the Long Fang Clan of Lycans on either side of The Veil. The heads of the clan might know the significance of my being the son of Belinda and Lionel Seckett, but it's been forty years since my parents' most remembered exploits, and they've been 'missing, presumed dead' for the last ten years, soon to be eleven, so those around forty years old or less might have less than a clue to what the Seckett name engendered.

It wasn't like I was traveling under an assumed name. I was too proud of my parents and my name to even consider that. It's just…well, folks are just too busy to pay much attention to history. Which is sad, considering how often we repeat the same dumb-as-all-Hells mistakes.

And no, I'm not contradicting myself. I don't use my actual first name for a few good reasons. Good enough for me, at least. Off the top, people in general don't have a clue as to how to say it correctly. M-Ah-Heese, rhymes with 'geese'. Seems simple enough to me. But you get tired after a while. The time for 'Maahes' will come. I'm good with 'Lyam' for now.

It was my Aunt Bezine's idea to name me Maahes, and she lobbied for it pretty hard. For some reason, my memories of times before my parents and Aunt Bezine left out on a 'No Big Deal' mission were difficult to recall clearly, but I do remember that as tough as Melene might be, she was a fluffy bunny when compared to Bezine. Bezine didn't put her foot down often, but when she did, folks on the other side of the planet felt the tremors. It was Bezine's idea to give me the name of the son of Sekhmet, the Egyptian Goddess of War.

Prior to her time as a deity, Sekhmet was simply the great-great-granddaughter of Eliondra, the General of the Atlantis Defense Force, and the one who sacrificed herself, and thousands of her forces, to ensure the survival of those Atlantean refugees that were able to make it to the airships that took the survivors off their small continent, as it crumbled into the sea. Eliondra made sure that a good number of her fellow members of the race created by the Atlanteans were included on the refugee ships, but there just wasn't enough room for everyone. The Atlanteans renamed the land they settled on *Eliondra*, in memory of her sacrifice.

Most of the warriors the Atlanteans bioengineered into existence grew and thrived along with the former Atlanteans, but some began to wander. One of those was Menchit, Sekhmet's mother, who made her way through The Veil, traveled up through Africa, and eventually found herself in what is known as Ancient Egypt. Sekhmet's mother considered the Egyptians moronic in their worship of a battalion of gods and goddesses who were nothing more than a bunch of natives of Lyrodrylle 'having a bit of fun' with the primitive humans. This didn't stop her from taking advantage of the situation, and the Egyptians were soon worshipping a new, foreign goddess that, the myths declared, came up from the Nubian Lands to lead the Egyptians in war. Her daughter, Sekhmet, decided to raise the ante and shaped herself as a goddess of War, Chaos and Retribution. Then, she began to quietly, or not so quietly, eliminate the competition. Sekhmet had two sons that followed her into myth, Maahes and Nefertum, but what went 'Underreported' in Egyptian writings but was fully laid out in The Pride's Chronicles, was that Mother and Daughter started having major issues. Sekhmet was the more popular, but Menchit's followers were the more inclined to annihilate everything in their path, in the name of their goddess. Seeing the possibility of both Upper and Lower Egypt being wiped out of existence, Sekhmet took an army of her acolytes and left, letting her mother use her name and assume the role of Goddess of War for both parts of Egypt.

Sekhmet and her acolytes made their way into and throughout the African continent, parts of Asia, and even the Americas. Eventually, her granddaughter led the whole tribe back through The Veil, landed on and conquered a pretty large island a few hundred miles off the coast of the Supercontinent Pangea, and founded the nation of Sekhmet's Pride, holding fast to the truth that they were indeed direct descendants of both Egyptian Lioness Goddesses, but to Sekhmet went the honor of the naming, for her choosing the welfare of others over fighting an Extinction-Level war that would result in everyone losing, and dying.

Once the word went out, all existing remnants of these bioengineered super-beings made their way to the new nation, and Sekhmet's Pride wasted little time in growing into a world power on Lyrodrylle. A nation of superhuman Warriors tends to make an impression on folk.

Bezine wanted me named for the first child of Sekhmet, a true Son of the Lioness. Also, she wanted to make a statement. Maahes was the name of a God. A *Lion* God. One who was dominant, never subservient. It's no coincidence that, of all the males born into The Pride, not one of them was ever given 'Maahes' as a name. Sekhmet's Pride is a Matriarchal society, from the Lioness, or ruler, all the way down to the sanitation workers and street sweepers, if there were any. Women ruled. The government, businesses, homes. Women were 'Lionesses', and men were simply males. Of all the men of that race, there had never been a man that was given the title, 'Lion'.

Until my father. And he more took it than received it.

Lionel Seckett accomplished this recognition for his deeds before, during and after *The Sundering*, which included the heroic acts performed by him, my mother and my aunts during *The Battle of Tandora Heights,* when they saved, virtually on their own, a whole division of The Pride's defense force from annihilation by two legions of ghouls, liches, and feral vampires that were supporting the last remnants of warlocks and hags of The Brotherhood of The Red Hand. As much as they resented his existence, it was of great benefit to the rescued lionesses that my father, like me, was raised outside of the direct influence of The Pride's bias and was able to reach his greatest potential, both as a Child of The Pride and as an Arcane Talent.

Melene enjoyed telling me her favorite part of the story. It seems that, after Dad was given so many medals and awards from grateful societies that he could hardly stand up straight, the hierarchy of Sekhmet's Pride began to look more than a little foolish and petty for not celebrating his efforts, for no other reason than he was 'A *male* who didn't know his place in the world'. They threw together a haphazard event, which was poorly attended, and made no bones about how he could consider their efforts as a great condescension for a mere male. To their shock, the ungrateful member of their weaker sex laughed in their faces, tossed the hunk of metal to the ground, and replied, "Thanks, but No Thanks. I don't go where I'm not welcome, and I don't take gifts from Strangers." He and his team, who were Mom, my aunts, and 'Uncle' Hal Bergen, walked off the podium, out of the city, to the docks, onto the ship that brought them to the island, and never looked back. It was a young girl of The Pride, holding her shocked mother's hand as they watched Lionel lead my Family out the gates of the capital city, shoulders back, head held high, who was only the first to say, "Did you see his eyes, Mama? How he walked? Was that a lion? A *real* lion?"

The worldwide embarrassment of the event stung The Pride badly. Patrina Journey, Lioness and ruler of The Pride, subsequently sent a representative to my parents and asked them to accept her apology and quietly accept more fitting awards for their efforts. My father was inclined to refuse, but his wife and guardians changed his mind. The Pride's High Council grumbled, but conceded. It went unannounced, so the rest of the population of the nation didn't know of it. To most of Sekhmet's Pride, Lionel Seckett was still an ungrateful male who didn't know his place.

So I understood where Bezine was coming from, and I appreciated it. I do appreciate the name. Melene thinks I dislike the name. I don't. I just simply like the way 'Lyam Seckett' sounds. 'Lee Seckett' sounds cool too.

But beyond that, and beyond dealing with people saying my name wrong all the damn time, I don't want to be considered a 'Son' of The Lioness because of my name. I want it because I *earned* it. I'll carry my name, proudly, when people see who I am, what I've done, and come to the conclusion that *I can't be anything else* but *a lion!* A true Child of the Goddess of War and Chaos.

Sekhmet's Son.

Until that day, my beloved Aunt Bezine, wherever you are— thanks, but no thanks. Not yet.

As is usually the case, there are those who see right through all the silliness and see you for who you are, and a ton of those were at the children's hospital that Trini's entourage visited after the photo shoot.

Trevor's House was one of the larger medical facilities my parents built a few years after the flood waters receded from the Tri-State Area, a tragic casualty of *The Sundering*. There were a lot of people who were homeless, sick and hungry. The Pentagram-sponsored efforts were generous and extensive, but there were still an uncountable number of children left orphaned and exposed to diseases that had gone dormant, but came back in force because of the severe disruption of the world. My parents considered themselves New Yorkers, and far past the usual concept of 'wealthy'. They couldn't leave it to others to help the children, so they bought out Forest Hills General Hospital, rebuilt it from the ground up, and had it full of children and families in need in just under three years. As was often the case for them, they owned it, did not charge the patients a dime, and made it clear to potential donors that this was not going to be a profit-based endeavor. It didn't take long for *Trevor's House*, named after the first patient that was admitted into the facility, to be recognized as one of the finest medical institutions on the planet, and the donations rolled in when it became clear that no patient was turned away, including the children of wealthy parents who had watched their children suffer agonies at other hospitals. It was kept simple for the medical staff and administration at Trevor's House. If you weren't there for the children, you weren't there for long. And considering the financial packages my parents put in place, those medical professionals became born-again nurturers with quickness.

The children, in between getting better medical service than anywhere else on Earth, were all die-hard fanatics for *Selene*. It did the heart good that when Megan suggested they drop by *Trevor's House* for a visit, the star's response was a spontaneous '*Hell*, yeah! Let's roll!"

Her boyfriend and his crew rumbled some, but those of Trini's family that were in the posse made sure to tell her Security Team that more than a few of Trini's childhood friends had spent time in the hospital for some serious issues, from Sickle Cell Anemia to

Cancer treatments, and all were better for the Hospital's top flight, open arms policy.

"Trini's become a donor as well, you know," Liza, Trini's younger sister confided to me as we loaded up in the transports.

"That's a pretty righteous thing to do!" I enthused with her.

"Yeah? I don't see you reachin' in *your* pocket!"

I simply smiled slightly at whichever of Jackson's cronies this one was. Didn't bother with learning his name. Wasn't worth the effort.

"People do the best they can, when they can!" Liza snapped at the nameless Were-Drone. "Trini don't care what other people do with their money. Maybe you shouldn't either!"

The drone wanted to respond, probably rudely, but my placing myself in between, with the correct facial expression, helped us to move things along.

It took just under forty minutes for us to arrive. Happily, Megan made sure to call ahead, so there was a small group waiting out front, and the facility was reasonably prepared for an 'Unexpected' visit. I took a quick look around and relaxed. My parents made sure that the hospital's security system and guards were about as competent as those employed by Blue Star, so I knew the grounds were secure, even ten years after their disappearance.

I think Megan was the only one who noticed that the hospital's Chief Administrator looked in my direction with a deeply puzzled look on his face, then with my brief shake of the head, focused on the celebrity heading towards him at speed. After the intros were made, we spent the next few hours visiting the kids, all of whom were almost levitating out of their beds and chairs when the widely smiling, laughing hip-hop star came into their view. I lagged behind a bit, so I could smile and joke with a few of the patients and medics that recognized me from my bi-weekly visits, making sure to let them know that I might be busy for a while, but I'd be back ASAP.

"You been here before?"

I looked up from the sweetie I was joking with and saw Tilsa and Karl, Megan's assistant, looking on with interest. I shrugged.

"Once or twice."

"Yeah, right," The little traitor giggled, then stuck her tongue out at my look. Tilsa raised an eyebrow as Karl chuckled.

"Look," I replied quietly. "You already know who I am, who my family is. And you do know they own and rebuilt this hospital, right?"

"Them building it doesn't immediately equate to you visiting enough for you to take sass from Little Miss here!" Tilsa snorted.

"Lee's my boyfriend!" the Wee One snapped, wrapping my thumb with her tiny hand. "He said so!"

"Yes, I did, Shari," I leaned forward and gave her a light kiss on her forehead. "And I meant it. You're doing better today?"

"Little bit," She sighed. "I don't like sleeping so much. And you ain't here when I wake up!"

"I know, Shari. I come when I can. And your body needs to get stronger, so you don't have to sleep so much. But Dr. Mdenge says you're doing much better. So you keep getting stronger, so they let you come home with me and Aunt Melly. Sound good?"

"Yep! You just make sure I get my own room. I'm too young for all that smoochie stuff!"

I grabbed my chest. "You're just stringing me along, Shari? I'm heartbroken!"

She smiled sweetly, then turned to her side. "You wait! I'll be the best girlfriend ever!" She dropped off almost as soon as she was finished talking. I made sure her blankets were just so before we moved away.

"That was a bit T.M.I.-ish, don't you think?" Karl tittered, until he saw the look on my face. From what I was told, I always had the same expression on my face after visiting my Shari, a look she never saw for herself.

Tilsa was quick to pick up the vibe. "Terminal diagnosis?"

I nodded. "ALS. Lou Gehrig's disease. Come to find out, it's not impossible for kids to get it. Just damned unlikely. Shari was diagnosed when she was nine. She's been here these past four years. She has no idea how long she's been here. Not even the medical people from Lyrodrylle know what to do with ALS yet. Everyone's surprised she's hung on this long." I looked up at Tilsa, not caring what my face looked like. "They shouldn't be! Shari's a tough, big-hearted girl. There's no quit in her. She believes she's gonna walk out of here on her own."

I looked down and away. "Even if no one else does."

Tilsa touched my shoulder gently. "C'mon, before they start wondering what's going on."

I nodded, and we caught up to the crew as they moved on to the next room. I spent the rest of the visit by the door, making sure there were no lurkers outside the room. The word mysteriously circulated to all concerned that I was working, not visiting, so everyone was cool, and Trini was absolutely terrific with the folks, so there were no awkward moments, and the visit was a for-real memorable experience for all those who allowed themselves to get caught up in the moment.

That didn't stop Liza from kicking me in the shin as we boarded the transports.

"That's for not telling me who your parents were!" she fussed. "And not saying you go there often enough to know just about all the patients by name."

"This was Trini's moment, Liza," I groaned. She was a good kicker. "I wanted her to have her time with them, Let her know how important she is to so many of them."

"Yeah, well, okay." She motioned for me to lower my head. I'd seen this before with others in Trini's entourage. When my head got to the proper levels, she kissed my cheek and nodded. "Thank you for sharing. Sis needs good times like this in her day."

I watched the pint-sized terror skip her way up the steps into the transport. The Chief grumbled, "Not sure what that was all about, but no more fraternizing on the job, Seckett!"

"You got it, Chief. My bad."

Chapter 4. Earning The Big Bucks

We were into the second week of our assignment when the balloon went up.

"I DON'T LIKE THAT BUNCH TO THE LEFT, CHIEF."

I heard Denny Pitts' voice rumble through my earpiece. I kept my eyes on the space to the rear and right of our Primary.

There was a heavy stack of people packing into *Talfi's,* the downtown club that was hosting the album release party for *Selene*, and it wasn't solely due to Meg's marketing skills. It didn't take me long to become a rabid fan of the amazing, outrageously unique new vocalist that was getting ready to take over the industry. Producers, groupies, some of the younger record execs, online music gurus. All of them were pushing their way in. To congratulate, to celebrate. To shop for possible deals. To see and be seen.

It took some work to convince Trini to keep her movements along specifically designated routes and locations in the club. One of the things I liked about the artist, as big a pain as it was, was that she hated going into the club's VIP lounge. "The stuck-up skanks wouldn't let me through the door when I was a nobody. Those saggy *putas* can bow down! All this pretentious, 'better-than-you' mess don't mean nothin' to me!"

Cool attitude, Hun, but that translated to not having a closed set of people near you, nor a controlled environment that was a helluva lot easier to keep secured. So here we were, amongst the folks, working our tails off to keep a distance of four square feet around the girl.

And it wasn't just the kind of 'Flavor of The Month' popularity she was getting from the crowd. Trini was about 5'3", slim but nicely curved, with long, midnight black hair framing a lightly tanned face that included expressive eyes, a cute button of a nose, and large, delightfully shaped lips. But more than her looks, her aura around her was like a banked fire, like she was only a moment away from exploding into a flame that would devour everything and everyone around her. And here were the moths, hovering as close to the flame as they could, all deciding that being near her burning personality, and her talent, was worth being consumed. Folk couldn't help but be drawn to her. How do I know this? Aside from watching her for the past so many days, I am a *Talent*, remember? I could *see* the girl's aura shimmering all around her, by the Divine!

"I see a few guys from the club's security moving in that direction," Chief Sykes responded, maintaining his post at the foot of the stairs, three feet to Trini's left. Tilsa kept in her place, three feet directly behind the artist, while Ben was on her right, Denny Pitts was up the stairs on overwatch, and I was lurking further back to the rear. It was up to Denny and me to stop or slow down any un-vetted individuals from entering the space created by the team.

We were all dressed in relatively fashionable, if conservative street gear, but it wasn't hard to notice reinforced stitching and ballistic material. Except for my duster, but then that was crafted and augmented in one of the more exclusive tailors in Tellerman, a prosperous nation in Lyrodrylle renowned for their 'specialty shops' industry. Tellerman was unique amongst all the nations of Lyrodrylle in that it was effectively a Company Town structure with a specific industry in control of the forty or so smaller cities and towns. Oxenburgh, for example, was a good-sized city that had twenty different mega-ranches and pretty much fed three-quarters of the whole planet beef, mutton, and various other cattle, and 85 % of the city's residents were involved somehow in the cattle industry. The other cities of Tellerman followed similar lines. If you were a herbologist, it was very likely that you lived in

Greenway, while furniture makers and others involved in the wood crafting industry found a home in Cedar Groves.

Just imagine a whole country full of specialists, customizers, craftsmen and women, factories of all shapes, sizes and functions, designers that seemed allergic to the 'production model' concept. It was the council members of The Pentagram deciding to hire droves of these individualists and challenging them to find productive ways to reinvent the broken wheel that was the Lyrodryllian economy that allowed the Planet to recover more swiftly after *The Sundering* than any thought possible. In this particular case, it took insane, inventive mavericks to create the heretical solutions needed to heal a broken planet. So effective were many of their solutions, The Pentagram adopted many of them, crossed over into Earth, and effectively threatened the surviving nations of that planet to follow The Pentagram's Program, or be left to deal on their own. It took a few years for the over-proud leaders to consider acceding to another planet's will, but after the remnants of Great Britain capitulated, the rest pretty much lined up and signed on the dotted line.

It was this, and the reasonable belief that there wouldn't be so much cataclysm to recover from if not for 'those damned Mysticlander abominations' that created the ever-simmering, continuous sense of tension between the two planets. It didn't help that the human populace was forced to accept that there was another planet, much closer than they imagined, and their myths, legends, and horror stories were actually slightly skewed documents of real events, with real beings that walked around or flew, with feathers, fur, sharpened teeth, conjuring spells, a peculiar thirst for blood, or rode on dragons. Most humans born ten or twenty years after *The Sundering* simply adapted and grew up into the new reality, but there were quite a few humans that were around to remind those naïve fools that it wasn't always this way, and those cursed 'Mystical Beasties' is the reason for the change. Never mind that the air quality was vastly improved, Earth's Environmental Issues were effectively solved, the overall quality of life around the planet had greatly improved, and the world economy was more stable than ever in its existence. There would always be those who longed for the 'Good Old Days'. When asked specifically the years of those good old days, the answers always depended on the speaker's race, country, or economic standing, so no two complainers could ever agree on exactly when those good days were, only that there were days in the past that were good, and the various speakers were mostly old.

But back to my very cool coat's origins. The design was originally a modified Australian Outback style, long slit in the back to the top of the thighs. The material was a secret concoction of wool, silk, and metal fibers that, when including the runes, incantations, and various other Mystical additions made the coat bulletproof, fire-resistant, repelled water, and gave it a really snazzy outer appearance. This particular garment came from Arcturas, a city in Tellerman known on both sides of The Veil for custom-designed clothing specific to the needs of those who often venture into harm's way. There were other Tellerman cities that catered to the needs of high fashion; Arcturas' most loyal customers were making their way under, or through a hail of bullets, not skipping down the runway. The tailor who put the duster together was a favorite of Melene's, who was known in the combat clothing community to break the unbreakable, tear the untearable, and 'by the Gods! How did you manage to get a hole in *this*?!' With my aunt taking on the occasional consultant job for the D.I.A. (read: enlightened mercenary), she continuously challenged these exceptional Crafters in finding some way of creating a set of gear that could survive Melene's ability to damage anything they put together. It was their 'Eternal Quest'.

Enough 'microfiber of your choice'-gathering. Focus on the job.

"Looks like it's flaring up, folks," Denny noted.

Happily, my mental excursion only took about three seconds of thought-time, so I wasn't completely out of pocket when I took in the situation unfolding before me.

"It does indeed," Chief responded, as we watched the two Security guys get tossed through the air. Somehow, the word got out and people started drifting away from the scene. More members of the club's Security were trying to get to the problem area, but they were swimming upstream, and the crowd was a hair-trigger away from panicked running.

"Lee, you're up. Everyone else, maintain perimeter."

"On it, Chief."

Here we go.

Just as I made it past Trini and the squad, a quartet of weirded-out women cleared the space and were about to do the dash towards our client. Their outfits were mostly ripped gothic, if that was even a thing, and their tall, bony frames swayed menacingly as they moved.

"Selene! Oh, Selene!"

"Your voice! Your music! It's beautiful! Too, too beautiful!"

"You have no right to this gift! The Gods didn't bless you!"

"Stop it! We must end your blasphemy!"

They kept on, yammering along that theme, flinging anything and anyone out of their path to their target.

Oh, Gods no. Why did Jackson have to jump in front of them? And where was his crew? Not having his back, it seemed. That said a lot, for one who would listen.

"Keep your filthy paws away from—"

Before he could finish the thought, the crazy chick in the lead grabbed him by the throat and sailed his behind over the crowd. I think I felt the floor shudder when he landed.

He's a Lycan. He'll heal up fine.

I stepped up into the space cleared by Jackson's launch. I didn't speak. Words were superfluous.

"You can't stop us! She must pay for her crimes!"

Lead chick reached out again. Instead of grabbing throat, her arm was snatched, made to bend in the wrong direction, and was used to punch herself in the throat.

The other three made their way around a weakly gurgling member of the team. Two tried to use their fingernails as claws, but the one further back pulled out a short sword. She was the bigger threat, then.

I ducked, then spun away from the grasping hands of the chick to my left, finished my spin between her and the one with the blade, used the momentum to kick the sword out of the armed woman's hands, then planted my feet and used my back muscles and hips to torque a right hook to the woman's face. I could feel the skull shatter under my fist. She was done.

All that happened in somewhere around two seconds, or less. Before the other two could react, I turned to their backs, punched the one on my left in her spine, shattering it, and snatched the last one by her neck and snapped it.

Four seconds. Four down and done.

Melene will be pissed when I tell her how slow I was.

I heard the Chief was about to say something, but I cut him off when I saw the far wall of the club begin to shimmer.

"Lock down!" I snarled over the com system. "'Ware to the rear!"

We trained for this, and the team was amongst the best. I motored up to Trini as the others turned to the rear wall and spread out.

"Down now Trini, please,"

"Lee?" she stuttered. I couldn't tell what shook her most; the situation, Jackson's launch, or her needing to reevaluate my presence on the team. Either way, there was no time for analysis.

"I've got you, Trini. Just get down, like we practiced. It'll be fine."

She still looked shook, but just a bit less so. She nodded, trusting me, and got down to a sitting position on the floor, and stayed still as I formed an opaque domed shield around her. Fully formed, it was gonna take a blast from a frag grenade to put a chip in it.

After that, I joined with my team as they charged the horde of Maenads that shattered the rear wall and made their way into the club, carrying clubs, axes, and a variety of melee weapons. It looked like there were close to three score of them, all from the other side of The Veil, making them more than a few percentage points stronger than the average human, and that strength was increased in their frenzied state.

But there was a reason Blue Star was top dog in the security field.

We worked as a team, quartering off a small number and tearing them down while a few of us held the larger number in check. They were too frenzied to realize that I was erecting temporary shield barriers to contain them, funneling them into the approach patterns that best suited our smaller number. There was no quarter given, no half measures. We used our own melee weapons because we were in close combat, and bullets could end up anywhere. I pulled out short-handled maces for each hand instead of swords because I wanted to cause breakage instead of blood. I wasn't interested in walking through pools of blood. Others on my team weren't so squeamish.

I focused on the flow of battle, blocking, breaking, dodging, bracing for impact, redirect, smash down. Check the dome, still intact. Smash again, dodge, shatter that limb!

I looked at the dome again, and saw it shake. No, the floor was shaking! Dammit!

"Chief! An attack from below the shield!"

"Go! We'll catch up!"

I cleared the mob just as the section of floor the barrier was sitting on dropped through a hole, and without a thought, I leaped in after it. Just as I touched down on the dome, a blast of Mystic energy smashed me into the closest lower level wall. That hurt. Good save, Duster!

"You should have minded your own business, wretched beastie!"

I looked up to see a Maenad, just as bony as the rest, so far around the bend she was doing laps, and her hair swirling around her like she was caught in the path of a tornado. Her glowing eyes told me that her weapon of choice wasn't going to be her fingernails or a club. That, and the bent staff in her hand.

"This is a Divine Crusade, You foolish tool of perdition!" she screeched. "Our beloved Deities demands it of us. We must seek out the blasphemers! The evil thieves of the blessed harmonies! They must die for their sins, and you will not—"

I had heard about enough at that point, so I returned serve with a Wind Whip spell and slammed her into a wall. I took a second to make sure Trini was secure, that second was long enough to have the hag recover and put up a shield, so my Solar Lance was blocked, but it still caused her to stumble back a few steps.

"What are you?" she screeched. "You are no human!"

I didn't bother with banter. That trash is for comic books and cornball movies. I focused on shattering her shield while making sure to keep a shield up around me. As my Maestra demonstrated often, "You need the third eye open and watching your back door!"

Sure came in handy, as I felt the assault come in from behind. Pretty heavy, must have been an uber-sized axe. Don't think it was a gun. Shield's fine. I refocused on the Talented skank in front. I still hadn't gotten to the point where I could properly ripple off a spell every second or less, but I was close, and I made sure to store a hella ton of Mana in my staff, so I kept at it. Pulling pieces of masonry from the walls and smashing into her shields. Another Solar Lance. Compressed air formed into bullets. It took less than two minutes to shatter her shield, then I leaped forward and used one of my maces to smash her skull into wet bits of matter before she could get up the energy for another shield. Such fun.

I spun away from her, saw that her distraction almost worked. There were more than a few spiderwebs of cracks along my shield over Trini, and they were pretty close to breaking through.

Pretty close wasn't close enough.

We were in the lower levels of the club. Just me and the five Maenads. No collateral damage issues down here.

"Rugitus!" I roared as I stretched out my right hand, and a thick wave of flames roared through the space and scoured my enemies until there was nothing left but ash. There's nothing like old-school Latin for getting your point across.

I waited another few seconds, then tapped my shield, allowing it to disappear. Trini was simply sitting there, ankles crossed, like it was just another day from around the way.

"We good?" she asked in a calm manner, even smiling a bit. The girl was a trooper for real!

"Relatively speaking, yeah, we're good."

"Good. I was starting to get a little worried about how much air you left inside the bubble."

"I did make sure to compress extra air into the space before I closed you in Trini. We discussed this already."

"Yeah, but that was before anything actually happened for real." She looked around the dim space. "Why are we in the basement?"

I was about to respond, but nah, whatever.

"Let's just get back up top, we'll do a debrief later."

I picked her up in a princess carry, and she wrapped her arms around my neck. I allowed myself to look at her. She looked at me and smiled a bit more before letting her head rest on my chest. I leaped up through the hole and returned to the upper floor. I was just returning her to her feet when Jackson came rushing up with the rest of his posse.

Oh, now *their mange-ridden hides show up! Is that 'Posse'? Or is that, P-, ah, screw it. Never mind.*

Trini! Are you okay? What happened? Where'd you go?" He grabbed the front of my duster and started growling. "I thought you all knew what the Hells you were doing! How did my Trini end up in a hole?"

It might've been the adrenalin still hyped up in my system, maybe it was the near calamity of my shield falling. Maybe enough was too much. In any event, I didn't stop myself from grabbing the offending oversized paw of a hand and squeezing. He winced, tried to pull his hand back, but was unable to. Then he looked at me, saw imminent demise staring back, and I could feel his nutsack crawling up into his stomach cavity.

"You really want to learn to control these urges of yours, Caine," I snarled. "You'll stay healthier if you do."

This was it. This was *scraggin* it! No more 'Mr. Professional' crap! I'm gonna—

Chapter 5. Trish Comes Calling
I felt a small hand lightly placed on mine.

"LEE," TRINI WHISPERED. "PLEASE, LET HIM GO. He just worries so much."

"I know," I sighed. *For you, he'll live.* I let him go. He couldn't stop himself from rubbing his wrist. I gave him another warning glare, then walked over to my teammates, who were huddled over Denny.

"Another swarm came, just after you jumped down into the hole. Denny got tagged pretty good with some crazy crab's club," Tilsa explained. I could see the rage barely controlled in her eyes.

"Concussion, pretty bad," Chief grunted. "Our medical team is coming. Police should be here soon. And the D.I.A."

"Do we need to do all this here?" I looked around the club. Looked like it was hit with a tornado. "We should get Trini under wraps."

"I'm aware!" The Chief snarled. "But we got to follow protocol, Lee! There's a lot of dead bodies lying around, if you didn't already notice!"

I swallowed what I was about to say. He's the Chief. He was right. And even if he wasn't right, he was still the Chief. So we waited. I spent most of the time watching Trini quietly chewing out her boyfriend and calming the rest of her people. She had risen a great deal in my estimation. She must have been on the edge of falling apart, but she kept it together for her people. Hella fine leadership.

Sucked in choosing boyfriends, though.

The business with the police and the D.I.A. was pretty harassment-free. Just long and involved. Thank All the Gods and Goddesses, the only dead bodies were Maenads. Club security, those that weren't treated like Frisbees, did an excellent job in getting the civilians, and themselves, clear of the ruckus. It took just over an hour to deal with all the questions from the NYPD, then the D.I.A. I walked around a bit after I was debriefed by the authorities, still coming down from the adrenaline, and as I rambled, I saw the curtain that led to the VIP lounge twitch. *Someone was up there.* I made my way up the stairs, pacing myself, no rush, see what was the situation before blowing up. I went up to the curtain. No one there. I went behind the curtain. No one. I was just about to leave out when I was grabbed by the collar of my duster, yanked through the entrance of the lounge, then assaulted by a delightful fragrance, a pair of arms like twin anacondas wrapping around my neck, and a luscious mouth that invaded my mouth and made me nearly swoon in ecstasy.

"Well, hello, lover!" a voice lilted sweetly when I was finally allowed to come up for air.

"Trish! What in all Seven Hells are you doing here?"

She pouted deliciously as she looked down into my eyes. "It's been nearly a week, Lee, without even a kiss and a hug! You can't starve a girl like that, you know. It's downright unhealthy!"

There was a ton of arguments I could have used, and I should have tried at least a few of them. But by The Gods! I missed her so scraggin' much, and I just grabbed handfuls of delightfully succulent flesh and kissed the Hells out of her. She moaned when I squeezed, and then snuggled in tighter.

She was a Werewolf. Lycans easily healed from physical assaults.

Patricia Ramsey was every bit a predator. 6'2", 180 pounds in her human form, built along the same lines as my Aunt Melene, except a bit rounder, a bit fuller in her chest, and not quite so chiseled in her musculature. But make no mistake. When she wasn't allowing herself to be manhandled by some reckless youth, the 208-year-old Lycan was tough. Cheap steak tough. She had to be. Being hard-core, ruthless and brutal when necessary came along with the package when you were also the Countess of Duerlin, and heiress to Clarence Ramsey's title and estate.

I met her about a month after my nineteenth birthday. It was about that time that I had grown in my skill and ranking to finally be able to use my Talent beyond my body's inborn immunity to magic, and my Aunt Melene decided I was able to get out there in the world without being taken out too easily. She invited me to accompany her to some charity event, and I had nothing else to do, so I suited and booted and escorted her to the gig. It was there that I met Patricia. She caught me staring (and possibly drooling) more than once, and since it was a charity event, and she was feeling charitable, she decided to engage me in conversation instead of having me tossed out for being too obvious a perv. I don't remember all that we talked about, I just remember being mesmerized with her wit, her hilarious commentary on some of the attendees, and her seeming to be thoroughly engaged with the thoughts of a less than Babe in the Woods. After that night, we seemed to somehow run into each other again, repeatedly, with the same level of attention for only each other.

Finally, I remarked that it seemed really weird that we kept showing up in the same places.

"Oh, it's not weird at all, Lee."

"No?"

"No. I'm stalking you."

"What? Me? But why?"

Trish looked at me without a hint of humor. "At first, my motivation was very clear to me. You are the son and only child of Lionel and Belinda Seckett. Those two are still rather powerful Talismans in the Arcane World. Having the ear, possibly the affections, of the heir to that Legacy would be of great potential influence for my Clan, Lee. In everything I do, my dear, I have to keep the needs of the Clan in my mind."

"Oh." I remember feeling profoundly disappointed from her words. "I'm not ignorant of such things, Trish. I just thought, just hoped there was something more than that with us."

I felt her hand raising my face, making me look into her eyes.

"There is, Lee. So much more than that for me. There will be no lies between us, Maahes Seckett. Yes, I used your given name on purpose. We will not ever announce the Banns. We won't be exchanging vows, lying on a beach for our honeymoon, celebrating silver anniversaries. My responsibilities to The Clan require a different path for me. But I like you, Maahes. I like you profoundly. I can see the warrior in you, and I can see the caring, nurturing soul inside the warrior's body, and when we dance, and you hold me close, I feel warm, safe, and so incredibly aroused at the same time, I can barely contain myself. I like being with you, I like talking with you, I like thinking about you.

So, no dreams of Happy Ever After for us, my dear. But would you accept Deliriously Happy For Now?"

I found that, yes, I could work with that. And so I gained yet another tutor in my life. And her lessons, and teaching techniques, were impossibly thorough, feverishly intense, and beyond magnificent. I spent the following three years in extremely focused; Advanced courses in 'How to Drive a Woman to the Edge of Ecstatic Madness'; 'When does "No" mean "No", and when does it mean, "Convince me, and you better be real, *REAL* convincing!" and the like. There were the other crucial lessons not relating to the bedroom, like: 'How to Deal with Useless Pieces of Animated Flesh without being arrested for Manslaughter'; 'When to use a Strategic Retreat to Achieve Ultimate Victory'; 'How to Recognize and Avoid a Loser before you are dragged down with them'; and one of toughest ones, 'How to Shine the Light in You Without Putting Everyone around you into the Shade?'.

We both graduated, in our own ways. And we loved each other, passionately. And we both knew that the last lesson was drawing ever closer: 'How to say "Goodbye", without Life being over?'

Until that final lesson, we laughed, loved, and celebrated each moment to the fullest. Damned fine teacher, that Patricia Ramsey!

"Dammit, Trish! I gotta get back to my team," I groaned as she rubbed herself against me. I swear I was seconds from ripping my clothes off, without the use of hands.

"I know, Lover," the fiend giggled. "I just wanted you to remember what you were missing while on this little business of yours!"

43

I shut off her giggles with one more tongue bath, one more vice-like grip of her wondrous physique, okay, just one more kiss. Okay. Somehow, I was able to release my grip on her, stumbled out of the Lounge, hauled a few deep, cleansing breaths, and made my way back down the stairs. The interrogations had been wrapped up, and everyone was standing around, watching me slowly make my way down the stairs.

"Anything up there?" Tilsa asked first.

"Thought I saw something. I didn't."

"Hmm." The Chief looked me over briefly, then nodded. "Waiting on you. Let's move out."

As we made our way to the exit, Jackson's head shot up. He inhaled through his nose once. Then again, then he turned to me his eyes narrowing.

"Something on your mind, Mr. Caine?" I asked firmly.

"I…no. Nothing. Nothing, Seckett."

"Alright, then."

Chapter 6: Out of a Job (Now), And Into The Money (Soon?)

As I cleared the entrance, I saw two of my favorite people standing close by our transports.

I WASN'T TOO SURPRISED THAT AUNT MELENE WAS CLOSE BY. She usually was. I don't see her. Ever. She's way too adept in stalking for that. But I don't think even she gets just how much she means to me. Since the disappearance of my parents and Aunt Bezine—and Hal Bergen, a human weaponsmith and close family friend who decided to take Melene's place on the team and head out with them, mainly because he was hopelessly besotted with Aunt Bezine (How did I even remember *that*?) —I've found myself able to feel Melene's presence whenever she was close by. I can't point to her. I just know, somehow. Since turning nineteen and finally beginning to go out, meeting people and socializing, I would have these moments when I knew she wasn't far away, keeping a protective eye on her cub. I think she might've figured I would resent her protectiveness, and there were a few times when maybe she could've given me a bit more room, especially when I was out with Trish (Or *in* with Trish, so to speak). But, being the hardcore mama's boy (or auntie's, I guess) that I was, I greatly appreciated her caring that much about me. And to be honest, New York City can be pretty intimidating when you're hitting the streets for the first time, even for someone with my training. My life was a very sheltered existence up to that point, with only the trips to *Trevor's House,* and the occasional outing to some gala event being hosted by Lion's Share Inc. to give me brief moments outside of my home. Of course, being the big, muscle-bound tough guy that I was, I'd never admit to anyone how reluctant I was to finally taking the training wheels off my life.

I was, however, quite surprised to see my Maestra next to her. Alistra De Vore had spent the past nineteen years as my personal trainer in The Arts, but I've rarely seen her outside of the dojo or in some form of learning activity. I have no idea what her life was outside of my training sessions with me. And she never gave the impression that she wanted me to ask. But you don't spend three hours a day, every day, for nineteen years with a person without developing some level of fondness. Maestra De Vore was a brutal taskmaster, but I loved her, and in her way, she was devoted to me as well.

My crew slowed as they saw the two women standing before them. One over six feet tall, dark-skinned, beautiful but intimidating, the other just over five feet, slim and fair-skinned, looking like everyone's favorite granny, until you looked closer into her eyes.

Trust me, folks they're both amongst the scariest people I ever did meet or ever will.

I made sure Trini was covered before rushing over, seeing how they weren't moving.

"What brings you here?" I asked after getting my proper hugs from both.

"We heard Talfi's was in the process of an unscheduled demolition," Alistra responded with a small grin. "I figured you were putting some of your lessons into action. I wanted to see how you were." She nudged Melene, who grinned at the smaller woman. "This big oaf here didn't want to interfere with your job, so we waited until everything seemed to be done."

"It's appreciated, Maestra," I sighed. "I think it went well enough, but, um…"

"Lee, we need to move."

I waved to Chief Sykes, then gaped as my aunt and Maestra made their way to the transport doors.

"You know who I am?" Melene asked my Chief.

"Yes, ma'am."

"Good. This is Alistra De Vore, Lee's Maestra in The Arts. We will be traveling with you."

The Chief was well aware that this particular assignment went well beyond protecting Trini Flores. That was the reason Blue Star's 'A Team' was given the assignment.

"Yes, ma'am. We already went through an after-action with the D.I.A., but it might be good to cover some of that ground with an agent of The Cadre."

"It would indeed, Chief. This agent is very interested in finding the source, instead of being focused on the puppets being sent out in the field." She watched as Trini, followed by Ben and the rest of her entourage, got into the second transport. "We will ride with your client, and you can fill me in. Ali, you ride with Lee in the lead vehicle."

We all got settled and our rides pulled out, heading back to Lower Manhattan.

The others looked on as my Teacher stood before me.

"You were saying?"

"I think…I took too long to deal with the Talent. And I allowed myself to be distracted." I admitted in a quiet voice. "There were others, hammering at the shield while I was dealing with the Talent. I don't think she was that strong, it shouldn't have been that hard."

"Er, ma'am, if I could say something?" Tilsa, all 6'8" and Valkyrie-esque, meekly raised her hand like she was in grade school. When Maestra nodded, Tilsa cleared her throat nervously. "I don't know anything about magic stuff, but we do have Talents in our agency, so I've seen some things. I think Lee's being too hard on himself. He did great in using his Talent in optimizing the field when we were in the big scrum, and we didn't take any real damage until he had to go after the client. I don't know what happened down there, but he wasn't down there for much more than three minutes before he came jumping up through the hole with Ms. Trini."

My Maestra nodded, then looked back to me, then placed her hands over the sides of my head. "Let me in, Lyam."

This was a major component of our training. Amongst other gifts, Alistra De Vore had access to Psychomancy, or mental magic. There have been many sessions when somebody looking through the door of the training salon would see the two of us, sitting in the lotus position on the mats, simply staring at each other. They had no idea what level of mayhem was happening on the mental plane. Though I didn't have much access to Psychomancy yet, Alistra had gone to great lengths to strengthen my mind, helping me to build massive walls of resistance to a psychic attack, teaching me how to form traps for those able to enter my mind, even when asleep or unconscious. And there were other techniques she shared with me, like crafting spells that emulated telekinesis, and connecting my mind with the strength of my soul, giving me the ability to project myself on the Astral Plane. I tell you, with no doubt in my heart, that the only reason why the worlds hadn't written whole libraries on Alistra De Vore has to be that she didn't want that kind of recognition. As she said, on more than one occasion. "Look where all that fame and recognition got your parents? Calling me for every fire that some schmuck could put out himself with a big enough bucket of water? No, I thank you!"

So, I opened the pathways Alistra taught me to create, and I felt her mind snuggle up next to mine. "Alright, my lad, let's look through the files, eh?"

I replayed the sequence of events in my mind, and we watched together.

"The big chick was right about those shield constructs. Good funneling, good. Didn't use any offensive spells?"

"I didn't want to make my Talent obvious on this mission." I replied. "The team knows, Trini and her manager, some of their followers. But I don't know who else might be watching."

"Good reasoning. Okay, let's continue. Hmm. That floor collapsed too fast for a weak Talent. Hmm. Yes. Looks like Solar Lance has become your go-to, yes. Took too long to remember to put up a circle shield, but in time. Okay, I've seen enough. Coming out."

I felt her presence leave my mind, and I shuddered a bit as I adjusted myself mentally and physically.

"First off, Lyam, you're wrong. That Talent was an initiate to the Beldame Mysteries." She turned to Tilsa and Denny. "You youngsters have heard of Battle Mages? Good. Those are Talents of The Light Arts. The Dark Arts have a matching designation. They call them the Beldamai—Beldamus for males, Beldame for females. This woman was the equivalent of an early Rank 5 Sorceress, and you took her down in less than two minutes. What does that tell you?"

I thought about it, relieved a bit in my heart for her evaluation. Then smiled. "It tells me that if I were ready for Battle Mage Trials, I would have been done in thirty seconds or less?"

She swatted me upside my head, which happened often. "Silly fool. But yes, I agree. Two things. One, your Ripple Effect is coming along nicely, but it's still too slow. You need to keep working on that. Two, you are strong in Fire and Earth, but unlike most Talents, you *do* have some access to Air and Water. Your Solar Lance is a great go-to spell, but you would have shattered her shield faster with an Ice Spike spell. I taught you that spell often enough, it should be in your short list inventory of spells you would select in a duel!"

"But I didn't have access to water!" *Geez, was I whining?* "I didn't think I ..." I stopped, looking at the disgusted look on her face. "Oh, damn," I groaned. "Gather the moisture in the air with a Collectis Aquis spell. Then freeze it into a spike and shoot it off with the Ice Spike spell!"

"And that should have taken all of five seconds, tops," Alistra nodded. "You big dummy."

She looked at my teammates, who appeared worried, or in disbelief, and snorted. She stepped away, all the way back to where the driver's compartment was located. "Show them," she commanded as she put up a shimmering shield.

Without standing, I invoked the Water spell, and within two seconds a small globule of water was hovering at eye level before me. Then used my right hand to shape the water and activated the Ice Pick spell, then released it. We watched as the sharpened spike of ice bulleted through the air, then exploded into my Maestra's shield, causing the barrier to shatter and Alistra to be pressed back into the compartment wall.

"That shield was the equivalent to the one you faced in the club. You see the effect? A sharp, precise attack, focused on a small area instead of splashing across the whole surface, caused the whole shield to shatter."

She sat down next to me and scowled at my teammates, who were exhibiting some small signs of protectiveness. "Before you two get your panties in a bunch, Let's be clear. This was his second throw down with a real enemy Talent. Someone strong enough, tough enough, and motivated enough to take him out. And he put her down in two minutes. I'm Gods-cursed proud of my boy!

"But he could've done better, and he said so before I did." She leaned forward. "This young fool *wants* to be a Battle Mage, more than anything. Wants to be just like his parents. He could live a happy life where he's at now, could even be like a Battle Mage without going through The Trials. But that's not good enough for him! He wants the title, the official registration, and all that cat-scat.

"Let me tell you something. Most of those conducting The Trials would tell him he's ready now, that he could undergo The Trials, and even have a bloody good chance at succeeding. But I don't want him to be good enough to survive The Trials. I want him to be strong enough, smart enough, I want him to be '*The Baddest, Skull-Crushing-est Death-Dealer on Both Planets'* enough to survive the life he'll have to live *after* The Trials! Whatever ocean of muck they throw him into, I want Maahes, Lyam Seckett to backstroke through it like he's chilling out in the local swimming pool!"

She looked at me, and I saw the love, the devotion. "Belinda was like a daughter to me, Lyam, I taught her, just as I'm teaching you. She didn't feel joy at being a Battle Mage. For her, it was just an occupation. Her joy came in raising her children. Her two boys before she met your father, then with you. That's what I want for you, my child. I want you to be happy, I want you to raise your children, and to have more time to do it than Belinda and Lionel did."

I gathered the slim elder in my arms. "I know, Maestra," I whispered into her hair. "I know, and I will. I swear it. I'll remember to live a life. I won't let the job get in the way of having a life."

"Better not," she snickered. "Or I'll track ye' down and kick your keester up and down the block!"

As we sat back, I noted that we were pretty close to The Karkarof, the luxury hotel that Trini was currently using as her place of residence. That pretty much said all you needed to know about Trini's prospects. The salary I was receiving from Blue Star for this assignment was substantial, but it might be just enough to afford a broom closet for a night in any of the Karkarof chain of hotels and luxury suites.

"Um, Ms. De Vore," Denny was asking. "I was wondering, what is this thing you were talking about, a ripple?"

Alistra leaned back. "Understand, I'm no Battle Talent. Can't abide by most of the idiots who use their blessings from The Creator to do harm to another being. But since this one intends to follow that path, I've had to adjust my teaching methods, somewhat. Anyway, The Ripple Effect is a highly prized combat skill with those who practice The Arts. You see, once you've established that you have Talent, or access to the pool of Mystical energy that surrounds us, let's just call it magic, or Mana, like in those Japanese comics, well after that, the use of spells has everything to do with the mind of the spell caster. When Lyam here casts a spell, he has to choose a spell, call its formation into mind, invoke it, then cast it out at whatever he is targeting. Saying all that out loud takes about ten, twenty seconds? Now, imagine him being able to go through all that mental prep, all those steps, in one second? In a fraction of a second? Then doing it again, a second later? Then again, then again?"

"Ah, yeah!" Tilsa enthused. "It would be like a ripple of spells, a wave of spells constantly going out from him!" I noticed her impressive bosom dancing with her enthusiasm. She noticed that I noticed, and smiled wickedly. That lady is gonna be trouble for a Brother.

"Yeah, like a machine gun!" Denny added, seemingly oblivious to the byplay between us.

"No mortal mind could ever ripple spells as fast as a machine gun," Alistra cautioned as we pulled up to the Karkarof. "But a semi-automatic? As fast as it would take for a finger to pull a trigger? Lyam here is pretty close to that. I want him closer."

"We're here." Tilsa smiled at my Maestra. "Thank you, Madame, there were a lot of things I was curious about regarding magic, and I'm glad to know more about my teammate here. I know you worry about him, but trust me, he can handle the weight. Once the word gets out about him, he'll be able to avoid a lot of fights simply by letting the bad guys know he's coming, and they'll run their tails off!"

I appreciated Tilsa's confidence in me. She was obviously a veteran to combat, whatever her past was. Having someone like her giving me the nod went a long way with me.

The Chief quirked an eyebrow at our laughing as we left the transport, but he didn't ask questions. "Tilsa, Denny, go with Ben and make sure Ms. Flores gets tucked in. I'll be up shortly. Lee, you're with me. We got a call en route. We need to go see some people."

Chief Sykes led me through the foyer of the hotel. I'm proud to say I didn't gawk at all the luxurious furniture and appointments tastefully gracing the interior of the space, but, By The Divine!, the place was amazing! I followed him towards the conference centers and entered after him into one of the smaller suites. Already sitting at the table were my aunt, Megan, Director Dellums, my present boss, Brian Foster, and two gentlemen I didn't recognize but could tell were Lycans. Both were showing some grey at their temples, and were in the 6'8"to 6'10" range, with muscles rippling from neck to toes. Even their eyebrows looked like they worked out. There was another present, someone I did recognize, but didn't particularly like. No, actually, I couldn't stand Billy Grantham, 5th Degree sorcerer. The smug bag of pus. The slight smirk on his face made it clear to me that he was pleased to be here, and was sure I wouldn't be. Friggin' clown.

"Take a seat, Lee."

Oh, I didn't like that calm, even tone my aunt used. It told me someone was pretty close to a violent death, and I prayed it wasn't me!

After I settled, Director Dellums leaned forward. "First, I would like to extend my congratulations on a job well done, and my apologies for doubting your capabilities. From what we have gathered from the debriefs from Chief Sykes and your other teammates, your actions were the key to the survival of Ms. Flores, and in the complete destruction of the Maenad Cell Group, with a highly beneficial addition that no innocent lives were lost and only a few minor to serious injuries." He turned his gaze to my chief. "I wanted to make sure that you were aware of the sentiments of the D.I.A. regarding Mr. Seckett, Mr. Sykes. The rest of this gathering does not concern you or your team, so you are excused."

"If it concerns a highly valued member of my team," Chief rumbled. "I'd prefer to stay."

"Not this time, Chief," Brian Foster interjected quietly. "I'll bring you up to speed in a little bit."

The chief huffed, gripped my shoulder briefly, then strode out. As the door closed, Dellums continued. "In your opinion, Mr. Seckett, is the threat to Trinidad Flores over?

It didn't take me long to reply.

"I don't believe so. We don't know how many beings are in this swarm of Maenads. There might be twice as many ready to descend on her. We don't know. Besides that, the going theory is that there is a Mystical Entity that calls out to people, drives them mad, then sends them out to do its will. Can we rule out the possibility that this Entity, if it exists, might decide to make a move on Trini itself, after its puppets failed?" I shook my head. "I wouldn't consider this mission completed until we could track down the source, if that is at all possible."

I looked around the table. Brian looked uncomfortable, Grantham's level of douche-ness only increased, the two Lycans continued smoldering, and Megan and Melene looked like they were ready to declare war. Oh, Boy.

My boss broke the stalemate. "Lee, as of this moment, you are no longer an employee of Blue Star Security."

I leaned back from the table, like I just got punched in the chest. Hard. "Why am I being fired?" I asked quietly. This was my first job! I didn't do it right?

"I'll tell you why," Melene snarled as she leaned forward. "Those two scat-bag Lycan turds are twisting his arm to fire you!" She pointed her hand in their direction. "The one on the left is

Henri La Croix, First Deputy to Duke Clarence Ramsey. The one on the right is Adolphus Caine, his Minister of Finances, and Jackson Caine's proud papa!" She snapped at the two when they started growling. "You even *think* of talking before I'm through, and your Duke will have two new positions to hire, and I'll have two new rugs for my house! First, Lyam, it's become public knowledge that you and Patricia Ramsey are an item."

"But they already knew!" I exclaimed. "They sicced her on me. She *told* me."

"Of *course* they knew. They were expecting her to twist you around her finger, get you nice and compromised so they could have some control over a potentially powerful heir to a prominent family. But she fell for you, and screwed the pooch. The point here is that the higher-ups may have known, but the rank-and-file didn't know *jack*. Not until tonight, when Jackson caught a whiff of her scent on you, then opened his big flapping jaws to whoever would listen." I stared at her in shock. She nodded her head. "Yeah, less than 90 minutes ago. It's amazing what you can do with cell phones and the Internet these days.

"In addition, Jackson's been whining about how you're trying to make moves on his lil' puddin', which of course is horse turds, but who cares about the truth these days?

"Finally, we get to the closed-circuit camera in the club, recording the whole damn battle, which gets kicked off with the cameras displaying big, bad Jackson being thrown like a flapjack, his lickspittle posse cowering like the limp tools they are—I SAID SHUT YOUR PIE HOLES!" She stared the Lycans down again. "Where was I? Yeah, and then it shows how you wiped out the first four in about two seconds. Well, it doesn't show it, but some genius who got a hold of the feed, please don't ask me how it got released, some other techno whiz-kid was able to put the action on slo-mo, and there we are with you, then you and your team—you in particular—mopping the floor with the crazy skanks while the big bad Weres are hiding in the rear and trying to wake up Jackson."

She slowly stood up and leaned on the table, staring at the Lycans. "Now, if these mobile buckets of pond scum were as smart and hardcore as they thought, they could have easily approached you in an above-board manner, offer the possibilities of a future alliance of mutually respected parties, and you would have been considered an official friend of The Clan, which would make anything Trish did with you an acceptable dalliance on her part before she tied the knot with whoever they have lined up. But because they chose to go the bone-brain route, now Trish is embarrassing The Clan with an unaffiliated cur that has shown up members of The Clan in public!"

She sat back down, still enraged. "Brian fought for you, Lyam. Don't doubt that. But Ramsey and his Clan are too powerful, even for a leading business like Blue Star. *That's* why you're being fired.

"But you two gentlemen better take this message back to your Duke. Since the supposed brain trust of your Clan set Patricia on her path, then you must have done *some* homework on him. At least as far as public records are concerned. So you would know that Lyam is just over two months away from his twenty-fourth birthday. That would mean that he's on the verge of receiving his full inheritance, as per the bylaws for descendants of races native to Lyrodrylle. He was born in this country, so he could have come into his full inheritance when he turned 21, but his parents wanted to dot the I's and cross the T's, so to speak. In any event, none of you furry butt-boys have a clue to what kind of inheritance he's receiving, but have you ever pondered on the origins of Lion's Share, Inc.?"

Everyone, including me, gasped. I knew my parents had a healthy investment portfolio, hence the nice big house in Southeast Queens, but what was she saying? What the unholy Hells was she actually saying?!

"Yeah, you might want to think on *that* for a minute or two. Tell your boss the Duke that, and tell him that instead of having a potential alliance with the Heir of the Seckett Inheritance, he's pretty damn close to establishing a good old-fashioned feud of The Clans!"

She sat back and watched the two massive Weres scramble to their feet and through the door. I saw that the smug look on Grantham's face was gone, replaced by a furrowed brow and a grim set to his lips. A lot like the look on Dellums' face.

"Lion's Share Investments holds 25 % of my company's stock," Megan whispered woodenly.

"Our company's under the umbrella of their Security Division," Brian choked.

They both looked at me, their faces paling. I think I might have dropped a shade or two myself. I turned my gaze back to my aunt, who was still in the midst of classic Lioness fury. I reached out and closed my hand over hers. "Melene, it's okay. I'm okay. We're okay."

Melene sighed, sadly, slowly letting go of the rage. "I'm *far* from okay, dear one, and have been for quite some time, but yes, I need to let this go. For now." She looked to the Director. "Finish this, Dellums."

"Er, yes." He nervously adjusted a tie that was already perfectly placed. "Yes, well, thing is, Lyam, due to the exposure from the recordings going out, the main reason why you were integral to this assignment no longer applies. You have been exposed to the world, so to speak—and, well, to lessen the friction that might be caused by your presence, it has been decided by me and Melene's superior that you should be replaced. Agent Grantham here will be taking over the Talent requirements of this case."

"Even though, as I've said now for the eighth time, that we have well-trained Talents on my staff already!" Brian Foster was just about to rise up and hit somebody. A very bad thing.

"Mr. Foster," I interjected, trying to project firm empathy, if that was even a thing. "Please, if I may. I am still very worried for Ms. Flores' safety, and we have no idea what angle any future attacks might take. If I'm being put on the sideline, then I would highly recommend someone of Agent Grantham's caliber. He has a great deal of experience dealing with unconventional tactics and is recognized in the Talent community as someone who can combat magical attacks successfully. And I do believe, if Ms. Flores is still a target, that magic will factor greatly in the next attack. Of course, I would also recommend creating a protective perimeter around Ms. Flores, and creating a tripwire defense, since one of the major goals of all of this is to permanently end the threat of Maenad attacks, but then, what do I know? I'm just an out-of-work bodyguard." I quirked an eyebrow. "I *will* be getting some kind of severance pay, right?"

"Uh, yeah," Brian chuckled. "I'll get it sent to your address. Alright, if you sign off on this guy, I'll let it go. But you know how touchy Talents can be, especially if they feel as if they've been insulted."

"Oh, I wouldn't know anything about that."

I hope I laid the sarcasm down thick enough for them to get the point.

"Well, if that's all for me, then I'd like to go home. It's been a difficult evening."

"Let's go," Melene confirmed, and we were pretty much out the door before anyone else could move.

"Well, *scrag* me," I muttered. "I done been fired!"

Melene chuckled grimly. "Remember the great quote by Marx."

"Karl?"

"No, Groucho."

I chuckled. "'I don't want to belong to any club that would have me as one of its members.' Yeah, I hear that."

✳✳✳

The next day was hella brutal.

Only ten days out of routine, and damn, it felt like a month by the time Melene and Alistra were done with me.

The good news? I got Melene locked up in a submission hold twice, and even knocked Alistra on her behind. Only once, though. Before, and after that, they straight up hung me out to dry.

In a break from the usual routine, Alistra sat with us after training, sharing our afternoon meal. She spent a lot of it shaking her head, as she watched Melene and I consume enough food for four people. When you have a pretty massive body, with a ton of muscles and a bullet train for metabolism, you gotta pack it in!

"And this is the main reason why I don't share meals with you Pride people!" Alistra fussed. "My God, I'm ten pounds heavier just watching you two."

"You could do with adding a few pounds, you bony crow!" Melene snickered back.

They jabbed back and forth as I finished my third steak and started addressing the few veggies left on my plate. I had been spending a lot of time thinking, since last night.

"Melene, could I ask you about what you said? About some kind of inheritance?"

She paused, put her fork and knife down. "Of course. What about it?"

"Well, I guess…what is it?"

Alistra snorted. "Melene! You never told him? Anything?"

"Ali, you know I don't like being reminded of all I—*we* lost."

"But Melly, the kid's gotta be ready!"

"I know I've been dragging my feet. I know!" My aunt sighed, then nodded to herself.

"Lee, there's no other way to say this. Lion's Share Inc.? Your family, you…well, you own it."

I almost fell out of my chair.

At the time, Lion's Share Inc. was number three in top multi-national, multi-world businesses. It was a monster. It had a multitude of divisions: Agriculture, Real Estate, Entertainment, Insurance, Investments, Banking, Science, Defense—the list went on. It was number three because of its charities and benefits division. Affordable housing, free and/or affordable health care programs, terraforming deserts…again, the list went on. At this point in its existence, it couldn't help but make money, and it wouldn't turn its back on those in need on either side of The Veil. Those shareholders who had a problem with the loss in profits because of the charitable efforts were bought out, at twice the going rate for their shares, and were then effectively blackballed from buying shares of the company again.

I read about all of this. Learned it all. One of the many assignments I was given, while I was attending the Cremon Eft Academy's satellite system, was to give a comprehensive study on a leading company in the business world. Melene made sure I chose Lion's Share as the focus of the assignment. And keeping to Cremon Eft's nearly impossible standards, I studied the scat out of the company. Even going in person and interviewing a number of the staff, managers, *and* two members of the Board of Directors. They all seemed quite pleased, even amused, by my interest.

Now, I have a pretty good idea why they thought it was so funny. Here's this fifteen-year-old kid asking all these questions about the business, as if he won't be running it in less than a decade.

Gotta say though, it *was* a damned comprehensive study. My professors complimented me on it a bunch of times when I graduated from the Cremon Eft satellite program two years later, sporting their version of a dual Bachelor of Science Degree in Criminology and Behavioral Science (most businesses and *all* educational institutions on Earth equate a B.S. from Cremon Eft as at least a Master's degree on their side of The Veil.)

"Melene, why didn't we have this talk before now?"

Melene sighed sadly. "I read your submission to Cremon Eft, Lee. More than four hundred pages long. You know all you need to know about Lion's Share and how businesses work as a whole. The only people who presently know more about the entirety of the business are Silverstein, Blake and Goldman. Family friends, as well as the lawyers who have been handling your personal portfolio two months after you were conceived. Fact, not just my opinion.

"You have developed yourself into a man who has a strong mind, a kind heart, and an inner drive to move mountains to achieve your goals. You didn't need to be raised with gold and jewels dripping out your butt cheeks to be ready for what's to come. You needed to have your mind and spirit right *before* you came into your inheritance, not after.

"And well, my dearest one, it felt...it feels like—well, if I talk to you about your inheritance, it feels like I'm giving up on Lionel and Belinda, and Bezine and Hal." A tear rolled down her cheek. "It feels like I'm admitting, that I'll never see them again, Maahes, and I'm just not ready to believe that. Not yet."

The food was forgotten as we shared our tears the rest of the afternoon. And after Alistra left, I took my aunt to her room and held her in my arms as the tears poured.

And I pondered my life. I got fired from my first actual job. A job I realized that I enjoyed and was good at. I've pretty much been fired as Trish's boyfriend, or courtesan, whatever role I was playing, without the courtesy of a goodbye kiss.

And I was filthy, stinking, beyond disgustingly rich. The only languages that *might* accurately describe how wealthy I was went extinct thousands of years ago.

And I would give it all away in less than a second for one more day with my family.

Chapter 7: Broken
The next day was Wreck. Literally.

WHEN IT WAS TIME FOR MY MAESTRA'S SESSION that afternoon, I was already deep in the throes of exhausted recovery from my morning session with Melene and my Samba master, Alekseyev Klitko, one of the few Weres I ever met that, if I needed to defeat him in less than an hour, I'd simply pull up a pump action full of silver slugs and blast the scragger. And always with the laughing for joy as his foot blasted me across the salon. But I got him, oh I tagged his behind good that day, a bunch of times. And what does he do? Picks himself up off the mat, shakes his head, then races across the space and bear hugs me breathless, kissing both cheeks, bouncing me around like I was a rag doll.

Hey, folks! Come see the Big Ole Chocolate Thunder being treated like Granny's favorite Cockapoo!

Russian Werebears. They can wreck your body, or your ego, and you can never tell which is gonna happen.

When I started crawling my way back to my feet, I noted that Alistra brought company, in the form of a dwarf. One I happened to know and like.

"Digby!" I limped over to greet him, grateful for the care he took in shaking my hand and slapping my shoulder.

"You've grown, lad!" he noted, his voice reminding me again of an avalanche in progress.

"Nah, you're just wearing lower heels."

"Hmph, still a knucklehead."

"I'll get Melene!" Alistra called as she made her way down the hall to the stairs. "Take Digby to the study."

"So what brings you, Mr. Crusher." I bowed mockingly and followed Digby into the library/classroom/study hall where I spent at least 6 hours a day, every day, for four years, as I attended the Cremon Eft Satellite System. With the monitors and hologram projectors of Eliondria's tech companies, it really did feel as if my professors were right there in the same space as me. Cremon Eft, for the most part, really didn't like their satellite program, preferring their students to learn on their campus, which was about the size of a small city. But no dice—Melene was not letting me out of her sight for too long then. Considering my emotional state in my teen years, I didn't fight her on it.

Digby settled into the low, heavy wooden chair he always sat in when he visited the study. We left it there for him. Digby isn't into a lot of padding, and he sure didn't like his legs dangling.

Considering he was four feet tall, near on four feet wide, and was a barrel-shaped being of muscles pushing other muscles out of the way, Digby had to be careful of where he parked himself.

"I saw the images, read the reports." He replied as he settled in, nodded to Melene as she and Alistra came through the door. "I wanted to hear it from you. So tell me, from the beginning."

And I went at it. When The Chief Nemesene of North, South and Central Americas tells you to jump, all you ask is, "How long you want me to stay up here?"

When I had finished, sharing my speculations regarding possible future attacks, he hummed to himself, nodded slowly, then smiled grimly. "I think I agree. I don't believe this is over. And it might graduate to a new level. This must be dealt with. If there is a source, an Entity, it must be found." He turned to Melene. "At this present time, you are my only available Deputy, Melene. I will need you to proceed with a team to seek out and eliminate this source, if it can be found."

He held a massive hand before she could speak. "I know what we agreed, and the agreement is still in effect. Now, it is time to see if it has been fulfilled."

"Oh, damn," Melene replied ruefully. "You're gonna go there?"

"I must, Deputy. Even if there were others available, you know you are one of my best."

"Alright." Melene sighed. "No use in putting this off. Me and Alistra?"

Digby smiled. "You know I wouldn't ask that of you. My team is waiting outside as we speak."

"Um, what's going—"

"SILENCE!" Digby roared. "Candidates are to be observed, NOT listened to!"

"Candi—"

"Did I NOT just tell you to be silent?" He stood and pointed to the door. "Report to the Salon and prepare yourself!"

Thoroughly confused, I simply followed Alistra and Melene as they led me into the training room. Before I could ask any questions, Digby came tromping in, followed by three other people. Two of them, a tall burly man and an even taller, somewhat muscular female were wearing clothing similar to mine; comfortable, reinforced stitching, no pockets or lapels, nothing hanging loose.

Fighting gear.

The third was carrying a large sack. She placed it close to the far wall of the salon, opened it, and began pulling out sorts of training weapons: swords, clubs, daggers, axes, and the like. When she was done, she turned to me. "Choose your weapons."

What in all Seven Hells? I already spent the morning being beaten like a piñata!

I turned to Digby. I couldn't speak, but I think my glare spoke volumes.

"You are being tested. Full combat. All out. Both opponents at the same time. Optimal outcome: Defeating both opponents. Minimal outcome, survive ten minutes of combat. Use of training weapons. Only rule: No permanent death."

Oh.

So, it's like that, then?

I nodded and walked over to the pile. I saw a short sword, falchion style. Two feet of blade, a broad bar covering the knuckles. That'll do. I returned to the center of the mat and saw that the woman was wielding a Wizard staff, while the man was sporting a long sword. "Where's his staff?" the woman asked. "You said he was a Rank 4 Sorcerer."

I pulled back the sleeve of my left arm, showed her my reduced staff, snugly nestled in its flesh sleeve.

"Oh. Well, then."

Digby clapped his hands once, sounding like a shot from a desert eagle. "Begin!"

I was already rolling under the spell sent in my direction before Digby could get to the 'n'. I threw up one of my stronger mobile shields, then proceeded to seemingly ignore the Talent. I was on my feet and braced, blocking the over-hand blow from the guy. Hard shot. I would've thought he hit like a girl, but Melene was the girl. Her sword strokes hit harder.

We just went at it. He was cursed fast, able to get that long blade hummin'! And strong. Must have been a native of Lyrodrylle, because he was too strong for a human, and I couldn't detect any augmentations on or in him. He was slipping my thrusts, as I got in close. Then I had to roll back from a snap kick, giving him the room he wanted for his sword. I rolled to my feet, just in time to feel my shield finally shatter under the woman's barrage.

Don't worry, sister. I was paying *real* close attention to you. And the interval between your spells.

They wanted to test me? Well, open the booklet to page 1, and let's begin.

I went balls-out and rushed the sword slinger. He wasn't ready. I smashed my falchion into his longer sword with brute force instead of finesse, and before he could recover, I brought my right foot hard into the side of his head. Then locked my left hand on his sword wrist, then hammered it with my sword.

You could hear the wrist snap from two blocks away.

The man was hardcore. And he had three other limbs that worked quite well, thank you. The Sorceress was still tearing up my clothes with her clockwork spells but must have realized at some point that I really was immune to most spells. She had to pull out the big guns.

Her first one landed when I was just about to slam my elbow into the big guy's jaw. And Divine's Sake!, it hurt. Made me stutter, and he was able to avoid the blow and send a knife hand into my gut. That hurt, too, but I ate it. And I took the next heavy-duty shot from the woman, some variety of ice spike. That hurt a lot too. So much so that I froze in place, stopped moving.

Mr. Man accepted the open invitation and put everything into a right cross that might have knocked me right the scrag out. Problem was, I was no longer there. I had dropped to the floor. He missed me with his punch.

And Ms. Lady, right on schedule, missed me with the Burning Spear spell she launched at the same time.

She didn't miss *him*, though.

And I didn't miss her, as I swiveled on my back and let loose a series of Chained Lightening Spells, first on her shields, and when they shattered, on her.

When she was allowed to collapse into a twitching pile, I looked to my other opponent and saw that he was already being treated by the stranger who carried in the bag.

"Well done, Candidate,"

I turned to Digby's voice. Then gulped. *Oh, Hells No!*

I watched him stride forward, wearing only the pants to his suit, his hairless, impossibly broad torso over-crammed with hairless, grey-skinned muscle. He had taken his shoes and socks off as well, and his broad, massive feet shook the floor as he walked. "Now we go into Round 2. Final round. Your task is simple."

He smiled a grim smile in his grey, crushed-in face.

"Get me off my feet."

Get a dwarf, denizen of the earth, imbued from head to toe with stupendous levels of earth magic coursing through his body, off the ground that his feet might as well be anchored to?

"Great. Just scraggin' great."

✳✳✳

Oh, well. Been here before.

Melene's sent me to the mat wrecked, broken, and immobile more than a few times. Alistra too. Any number of my unarmed combat masters have torn me to shreds when I was younger. One of my Blade masters even cut my hand off completely. Took two months for that one to grow back. *Thank you, Ancient Atlanteans, for including Regeneration in the genetic gift basket you put together for my bioengineered ancestors. And for the portable Regen units your descendants invented.*

Yeah, there I was, laid out in my house's private infirmary with tubes running in and out of me, with my torso, both arms and one leg temporarily cast and immobilized. Organs severely bruised, but thank the Creator they weren't lacerated this time, cause that *really* sucked. Pissing a river of blood is *not* a good look.

But hey, everyone else seemed to consider me their MVPB: Most Valuable Punching Bag. Why not someone else I looked up to with a great deal of fondness.

Well, I did get him off his feet, though.

He was nowhere near as fast as me. He didn't have to be. I came in with a sweetly arced left cross, right in the proper part of the jaw, the guaranteed knock-out spot.

And shattered my wrist and broke all my fingers. Before I could react to even that bit of horror, his right hand hammered three shots into my ribs. His being a dwarf aside, I still couldn't believe they broke so fast. I'm a Gods-blasted superhuman child of The Pride! What the *Wreck*?

I retreated, he advanced. I put up one of my strongest shields, but it took him only five colossal shots to bring it down. I tried to grab his left hand when he slammed down with a hammer blow, but he caught my wrist with his other hand and twisted it the entirely wrong way. Both arms effectively out of commission. I backpedaled, he kept coming in. I was beyond agony. And it was so cursed hard to breathe. I gathered myself, focused, and slammed a stomp kick into his leading leg. It didn't move. Then he dropped a boulder of an elbow on my knee. I also blew chunks from the agony of my knee being shattered.

I fell, crawled away, but he kept coming. Relentlessly closing in, lifting his foot, stomping forward, lifting the other. Juggernaut style. Always closing in. Lifting those damned, tree trunk stumpy legs forward.

Lifting them up, then forward.

Up.

Off the floor.

I focused. Oh, by all the Gods and Goddesses, did I focus. Then I sent out my shield.

Not over me.

I sent it flat on the floor.

I shuffled back, and he came on.

One foot.

I shuffled back some more.

He bored in. Took another step.

Two feet.

I stopped shuffling.

He stood over me. He raised his massive arm, his fist a wrecking ball.

"Do you concede?" he rumbled as he stood above me, eyes cold, fist ready.

"No. I've won." I could see the blood dribbling on my chest. I spat my mouth clear.

"You've won?"

"Yes," I gasped. "Your feet, ain't on the ground, anymore."

"What are you—" was all he could get out before I used whatever Mystical Energy I had left into lifting the shield, and Digby, off the floor, smashing him into the ceiling, then flattening him to it, closing it around his body. I kept closing it in, tightening it around him. Eliminating every possible crevice, every little space.

Including air pockets.

"Maahes! Stop it!" Melene was screaming. "He can't breathe! Release the shield!"

"*I* can't breathe!" I snarled. "Why should he?"

Melene pulled me in, made me face her. "Because you're not *that* guy! Because you do not kill if you don't have to. Maahes, please, let him go. Don't be that guy."

She was right. I wasn't that guy.

I sure scraggin' considered it.

I released the shield. Digby came crashing to the floor, and I went crashing into the blackness.

Chapter 8. In Recovery

It took a few hours for me to come out of unconsciousness.

AFTER THAT, FOLLOWED A DAY OF ANGRY THOUGHTS and cold responses to whoever came to 'see if I needed anything'. Of worried expressions and angry silences. The following morning, Alistra came into the infirmary. She didn't bother trying to offer some kind of greetings. She had probably grown tired of the cold reception. She simply said, "The device is ready, you need to be moved." Then, she wrapped me up in a shield and gently moved me out of the infirmary and down the stairs. It seemed they remodeled the basement to include a full-body Regen unit, one of the greatest pieces of technology ever invented by the bioscience engineers of Eliondra. They have smaller units that can fit around the limbs, but with multiple fractures, organ damage and shattered ribs, the full-body unit was required to make sure the body healed evenly, as well as rapidly.

Some stranger was standing by the unit. Tall, thin, bald, pinkish skin, and wearing a lab coat.

Of course there was a lab coat.

"Hello there, Mr. Seckett." His voice was too damned cheery. "I'm Kral Doljon, I'm here to supervise your recovery. Normally I wouldn't be needed, the unit pretty much runs itself. But this is new territory for everyone here, so I'll be tutoring you all on how

68

to use the unit while making sure you progress properly through your recovery. Do you have any questions?"

"No," I replied.

"Yes." Melene came into view. Lovely. "How long will he need to be in the unit?"

"He should be fully recovered in less than a month." The Tech replied.

"That soon? That's wonderful!" Melene looked at my unexpressive face. "Isn't that good to hear, Lee?"

"Just swell," I answered woodenly, bringing a frown to my aunt's face.

"Don't you want to recover, Lyam?"

"I don't know. I'm kind of diggin' not having someone kicking the piss out of me at the moment. Not real happy with the idea of being put back into this thing right after I get out of it."

My voice had gone from dull and bland to snarling rage by the time I was finished. One could assume that I didn't take my latest massacre well.

Melene reached a hand out to me, and just as I had done before, I turned my face away. I heard a sigh, and then footsteps passing up the stairs.

"That was cruel, Maahes," Alistra hissed.

"And what do you call what happened to me?" I snapped back. "Therapeutic?"

"No," my Maestra came right back with heat. "It's not therapeutic. It's exactly what you need to get used to, since you want to be a Battle Mage so bloody bad. *This* is the cost of admission!"

"Yeah? Well if it's gonna be friends and family shattering limbs all the scraggin' time, then maybe I *should* rethink the whole damned thing, like you say all the time!"

"Um, I'm sorry to interrupt," Kral interjected before Alistra could speak. "But we really should get him into the unit. If you place him in position, I can remove the temporary casts and clothing, and we can get him on the way to healing up!"

"Yes, you're right," Alistra huffed, annoyed. "Sorry."

She laid me on the unit's bed. Pretty comfortable, all things considered. "Can he eat while he's in this thing?"

"He'll have to. He can't leave the unit until he's completed his recovery."

"Yes, of course. Lee, would you like some music? Any reading material?"

"No, thank you."

"Yes, well, I'll go see about your aunt, then."

"Yes."

Kral waited until the door closed at the top of the stairs. "Those two care a great deal, you know."

"I know that."

He didn't expect me to agree so readily. "If I am allowed to ask, what in the world happened?"

"Digby Crusher happened. Some kind of testing or something. Not even sure what I was being tested for!"

"Digby Crusher did this? Very strange. He seems such a kind, gentle soul."

"Surprised all Seven Hells out of me, too!"

"It seemed so much more in character for him to demand this unit be rushed to this house without delay. Paid for it, the shipping, setting it up, everything!"

"Yeah," I grumped, "I'll pay him back for all that. From what I'm told, I can afford it."

I felt him staring. "I would think you far too young to be so jaded and bitter. I hope I don't offend you too much." He seemed nervous about my reaction. I actually surprised myself with my chuckle.

"That's one of those comments that's always struck me funny."

"What's that?"

"'I hope I don't offend you too much.' Is anybody measuring how offended a person should be? How much is too much offense? Is there such a thing as being offended ju-u-u-ust right?"

Kral chuckled. "How about, 'It's always darkest before the dawn,' when any idiot with a pair of eyes knows that it's darkest at *midnight*, and it's only getting brighter after that?"

I snorted with him. "And then there's, 'It takes one to know one.' No, it don't! If a whole squad of people are standing there, watching you make a complete blinkin' fool of yourself, do they all have to be idiots to know you're an idiot? Really?"

I've only seen Kral Doljon once or twice after that time, for only passing seconds, but there will always be a warm space in my heart for him. For getting me to laugh again. For talking to me about life in Eliondria, how folks on the other side of The Veil see humans and how they react to the still existing undercurrent of fear and resentment humans feel about 'Those Mysticlanders.' Sharing with me the quirky behavior of Simel, the man he loved and missed every day, every minute. So many things.

Especially the healing. Not the body. Helping me to heal my heart, my mind. My soul.

I wish there were more Kral Doljons on either side of The Veil.

I wish I could be more like Kral Doljon.

I couldn't be Kral Doljon. I could be a better me, though.

***

This wasn't the first time I found myself Astral Walking in my sleep. According to Alistra, it's safer than normal sleepwalking because the mind is actually conscious, though in a more relaxed, imaginative state. One could delve deeper into the dream state and bring a whole lot more order and clarity to his dreams. Or he could meander around in the 'Real World' and send out his astral body damn near anywhere in the world.

After nearly two weeks in the Regeneration device, I decided to do a walkabout around the house, see if there'd been any changes beyond the remodeling of our basement. I had a lot of love for this house. My bedroom, which I was told was larger than most studio apartments in NYC. The warm, comfortable feeling of sitting by the fireplace in the living room, the training salons that took up more than half of the outsized main floor.

I was just about to go into the study when I heard voices. I stayed in the hallway and listened. One of the voices, speaking in a broken stuttering tone of pain, belonged to my aunt. The other, calm, reassuring and caring, belonged to Lucy Helsinger, one of the very few people my family loved more deeply than any other, one we trusted with our lives. And just happened to be a 2nd generation Vampire.

Vampires, on the whole, are not a lovable race of beings, but the vast majority of horror stories told and repeated about the predators involve 4th generation Vampires, or 5th and 6th Gen., which were pretty much mindless beasts at that point. 2nd gen. Vampires, being closest to the progenitors of the race, require much less blood to survive, are many times more powerful than even the next generation, and, as far as Ms. Lucy knew (or would admit), there were only three other 2nd gen. Vampires left besides her. Since 2nd gen. Vampires' only reaction to sunlight was a slightly annoying case of sunburn, Melene and I were visited by Ms. Lucy often. My aunt preferred we didn't visit Ms. Lucy though, because she lived in New Arcadia, a pocket dimension located pretty close to the center of Brooklyn, and the place came with too many memories Melene preferred to not deal with. And as was usually the case, I accepted my aunt's word like it was gospel.

I spent a whole lot of the time recovering in the Regen device thinking about a lot of things I simply accepted with little or no questioning on my part. Was I really that big a clueless, naive moron? A wind-up warrior, built to follow orders and question nothing? Or was I simply learning that Blind Faith in all things was potentially hazardous to my health? And that real 'Trust' was a two-way street? That I would trust someone to tell me the truth, but that someone had to trust me with the truth?

But, I'd never heard my aunt sound so lost. So broken. The walls of anger I built up in my heart, the walls of resentment, all of it crumbled away as I listened to my loved one's sorrow. In all truth, Melene was everything to me, and it destroyed me to feel as if I could have anything to do with bringing her any kind of pain.

"And now, he hates me!" *Melene sobbed.*

"He doesn't hate you," *Lucy soothed.* "He couldn't hate you. He loves you more than breathing. He simply feels betrayed by those he loves. You, Digby, and even Alistra, bless her heart. He loves you all so very much, which means, for someone with deep passions like Maahes, the feeling of betrayal goes deep as well."

"I can't lose him, Lucy!" *Melene hiccupped in a broken tone.* "He's all I have left! I can't lose my *Son* too! I can't!"

'Son'? What is she saying? I've seen my birth certificate, and it's got Lionel and Belinda listed as my parents. She didn't say I was like a son to her. She said, "My son." Huh?

"I know that, Melly. We all know that. But all Maahes knows is loss, and a daily regimen of pain and drills! Every day, another level of back-breaking effort. Always expected to excel, always wanting to meet your expectations, while you keep moving the bar higher! I did warn you that it might become too much for him!"

"I know it, Lucy. I know. But he is a Child of The Pride! More than that, He's Lionel's Son! He is beyond anything ever seen on this planet, and Lyrodrylle as well! Before Lionel, there was never a Child of The Pride that could use magic. Lionel scared all of them, Lucy, all the way down to their bones. Can you imagine how they'll react when they see his son, who can do even greater things?"

Melene gasped for breath, then continued in her broken tone. "Yes, I pushed him. I pushed him harder than any being not of The Pride. Just like I was pushed when I was younger. Just as Bezine was pushed. You know the level of brutality cadets had to endure in the Burning Sands Training Academy, Lucy."

"Yes, Mel, but you had Bezine to share the load, and other cadets to commiserate with. You had the occasional Weekend Pass to relax and let your hair down. And after that, you had Lionel, then Belinda. Then, you had Maahes.

"You had a life outside of training and war. A wonderful life. Even I was envious of the life you all shared. Why'd you think I hung around you Big-headed Warrior types? I wanted to share in it, at least a little.

"But what kind of life has Maahes lived, Mel? It's been nothing but drill and discipline. Blood sweat and tears. No breaks, no happy memories. No friends to share his thoughts, his fears with. By The Creator, Mel, even the Christian Hermits have their God to pray to! Mas has had no one to run to, to lean on when he's pissed off with something you said or did. He can't have that kind of relationship with Digby, or Alistra, or even me. He has no one."

"He had the girls, didn't he?" *Melene snapped defensively.* "He had them in his life!"

"Did he?" *Lucy whispered.* "Does he remember that? Or is it an occasional dream that flits through his mind every once and a while?"

"You're right," *My aunt sighed sadly.* "Even that, we took from him. Oh, Lucy, what can I do? How do I fix this? I can't lose him too!"

"You'll never lose him, Mel. He loves you too much. But you will need to give him space. Let him begin to build a life of his own. And he needs to know *everything,* Melene. In the eyes of both sides of The Veil, he is a mature adult. It is time for him to receive his *full* inheritance, and not just a pile of money and a Multi-Planetary Conglomerate to play with!"

"Yes," Melene whispered. "It's time."

I drifted back to my sleeping body as they continued talking. I had a whole helluva lot to think about. But amongst the myriad of thoughts, two stood out the most: Ms. Lucy was right. Melene is everything to me. I do *love her more than breathing, and she'll never lose me. It's time that particular wound was healed as well.*

And, who or what did they mean by The Girls?

***

Only a week later, Kral shut down the device and I was able to stand up and stretch. Physically, I felt perfect. Even stronger, more flexible than when I went in. I said as much to Kral, who replied, "Even with your genetic ability to heal from just about anything, there are still imperfections, even at the molecular level. Muscles torn, bones broken, organs damaged.

"Now, your muscles are going to continue to have microscopic tears as you continue to develop them, but as for your bones and organs? Those my friend, are pretty much back to 'Showroom New'!" He waved at my arm. "Excepting that flesh sleeve you already built into your arm, though. The regeneration device didn't recognize that as a wound, so it left it alone. That *was* a deliberate body modification on your part, wasn't it?"

"Yes. Thanks, Kral. For everything."

He saw me looking around and nodded to an open space behind the machine, where a set of sweats and slides were placed on a bench. I smiled my thanks and went to put the clothes on. No need to swing too freely in the breeze, even when in your own home. I made my way up the stairs as the tech continued shutting down the machine. I was looking for Melene, and I could feel where she was.

As expected, she was sitting on a couch in the living room, reading through documents she printed into hard copies. She looked and gasped a little when she saw me cross through the threshold, but she didn't speak. All she did, all she seemed able to do, was sit the papers on the tea table next to her, fold her hands together, and look up at me.

No waiting, no drama, and no cat-scat. Whatever went down, this was Melene, more than just my aunt. She was like a mother to me, and I loved her with every fiber of my being. Accepting that truth, I sat down next to her, draped my arm around her shoulder, and gathered her into my chest.

"Maahes," She sighed fearfully. "Oh Maahes, I'm so sorry!"

"Me too," I replied, gently kissing her on the top of her head. "But we're Children of Sekhmet, Auntie. We heal, from every wound. So let's heal."

"Yes," she responded warmly, in happy relief. "We'll heal together."

We must have sat there for hours, just holding each other, healing. Just before we made our way to the kitchen, because we were both starving, I asked, "Melene, who were The Girls? Am I really just imagining that they were real?" She didn't reply immediately. I waited.

"No, Lee," Melene sighed finally. "They are not simply dreams of yours. They do exist, and we'll talk about that, and so many other things. But not yet. Soon. Can you wait until it's time?"

"Well, since you've *finally* let me know that I wasn't crazy and had imaginary friends," I replied archly, earning a light punch to the ribs. "I suppose I can wait a little longer."

"Thank you," My aunt whispered gratefully. "I love you, Maahes. So very much."

"And I love you," I replied, then whispered, "Mother."

She cried. I held her tenderly. Then, we dried our tears, and made our way to the kitchen. We fed our hearts, and now it was time to feed our bodies.

Chapter 9. Big Shoes, Big Enough Feet?

It took a bit, a couple of days, but my mind, heart, and Auntie healed up.

IT WAS JUST TOO SCRAGGIN' TIRING to stay angry. Especially with someone who dedicated the last quarter of a century exclusively on me becoming everything I could be. No way she deserves that, and I'd like to think I'm a better man than that.

After that, some routines were restarted, if adjusted a bit. And some new activities were introduced.

We continued my daily training regimen, but both my combat sessions and Talent training were reduced by an hour.

Instead of the 'Unto Death' approach of before, My combat sessions was more focused on honing learned skills and developing my own particular fighting style, merging the lessons I learned from Sambo, Krav Maga, Muy Thai, and Tai Chi Quan, amongst others, to create for myself a style that was fluid, open to growth, adequate regarding defense but primarily aggressive. And violent. My Masters, Melene and I agreed that, due to the genetics of my race and the shields I can generate with my Talent, I had a natural level of defense that would protect me from most levels of damage, so it would be best for me to focus on attack, to assume that I would begin most conflicts outnumbered by my opponents, so I should develop my best personal method of immobilizing multiple targets in the swiftest, most efficient manner. That was immensely helpful to me; instead of spending the time trying to gather in a plethora of techniques, I was able to focus on specific pieces from different techniques that I excelled at, merge them into a chimera-like system exclusive to me, so that my own, best practice rapidly came into being.

Alistra followed the same new theory in my Talent training as well. We both realized that one of the key factors in my 'Ripple Attack' being just a hair too slow for both our ideal, was the time my mind took to go through the vast inventory of possible spells and putting them into effect. We decided, instead of constantly choosing amongst the hundreds of spells I had mastered, to slice it down to twelve or so spells, across the Elemental spectrum, and put them on mental 'Speed Dial'. Three spells of the Fire element, three with Earth, Two of Water, One of Air until I grew stronger in that Element, and the last three combo spells like 'Chained Lightning' and my pseudo Telekinetic spell.

And, of course, there had to a slot for 'Thor's Hammer', a spell that, at full strength was one of the most powerful ever imagined. The Hammer was such a destroyer, I learned it, studied it, but never used it. I didn't hate an entire town or village that much.

After we made that adjustment, my Ripple of spells went from one spell every second and change to half a second. It was an excellent combo of hardcore spells, coming at an opponent every half a second.

As Alistra pointed out, "You already have a wider variety of spells than most of the top-gun spell slingers, Lyam. Those in the rapid-fire game usually put their focus on speed and power, not diversity. After all, a gun usually fires only one kind of bullet, y'know?"

It was a good thing the time spent on daily training was reduced from eight to six hours while at the same time a great deal more productive. It seemed that the level of interest in who I was, where I was going, and what I was doing had increased dramatically.

For starters, there was Digby, who came to visit after I was done in the Regen Device, eight days earlier than expected.

It was awkward at first. I was still a bit pissed with him. But Digby was Good Peoples, and we had history together.

We stared at each other for a few seconds, as Melene, Alistra and two of Digby's assistants stood off to the side. Silent. Digby sitting, me standing before him. With a grunt, Digby cleared the ice.

"Sorry about that." He rumbled. "You were expected to submit, after I took out your ribs. You wouldn't quit. You were supposed to." He shrugged, his shoulders emulating the continental shelf shifting.

"Why, Digby?" I asked. "What was it for?"

"Because," He responded slowly, deliberately. "It's important for a Nemesene to know his limits, to realize that there are some battles he cannot win on his own, and when to retreat, so he can fight another day!"

"Oh," I replied.

"Yes, 'Oh'!" Digby roared. "And just like I should've expected from the son of those two maniacs, you screw up the whole cursed lesson. First, by *not* giving up, then by finding a stone-munching way to *WIN!*"

The frozen tableau was wrecked by the quiet snickering of one of the strangers that came in with Digby. Digby looked at him, was about to snap off a comment, then wearily shook his head and sighed. "I really should have known better," he noted grumpily.

I didn't know what to say to that. "Um, my bad?" I offered, shrugging my shoulders.

Digby slowly stood up and looked me over. "This hair on your face. On purpose, or lazy?"

"On purpose."

"Hmph. Of course you won't let it grow to its greatest possibilities, like the rest of these heathens, but it's a start. Looks like you finally took the training wheels off."

I kept my verbal ripostes to myself, our reconciliation was newly hatched. Digby continued his inspection. "The unit did good work. You're taller."

Huh? That again? "I'm taller?"

His eyebrows furrowed in focus. "Six feet and a quarter of an inch, in these humans' primitive scale.

"Well, okay, I guess," I replied.

"You're probably going to top out at 6'2", 6'3" at the most. If you don't get your pebble-brained self killed permanently first!" he growled.

78

"I do apologize, sir. But I had no idea what the Unholy Hell was going on! I still don't, to be honest. All I know is a dear friend of the family had suddenly gone berserk and siccing his war dogs on me. Then he strips down and starts to wrecking-ball my carcass in my own home! What the scraggin' Hell was *that* all about? Um, sir?"

"It was a part of the deal I made with my Chief, Lyam." Melene stepped forward. "I've never left The Nemesene Cadre, Lee. A Nemesene may grow too old or too permanently injured for field work, but we rarely actually retire. Your parents, Aunt Bezine and I, we weren't simply a part of The Cadre. We were a team, a four person Unit serving as a Forward Area Strike Team. FAST units go into enemy territory, behind the lines. We do reconnaissance work, infiltrate, identify enemy positions, sabotage, assassinate, take out command structures, and basically cause all manner of mayhem. And I have no problem saying that we were the best damned team ever in The Cadre.

"After the two worlds began recovering from *The Sundering*, Lionel and Belinda started dabbling in High Finance. They wanted to create a nest egg for us, just in case. But while they were growing their nest egg into Lion's Share Inc., we were still on active duty, and we'd be called in for just about anything, with little to no warning, at any given moment in time.

"That changed when you were born. We wanted to take some time, live as a family instead of a commando unit. So we twisted our Chief's arm, kind of forced him to allow us to go on sabbatical, until you had grown into maturity. When that time came, you would be given the option of either joining The Cadre, if you were skilled enough to do so, or to live your life independently, however you chose, but the rest of us would return to active duty."

I looked at her, feeling a dark pit in my gut. "So, all this time, all this training, all of it was for making sure I could stand on my own? So you could leave me behind?"

"*Maahes!* No!"

I could barely breathe from the force of Melene's hugging. "Our plan was to have you join us in the field! You *are* a Lion, Lee. There's no way we could believe you wouldn't want to face the challenges, go to strange, new territories, and charge into danger by our sides. Then, when *you* felt you were ready, you would leave *us*, to develop your own team. Your own Pride, with you as The Lion, leading in courage and wisdom, as you were born to do."

I leaned back from our hug. "You know, we *really* should've had this particular chat a few years ago!"

"I know," She replied sadly, stroking my face. "I wasn't ready. I'm still not, to be honest."

"Yes, well," Digby interjected firmly. "Ready or not, his time draws nigh, and there is that business of the Maenads that is still not resolved to my liking. Maahes Seckett, you have expressed a desire to join the ranks of The Nemesene Cadre in the past. Is this still of interest to you?"

I took a moment.

Yes, I was the Heir to the Lion's Share empire, and that was massive, not to be ignored or treated lightly. But the Board of Directors, and our personal lawyers, were chosen specifically by my parents because they could be trusted to build the company in their absence, and to not cross the line into dirty, unethical business practices that would tarnish the name and reputation of the business. In the final analysis, I wasn't interested in serving as a figurehead that would rubberstamp whatever proposal they *might* remember to put on my desk.

And Melene was right. Just the thought of getting out into the field was making me burn with anticipation. I *wanted* to get out there and *wreck* it to the bone! I wanted to hunt!

And grow into being the leader of my own stone-cold wrecking crew? Oh, yeah. I could see that. Very clearly.

I looked to my soon-to-be boss. "Yes sir, Mr. Crusher. I very much want to join The Cadre."

"Good." He nodded once. "Maahes Seckett, I bid you to take a knee. Melene, you know what to do."

Melene gasped. "Truly? But I thought, but he's just…"

"You saw him, Melene. Tough enough to take horrific blows, Courageous enough to face his fears and not give up, and Sneaky-smart enough to find a way through a window when the front door is blocked off. Like Belinda and Lionel. Like you, Melene."

I didn't understand that bit, I just knelt there and kept my mouth shut as Melene stood behind me and placed her hands upon my shoulders.

Digby nodded once, then began speaking in his deep, resounding voice.

"We have before us as Candidate, Maahes Seckett, also known as Lyam, or Lee Seckett. It is Maahes' aspiration to join The Nemesene Cadre. Who speaks for this candidate?"

"I do," Melene responded proudly. "I, Melene Alabato Seckett, declare that Maahes Seckett is of strong mind, heart and character, that he has excelled in the varied training activities in preparation for consideration, and he would be a credit to The Cadre."

"So be it. Maahes. If there is any doubt in your mind concerning this decision, please express them now. *Is* there any doubt in heart, mind or spirit?"

I gulped. "There are no doubts, Sir."

He nodded, reached into his suit jacket, and pulled out a badge. I gulped again. *By the claws of the Goddess! That's a full Deputy's badge, just like Melene's. No wonder she was shook!*

The badge was oval, about three inches long and two inches at its widest. In the center was the five pointed star representing The Pentagram, the chief governing body of Lyrodrylle. Centered within the star was a set of scales. Next to the upper point of the star, on the left was a sword, and on the right was a stick with lines, representing a measuring rod. And below the star was a series of indecipherable runes that, according to my aunt, was from a beyond ancient, unused language that spells out *Nemesis.* The whole thing, like Melene's, sported a burnished, old gold finish.

He held out the badge to me. "Those that choose to aid Nemesis in her eternal pursuit of Divine Retribution do so because they burn for Justice. Do you feel that burn, Candidate? Do you burn for Justice?"

"I do," I responded, surprising myself with the intensity in my voice. "I do so burn!"

"Then place your hand upon your shield of office, and when you feel that burn, keep it there!"

I honestly thought he meant that metaphysically. Er, no. I followed directions, felt the cool metal badge under my palm, then, seconds later, there was an itching sensation, followed by heat. Then hotter, much hotter. My instincts told me to lift my hand and run to the nearest bucket of water. But he said, 'Keep it there!" So I did.

Oh Gods, I felt the flesh on my hand melt under the raging heat. I wanted to scream, I wanted to weep with agony, but everything that was *me* was frozen, locked into the torment my hand was feeling.

I looked up from the impossible, enduring pain. I looked to Digby who was the source of this agony—then I saw it. The air behind Digby began to shimmer, like an emerging mirage in the desert heat. Then the shimmering stopped, and she was there, standing tall over Digby's shoulder. Her hair was black, and long. Her eyes were a flaming red. Her face was beyond any mortal description of beautiful. It just *was,* and that's all that could be said. She must have been a goddess, but instead of some white, diaphanous gown, she was dressed in leather. Green and black, reinforced leather, with bronzed metal plates strategically placed in possible areas of vulnerability. She was dressed for combat, up to and including the grim, penetrating expression of resolve on her face.

I looked at her, looked into her burning eyes, and didn't blink. Even deep in the throes of horrific agony, I wouldn't blink, because I knew, somehow, that she didn't want me to. She wanted me to take it, and keep on taking it, until it was done.

So I took it. And didn't blink. And we stared into each other's eyes, seemingly for centuries, until her face creased slightly into a grim smile. Then she nodded, once, and faded away into the air.

"It is done."

I shook myself, refocused. I kept my eyes on Digby's face. Too afraid to look at my hand. Digby smiled. "It is alright, Lyam. Take up your shield."

I gulped, looked down.

My hand was perfectly fine. No melted skin. No blackened bones poking through. Not even any scorch marks. I took up my badge. It felt good. It felt *right*.

Digby chuckled. "Good thing you really had no doubts, eh?"

"I saw something. Someone. Who was she, Digby?"

"You saw the Goddess, Lyam. You saw Nemesis. Out of all the false gods and goddesses the humans had worshipped, Nemesis, The Creator's avatar for Divine Justice, is the one of the very few who exist by The *Creator's* Design, not any mortal being. And unlike the false deities The Cadre dealt with, Nemesis does not seek worship. She doesn't need it. She seeks justice, and she has accepted you to be one of her fellow seekers of justice, and dispensers of just retribution on those who break the peace of our two worlds."

"Damn, sir, does everyone in the Cadre have to go through that?"

"No. Companion Agents, and the lower ranks, go through a less intensive bonding process to The Cadre. Intense, but nowhere near as much as those of Deputy rank or higher.

"You see, a Deputy rank is essentially a *command* ranking. You can now officially form and lead your own unit of two or more. Any unit of ten or more usually needs the leader to have a *Deputy Primus* ranking, or *Deputy Centurio,* but that's not a hard and fast rule."

"Deputy Primus?" I asked. "Deputy Centurio?"

"Basically translates to Chief Deputy, or Lead Deputy, but the Cadre heads like using the humans' Latin when they can get away with it. Same with Deputy Centurio, which is the first command rank of a Battle Mage in The Cadre."

"But, Digby, why a command rank? I'm not ready to command anybody."

The elder smiled. "That's the *first* question your mother asked when I brought her into The Cadre. She did alright. So will you. Besides, I had to. There were witnesses, Lyam."

"Witnesses?"

"To your test. As I said, you were supposed to concede, because it was presumed that it would be impossible for you to be able to succeed, *because nobody has before!*"

"You mean, I, but you, but... Well, scrag it."

"That's what I said." He gestured forward the man that was snickering before. His walk was graceful, but firm, resolute. His eyes twinkled with suppressed mirth, but his face was full of creases and old, healed-over scars. He reached out his hand as he approached. I *knew* him, but from where?

"Congratulations, Young Man!" He grinned. "Your Maestra showed me your test through a telepathic link. Very inventive solution, kid! Sneaky and underhanded, in other words, perfect! You might be more ready than she already thinks you are!"

"Thank you, sir! Er, ready for what?" Digby answered for him.

"This is Karl von Brunner. He is no longer a field agent in The Cadre. He is a retired Battle Mage. By choice. You might not remember, but Maestro was your actual first Talent trainer, a few months after your first birthday. Three years in, he decided that you needed a stronger, more diverse development in the Arcane before you focused exclusively on Battle Arts. Happily, he and your parents were able to convince Maestra Alistra to return, and help another Seckett to find their way through The Arcane Arts, as she did for your parents.

"Now that you have that depth of knowledge, he will be joining with Maestra De Vore in preparing you for your increase to rank to 5th Degree Sorcerer, then for undergoing The Trials for the Battle Mage rank. Before you ask, this is per your Maestra's request. She has made it very clear these past nineteen years that she is not the best teacher for combat training. I've seen the results of Maestro von Brunner's efforts. He's a much better teacher than he was a Battle Mage, and he was a *highly* accomplished Battle Mage. This will be an ongoing effort that will have to fit in around the assignments that you and Melene will be dealing with.

"Because, as of today, you are both on the active duty roster."

I nodded, taking it in. "As you say, Sir. What's the first assignment?"

"The *prime* assignment is this stone-blasted Maenad thing! I've got an itchy feeling in my beard. My instincts are telling me this isn't done! But we have no leads yet, so we can't move on it at this moment. Until then, you must keep yourselves ready for whatever other issues may pop up in my territory. Brushing up on your language skills would be of immense help to you."

He reached into his jacket again, and pulled out a leather sack. It had a flap closure and loops so it could be fitted on a belt.

"This is a gift for you, Congratulations, and welcome into The Cadre, Deputy."

"Oh no!" I almost squealed like a two-year-old. "Is that what I think it is?"

"Yes, Lee. Your own portable dimensional pocket. I make sure that all my Command rank personnel have at least one of their own."

"By The Goddess. Thank you, Chief. Thank you!"

I was trying to be cool, but Gods and Goddesses—a PDP. My own PD-scraggin'-P!

"You know how to attune it to your personal use?" Melene asked as she looked at me passing my hand lovingly over the leather exterior. "Because of this immunity thing, I needed both Lionel and Belinda to help me get attuned to mine!"

"Go ahead, Lee," Alistra offered. I'll be here in case you need help."

"I think me and The Old Man got it," I snorted as I willed my Staff from its sheath in my arm. It flared out to its normal size and length then vibrated slightly in my hand, the gemstones placed along the shaft glittering with the subtle movement. I suppose I called my Staff 'The Old Man' because it was made of Tellerind wood which, the legends say, was native of Atlantis and was imbued with Mystical properties far beyond any other wood used for making Wizard staffs. A lot of Talents give their staffs names. I haven't. I figured if The Old Man wanted to be named, he'd tell me what the name would be, somehow. Someday.

I opened the flap of the PDP, stuck my right hand in the space, and then gripped my staff tightly. I felt the staff begin to shudder rapidly, closely followed by a smooth, warm but firm grip on my hand in the space. After about twenty seconds or so, I felt my hand being released, and the Staff stopped vibrating.

I had to try it out! I ran to one of the book shelves, and grabbed a nice, massive tome. *History of Commerce in Ancient Lemuria.* Perfect! I pulled back the flap. The opening was nowhere near wide enough to simply slide the book in, so I turned it on an angle and slid an edge of the book into the opening of the PDP. Once the edge got into the opening, the rest of the book vanished!

Now, the crucial part. I reached into the pouch, thought about the book title—then I felt it in my hand! I pulled, and the opening flexed itself around the book so I could finish pulling it free.

"Oh, Hellz yeah!" I punched a fist into the air. PDPs are so smokin' killer!

Even Digby was chuckling at my display. "And he's one of my Deputies," he sighed.

"Okay, we'll be on our way. There's much to do, for all of us. So let's get to work!"

Soon, it was just Melene and me in our home. She was me eyeing in such a way, I thought I had left my pants undone. "What I do now?"

"Nothing, dear one. I was just thinking that we should make a call to Anders Krieg, the family's exclusive tailor in Arcturus, Tellerman." She smiled at my puzzled look. "The shop that put together your duster?"

"Oh. But why?"

"Lee, did you think you would be going into the field wearing a pair of jeans and a tee shirt?"

"Um, no?"

"That's right, um no! In fact, we need to look over everything. Apparel, Footwear, you've already got storage capacity taken care of, and your revolvers are fine for training purposes, but in the field, you *must* be able to shoot more than five shots before reloading." She sighed at my hangdog expression. "Okay, maybe, *maybe* as a backup piece. But something along the lines of a Desert Eagle has to be your primary. Actually, Hal's armory in The Bronx has done absolutely brilliant work in using Lyrodryllian-sourced metals to develop reinforced alloys, and they've created .55 caliber that looks the same and are…"

She was right. I sighed as I followed her into our weapons locker, then to our gear caches.

A whole helluva lot to do.

Chapter 10. Clubbin'

I LOVE MY AUNT MELENE.

SHE MEANS THE WORLD, STARS AND SUN TO ME.

But there are times ...

And one of those times came a few days after I was placed on The Cadre's active roster. No other assignments had been given yet, so I continued my training, with the addition of Maestro von Brunner. He truly was a Hella-scary Arcanist. He used his portion of my Talent training sessions to focus on Area of Effect spells, spells that could do serious wreckage to a targeted area, or on multiple enemies instead of a single enemy. He stole the terminology from the multitude of computer gaming programs that had become addictively popular at the time.

"As a Battle Mage, it's almost guaranteed that it you will be outnumbered, probably by a large margin." He explained. "You don't want your enemies to be free to line you up for a shot while you're busy with only one or two."

And Digby was right, he was a great teacher. In only three days he was able to evaluate the shift in focus Maestra Alistra and I had decided on, jumped right in, and ratcheted it up even higher.

Those sessions, and the combat sessions were going very well, very productive. And he helped me to streamline the mental incantation for Thor's Hammer, but recommended to keep it as a *coupe de gras*, not on the rapid fire list of options. "It's bulky by necessity, Lee, so it's still gonna take time to put it into effect. And don't get it twisted, young man. Battle Mages have to be careful about collateral damage, especially since those piles of dung in The Red Hand used the *Canferashon* and came close to destroying all life on both planets."

"Maestro, do you have any idea why they did it?" The man sighed, wiped his wrecked face for a bit. "No one knows for sure, Lee. And no one who ever found a member of the cult ever kept them alive long enough to ask. I have a theory though. I've pondered it often.

"The history books you've read told you of the race that made up most of the members of the cult, right?"

"Yes," I nodded. "The Ellovysians."

"Right. Those twisted wastes of animated flesh. Nearly as good a breed of Warriors as the Lionesses of The Pride, and top-flight Magicians. Beautiful to look at. And the most foul, evil-minded piles of donkey dung ever allowed to breathe free air. They experimented on sapient beings, Lyam. Sometimes to discover something. Sometimes to try out a new theory. Sometimes just because they scraggin' enjoyed seeing the agony on their faces.

"Anyway, I strongly believe that the Ellovysians somehow convinced these Red Hand idiots that they would somehow survive the wreckage of the spell. Ellovysians were big on discovering and exploiting pocket dimensions, and I believe that just about all of the members of that race tucked themselves up in a pocket dimension, and are either waiting for the dust to clear from the ruins and take over everything, or, and I pray this to be what happened, the pointy-eared tools forgot how to reopen the dimension, and they're stuck in it forever!"

I sat there, thinking about it. Ellovysians were universally hated. For damn good reasons. No one had a strong theory on why they seemed to have all disappeared, though there is a growing sentiment that there are still a few, or more than a few, in hiding. I shuddered.

"Sir, what if your theory is the answer? And they somehow find a way out of their pocket dimension?"

"Hell on Earth," the Maestro sighed wearily. "And on Lyrodrylle. Straight-up Hell."

In between me worrying about a sudden appearance of the Ellovysians, or Elves, a derogatory term used to describe the race, Melene, outside of training, was driving me nuts!

If it wasn't getting the gear together, it was going over, yet again, the geography of North, South and Central America. And the languages. And the cultures. And the population centers. And best available modes of transportation.

Then there were the stories she shared 'From The Files of The Cadre,' using them as object lessons for what to do and not do in the field.

Then there was the review of the multitudes of beasts, monsters and undeads; their abilities, eating habits, habitats, preferred modes of attack. Vulnerabilities.

You get the drift.

It was a Friday night. Most everyone my age was getting ready to go clubbing. I was studying the mating habits of the flightless cockatrices of Ketzel, when I realized that this was a truly balls way of spending a Friday night. I closed the book, carefully put it back on the shelf, turned to my beloved aunt and said, "This is cat-scat. I'm going out."

She looked up, saw the 'Dazed and Crazed' expression in my eyes, and said, "Yes, this might be a bit much. Go. Have fun."

I kissed her forehead, and pretty much flew out the room. Forty minutes later, I was clean, groomed, geared, and calling Megan Trasker. I figured she, if anybody, would know of a place I could just chill.

"Oh my GOD! LEE!" The woman actually did scream. "How *are* you? Where've you been? Nobody's heard from you, seen you anywhere, it's like you just got swallowed up by the earth or something! Where are you? What are you doing?"

I tried to reply, but she just hit third gear.

"Whatever it is, CANCEL IT! You have to be here. You absolutely must! You can't just disappear on people, Lee."

"But where's here, Megan?"

"Dante's Retreat in Brooklyn! You have to be here! Trini's performing! She's been asking about you almost every day!"

"But Jackson and—"

"Yesterday's stinkin' trash!" *Back to the high decibels*, I sighed. "She dropped that loser after I told her about the meeting. She was so pissed. Say you'll come! Are you coming? Are you? Are you?"

"Yes, I'll come!" I pulled the cell phone away until she stopped screaming. "But if you're gonna be blowing my eardrums out, I won't hear the performance."

"I'm sending a ride to you now! Are you at that address in Queens? Good! Don't move! It'll get there in twenty minutes! This is good. This is GOOD!"

We spent another five minutes agreeing on how good it was, then I ended the call, slipped on my favorite (see: only) black duster, and decided to slide my short barreled, S&W 500.50 cal. in my PDP.

Because you never know.

Staff in its skin sheath, .50 cal. in a handy pocket dimension, wallet full of large bills, and wintergreen breath mints in my pants pocket. I was good to go.

I had just enough time to deactivate the protections surrounding my home. The Secketts try to minimize taking chances. Melene would reactivate the security network of spells, runes and everything else after I left. The driver-less electric was right on schedule, and I slid into the backseat. It took off before I could speak. Preprogrammed, it seemed. Like the brilliant work the Technomancers of Eliondria achieved in creating the PDP, and the fact that every other car on the road, with or without drivers, were electric powered and not the toxic, destructive gasoline of the past, there had been a great many innovations, almost miraculous at first but perceived as commonplace today, innovations that have greatly increased the quality of life for nearly every sapient being on Earth today.

It's just a horrid, horrid shame that it took *The Sundering* for these innovations to be introduced to humans.

Billions died when The Veil collapsed, causing the two planets, Earth and Lyrodrylle, to occupy the same spatial and dimensional space. The Veil allows the two planets to be connected, but existing in two different dimensions. A great many Lyrodryllian theorists had pondered what would happen if The

Veil was not there to keep the planets connected through Veil Waypoints. Most came down on the side that believed the two planets would go their separate ways, never the twain to meet.

As the citizens of both worlds discovered, they were wrong.

I felt myself filling up with an unexpected melancholy, as my transport smoothly exited The Belt Parkway and made its way up to Atlantic Avenue. I looked out, saw houses that must have been there for sixty of more years, and the newer, different single and multiple occupancy residences sprinkled in amongst the crowd. The architects that came from Lyrodrylle to assist in the recovery tried to design the newer buildings to blend in with the existing structures, but after all the cleaning up, after the resurfacing of all the streets and highways, with the remodeling of the local green spaces, the resulting appearance of so much of the Outer Boroughs just didn't flow. The newer structures felt like semi-hostile invaders, and the existent houses and buildings just looked so tired and out of step with the 'new normal'. So much gained, but so damned much lost. There were a great many archived pictures and video recordings of New York City before *The Sundering*, but they did little to convey the energy, the vitality of the people, of the streets. NYC is still the city that never sleeps, don't get me wrong. It's just that, so many souls, so many amazing stories, so much potential for greatness. Lost, forever.

Shake it off, Bruh. Save the 'woe is us' thoughts for when you're not going out to enjoy being around other folk.

Dante's Retreat was a relatively new club/performance space in what was the East New York section of Brooklyn. As was the case in so many parts of the planet, there were significant changes. It was located on Atlantic Ave., but the entrance was on Wyona Street. It took up almost half the block, and from what I could see, it was bursting at the seams with folk looking to get in. Well, why the Hells not? At the very least, it had a unique look that had to attract interest. The Security people at the door were dressed in leather outfits, including hoods and masks, looking like medieval torturers and executioners, and I hoped with all my soul that the dandies dressed up in variations of the human's Renaissance period were staff. I sighed in relief when I noted that those on and around the long line to get in were dressed in the latest gear. I didn't feel a need to get extravagant, so I went with pair of straight leg wool trousers in black, a pearl grey, collarless shirt jacket, and my usual ankle-high, lace up boots and black duster. Cleaned and polished, of course. Casual, comfortable, and stylish enough. At least for me. I really didn't like close-fitting clothes. And I truly loved my boots. I have about four or so pairs of the same style. Inch-high heel, round toe, styled to look like upscale dress boots, but with a reinforced metal plate across the toes and lined throughout with Crolineum, yet another innovation from those wacky scientists in Lyrodrylle who decided that the bullet-proof liners invented by humans just wasn't flexible, thin and protective enough. In essence, I wore my combat boots whenever I left my home.

Because you never know.

I started towards the entrance, figuring that, with Megan sending the ride, she probably made sure to have my name on the guest list. Sure enough, I took no more than two steps before I heard the cry of the banshee. Or in this instance, Karl, Megan's assistant.

"LEE! Over here!" He ranted as he ran over from the doors. "Don't even *think* of getting on that line! Megs would kill me!"

The daft fool actually jumped into my arms and kissed me on the cheek. He's so lucky I liked him. "Um, Karl, you do know I don't go that way, right?"

"I know," He pouted, "But there's always hope!"

"You're such a fool!" I chuckled as I carried him to the entrance. In the short time I was on Blue Star's Team, Karl was Good Peoples with me. Funny, outlandish, a bit of a queen, really, but sharp and focused when it came to scheduling, accommodations, transports, and other potential logistical nightmares. And the faces he would come up with when Jackson or any of his crew were nearby? Priceless.

After I set him back on his feet, him resisting all the way, He led me through the doors and he gave me a rundown of current events.

"There was another attack, a week ago." He whispered as we passed through the interior, designed to reflect, in a somewhat sanitized way, the various rings of Hell, with the dark lighting, strategically placed torches, and caged up captives in shredded clothing and writhing in agony. I prayed fervently that they were paid employees of the club. There were those clubs in The NYC that catered to those non-humans that thrived on the pain and agony of others, but they were more discreetly located and concealed.

"It was hushed up, thoroughly, by the D.I.A. It was awful, Lee. Denny was injured pretty badly, and ten people died!"

"Where?"

"Greta's Boutique. A lingerie shop in SoHo. Trini just wanted to do a little shopping!"

I put my arm around Karl's shoulder, I could feel him shaking. I wanted to tell him that it would be alright, but I couldn't. I was off the team, and I wouldn't make assurances I couldn't enforce.

"Denny's recovering okay?"

"Yes. His Agency has one of those Regeneration gizmos. They got him in it in time. He should be up and about in another two weeks."

"But what about Grantham? Where was he?"

Karl looked at me with dead eyes. "He's the reason for the ten civilian deaths! He dropped a spell, and it destroyed the whole freakin' store. And acts like he did us a favor in putting a shield over us first. Ham-handed Nazi!"

I was shook. That wasn't Billie Grantham. He's an egotistical, conceited prick that thinks the sun shines out his cheeks, a glory hound who takes the majority of credit for a minimum of actual participation, but he's a monster of a Sorcerer! He's skilled enough for a 5th Degree Sorcerer ranking easy, but hates the idea of someone 'Superior' to him telling him what he can and can't do. Being on the receiving end of his skills too damned many times, I personally wouldn't spit on the stuck-up blowhole if he was on fire, but I respected him highly as a Talent.

"Do you have any idea what spell he used?" I asked worriedly.

"I heard him talking to a Director," Karl gulped. "Something about a 'Hammer'."

Oh. Hells. No.

You don't drop 'Thor's Hammer' in an urban setting. Not unless you were on a real creative, and real scraggin' stupid demolition team. Thor's Hammer is the ultimate AOE attack spell, used only when you're surrounded on all sides by a regiment of enemies and you've completed your Last Will and Testament. Imagine a bolt of lightning, about the size of a subway car, slamming down in the midst of a village, or town. Total devastation.

Thing is, even with the Hammer, Billie Grantham was a meticulous breed of Talent. I would know, because the douche dropped Thor's Hammer on me! Twice! But his skills were of such a high degree of control and preciseness, he could taper the power of the spell so that instead of wiping out fifteen city blocks, he could put in just enough strength to smash an up-and-coming newbie through the floor of his home salon. It's been a couple of years since our last simulated battle. I guess the level of difficulty in beating me had grown to the point that he didn't want to try his luck a third time. Me learning the spell as well, might have also had something to do with his not accepting any more invitations from Alistra and Melene for assisting in my training sessions.

Tool.

Point being, even if Grantham dropped the Hammer, he should have been able to control its level of intensity—much more than it seemed to be the case. I was about to ask another question when I was suddenly waylaid by a rather nice load of wriggling flesh.

I don't remember ever kissing this particular mouth before, but the experience felt quite delightful. Warm, full, and aggressively battling my tongue for supremacy. This was one Hells of a kiss!

Please don't be Karl!

Thankfully, no. I don't think Karl had an impressive set of lungs to press into my chest. Besides, the smirky fool was standing right next to me. After another few seconds of oxygen deprivation, the arms lessened their grip and I was allowed to pull back and start breathing again.

"Umm, that was definitely on my to-do list," Megan purred as she slid back to the floor.

"Well, hello, Megs! Gotta say, I had no idea you were interested."

"Interested! I wanted to lock you in my bedroom for a month two minutes after I met you, stud." She ran her hand across my jaw and lips. "You're letting a beard and mustache grow! Pirate Look. I like, a lot. Adds character and mystery. But not too much? It can tickle in a not-nice way!"

I quirked an eyebrow. "I'm still stuck on two minutes."

"I wanted to make sure you weren't into Karl first."

I cast a lecherous gaze at the assistant, who started laughing at the look. "Well he is a sweet bit of eye candy, but no. I prefer to be the only car on the road with a stick shift."

"Well, I do hope to get a chance to take you for nice long drive in the near future?"

"Oh you both make me ill!" Karl groaned as he led us further into the club, giving me the opportunity to see, and feel Megan, as she refused to let go of my arm.

Because, to be completely honest, I didn't take the time to look at her when I was on the job. Well, look, I guess, but not *see* her, if that makes any sense. Like my aunt, for example. Melene was 6'3", and from head to toe, she was a hetero males' fantasy of so stacked up top, with a wasp-thin waist, wide, flaring hips, and so much junk in the trunk, it was if parts of her came into a room two seconds before, and after, she did. All this, sheathed in a powerfully sculpted musculature, so much so that there wasn't the least bit of hanging, sagging or excess at all. All this was true, and I was with her every day. But I don't *see* her. I don't gaze upon her perfect flesh and have…*thoughts.*

Look, *Anybody* that knows anything about natives of Sekhmet's Pride know that the race as a whole could be considered inveterate horndogs, to borrow from local human slang. This goes for both male and female. But there are limits, and we do respect barriers. Well, I do at least. I suppose it might be too much time amongst you humans and your twisted version of 'morality' that you rarely follow yourselves.

I mean, *ewww,* she really is like a mom to me, guys!

Besides, unlike the vast majority of modern-day Cro Magnons scampering about on both sides of The Veil, when I have a job to do, *I do the job,* and everything else is a distant second.

I used that focused line of thought when I came into the Security gig. Megan was a boss, Trinidad Flores was a client, and that was that. And unlike the way she was dressed tonight, Megan assisted in that focus by wearing dress suits and pants suits that deemphasized her figure. Very stylish, but very professional. But Holy Hell! Those outfits had a good bit to deemphasize. The sleeveless 'little black dress' was pretty close to form-fitting, and it was a very impressive form. At 5'6", with long legs, nicely curved hips, and a healthy pair sitting on top of a flat stomach and narrow waist, the 36 year old woman knew I was getting an eyeful, and the smile on her face made it clear that that was according to plan.

"But why did you just disappear like that, Lee?" She asked over the music in the club. "You had nothing to be ashamed about!"

"It wasn't shame, Megs. It's complicated, but basically, I've got a new job, after having to go through a back-breaking interview. Emphasis on 'breaking'."

"Oh, what is it?" She squeezed my arm tighter, smashing it into her chest. Oh My.

I looked her in the eye. "Keep it to yourself? For now?" When she nodded, I leaned closer to her ear. "The Cadre."

Her eyes near-on bugged out of her head. She silently mouthed, "Nemesenes?" I nodded.

"*Wreck* me!" she gasped.

I smiled at her using slang from the far side of The Veil. "Is that a request?"

Her mouth smiled slowly. "And if it is?"

"I've been known to do requests in my shows." I returned her smile as I replied.

She squeezed my arm again. "So glad you could make it! You and your new facial hair."

She led me through a set of doors, down a short hallway, then into the performance hall. Looked like it seated around a thousand. Pretty big club, to fit in a dance floor, a cocktail lounge, a smallish bistro and a concert space which, going by the steps Megan was walking me towards, included the requisite VIP room.

"You can watch her from up here. I don't want her to know you're here yet. I want it to be a surprise. She'll be going on soon. You hang here, enjoy the show!"

"Where's the crew?" I asked worriedly.

"The Chief and the others are backstage, Tilsa's with her in the Dressing Room. Grantham's wandering around the club. 'Overwatch,' he called it." Megan sniffed. "Whatever. I gotta get to Trini. Sometimes she gets too amped before hitting the stage. Gotta make sure she's relaxed."

"Go on, Megs. I'm good."

She leaned forward and gave me another toe-curling kiss. "I'm expecting nothing less than 'Brilliant' later, Stud!"

I watched her sway out the door. There was indeed some junk in *that* trunk, and she knew it! Even with the professional gear, I'd a paid attention to that lady if she walked like *that* before now!

"Well, it seems you bring out the, *best* in her, one could say?"

I turned to the voice, and saw Billie Grantham, and his requisite opera cape, standing towards the rear of the VIP Lounge. He wasn't smiling. No smirk in evidence. He seemed very focused on something. Hope it wasn't me—I wasn't in the mood for his garbage.

"She told you about the incident?" I nodded. "Caught a healthy slice of Hell from every direction on that one. It wasn't one of my shining moments."

I moved to a seat closer to him, I didn't feel like others needed to hear us. I sat down, then looked up at the man. "We're both Talents, Billie. We know the deal. You know I know what you're about. *What in Cracking Hells happened?*"

He sighed. "That's the thing of it, Lyam. *I don't know what happened!* It wasn't that big a mob. Only about forty or so. And they couldn't even all fit into the shop! The other four were focused on close quarters action, I was keeping the area disciplined, funneling the attackers, like you did.

"Suddenly I had a feeling of vertigo, it was just a second, but everything felt all twisted inside. After that, I guess I decided that a nicely rationed amount of Thor's Hammer would end the issue. Quick, fast, just need to hose down the streets after."

"But it wasn't nicely rationed, Billie."

"I know," He groaned. "I could feel it. I can't explain why it was so powerful. All I could do was throw up the strongest shield I could and place it around as many people in the boutique as possible." He grimaced. "It worked, mostly. But there were some casualties."

"Billie, I want you to think hard. Think about how you were thinking at the time. Were you thinking about Thor's Hammer while you were throwing up the screens and blocking shields, or did it come to mind later? *After* the feeling of vertigo passed?"

I watched him as he mulled it over, his forehead wrinkling in concentration.

"Oh, damn it straight to Hell," he whispered. "I got *jacked*!"

I nodded. "I'll bet the Talent I killed would have said the same thing. If she lived."

"But I saw the body. She looked as cracked out as the rest of the crazies."

"She was probably under an influence a lot longer than you were." I thought about it some more. "I'm spit-balling here, Billie, but maybe her takeover was slow, gradual, hard for her to notice, until she was completely taken over. But you felt a hard twist. A shock to your system. Possibly because of the short space of time, possibly because the influence had to travel over a longer distance to reach you."

"Damn!" He snarled heatedly. "Damn, Damn, DAMN! Someone invaded *my* head? Took *me* over?!"

I shrugged. "It happens."

"Why didn't it happen to you?"

"If all this isn't just intellectual exercise Cat-Scat, then I would suggest that whatever we're talking about already had a Talent puppet. Maybe it can only do one at a time?"

"*Damn it*. What do I do now?" We saw the lights dim, and an off-stage announcer began hyping up the crowd. "I can't get checked out now! All these people, and I don't know if I'm in control!"

"Don't worry." I replied as I got to my feet.

"I don't want to hurt anybody!"

"You won't."

"How can you know that, Seckett?"

"Because I won't let you."

"You? How are you—"

He didn't finish his thought, due to a sudden loss of consciousness by way of a right hook to the nerve cluster near his jaw.

"And now, ladies and gentlemen! Here she is...*SELENE!*"

I dragged Grantham's body with me closer to the front of the lounge, took a seat, and watched the performance.

Chapter 11. Heroes

It was the best show I'd ever seen.

TRINIDAD FLORES WAS BORN FOR THE STAGE. She was beyond human description. There *had* to be some touch of the Arcane in her ancestry! No wonder the Maenads were trying so hard to take her out. I think I finally got closer to the twisted logic. Something that beautiful, so close to perfect—it couldn't be allowed to exist in the mortal realm. It had to be released from this plane of existence, and sent on to the Elysian Fields, to Paradise. To Heaven.

I found myself laughing, and touched to my core, by how she began her show. The lights came up on three tall, huge men and a woman of the same proportions. Strong, muscled, and wearing masks, along with stylized Security uniforms. Trini's voice came from off stage as the four stood unmoving on center stage.

"This is how I be living now. Haters trying to shut me down. Sleaze-ball slave owners trying to keep a Sistah on the plantation. Turncoat skanks trying to rob me of my voice! But it ain't gonna work, haters. You can't shut me down. Holla if ya' hear a Queen spittin' the truth!"

The crowd screamed in response to the command.

"*¡Los Tontos Malvados no Pueden Retenerme!* They can't lock me down in they box. Holla!"

The walls vibrated from the screams.

"You can't close me down! You can't lock me up! And you damn sure can't shut *La Reina* up! I GOT THE THRONE NOW,

HATERS! *The people don't hear you!* No matter how loud you HOLLA!"

Straight pandemonium erupted all around me. Even the service crew were screaming and crying. Me too. Well, not the crying part. Not much.

"'Cause I got me my posse, and they got my back!" Another roar of acceptance. "'Cause I got me my crew, and they got my back!" The crowd raged again, then the stage suddenly went black, and her voice, in lower, softer tone, said, "And I got me my hero, and he won't let me fall."

The lights came up again on the stage again. The band kicked into gear, and the four security types had formed a small corridor, two by two. Then we watched, mesmerized, as someone new came on the stage from the side, carrying something. He was tall, muscled, and wearing a long black trench coat with a hood covering the top of his face. He turned to the front of the stage, and the crowd went into paroxysm when they saw that the man was carrying their *Selene,* His strong protective arms cradling her securely, while she had her arms wrapped around his neck and her head on his chest.

I collapsed into my chair. The tapes had gone viral…everyone had to have seen them by then. They had to recognize the visual she was creating. They knew what she was saying, and to whom she was saying it.

I watched as he gently placed her on her feet, they embraced, and then he walked off the stage. She stepped forward, faced the crowd, and said, "Even the Queen needs a hero sometimes."

The crowd roared in agreement.

"And I ain't talkin' 'bout somebody who's gonna hover you all the time! I ain't talkin' 'bout someone gonna stop *La Reina* from doin' her thing, ya heard!"

She had them in complete thrall as she worked the stage.

"I'm talkin' 'bout a REAL hero! Someone who'll let you stretch your wings, and fly on your own. Stand on your own two, and call your own shots. Someone who gets it that a Queen just gotta do what a Queen gotta do. Holla!

"See, a real ride-or-die hero knows that sometimes, all a body need to know is that when it's time to put in work, They! Got! Yo'! Back!"

She drew further to the edge as the crowd roared back in response.

"Everybody needs a hero!" She leaned forward. "A hero," she paused, she willed them in. "A hero, JUST LIKE YOU!"

Oh, lords and ladies! She hadn't started singing, and already she'd achieved delirium.

"You can be a hero. You can be somebody's hero. We can all be heroes! Are you wit' me? ARE YOU WIT' ME?!"

She began stomping around the stage as the band, and the Security types stomped right with her as she further amped up the crowd (If that was even possible) and the band shifted into a hard-edged Funk Groove!

"C'mon! Let's be Heroes! C'mon!" She started jabbing her finger at people in the audience. "You gonna be a hero to somebody? You? You got my back? I know *you* got a Queen's back! Yeah, I'm talkin' to you. Throw it up! Throw it up high! C'mon! Let's be heroes! Let's be heroes! And let's tear this Mutha DOWN!"

The next two hours were a revelation. She sang. She rapped. She brought the lights down for a spoken word set. She tore hearts to pieces with songs of love and loss. She inspired. She flowed into Spanish, French, Creole, never missing a beat, never losing one completely enthralled vassal of her Queendom. She briefly segued into a brief comedy routine, laughing about her own 'All Mighty Hiney-Highness', and we were allowed to laugh with her, understanding the message of not taking yourself so damned seriously. And we loved her for helping us to laugh at ourselves too. Then the band started jammin', the old-school D.J. on stage started scratchin' and the crowd went berserk!

She ended up doing two encores. The crowd was on the edge of riot, and wouldn't let her leave. Finally, at the last, she came back out for the second time.

"Y'all makin' a Sistah put in extra work! You puttin' out extra bucks!" The audience howled, and some started throwing money. She picked up a bill. "Yo, what's up?! That's a five! What you sayin'? I'm a low-budget *puta*?" She shushed the crowd. "But serious, though. I'm done. But I'll do one more for ya'.

"This is an old-school piece written by Patti Labelle—yeah, I know you know *that* Queen! Now, respect due to royalty, most of us in the business don't even touch this song. But I'm feelin' it, though, and I'm feelin' all of you! So I'm gonna give it a shot!

"And I'm dedicating this song to all of you. All my peoples. And I'm dedicating this song to you, Lee, wherever you are. You ain't asked for a damn thing, but you gave me my life. Thank you, for being a hero when I needed one."

You are my friend.
I never knew it 'til then, my friend.
You hold my hand
You might not say a word
But I see your pain when I show my tears ...

I knew the song. I loved the song. I had both Patti Labelle's version and Sylvester's in my audio collection, both live versions. It was sad that this was one of the few recordings Sylvester was able to do before he was gunned down by a psychotic homophobe.

Now I gotta add another version to my collection, I decided as the tears rolled down my face.

Been around, been around, been around
I've been looking around and you were here all the time...

Thunderous applause, cascades of tears, complete strangers hugging each other, leaning on each other for support. It was a cathartic moment for us all. I so needed this moment.

And you missed it, Billie, I sighed as I looked down at the unconscious Sorcerer. *Ah, well, I'm sure you know someone who's good with healing spells.*

Chapter 12. After The Dance
About fifteen minutes later, Karl came up for me.

I HAD ALREADY SET GRANTHAM DOWN in one of the couches in the Lounge. I had called one of the numbers I had for the D.I.A., and someone would be coming for him shortly. Karl led me through the service area, and we soon arrived near the dressing area. There was a throng of people outside Trini's dressing room, most of whom gasped and whispered frantically as they stepped out of my way, clearing a path to the door. The few that didn't recognize me were snatched back off their feet. I could hear Trini and Megan through the door.

"But I'm *tired,* Megs! I can't see nobody. All I wanna do is get something   to   eat   and   go   to   bed."
"And you will get something to eat. And you will go to bed. Seeing one bloody fan isn't gonna stop that from happening."

"But *why,* Megs? Why you gotta pull some smack like this after the hardest show I ever done?"

"Because," Meg giggled. "Because the show ain't over!"
"What you talking about?"
By that time, Karl was turning the knob on the door.
"What the Hell, Karl? You gotta—oh, my God! Lee?!"
"Hello, Trini," was as far as I got, before the petite powerhouse wrapped herself around me and hugged with all she had.

"Lee! I missed you." She leaned back her head. "Were you here for the show? Did you see it? Did you?" Her look focused. "You growin' that hair on purpose? If not, you should."

"I saw it all, Trini. I don't have the words. You were beyond brilliant."

"I'm so glad!" She wrapped me up again, and then leaned over enough to swat Megan with one of her arms. "*¡Puta!* This why you cheezin' all damned night? I hate you!"

"Just wanted to get my cut off the top," Megan giggled. "You know how us managers are."

"Skank!" Trini grinned, eyes twinkling. "How was he?"

"Just a kiss so far. But the toes tingled, and the panties were just about to drop!"

"Hmph." She turned back to me. "I'm gonna kiss you, cause I really, really missed you, and because you saved my life, and I never actually said thank you. But don't fall in love or anything, okay?"

I looked around at the smirking Security team, Karl holding his sides in suppressed laughter, and Megan sporting the grin of a Cheshire Cat. "If you say so," I sighed dramatically, then got a two-hand grip on the good stuff, and kissed the Unholy Hells out of her. Unlike my reaction to Megs' sneak attack, this one was a premeditated, Moments-Away-from-Wrecking-Furniture kiss. The kind of No Holds Barred kiss that made promises you better be ready to keep! The shudder that I felt cross her body told me she got the memo.

"Um, oh yeah, okay, um." She gasped brokenly. "That, um, yeah."

"Me next!" Tilsa hollered. "I want one of those. I missed you, too!" She breathing heavy with enthusiasm, her rather substantial bosom bouncing with her antics. She was acting sexy-silly on purpose, I just knew it. I *did* consider her request until Ben came in with, "Well, damn, Lee, I wouldn't mind getting' one of those too!" Giving us the space to laugh and move on. But that Tilsa. Hmmm...

"Um, yeah, I think he's gonna be too busy for that." Trini replied, rather pointedly indeed. She looked into my eyes "You gonna be too busy, right?" She whispered.

"Still want to get something to eat and go to bed?"

"I'm really hungry, Lee, I haven't eaten for hours."

"Then we get you some food, then Megan and me will tuck you in."

"Megan and you? But…" Her eyes widened. "Really?"

"Trini, trust me. You're gonna need all the help you can get."

"Oh, um, yeah. You might be right."

***

The Karkarof had a great deal of experience with dealing with guests who were in desperate need of a feast at all hours of the night, So with a judiciously placed phone call from Megan, the hotel's dining room was reopened and had a ton of food waiting, Buffet Style. Including Trini's entourage, Twenty people piled into the dining room, and then proceeded to pile into the food. Everyone seemed to be healthy eaters.

We spent hours talking, sharing, decompressing and laughing. I explained how and why I had to go into the Regen Unit for three weeks, hence my apparent disappearance. The Security folks groaned in complete empathy. Karl and a few of Trini's family members turned a little green and slowed down their food intake until their stomachs settled. Megan shared with me how well Trini's sales in records and merchandise was going, which was way past phenomenal, and that they were close to contracting with one or two other acts and putting together a national tour. While we were eating, Chief Sykes got the call that Billie Grantham was undergoing treatment and another Talent would be arriving within the hour. I immediately called up Alistra, but she had already gone to the D.I.A. grounds and was involved with the activity concerning Grantham.

It took a while but everyone was finally finished eating, and we piled into the elevators.

"Um. I'm usually pretty close to where Trini sleeps, Lee," Tilsa noted.

I smiled. "Not tonight, Tilsa. I got this."

She sighed. "Damn, I was hoping…"

For a moment, as I looked at Tilsa, it was if another woman was superimposed over her. Shorter by an inch or two, skin of coffee with cream, body full of the wondrous, voluptuous curves, sheathed in long, sculpted muscle that I finally had to admit to myself was my ideal. I felt my breath hitch at the vision, and then it was gone. I cleared my throat, a bit unsteady. "Not tonight, M'Lady, but soon," I promised.

She smiled, as if she was well aware of what just happened. "I'm gonna hold you to that, Lee."

There was just a hint of added sway to her walk as she left the elevator. *Had to be deliberate. Mean lady!*

Soon, it was only Trini, Megan and I as we went up to the penthouse suite. Megan looked relaxed. Trini, a little nervous, but eager. I don't know how I looked, but I'm sure we all had the same expression on our faces when the doors to the penthouse opened.

"What the Hell is THIS?!" Trini screeched while Megan groaned, "Oh, for God's sake!"

While I growled, "Trish! What in all Seven Hells are you doing here?"

There she was, my Ex, I think, leaning in the doorway of the suite, dressed in a sheer, full-length negligee, with a glass of champagne in her hand. "It's bloody well about time you all showed up! What kept you?"

"Who's this Trick?" Trini snarled. "And how did she get into my suite?"

"This is Patricia Ramsey," Megan sighed wearily. "Werewolf, Countess of Duerlin, heir to The Ramsey Estate, Lee's *ex*-girlfriend (she put heavy emphasis on that one!), and one of the two main reasons Lee was fired from Blue Star Security."

"Ah-ah-ah," Trish tsked as we left the elevator, wagging a finger at Megan. "Let's not leave out the most pertinent parts of the introduction, eh? Cougar-At-large, trainer of callow young men into masterfully skilled lovers, and the *main* reason why you two are about to have a night neither of you will ever forget."

"Trish, why are you here?" I sighed wearily. I was so not ready for this.

"Because we did not say goodbye properly, Lyam," she answered, all her bluster gone. "I know it's goodbye, my dearest, but I refuse to let it end as they would have it. We will have our last, glorious moment before we must walk away from each other forever." She smiled, sweetly. "And it would be wonderful to walk out the door while these utterly bewitching ladies are walking in!"

"How'd you even get up in here?" Trini asked heatedly. "They monitor who uses this elevator, and the door has a security lockout!"

In answer, Trish flexed her hand, and her nails grew into long, thick and pointed daggers. "Easy-peasy. I went up to the rooms two floors below, then out the window, climb up the side of the building, and *voila*!"

Megan's mouth was gaping. "You wanted some of this guy *that* bad?"

Trish's eyes smoldered. "Trust me, darling, he's worth every inch of that climb!"

Trini kicked a stool in frustration. "This ain't right! I was kinda okay with sharing with Megs, she's cool with me. But I don't know you. I thought this was gonna be, you know, special, and, and…"

She took a step back when I turned and stared into her eyes. "Trinidad Flores, your performance tonight was beyond words. You deserve to be treated like the Queen you are! Never doubt that I will do everything and anything to show you just how much a queen you are.

"And you, Megs, you are a treasure. You've worked so hard for Trini and her family. You give everything you've got to make sure she succeeds. Well tonight, you will be served. You will be the focus of attention. You've earned that, and I'm the one to make sure you get it!

"As for you, Trish. You're right. You have taught me so much. Perhaps I am a Master now, and I owe that to you. But you left your scent on me, and that fool Jackson caught it. You betrayed me, Trish. For that, you must be punished. You will not be on center stage for this performance. You will serve me, and serve these beautiful ladies, and if you please me in how you serve, then perhaps, I may allow you *some* fulfillment. Accept this, or walk out the door, or crawl out the window. Choose now!"

We locked eyes. She was a strong, fiercely proud woman. But she knew me. Better than any other, even Aunt Melene, in this particular arena. She saw the will to dominate in me, and she used every trick in the book to make that trait flourish. She knew how relentless I could be, and even at the end of our time together, she loved me for it.

She bowed. Low. "I choose to stay, and obey you, Maahes."

"*¡Dios Mio!*" Trini whispered.

"Then you may begin by getting a glass of champagne for Megan, and help her undress. I will be giving Trini her shower, and when she is done being cleansed, I will assist Megan."

I took Trini's hand. "Come, my Queen, let me take care of you."

All three women were swept up into The Perfect Storm of the superhuman levels of endurance of Children of The Pride, Trish's extensive training in Bedroom Gymnastics, and my relentless will to dominate and conquer in every field of endeavor. I didn't know what Trini and Megan's experiences were before me. I didn't care. Our feast was measured in hours, not seconds or minutes. Even in my young adult mind, I wasn't about to proclaim myself the greatest ever born. But Patricia Ramsey was an excellent teacher, I was a very motivated student, and I submitted my Doctorate Thesis with my ladies, until well after the sun rose in the east.

My every caress, every kiss, every tender request and passionate demand was focused on them and their pleasure. They felt so very perfect, their energy was so beautiful, I felt my very *Soul* demanding that I give over everything I was, everything I learned, just scraggin' everything, to their Bliss. Gently washing them in the shower, smoothing out the kinks and pulled muscles with their massages, I revealed to them my focused, mountain-high passion for each one of these fascinating models of perfect womanhood, over, and over.

Megan and Trini considered themselves thoroughly taken care of after an hour of festivities. Trish only smiled at the poor, addled dears and chuckled. "Sweeties, you might want to limber up some. That was only Round One! Now remember, Lee, they can't heal, as I do. A bit more gently? Yes. That's it. Fenrir's teeth, I'm going to miss you!"

My heart winced, thinking of Trish leaving my life. As would Trini, and Megan. They had their own stories to write into the

Universe, and I knew I was only in a few of their chapters. Trish helped me to understand the difference between 'Now' Love, and 'Forever' Love. This was nothing else but 'Now', and we all knew it. So, without words, we all agreed to pour a spoonful of 'Forever' into this 'Now' Feast, so we could look back, and reflect on a Perfectly Divine Meal in the years to come.

We left the world behind us, as we took the passionate journey deep into their desires, their needs, their barely imagined fantasies. Individually and together, flowing from tenderly nurturing to wrecking the bed frame (and any other close-by furniture), we left no wondrous stone unturned, no exciting path unexplored. We shared our tears, our laughter (we gave Trish the beating she deserved, and craved), we shared our screams to the heavens as we exploded into ecstasy, and then began the blessed cycle all over again. I gave, I gratefully received, I demanded, and reverently offered, so My Ladies could know beyond all doubt that they were worshipped, catered to, dominated, and so very deserving of the absolute best I could give. And they gave themselves over completely to the moment. I could feel it, all the way down to my bones. They allowed themselves to fly, to take themselves to the edge, then leap into the blessed Aether of unimagined bliss, trusting in me catching them in loving arms.

I took my time. It really isn't that difficult for a reasonably healthy male to satisfy himself, if that's all you're about. But, to see the Bliss on their faces, the strain on their brows as the passion builds, the miraculous release, with the tears that follow. To feel the fire beneath the surface of their exquisite flesh, to be the cause of the racing heartbeats. To hear the gasp, the hitch of inhaling breath, then the slow, deep exhale of contentment. There are no words. Nothing I could ever say or write could ever capture the feeling of bringing this Bliss to My Ladies. As the bard Shakespeare put it, these wondrous blessings of The Creator 'Died' a multitude of times, and they deserved every Blessed little death.

Trini's fire was set free to consume her and us all. Megan's passions were torn loose from the cage of her own will, and she howled and screamed with every climactic explosion. And Trish, she wept, hard passionate tears as she gave her great, untamable will over to her Master. They needed, they begged, they demanded, and I gave them all I had, all I learned, all I dreamed. I gave, until they could take no more.

I left the three of them in intimately-induced comas, curled up around each other on the bed. I was pretty washed out myself, so I laid out on a bed in another part of the suite and caught a few hours of sleep.

Yes, I was damned proud of myself, if you were wondering. All three of those ladies deserved the very blessed best any man could ever give. Doesn't everyone deserve a moment when fantasies they didn't even know they had are fulfilled? When dreams are realized in their entirety, instead of lame excuses given over and over again?

I made a promise, I delivered, so I took a nap.

Chapter 13. A Tough Old Broad!

When I woke up a few hours later, I noted that they were still asleep.

AND MY EMPTY BELLY WAS PISSED! It's been a long time since I felt this hungry. Food, most definitely.

But, first things first.

Yeah, I called my aunt.

She was worried, but didn't go too ballistic with me staying out all night without giving her a heads-up.

"You *are* a Child of The Pride," She chuckled. "These sorts of things tend to happen with us. When we go out on *that* kind of hunt, the prey generally line up and wait to be eaten."

I shook my head. "I really don't think I'm supposed to have this kind of conversation with my mother figure, Melene,"

"That's your Mother's human genes talking, Maahes. So many humans are such prudes and liars. But don't worry. Take the day, just be ready to get back to the grind tomorrow." She snickered. "Or when they wake up!"

"Auntie!" I gasped. She was still laughing when she disconnected.

But you know, she might be on to something, Hmm…

No. Food first. A shower, then food. Yes. As I picked the suite's phone for room service, Trish strolled into the bedroom I was using. She was dressed, her hair was styled, and she looked miserable.

"I needed that, Lee," she whispered. "One last glorious moment. You were magnificent! To think that I helped you to become so masterful, so *God-like*. But so caring, so gentle. So loving. I felt adored by you, Lee. Like I was the most beautiful, the most precious woman in the whole universe. We all felt that way. We all felt as bright, as worshipped as stars in the night sky."

She smiled through her tears. "That, my lovely man, is the proper way to say goodbye." She gulped. "I have to go. I'll cherish this always, my love. Thank you."

We kissed, we held each other tenderly, lovingly.

And then, she walked away.

I wasn't hungry any more. I laid in the bed. And I cried. I wasn't quite 24 years old. I was still a kid, when all was said and done, and my first love, who I still loved, just walked out the door.

I gave myself an hour or so, and then I picked up the phone and called room service.

"I hope you're calling for some food, Stud."

Wrapped in a bed sheet, Megan strolled in the room slowly, as if she was remembering how to walk in a straight line. She just made it to where I was sitting on the edge of the bed, and plopped herself down on my lap. Her hand brushed gently across my face. "Tears, Lee?"

I nodded. "Trish said goodbye."

"Oh, Lee," She sighed as she hugged me. "When I think of all you've done, all you will be required to do in the future. I so hope you have somebody in your life that can face it all by your side. It's too hard to live this life alone." Her smile had a trace of bitterness. "Take it from one who knows."

We kissed, and I was grateful for its gentleness.

"I wanted to tell you that you were right, Stud. I NEVER in my life had an experience like that before. Thank you so very much for letting me feel so free, so out of control! And no one has *ever* made me drop dead from exhaustion!" She moved herself to sit next to me.

"Now, what about something to eat? I'm starving!"

"Me too," Trini grumbled as she staggered into the room. Baby Girl looked thoroughly turned inside out. She stumbled up to me, forlornly raised her arms, and waited for me to lift her up and cradle her.

"You turned me out, Daddy," she whimpered into my chest. "I think my kitty is broken!"

Meg giggled. "I know what you mean, Trini. I think I'm gonna need that surgery, the one that tightens up the muscles down there?"

I almost couldn't walk this far!" Trini murmured, and then kissed my cheek. "Thank you, Lee. I did feel like a Queen." She giggled. "I ain't gonna make just a song about this. I'ma do a whole double album! The peeps are gonna be trippin' hard."

"You are very welcome," I replied. "Both of you. I really enjoyed the hell out of that. You two were amazing!"

"Better than Trish?" Trini asked in a small voice.

"Unique. Original," I turned Trini's head so we could look at each other. "Tell me Trini. Honestly. Who's most important in your band? The drums? The bass? Keyboards?"

She shrugged. "I need them all for the music I'm putting together. They all bring that special flavor! It wouldn't sound right if one was missing. I can't choose."

I smiled. "And there's your answer. To that question, and the other two or three you were about to ask."

She huffed in frustration, and then snuggled in again. "Yeah, that was a straight-up masterpiece, wasn't it?" she admitted with a sniff.

We ordered a ton of food, and snuggled a bit more before I made my way to the shower. I was in the midst of shampooing my hair when Megan came in. Close to frantic.

"Lee! We've got to go! All Hell broke loose downstairs!"

I jumped out the shower and began throwing on my clothes. "What happened?"

"Some whacked-out magic user is wrecking the lobby!" Megan was pretty much dressed, sans undergarments and her shoes. "They want the guests to evacuate the building! They're afraid of possible structural damage!"

I finished with my pants and was about to button up my shirt when I heard the ping of the elevator.

Oh no!

I raced past Megan, motored into the living room area and leapt in front of Trini just as a volcanic blast of fire tore into my shirt, and me.

I shielded Trini before turning to face-

My Maestra.

Well, isn't this swell?

***

"Out of my way!"

That was definitely not Alistra's voice. That was definitely her body though, even if it looked a lot messier than normal. And from the burning sensation in my back, that was definitely her Talent.

"I will not fail. She will be silenced!" The being within my teacher screeched as she sent another Electro Spear. This one I was able to block. I wanted to beg her to stop, plead with someone I cared for deeply to let go of this madness. But it would be a waste of time and effort. Alistra wasn't in the driver seat.

Nor could I play defense. This being had control of a Scary-Powerful sorceress. She wouldn't take long to batter through any defense I could put into play.

"Alright," I snarled, "come high, or don't come at all!"

Wait, how did I remember that? When did I learn to play Bid Whist with my family?

Never mind. It was time to put in work.

Instead of shielding her next attack, I rolled under it, towards her, I finished the roll, planted my hands against the shield she dropped into place and slammed an Avalanche spell into her. She was shielded, but it still slammed her into the wall. In the very brief window of time, I used my pseudo-telekinetic spell to shove Trini in the still open elevator. I looked to Meg.

"Get out!" I roared, and blocked the spell my possessed mentor sent towards the women. Before she could send another spell, the doors closed.

"Noooo!" she howled. "You! You did this. Again. I see you! You will not stop me again!"

"Eat scat, scraggin' thief!" I shouted back. And we went at it.

She was powerful, but it was power without the skill, without the experience of my Maestra.

Which didn't help a lot, as I found myself leaping over a couch and feeling the scorching heat of her Flame Whip spell. I blasted a Solar Lance back at her, she caught it with an Ice Wall defensive spell and hurled a Prism spell, blinding me just long enough to slam to more powerful spells at me.

I huddled under a strong shield, taking the hits, until my vision cleared, Then I pulled my S&W 500 out of my PDP.

"You can't hide forever!" snarled my enemy. "I will kill you!"

I didn't respond. Why waste the breath? I took a moment, formed my spell, then rolled into the open. Before she could serve up another scorcher, I lifted my revolver and squeezed off all five shots, sending .50 cal. shells into her shield. The fourth bullet shattered her shields, the fifth plowed into her right shoulder, flipping her around, slamming her into the wall, and forcing her to slowly collapse to the floor.

I released the Ice pick I had prepped, and walked over to the crumpled Sorceress.

Now comes the real battle.

I stood over her, unspeaking. I didn't have long to wait. Her eyes opened. She looked up at me, and snarled, "You fool!"

Then she pushed her way into my mind.

***

I felt her presence. It was a her. Whatever it might be now, it began as a female. She slithered. She oozed. She searched for a handle, but couldn't find one. She tried to turn into another avenue within my mind, but found herself trapped in one of a multitude of traps Alistra helped me to build in my mind.

She tore through it. Easily. But there was another. And another. Always another. She roared in frustration! She gathered herself in, then exploded through my mind, destroying all remaining traps at once. That was no longer an option for me. But she expended so much energy. How much did she have left?

Enough to make her way further into mind. I could feel her sense of impending victory. She would take over my mind, force me to kill Trini. She would triumph! Her Celestial brethren would cheer her victory! Why did they leave me alone? They should, they...

No! What is this? A wall? A wall in his mind? How could this be? How high is it? I can't see the top of it! How wide? No! How could it be endless? *How could this be!*

I'll break it down. Yes! I'll break this wall, then, I'll break him!

She tried, and tried. And kept trying. I felt her blows on the walls in my mind. Felt her hammering away at the protections my wonderful teacher helped me build, day by day, year by year, for over eighteen years. I felt each blow, because they were blows to my consciousness, and because I was leaning on the other side of those walls, pouring my will into each brick, refusing to quit, refusing to allow the slightest chip in the surface. She kept hammering, I kept reinforcing, seemingly for decades.

Then, I felt her presence flying away, heard her howling in fury, in murderous frustration. In depthless sorrow. Soon after, I felt her presence in my mind no longer. The invader was gone.

Replaced by a familiar friend.

She knocked on the far side of my walls. "All clear, Lee," Alistra called. *"You can come back to wakefulness. Nice walls. Good thing you kept building them."*

"How do I know this isn't a trick?" I called out in my mind.

Outside my mental landscape, I heard a gruff voice respond to my question.

"I've got a pair of .45 cal. Peacemakers pointed at both your heads. If either of you twitch weird or talk funny, I'm blowing your heads off!"

That's my cue! *I decided, and made my way back to the conscious world.*

Chapter 14. Who's in Charge of <u>This</u> Mess?

When I returned to the waking world, I found myself surrounded.

STANDING ABOVE ME, with an antique revolver pressed to my temple, was Maestro von Brunner, and I saw that he did indeed have a matching handgun pressed into the side of Alistra's head, which made the healer working at her side very nervous. There were a dozen more people in the shattered suite. All of them looked as if they were in the midst of some kind of work, but they were very carefully staying still, watching. Big guns pointed at people's heads can have that sort of effect, I supposed.

"Lee?" he snapped. "You the only one in there?"

"I think so," I answered slowly. "I'm not sure."

"I'm sure," Alistra groaned. "I sent the other packing."

"All right." The retired Battle Mage put his hand cannons away. "Now, what in all Seven Hells happened here?"

"The entity possessed me, tried to kill Trinidad Flores. Lyam stopped her. We battled. My favorite student nearly blew my arm off, thank you so very much! Then she tried to get into Lee's mind, take him over. He stopped her cold, then when I regained possession of my mind, I chased her off." She shook her head disgustedly. "Just the sort of idiocy I've been avoiding for three hundred damned years!"

Von Brunner shook his head. "Alright, here's the $5,000,000 question: How in all worlds did she get latched into you?"

"Greta Dearling!" Alistra's tone dropped the temperature in the room ten or more degrees.

"Greta?" The Maestro seemed horrified at the name. "How did she have anything to do with any of this?"

"Because of that great fool of a director, Dellums!" Alistra raged. "I don't give a tinker's damn that I'm surrounded by all you D.I.A. agents. His insistence that a Medium be present at Grantham's treatments, and her of all people on this side of the Universe, almost got me killed!"

"You're gonna have to explain that one, Ali."

"Dellums insisted on pulling a bunch of different supposed 'experts' in the Psychomancy field to work out a plan of clearing Grantham's mind. Somehow Greta got invited. The complete idiot started grandstanding, as she always does, and convinced everyone to go into the room they were holding Grantham in, gather in a circle around him, and invoke a Seeking Eye incantation."

"But, Ali," von Brunner grumbled. "For that spell, you need someone to stay back and protect the minds that have dropped all their internal protections."

"Got it in one, Sherlock. And you get only one guess to figure out who was supposed to anchor everyone else? Wrong! I was supposed to do it, but Greta pouted and sniffled, claiming that since she was the one who suggested the spell, she should be the anchor. And that jerkwad Dellums fell for her waterworks!"

Alistra continued in between her winces while her arm was being treated. "So there we are, ten of us sitting there with wide-open minds, while whatever the Hell is sitting in an unconscious Grantham happens to be wide awake. Greta's doing a piss-poor job of anchoring us, no great surprise there!, and the whosit in Grantham picks a mind, any mind, and here we are."

"Oh, Gods and Goddesses," Von Brunner groaned. "That Gods-cursed fame whore is gonna have to pay for her stupidity this time!"

Alistra grunted in agreement, and then turned basilisk eyes at me. "And speaking of almost killing me, what were you about, blasting at me with that bazooka?"

Yeah, that kinda sucked, didn't it?

I shrugged at first, and then when her frown deepened, I broke it down for her.

"I figured that if I wounded you severely enough, the entity would leave you. If it just ran away, that would be fine. We'd track it down eventually. If it tried to take me over, I'd be prepared for the attack. I figured you were caught off guard somehow, that could have been the only way you would be taken. I had my barriers up, and I figured I could hold it off until you revived enough to help me out. If I couldn't hold it off, well, I don't know, but at least Trini and everyone else would have gotten free by then."

"Too flipping chancy for my blood. And how did you know I would revive from a mental assault, while bleeding to death?"

"I didn't know, but I figured you were too tough an old biddy to just quit. It was just a shot in the arm, after all!"

"Hmph. If you were gonna be so damned cold-blooded about this, why didn't you just blow my head off? it probably would have been too traumatized to enter another mind!"

"You're my Maestra, Alistra. And my friend. I could never kill you." I smiled. "At least, if you bled to death, I could think of that as a mistake."

She looked at me, thoroughly irritated, then looked to von Brunner. "Can you believe this fool?"

He shrugged. "You and Melly trained him to be a hardcore, nut-crunching warrior. He reviewed the available info, made a calculated risk, executed the plan, and it came out pretty much the way he planned it. I'd think you'd be proud of him." His brows furrowed in thought. "Except for the targeting. He really should have just blown your head off, and not take any chances, but I guess we could go either way with that one."

"Not helping!"

"Maestro, do you have any idea how long we were dealing with the enemy?"

"Ms. Flores and Ms. Trasker were escorted out of the building about three hours ago, so I'd say about that long."

I frowned at that. "What took so long for a squad to get here? Everyone knew Trini was the target!"

"If I may?" One of the women agents in the suite stepped forward and introduced herself. "Deirdre Smalls, Special Agent in Charge for this scene. Ms. De Vore left the D.I.A. headquarters a disaster zone before she made her way here. No fatalities, we were pretty lucky there. But the interior of the building is mostly destroyed, and at least a hundred agents and support units severely injured and/or traumatized." She sighed. "It was all we could do to put together a team and scramble over here."

I had gotten to my feet by that time. After scrambling around the wreckage, I was able to locate my duster and boots. I laced the boots together and put them around my neck, then put the duster on over my shredded shirt. My trousers were pretty torn up, but I was mostly covered, and my PDP was still looped through my belt, so it would do for the time being.

By the time I collected my gear, I saw that Alistra had a mobile Regen unit attached to her shoulder, and they had her on a rolling stretcher.

"Where're they taking her?" I asked my Maestro.

"We elderly Talents established our own private treatment center uptown about eighty years ago. I know, you never heard of it. You're not supposed to." He smiled. "At least, not for another seventy years or so. Her family's meeting her there."

"Family?" I gaped.

"Understand, kid. As much as you know about Ali, there's a ton more about her you might never know. Alistra de Vore is a Purist type of Talent. She studies The Arts for the inherent beauty of it. She's never agreed with the philosophy of using The Arts in the battle arena. She loves your family, Lee, but she was never comfortable with their militaristic application of their Talent. How we've become such good friends is still a mystery to me. She's told me on a few occasions that you have a great mind for studying The Arts, but she knows you won't go that route, at least not for a while.

"So, yeah, she's kept her family separate and apart from all this gung-ho mess. Damn shame, if you ask me. A couple of her grandkids have the makings for Hard-Core Battle Mages!"

I felt hurt, for a bit. But, yeah, look at this wreckage all around us! However she felt about me, about my family, it would be clear to a blind man that things tend to get broken around us. If you weren't about that kind of life, why would you introduce your kin to it?

All that mattered was that my Maestra would be surrounded by loved ones and she would recover. I looked to Agent Smalls and told her I was leaving.

"Sorry, Mr. Seckett, I'm afraid you have to stay until Director Dellums arrives."

I sighed, and reached into the inside pocket of my duster. "No, agent. I'm sorry to pull rank, but I don't answer to the D.I.A., and I will not be standing around barefoot and indecently exposed." I showed her my Shield. She recognized the significance swiftly and backed off.

"Now, I will be going to my home, getting some food, pulling myself together, and I will then make myself available to the D.I.A." I turned to Maestro von Brunner. "Will you be staying with them?"

"Kind of have to. They're paying my consultant fee to assist their investigation."

"Well, they hired the best—this time at least. What about the NYPD?"

"The D.I.A. put the whole building on lock down. Police units weren't allowed to enter. They're handling crowd control."

"Got it. Okay. See you later at the house?"

"Tomorrow, bright and early. Try to keep out of trouble, kid."

I smiled. "Now how in All Hells am I supposed to do that? Trouble seems to be The Family Business!"

***

When I left the elevator, a small stampede hurtled in my direction, with Trini and Megan in the lead. They were dressed in baggy, mismatched gear that was scrounged from just about anywhere.

They didn't speak. They just ran, and then latched on as I folded my arms around them. Chief Sykes and the team followed close behind.

"They wouldn't leave until they saw you," He explained when he saw my stare. "We wanted to make sure you were okay too. The area's been secured the last two hours. Except for those agents upstairs, we're the only ones in the hotel."

"Good. Any fatalities?"

Sykes grimaced. "Two. Out of a possible four hundred fifty. Both maintenance workers who couldn't get out of the way of an elevator cab in free fall."

"Oh, Man." I looked down at the two in my arms. "How are you, darlings?"

"Oh, just fine," Megan sniffled. "Just another day in New York."

"I'm real tired of all this garbage," Trini muttered. "Maybe I need to chill for a minute, let you people get a handle on whatever this is." She looked up with tears in her eyes. "My family almost died, Lee. My sister! My cousins!"

"I think you're right."

Megan nodded too. "Trini going under wraps would probably help her popularity go through the roof, as long as it's not too long." She looked up and winked. "I am her manager, Lee. I'm paid to think like a mercenary."

I chuckled. "Don't worry. I won't let anybody know how big a softie you really are."

She snorted in reply. "Nobody'd believe you anyway."

I nodded to Chief Sykes. "I'm taking these two to a secure site. You folks are still on the job, so I figure you'll be coming along."

"Of course we're coming!" He snapped. "You're sure this site of yours is secure?"

"Very."

"Then why didn't we have this place available before now?"

"It's my home."

That made him pause. "Okay, I can see that." He nodded to the team, and they created a protective shell around us three. The Chief offered that there had been a Security transport waiting for them outside of the police perimeter for the last hour, so we made our way out the door of the hotel.

It was complete bedlam out there. Camera bulbs were flashing like mad, camera crews were stacked toward the front of the hotel, just on the other side of the metal barriers the police had set up. Beyond the camera crews, a swarm of fans and onlookers were screaming and waving hastily scrawled signs. I could even see more than a few remote controlled camera spheres hovering in the air above the crowds, making it clear that the press agencies operating in Lyrodrylle came out for the spectacle as well. A famous, high-rise luxury hotel gets wrecked. A wildly popular young, beautiful performer is almost assassinated. Two fatalities. Yeah, it had all the elements for the online rumor mills, newspaper headlines and the endless news cycles.

A police officer wearing a lot of brass stepped rapidly into our path. "Deputy Chief Warner, Operations," he announced brusquely. "You're this Seckett joker that's been causing all this destruction to my city?"

"No, sir," I replied politely. "I am the Deputy Nemesene presently on site, making me the one in command of this location until I leave it, per the Restoration Addendum to the Accords agreed upon by The Pentagram and The United Nations."

"That don't cut no ice with me, Junior," He snapped back, ignoring the shield I displayed. "You're coming with me to 1 Police Plaza. My bosses are getting tired of all this wreckage going down, and they want answers now!"

"Sir," I kept my cool. It really wasn't his fault. I'm sure they were simply trying to do their job and were getting nothing but kicked to the curb by the D.I.A. "I have no problem at all with meeting with your Chiefs, but this is an unsecure area and these ladies need to be taken to a safer location. When they have been placed under protection, I will make all haste to your headquarters."

"You're not hearing me, Boy (Oh, He didn't go there, did he?). I didn't ask or request a damned thing. I got forty officers available on site, and a few hundred more on the wire, and that means you'll be going with me, either on your own two feet or in hand cuffs!"

Instinctively, Trini and Megan stepped back to the Team. I calmly put the badge back in the liner pocket and looked the brass in the eye. "I've been as polite and accommodating as I'm gonna be, Deputy Chief. But you had to go and insult me, in front of witnesses, with the cameras overhead recording everything, and then threaten me. You want it to go that way? Okay. Let me reply in kind. Your laws make it clear that you're out of line, I'm not going to let you strong-arm me, and any wreckage I was involved in was a display of me showing restraint! If you continue trying to flex your muscles with me, I'll be forced to show you just how much wreckage I can cause this city!"

I tried, but he just had to force me to check him. He looked at me, and at the destroyed clothing. I supposed he pondered on what it took to smash up a massive building like The Karkarof and walk out without any obvious wounds, and blinked.

"A police escort will follow you to this secure site, and then will escort you to Headquarters." He muttered. His pissy face was wiped away when Trini moved forward and hugged him.

"Thank you, sir," she offered meekly. "I'm really not feeling very well."

The gruff officer hesitated, and then lightly patted her on the back. "Sorry to hear that, young lady," he grumbled. "I'm sure this, Deputy, will take care of you." He swallowed. "My kids love your music." Trini just nodded and went back to being gathered in Megan's arms.

"Well, you heard her!" the man barked at me. "Get moving! Can't you see she's in distress?"

"Thank you, Deputy Chief." I nodded, then led my people to the barriers, which seemingly moved on their own to create a corridor of open space that led to the security transport that was waiting on the curb. The officers kept the crowds back as we made our way through the horde. Some were screaming 'SELENE!', some reporters were throwing endless questions. As far as I was concerned, way too many were howling out my name and begging for responses to their questions. I suppose the days of 'low profile' were, indeed, officially over.

We finally stumbled into the vehicle, and made our way to the entrance leading to the Brooklyn Bridge, followed by four squad cars with their lights flashing. There wasn't a lot of talking as we made our way through Brooklyn and into Queens. We were all on the ragged edge at that point. I did make sure to call Melene and tell her that we were having company.

"The entrance will be clear. Hurry home, Maahes," she replied warmly.

"Lee, what did she mean, the entrance will be clear?" Tilsa asked.

I smiled at her heightened hearing. "Our home is in a private cul-de-sac. At the end of a single street. My parents and few of their Talent friends put down a perimeter a mile around it. Nothing on the ground, or in the air, or beneath the surface, can see into or enter that space unless we activate the spells that allow unauthorized vehicles to come onto the street and make their way to the house. The neighbors on the street were annoyed at first, but they grew to love the level of security, as well as the population of rodents, stray animals and pigeons being wiped out seemingly overnight."

"You mean, if one of these cameras buzzing around us," Chief pointed to a few of the remotes trailing behind us. "If one of these tries to record where you live? What happens?"

"They'll be knocked out of the air about a mile from the entrance, or if they sneak in with one of the patrol cars, they'll see an empty lot, then short circuit."

The Chief nodded. "That's pretty secure, all right. The airspace too?"

I nodded back. "My family made enemies. Bad ones. Had to be lured into the field for any of them to have a chance at getting my folks."

We were pretty quiet after that. It wasn't too long before we entered the block and rode the length of it, with the squad cars following. I saw that the gates onto our property were open, and the transport followed the cobblestoned path until we arrived before my three-story home.

"Looks like you're missing a drawbridge for this pile of bricks," Ben muttered. "Lots of company?"

"Rarely, actually, aside from my trainers."

"Just you and your aunt rattling around this fortress?" Megan wondered.

"There used to be more than just us two," I responded woodenly as the vehicle came to a stop.

"Oh, Lee, I'm so sorry," Megan gulped contritely as the door to the house opened. I simply nodded, made my way out the door of the transport and got my hug and kiss from my aunt.

"This was not what I had in mind when I said to take the day off!" she scolded gently, then looked me over. "I heard about Alistra. Are you okay?"

"I'm fine, Melene." I gestured to the crew behind me. "They followed me home, Auntie! Can I keep 'em?"

Her eyebrows quirked. "Would that be including the officers of the law?" She gestured at the police who were making their way towards us.

"Um, no, Aunt. They're here to take me to jail!"

"Ma'am!" One of the officers, a lieutenant, stepped forward hastily. "The Deputy knows were just here to escort him to Police HQ. The Chiefs need to have a better idea of what's going on, and nobody's talking to us."

Melene nodded. "Your Chiefs will be receiving a very politely worded letter of apology from the Chief Nemesene of this Sector. We know we have been remiss in making sure you have been informed of our investigation regarding the attacks on Ms. Flores, and Deputy Seckett will be happy to sit with your bosses for as long as they require. But I am sure that they would prefer the Deputy to be properly dressed, and to ensure that his stomach won't be growling throughout the interview?"

She gestured to the door. "I laid out some refreshments, for whoever might be hungry, so please, welcome to our home. You too, officers. Please don't think I'd be happy with you sitting in your cars or waiting outside while we're inside stuffing our faces!"

Her welcoming tone, and her gracious smile, ensured that she was followed by everyone through the large foyer and into the dining room, where the massive table groaned under a ton of food. Deli offerings, a variety of sliced meats, fruits, salads, even a vat of clam chowder. Everyone dug in without another word.

"How did you put this all together?" I asked in wonder.

"You really don't pay attention, Lee," She snorted. "I'm cooking stuff all the time. When it's not just the two of us eating enough for a family of six. We're feeding your trainers, I'm sending dishes to the Civic Center a few blocks away, or participating in the pot luck dinners being given by the various churches and block associations in the neighborhood. Just because we don't attend their events too often doesn't mean we aren't appreciated."

After a solid half hour stuffing my belly, I made my way upstairs, showered and dressed, and declared myself ready for the trip back to Manhattan.

"I'm sure my aunt will make you folks comfortable." I smiled at the folks. "She saves the beatings and foul language for me."

Chief Sykes stood up from his chair in the living room. "Ms. Alabato? I'm a little confused. I was expecting to see you at the hotel, like you were at other sites when Lee was involved. I was wondering why you weren't there."

Melene smiled. "Before a week ago, I was keeping an eye on my nephew. As of this week, Lee is a Deputy Nemesene of The Cadre. As such, he has command authority wherever he is. As a senior Deputy, if I entered the scene, he would have to hand command over to me. So, it may make me a lot more worried, but he was given that level of authority for a reason, and I have to respect that."

Even the police nodded to that, and after a few hugs and kisses, they walked me to the squad cars. I got in with the lieutenant and we were on our way. As we made our way from the Belt Parkway to the Van Wyck Expressway, the lieutenant cleared his throat. "Your aunt is a very gracious lady, Deputy, if you don't mind my saying so."

"I don't mind. I agree wholeheartedly."

"In fact I'd say she's pretty close to perfect. A man would consider himself blessed to have her in his life. I guess, I was just wondering, how the Hell is someone as amazing as her not married, not even in a relationship with somebody?"

I thought about his question. I thought hard. Then I thought about some things I thought were strange. I thought about how aggressive Children of The Pride tended to be regarding Sex. I thought about how she saw me as her son. I thought about my fuzzy memories that every so often let loose a memory that seemed to make no kind of sense, unless you considered it from a different angle.

And I thought about the marathon session of uninhibited passion I just shared with three different women, all at the same time.

"Y'know, Lieutenant, I'm starting to wonder. Maybe she was married. Possibly still is."

Chapter 15. Roads Less Traveled

I chalked up the almost pleasant discussion with the police to the letter that proceeded me.

UNLIKE SO MANY OTHERS IN CHARGE OF AN ORGANIZATION, Digby had no interest in measuring testosterone levels. His focus was on getting the job done. Everything else was a waste of his time, energy and resources. And as he pointed out before, he had very few resources available to him at that time. If the NYPD brass required him to eat a little crow, Digby would whip up a feast of the blackbirds.

Of course, it didn't hurt to do a little bit of judicious "throwing under the bus" with the D.I.A. Frankly, they deserved it. Having national-level pull for your organization didn't immediately mean that you were sharper than men and women employed by an organization that had been investigating crime for nearly two hundred years.

I laid it all out, top to bottom, made clear what was fact and what was speculation, reiterated that The Cadre had absolutely nothing to do with the boutique catastrophe, and asked if they had any details or insights that could help move the investigation along. It was politely pointed out to me that the NYPD had a whole division of officers that were of Mystic Lands heritage, and that if the force was approached from the beginning, there might have been a great deal less damage caused or lives lost. I made sure to take a few bites of that humble pie as well. They were right, why waste time with posturing?

After they stated that the Department apologized for the improper actions of the Deputy Chief, I responded with an apology as well, citing stress, concern for Trini and Megan's well-being and not having eaten for close on seven hours, which led into a discussion on a number of races of Lyrodrylle, and The Children of The Pride specifically. And, just FYI, how people of Lyrodryllian heritage considered the terms 'The Mystic Lands', or 'Mysticlanders' the same way indigenous people felt about 'redskins' or Afrocentric people felt about 'porch monkeys.' I hope they got the point.

In any event, they looked a lot less stern than when I came in. We shook hands, I suggested the possibility of organizing a liaison relationship with my boss, and they pulled out one of their nicer unmarked vehicles and gave a lift home.

When I came through the door, I heard a lot of noise coming from further in the house, and followed it to the weight room, towards the rear of the main floor. I watched as Melene walked all members of the Security team through a series of lifts. They seemed to be having a helluva session, so I quietly made my way up two flights of stairs, to the upper floor that was designed into a loft-style bedroom suite for me. With all the space, the access to technology, the maxed-out shower and in-floor bath, it was hard leaving my room when I was younger.

Of course, if the bed was full of two beautiful women in my tee shirts and panties, watching the latest news reports and sharing a bowl of potato chips, when I was a kid, I'd a nailed the door shut!

Well, no, still had to eat. But you get the point.

I walked in. We smiled together. They helped me undress. Then they assisted me in testing the soundproofing materials in the floor and walls.

A couple of hours later (I really was pretty tired), we were cuddled and watching the holographic monitor together. They were rehashing that morning's events. I noted how small Megan and Trini looked, huddled under my arms, clutching my coat around themselves. And I observed how even then The Chief, the team, and me, all had our heads on a swivel, eyes darting, looking for possible threats. They were among the best in the business, for real. I felt proud that I was a part of team, for a little while at least.

Next came the talking heads. The ones who spent hours shaping opinions and telling you how to think. Some of them at least had linked the tragic deaths of the other artists together finally. One floated the idea of the attacks on Trini being a publicity stunt, and was promptly crucified. I strongly suspected that Valerie Franklin would find it difficult to find her way back to the pundit chair. Trini flipped the channel, and we found ourselves staring at, me.

I really hadn't realized the loose curls of my heavy, dark brown hair had reached the lower part of my neck. Lately, all I did was brush it back and down, and it behaved. It needed a trim. If I wasn't wearing a helmet, long hair could be a liability.

It was a mostly side shot, and I had a nearly smiling expression on my face. Somebody might have taken a shot of me at Trini's performance.

Whatever.

This particular segment seemed to have me as the focus: Who I was, what I was about, where did I come from, yada, yada. We watched for a while, laughed at a few of the more outlandish speculations. Then Megs turned the monitor off.

"Lee," she sighed. "We have to talk. About us."

Now, I'd only recently begun the business of dating, but my straight male instincts informed me that when a man heard those words, it was time to run like your tail was on fire.

Nice to drop a bomb like that on a brother, in his own bedroom, after a couple hours of blowin' your back out.

"Alright." I sat up. "What about us?"

"I need to know, we both need to know, where we stand. What your intentions are." She looked to Trini, who nodded slowly. "You see, Trini's about to go global, on two different planets. And being the manager for her, well it takes everything I got. And we um, well…"

I nodded. "You need to know if I'm gonna pull a Jackson on you. On either of you. Am I gonna try to lock you down, clip your wings, that sort of thing?"

"Well, yeah," Trini murmured worriedly. "See, this thing right here? I've never felt this way before. Never! But Lee, I gotta do my thing. And Megs here, she's my right hand in this. We both gotta do what we gotta do, know what I'm sayin'? And if you, well, if you're gonna be my man, or Megan's or both, I don't know. Man, this is unreal, you know? But if, you know…"

I held up my hand and shushed her. I shook my head. This is where it gets rough. "I'm not your man, Trini. Not yours either, Megs. We might like each other," I said to their shocked faces. "We might even love each other, a lot. And we can have precious moments like this morning, and just now. But we can't date. Not in that way."

"But, but why?" Trini's stumbled out of her mouth. "I mean, I didn't think you'd treat me like Jackson did or nothin' I thought, if we laid it out, you'd be cool. But, we can't date?" Her eyes narrowed, grew hard in their look. "It's that Trish skank, ain't it? You still ain't over her. Right? It's her, right?"

"In a way," I raised my hand before she could explode. "Chill, Love. Let me explain." I got out of the bed, threw on a pair of gym shorts, then sat down in a chair near the bed, facing these two beautiful women. "When I say, 'in a way', I don't mean that were not over. We are. We still have a lot of love for each other, but we're done. But she does have something to do with where I'm at with you two for a simple reason. The same reason that you two felt that we needed to talk."

"It feels like you're all over the place, Lee," Megan grumped. "We wanted to see if you were okay with allowing us the freedom to do what we need to do for our careers! What are you talking about?"

"I'm talking about the kind of people we need in our different lives, Megs. This morning, when my teacher came in to kill you Trini, probably both you and Megs, What was your first reaction? What did your instincts scream for you to do?"

"Run," she admitted in a small voice.

"Megs?"

She sighed. "Honestly? Just us talking? Run my ass off!"

"And that's what I'm talking about, Meg. You two need someone in your lives that will allow you the freedom to reach the highest heights of your fields. I, on the other hand, need someone in my life who will see me running into danger and run into it with me. That their first thought will be to have my back, and save me if they need to.

"I can see the road I have to travel, Trini. It's a hard road. And it'll be a lonely road if I have to walk it alone. My road isn't your road, Megs. I won't expect either of you to walk it with me.

"Trish? Yeah, she's a natural born Rough Rider. She could walk my path, but her road is full of obligations and commitments. So no, we won't be walking the road together.

A tear slowly fell from Trini's eye. I gently wiped it away.

"You have to know that you two are the only women who have been here. Not even Trish got this deep into my space. You're here because I care so very deeply for you, and need you both to be safe. I believe I always will. But this is all we can share, Ladies. All we can have is now. Right here, today, you have my complete attention and devotion. As for tomorrow? I may have to begin that walk into Hell, and I need you two to give me the freedom to find the One to walk into Hell by my side."

We all had tears by then. Meg sighed as she slid off the bed and onto my lap. "I wish I could walk that road with you, Lee. I know someone has to. There always has to be somebody who'll run to danger instead of away from it. But I'm not the one who would do it, not by choice. And I know me, Lee. You'd give me the freedom to do whatever I wanted to do, but I would begin to resent you always being in danger. I would begin to think you preferred fighting the monsters instead of being with me.

"And just like Trini, you're just getting started on your career path. We talked so much these last few hours about how to let you down easy, hope you wouldn't get all Neanderthal and start shutting us down. Right, Trini?"

"You're right," Trini breathed. "We didn't want to lose you Lee, we just needed you to let us be free. Y'know?" She sniffed. "Didn't think that that freedom had to be a two-way street, though. Ain't that some kind of hot mess for a Sistah to work with?"

I leaned to her, kissed her sweet, warm lips. "Songs like some lyrics to a new song, my Queen."

"Screw you," she giggled between tears.

"Your wish," I replied as I tossed Trini into the bed and proceeded to put in maximum effort.

✷✷✷

"They both are absolutely amazing, Maahes."

I nodded in reply as I continued eating my bowl of cereal. Sometimes, you just needed to come down to the kitchen and make yourself a bowl of sugar-packed pieces of toasted wheat, swimming in a lake of cold milk. It helped with gaining clarity. I heard Melene coming down the stairs. She had beaten the Team to within an inch of their lives, and Trini and Megs were deep in recovery sleep.

She made herself a mug of tea and sat with me. I noted that, since me being deputized, Melene's been calling me Maahes instead of Lee more often. And I noticed that I didn't mind. Hmm.

"They seem to care a great deal about you already."

"I feel the same way about them. Their safety and happiness are very important to me."

We sat in silence for a few minutes, thinking thoughts.

"But neither are the One." She stated.

"They aren't built for it." I agreed. "They are tough, though. And strong. And amazing in a lot of other ways. But I need someone who can walk with me, not wait for me to come back."

She nodded, and we were quiet again for a while.

"Someone?" she asked with a grin.

I shrugged. "One, a dozen, or fifty. I just really hope I don't have to do this alone," I whispered. "Dad had Mom." I looked up into her face. "And, I'm starting to suspect, you and Bezine." Her eyebrows lifted, but she didn't deny it. "I want that for me, Melene." (I almost said, 'Mom'). "I want to believe that she's out there, or they. I don't know. Just that I find her. Or them. Or, whatever."

"You will, Lee." Melene promised. "Just keep your heart open, and believe."

I ate my cereal, she drank her tea, and we thought our separate thoughts.

Separate thoughts, but very likely the same topic.

Twins.

Chapter 16. Well, Hello, Della

Two hours later, and they were still staring.

WE SAT AROUND THE DINING ROOM TABLE. All our guests were eating. I was inhaling. There's a difference.

It was late in the day, and it was a great day at that. It was late October, the green was turning gold, and the wind blew a touch more coolness. My favorite time of the year. I started my day as normal. A full-out, twenty-mile run. Hit the salon, stretching for a half hour or so, depending. Then three hours, down from four, of honing learned techniques, walking through combinations, and then applying them at full speed. Over and over. Walk through the movements in my mind, lock them into muscle memory. Allow them to become as without thought as breathing. Then watch the flow, nothing jarred, abrupt, control the flow of movement.

After that, a half hour of recovery, meditation, relaxing. Then, three hours of working with Maestro von Brunner. In his opinion, the rapidity of my Ripple was fine and would eventually reach the quarter of a second per spell target I hoped to achieve. Most spell slingers were satisfied with half a second, even a full second per spell. But what he wanted me to focus on was using the shield as a weapon. We spent most of our time changing the shape, size, width of my shields. His theory: With my inborn immunity against all but the strongest spells and Talents, making my mostly unseeable shield as a weapon instead of a layer of defense I didn't always need could be a game changer. Having my shield edges as thin as possible, so it could slice as well as protect, would give me an unexpected advantage. An opponent would literally not see it coming.

After that, my training day was usually done. But since we had guests, it was decided that we would go to the local green space, a nice little mini-park full of trees. Melene and I brought our supplies of practice weapons and paintball guns. Then we split up into two teams and played 'Hide the Flag' into the night, with Megan and Trini serving as each teams' 'Flag'. Flags that had their own paintball guns and could protect themselves. Everyone was coated with paint, filthy as hell, and laughing our behinds off as we made our way back to the house. It was a good day.

My aunt decided, while we were out running around in the woods, that she was feeling Italian, so she called one her favorites, ordered a massive spread, and timed it for it to arrive about a half hour after everyone had their turns in the various showers in the house. Goodness knows there were a bunch of them!

So there we were, surrounded by angel hair pasta, mountains of garlic bread, broiled meats and steamed lobsters, steaming bowls of sauces, eating, talking, laughing, staring and being stared at.

"Lee." Ben swallowed his bread and continued. "This morning, and afternoon. You do that every day?"

I nodded, and continued eating.

"No breaks?"

I looked and smiled. "Took a break yesterday. See how that turned out?"

"But why go so hard? Every day?" Megs wondered. "And you say you've been doing this for close to twenty years?"

I leaned back. "I remember the second day on the job with all of you. Trini there walked into the studio at seven in the morning. She spent three hours in there. Warming up her voice, running scales, vocal exercises, mouthing exercises, changing her rapping cadence, making sounds that would scare birds and small children."

I caught the piece of bread Trini threw while the rest chuckled.

"And was she done? Nope. Off to the dance studio, another few hours. Stretching, gymnastics, ballet, jazz, hip hop, solo, small group, all that.

"After that, she goes back to the suite, gets a little something to eat, works with you over some business issues for an hour or so, then proceeds to bash out lyrics, vocal arrangements, key changes she wants for the band, studying poetry.

"She spent the whole day like that, Megan. And I'm sure most of her days are like that, when she's not doing a promotional, or performing, where she puts in even more hard core work. Did you ever ask Trini why she was doing that? Or did you already know the answer?"

Trini giggled. "I do that 'cause I'm La Reina, fool, and I wanna stay that way."

We all bowed and intoned, "All hail the Queen!" and laughed while Trini waved her hand, princess style.

"So," Ben continued. "You train that hard, that long, because your career demands that much?"

I nodded slowly. "The career I want. The Life I expect to live. Yeah, it demands that much work, if I expect to live it more than a few years."

"But, why would you want that kind of life?" Denny asked. "Not even the Special Forces soldiers work that hard! I should know, since I retired out of the SEALs eight years back!"

I smiled at the veteran warrior. "The SEALs protect the interests of this country. Nemesenes protect the safety and well-being of all peoples, on both sides of The Veil. And just like you felt the call to be a SEAL, I feel it to be a Nemesene, and do all I can to help those who can't help themselves, wherever they may be." I shrugged my shoulders. "Sounds as corny as hell, I know, but it's how I feel."

The crew around the table had varied reactions. Tilsa looked at me and smiled warmly, before returning her attention to the lobster on her plate. A few, particularly Megan and Trini, still looked slightly confused.

"The thing you all must understand," My aunt offered, "Well, all except Tilsa, is that humans act as if people of Lyrodrylle suddenly arrived just before The Sundering, only sixty years ago.

In truth, sapient beings of our planet were here on Earth since humans climbed down from the trees.

"You see, as many wars and catastrophes as there were on Lyrodrylle, we never suffered a dark period, where the great achievements of prior cultures were lost forever. Only a very few of the wonders of ancient civilizations like Lemuria, Atlantis or Nemedia were lost. A great many of their discoveries and technologies are still available to us.

"Consequently, when we made our way through The Veil, and saw that humans were beginning to evolve, you were considered primitives that would be fun to play with, almost like pets, and the humans who knew no better, saw the Lyrodryllian visitors as gods and goddesses. Titans. Mythic, all-powerful beings to be feared or worshipped."

"Oh, Hell no!" Megs snapped harshly. "The Earth wasn't nothin' but one big friggin' petting zoo to these sleazebags?"

"Yes, it was inexcusable, My Dear. So much so, Nemesis, a real Celestial, brought into existence through the Divine Will of The Creator, decided that it was past time to do something about it. She reached out to a number of truly heroic beings, and led them to form the Nemesene Cadre, an enforcement organization. The mandate of The Cadre was grown since its beginnings, but the first and most important mandate has always been to eradicate the destructive behaviors of Lyrodryllians regarding humans.

"But both planets are quite a large area for so many field agents to monitor. There's just never enough of us around, and terrible things have happened because of that truth."

The Chief, listening intently, leaned forward. "Terrible things, like?"

Megan sighed. "Sodom and Gomorrah."

Denny Pitts almost choked on his food. "Lyrodryllians destroyed the cities?"

Tilsa snorted. "Nah, The Divine Creator sent his angelic hitmen to wipe the towns out, but it was Lyrodryllians acting like complete retards that caused The Creator to order the Hit."

Her demeanor felt a little off to me. More aggressive, more assured than she normally seemed outside of combat situations. I was probably just making it up in my head, was my conclusion. No one else seemed to notice anything.

Ben did look at her funny, though. "You knew this?"

"She waved at herself. "Hellooo?" Big tall chick? Mother from Land of the Giants?"

"What else?" Megan asked worriedly.

"Two plagues. The Antonine Plague in ancient Rome was caused by failed experiments by Jusseline alchemists. The Cadre had to wipe that whole Society of diseased perverts out of existence. And you've all heard of The Black Plague."

The Chief wiped his face. "I'm afraid to ask, but…"

"Ellovysians," Melene's face was momentarily full of stone cold fury. "They dumped a thousand tons of exotic waste on the lands of Central Asia, treating the area like a land fill."

"Elven scum!" Tilsa snarled, her expression exactly matching Melene's

"Well, damn," Chief whispered.

"Those were times when the Nemesenes came up short. For every tale of failure, there's at least two hundred stories of success. Stories that will never be recorded in human history books, due to our original mandate. You weren't supposed to know there was anything to be saved from!"

Ben began nodding, and pointed a thumb at me. "And this one wants to, what? Stop the next Vesuvius from exploding?"

"Couldn't stop that one. We tried, lost three agents there. That mother was ready to go without any help. But yes, I get the question, and yes, if that is required to save as many innocent lives as possible."

"Oh. My. God." Megan held her face in her hands. "I understood what you were saying before, Lee. I did. But hearing this? Visualizing all that happened, and all that was prevented from happening?" She shook her head. "You're right, Stud. There's no place for me in a life like that."

"For real," Trini intoned, her face awed. "That's bananas! Yo, even a Queen like me gotta stay in her lane." She looked up at me, her face shifting gears. "We can still be wreckin' the bed frames though, right? I mean, when you're in town and not too busy?"

Both Tilsa and Denny exploded their food across the table. Megan just held her head, shaking it in woe.

Melene smiled wickedly. "I begin to wonder if you might have trace elements of The Pride in your ancestry, You Delightful Little Minx!"

***

The morning came, and I was walking out the door for my morning run. I noted that someone was leaning in the gateway, sparking my alarm a bit. As I drew closer, I saw that it was Tilsa, in familiar sweat gear.

"Your aunt let me borrow some stuff," She explained when I drew closer.

I gulped. The roomy Security gear the team wore was effective camouflage indeed. From the forcibly contained bosom to the generous hips and long, powerfully muscled legs, the woman was packin' an arsenal! She looked just as my aunt normally does in the gear, which was beyond mouth-watering, but she didn't have the same impact on my senses.

"You're staring," Tilsa chuckled. "That's rude."

I looked up at her. She had a pleasant, open face. More handsome than beautiful. But her sea-green eyes were bewitching. You could... wait. Weren't her eyes blue? I blinked, and yes, blue eyes. Um. Yeah.

"You really can't blame me for staring, Tilsa," I replied. "I'm just a horny little kid who hasn't learned how to behave around adults yet."

"The expressions on Trini and Megan's faces say otherwise, buster." She smiled. "Tells me you learned plenty."

I cleared my throat. I wasn't ready for the full court press. "You wanted to run with me, Tilsa?"

"Yep, can't afford to sit around too much. Can't lose my edge."

I shrugged. "All right. Let's get to it."

Back into Work Mode, I focused on stretching out any kinks, slowly warmed up my muscles, and with a nod to my morning partner we went at it, full out running.

I'd done my research. The giants of Jötunheim were deserving of their reputation regarding strength and resiliency, but were not particularly gifted with surpassing speed or endurance. So when I saw Tilsa keeping up with me, stride for stride, with little effort, I was pretty damned shocked, to be honest. Then I felt challenged.

I nodded to her. She smiled, and then we kicked in the afterburners.

I never pushed my run as far, or as fast, as I did that morning. I normally kept to around the mid-thirties mph on my runs and a twenty mile limit. With Tilsa keeping step for step, I know we hit over fifty mph, and we doubled the distance. Just because we could.

It had been so long since I had someone to run with. Melene considered road work boring, and preferred using the high-tech cardio machines in our well-appointed gym. It wasn't until I had a partner go balls-out right by my side that I considered that Melene might have had a point.

I could tell Tilsa was close to collapse when we made our way through my gate. I was too. It felt amazing!

"Dido's Tears, Dude!" She panted. "You do that every morning?"

"Nope, something special, for you," I wheezed in reply.

"Why?"

There were a few smart-ass replies I had on tap, but I decided on honesty. "Because it's been a scraggin' long time since I had someone to run with, I enjoyed being with you, and I didn't want it to end."

She didn't respond immediately. She looked at me intently, and then smiled. "I really don't think it will ever end, Lyam. Not between us."

Before I could respond, she hopped up and swiftly made her way into the house. I saw her determined stride, puzzled by her words and attitude, then shrugged, and went into my stretches. A lot achier than usual, but so worth it. But, according to my research, it was a morning that should have never happened. No full member of that culture could have kept up with me, much less a half breed or less. Therefore, one MUST conclude that she isn't really a partial descendant of the giants. Then, what was she, really?

Something to ponder in the very near future. I didn't get any 'danger' vibes from her in the least, so I'd table it till later. Melene and this morning's Maestro wouldn't appreciate me being late for Combat Training.

I stopped abruptly when I reached the salon. In addition to Melene and Master Chu, my Tai Chi Chuan Sensei, Chief Sykes and the whole team were there, all of them staring at Tilsa, and the sharp commando knife in her hand.

"Good, you're here," Tilsa noted in a pleasant, scary (to me) tone. We can proceed."

"Proceed with what, Danville?" The Chief barked. What do you think you're doing with that knife?"

"I'm handing in my resignation, Chief," Tilsa replied with enthusiasm. You could almost hear the giggle in her voice.

"Resignation?" Sykes spluttered. "You can't do that! Not while we're still on assignment. Not with our Primary still in active danger. And damned sure not without two weeks' notice!"

"I really am sorry, Chief. You guys are great teammates, and I'd like to think friends as well. But you have to understand, I was tasked for an assignment before I walked through the doors at Blue Star."

"You don't say," Melene interjected. She seemed way too calm for all this. "And could you tell us, Tilsa, what your assignment was?"

The woman smiled. "Not what, Captain Seckett. Who. And not was. Still is."

One of Melene's eyebrows lifted. "My. It's been a long time."

My sensei finally spoke. "Still active?" he asked Melene simply.

"Retired. Well, inactive, actually."

I felt like my head was about to explode. "Will somebody tell me what is happening here? Am I going to be beaten to a pulp again?"

Tilsa smirked. "Not unless you're into that sorta thing, big boy."

"I thought you said you were a Deputy, Ms. Alabato," Ben noted, speaking over his team leader.

"I am a Deputy. For The Cadre. I had another job before that, and another rank."

"Um, I'm actually more concerned at why Tilsa has that knife," Denny pointed out. "Maybe it's just me?"

"The knife is for a little surgery, Denny." Tilsa held up her left arm and pulled up the sleeve. "On me, people. Don't worry so much. The implant is pretty close to the top of my skin."

"Oh, damn! Are you serious?" Ben groaned as we watched Tilsa slice into the inside of her forearm, lengthwise. Everyone, Sensei Chu included, was used to spilling blood. Still gross, though. Tilsa dropped the knife and began digging into her arm. After a few seconds, she pulled back her right hand, showing us all a small, oval object. It was flat, about two inches long, and seemed white and smooth under the blood.

Seconds after she removed the object from her arm, she seemed to shift, melt, and remold herself. When she was done, I beheld a Goddess!

A bit shorter than before, the woman stood proudly before us, sporting a large, magnificent bust that had to put her sports bras in acute stress, washboard flat abdominals, a small waist that flared out to a wondrous pair of hips. All standing on long, delightfully muscled legs and perfectly shaped ankles and arches. All of that curvaceous wonder tightly sheathed in long chiseled muscles that somehow added to her allure instead of detracting from it.

And her face? The face in profile was beyond words. The long but delicately crafted nose, arched eyebrows, long, thick eyelashes, the firm yet graceful cheeks and chin, and the large, full, curved lips, all of it combined in a skin shaded like lightly creamed coffee creating a face that matched her mind-blowing physique in the new bar of perfection I had in my mind regarding to the 'Perfect Woman', at least how she would look. Her curves prevented from sag by an abundance of sculpted muscle, without the muscles losing the beauty of their form through excessive bulging.

She looked at me, turned her head, and smiled. And I saw the long, puckered scar that ran down the side of her face. And I saw that the left side of her face didn't move with her smile, like it was stiff, stone-like. I couldn't stop myself. I flew to her, and gently cupped her face in my hands, staring into her sea-green eyes. "Who did this to you?" I whispered harshly.

She blinked at the heat in my voice. "An enemy," She responded gently. "Unreachable for now, but her time will come." She bit her lip, worriedly. "Does it, disgust you?"

"How could it?" I replied, feeling out of breath. "You're perfect. Your face, your physique, your sense of humor. And you can run beside me." I gulped, took a breath. "You have the face of a warrior, the face of a victor, not a victim." I continued staring up into her eyes, her face, as I ran my hands through the long, smooth, honey brown hair that suddenly appeared, framing her face perfectly. "What is your assignment, Tilsa?"

"Della," she replied in a low, warm tone. "Della Manville, of Sekhmet Pride's Guardian Division. And you are my assignment, Maahes Seckett."

I smiled. "I told you, my friends can call me Lee."

She smiled back. "Am I just a friend, Lee?"

"I really, really, don't think so."

Chapter 17. Duet

It was time to get to work.

THERE WAS MUCH TO TALK ABOUT, a lot to reveal, but as both Melene and Della pointed out, enough time had been taken from training. Melene shooed the others out of the salon, leaving me with Master Chu. And Della.

"Is this my new normal, Della? I asked, as she wrapped a bandage around her arm.

"Not so much, Lee. I just thought it might be good to finish my 'Great Reveal'. She smirked. "My keeping up with you this morning wasn't my only surprise."

"Enough talking!" Sensei Chu snapped. "Begin!"

I went to work, and Della flowed right in with it. I forgot about her, about everything, as I opened my third eye, my inner eye, and looked even deeper into my movement. Watched the muscles pull, the limbs stretch out, the forms flow from one to the next. Slowly, focused, graceful. Ever since Alistra helped me with those aspects of Psychomancy I could adopt into my repertoire, I find my forms in Tai Chi had progressed in proper positioning and alignment that much more rapidly.

And I could feel the potential strains, and heal them as I went along. It made me almost piss my drawers when I discovered the ability to heal myself and others, albeit to a limited degree. I'd never be considered a 'Healer' Talent, but having even a mediocre access to that form of magic had to be of major use to a Warrior type.

Sooner than I realized, I had completed the hour-and-some routine my Master required before I went into Combat training. I stood up from my forms, and saw Della waiting, smiling.

"You didn't even notice me," She pouted.

"If I did, Master Chu would've beaten me black and blue." I responded.

"Correct," Snapped the Elder, though his eyes laughed. "You are quite developed in your practice, Ms. Manville. Almost at the level of this clumsy ox here."

"Hey!" I protested. I was, of course, ignored.

"I'm sure you didn't have to be beaten as many times as he has to reach your level?

Della bowed respectfully. "I don't know for sure, Sensei. I did all my training at The Burning Sands. We get beatings for any number of reasons. I'm not sure which beatings were for my training in the forms."

Master Chu smiled. "As long as your Masters know, that is all that's required." He clapped his hands. "Now, face off!" We did so, bowed to each other, and proceeded to beat each other to a pulp.

Well, it felt that way. Very different from how she presented herself at my Blue Star tryout. I was stronger, she was faster. I was more aggressive, she was more agile, and elusive. She was four years older, but I'd been in training since I was four, so it was a wash. She slammed me into the mat, I knocked her half-way across the salon space. Her knee lifts were devastating to my ribs and abdomen, my knife hands cut off her breathing. There were a couple of openings for a killer hook punch into her jaw—I just couldn't pull the trigger. I know she let me off the hook a time or too as well. I felt it.

We weren't trying to destroy each other, we were just continuing our introduction to each other, and I was thrilled to meet her.

"Tingzhǐ!"

We stopped, bowed to each other, and faced the Sensei.

"You dance like you're on stage instead of battle like warriors. Bah! I'm done with you both." After a few more harrumphs, he said, "But you complement each other already. That is good. I will inform your Masters that we need to begin including small group tactics into our training. Maybe if you're not facing each other, THERE WILL BE LESS DANCING!" After a few more huffs, he made his way out the salon.

"That bad?" Della wondered.

"That good!" I chuckled. "His usual response is to tell I'm a heavy-footed buffoon who drags his carcass through each combo, followed by a few well-placed swats on the back or shoulders with the cane in his hand."

"Oh, well, glad I could help,"

"Me too. Alright, I'm going to shower and change, get ready for my Talent training."

I could see, or imagined seeing, her wanting to ask if she could join me in the shower. I appreciated her resisting. Trini and Megan were important to me, and before there were changes in expectations, they deserved the respect of me talking with them first. I liked them too much to disrespect them like that. Even loved them, at least enough to not want them hurt.

But I did indulge in a full-body hug with my new guardian before I went. Oh my Goddess, she felt perfect!

When I returned, Della was sitting with Maestro von Brunner, waiting for me.

"It seems you've found the first member of your team, Deputy. It is perfect that she is of The Pride, Lee. Unlike you, her natural immunity to magic has not been compromised. So, with her indulgence, we're going to include her into your training."

"Excellent! Um, how?"

"Simple. She's going to attack you, and you're going to stop her." He smiled. "Using nothing else but the one thing that can't affect her in the least."

"Oh." I observed Della cracking her knuckles, smiling in eager anticipation.

"Shall we begin?"

It took two hours of running and being beaten within an inch of my life, but I figured it out. Lighting her clothes on fire, using my pseudo telekinetic spell to pull her pants down to her ankles causing her to stumble and fall. Using the same spell to pick up and throw objects at her. Earth spells to pull up the boards of the floor or creating holes, causing her to fall to the basement. I learned to think faster, more strategically, while she learned how to think faster and avoid my traps.

A good time was had by all, including Maestro von Brunner. I'd never seen him laugh so hard or so often.

"Really?" Della fumed. "You had to pull my top over my head?"

"Yeah, well the big, goofy smile on your face while you were smacking me around convinced me," I shot back.

"I was just happy to be in your company," Della snickered.

"You both did very well," The Maestro interjected. "Good display of innovative thinking and strategizing on the fly. Lyam, you might want to include sharp objects in your arsenal, use them to attack opponents like Della. Remember, you're naturally inclined to aggression. You have excellent defenses, but you are not a defensive-styled fighter. As for you, Ms. Manville," The Maestro smiled and bowed. "May I say that you are an utterly captivating example of Pride Perfection, and I would advise investing in flame-retardant gear if you're going into the field next to him?"

Della laughed warmly and mockingly returned his bow. "I'm glad you enjoyed the show, Maestro Lech!" She sauntered towards the door. "I'm hittin' the showers, and finding something less crispy to wear."

We watched her leave, and then we looked at each other.

"Good Lawd!"

"For real."

***

I found out later that Melene had supervised everyone in our home, including the ladies, in a series of exercises and weight training while I was in my routines. By the time we sat down for a meal that evening, everybody looked like worn-out Hell.

"I can't lift my arms," Trini moaned. "Somebody feed me? I'm so hungry!"

I chuckled and helped her out. "You're gonna thank Auntie for it though!"

"But I don't want to get all big and bulky!"

"You won't," Melene assured her. "I've seen you on stage, Trini. You are spectacular. But you are going into bigger venues. Longer shows. You need to be at your peak so you don't wear down towards the end of your performance. I know you're already a very hard worker. I'm just showing you something to add to your development routine. As will Señor Cantalano tomorrow."

Trini spat out her food. "The voice teacher? He's coming here? Tomorrow?"

"He's a sweetheart, and he loves working with dedicated students. He'll adore you."

"But he refused to even take my calls," Megan insisted as she groaned through her meal. "He didn't even let his assistant pick up the phone!"

"He's a pushover, but Ernesto's assistant is an unholy terror!" Melene snickered. "The very best gatekeeper in all creation. Don't worry, Trini, Diego will appreciate how seriously you take your training and you'll have him wrapped around your finger too."

"How do you even know him?" Meg asked.

"He was in a very bad place fourteen years ago, and Lee's mother helped him sort it out."

I know there was a lot more to it than the way Melene was acting, but it wasn't my story, so I didn't ask for details.

Trini sat back in her chair, looking at my aunt and me. "You're really beautiful, Ms. Melene. You both are. You both just seem to give, and keep on giving!"

Melene smiled. "You have a precious soul, Trinidad Flores. Makes it easy to give to people like you." She looked around the table. "These past years have been very hard on Lyam and me. We're still going through it. But having you all here, listening to your laughter and even your grumpy comments," she smiled at a reddening Sykes. "I've realized just how much I miss more than

151

just myself and Lee at the table. You've brought some needed fresh air to this oversized barn, and I appreciate it, more than I can say."

She leaned back in her chair and sighed. "And now, my dears. We have to talk seriously about what happens next."

The Chief frowned. "What happens next?" Melene nodded.

"My boss informs me that they have finally discovered a possible location for the source of the Maenad attacks. It's on the other side of The Veil. As one of his very few agents of command rank in this general location, I must take a team to seek out this source, and end it, if at all possible." She paused. "And Lee has to come with me."

The table was silent, as the folks, including me, digested that bomb.

"So, we have to go?" Trini asked in a small voice.

"Trini, you can't leave," Melene replied. "You're still in great danger. Chief Sykes, you and your team, and Megan here, you can decide to leave if you wish. You all have lives to live, but The Nemesene Cadre has officially taken over this case, and my Chief has mandated that Trini be kept in a secure location. Either here or at his headquarters. That is non-negotiable.

"I felt that you might be more comfortable here, Trini, but the choice in location is yours. It's pretty much the only choice you have, until this crisis is over. I'm sorry it has to be this way, My Dear."

Trini nodded solemnly. "If I go back out there, and you two are off hunting this whatever down, then we're all sitting ducks, ain't we?" She looked around the table. All of us. "The last two times, we're lucky none of us died. I miss my family, but they're all safe because I'm here. I can't deal with any of y'all dying because I got hard-headed."

"Blue Star hasn't pulled this detail, Trini," The Chief rumbled. "And we wouldn't leave you if they did!" Trini smiled at his vehemence. "So, you're just leaving a bunch of strangers in your home while you two go traipsing off somewhere?"

Melene smiled. "Not completely. A few members of The Cadre have been assigned to assist and keep an eye on things. And my chief will be coming through here often, until we return."

"Three will be heading out," Della interjected lowly but firmly.

Melene smiled, "I know, Guardian."

"We never did have that little chat, Tilsa, or whoever you are!" snarled the Chief. "Just who the Hell are you?"

"Yeah, and where is Tilsa?" Megan asked, confused. Then it started to frame up for her. "This is Tilsa? What happened?"

"All right," Della sighed and leaned her arms on the table. "Here it is, A to Z.

"For reasons that have never been explained to anyone, The Lioness, basically our Queen in Sekhmet's Pride, has always had a personal interest in the Seckett Family. When Lee's father was discovered living in this city, she sent a pair of Guardians to serve as bodyguards. Guardians are a somewhat secretive branch of The Pride's Military. Elite forces. Guardians answer only to The Lioness and her designates.

"The Guardians were mandated to stay by Lionel's side, protecting him. Keeping him safe, advising him, for life." She smiled at Melene. "How did that work out, Captain?"

"Abysmally, at times," Melene answered with a smile. "Beyond my wild imaginings at other times. We thought we were assigned to babysit a mewling, weak-minded male of the Pride. We had no idea we had a true Lion on our hands! We were clueless on how to handle Lionel in those first few years."

Della sighed. "Yes, that was my same thought, when I was given this assignment. That's why I rebelled." She looked around the table. "Four years ago, The Lioness decided to treat Lionel and Belinda's disappearance as permanent. I know you still hold out hope, Melene, and you should. But The Lioness doesn't operate on hopes. She decided to send another set of Guardians, for Lionel's son. Me as lead, since I've had experience, and two rookies to grow with our Primary. But the other two were pulled off the assignment just before departure, and it was never explained to me why.

"I didn't want to come here. Away from my fellow warriors, surrounded by weakling humans and your judgmental attitudes regarding a female's right to a happy sex life, and men having such an unacceptable level of authority over women. Even worse, stuck here for the rest of my life, catering to a weak, useless male of my race—as if he had any real purpose for breathing except as a sperm donor!"

She looked around the table, at the horrified expressions on the others' faces. It wasn't news to me. Melene had long ago taught me of how men were seen and treated in The Pride Society. One of the reasons I never asked if we could visit our supposed homeland. As far as I knew, I had no reason at all to go and put up with institutionalized sexism.

"That was how I thought when I arrived, less than three years ago. I decided that I would keep an eye on Maahes, but from a distance. I used my connections in previous assignments to have a disguise device implanted in my arm, change my appearance, and then spend some time seeking employment." She brushed the long, cruel scar on her face. "I'm not well known everywhere, but enough descriptions of my particular face ornament have circulated enough in some low circles, and I didn't want to deal with kind of annoyance. I was hired by Blue Star and made my way to Chief Sykes unit, because your unit doesn't go out except for high profile, highly sensitive cases, leaving me enough free time to observe the Seckett male, when I got around to it. I didn't know what to do when I realized that I couldn't observe him because of the level of security around this home and because of his limited activities outside the home. Very annoying.

"So, you can all imagine my shock when a highly trained, highly Talented young man is brought in on this special assignment, signed off by the D.I.A. and The Nemesenes, and the man just happens to be the weak, useless, thoroughly submissive male I was sent to Guard! You all would have laughed if you could see what was happening in my skull. All my preconceptions, wrecked on arrival!

"Our boss chooses me to try him out. I figure, if I used the strength of the being I was using as a disguise, I would easily display how inadequate this male was. Instead, I was proven wrong, and humbled. He goes on to show ridiculously high levels of skill and training. And I felt a stirring in me. Lionel proved himself to be more than what we of The Pride considered possible. Could this be true of his son?

"Then that day when that scraggin' moron Jackson smashed Lee through that wall. I almost killed the Lycan then and there! But instead, I controlled myself. I watched you pick yourself up,

154

and calmly walk back across the street. I saw that look in your eye, Lee. You were well aware that you could tear him to pieces, easily, but you held yourself in check, you chose to be a professional.

"I saw that you were strong enough to choose not to kill, the greatest of strengths for a true warrior.

"I was ashamed, Lee, and I had to find my way to your side. If you'll have me."

Della looked around the table again. "I know, Ben. Feels like we crossed way into the Too Much Information Zone. But Chief, I need you to understand, all of you, that this is not just a whim or a case of infatuation. We females of The Pride are a created race, as you've probably been informed. The Ancient Atlantean bioengineers and Enchanters combined all their impossibly advanced skills and learning to create a race of Warriors, built to be stronger, faster, more agile, and more gifted in the art of war than any other race that ever existed. It's not boasting; it's simply historical truth.

"During the process of our coming into existence, the Atlanteans added a multitude of specialized adaptations to our genetic code. One of the primary additions is the instinctual behavior of the creature they knew as lions. The Atlantean Lion was very similar to the species you know today, at least in basic appearance and behaviors, but they were the size of today's polar bear, were far more intelligent, and, according to what we've been taught, they were nearly suicidal in their level of loyalty to those they consider a member of their family, which was also termed The Pride.

The females were not targeted by the Atlanteans to be their protectors, but some glitch in the genetic code made it necessary for the women to step up. So they did, to the point where the females, the lionesses, grew to be the dominant sex of the race, and the males became submissive. And, more than forty thousand years later, even after Atlantis sank into legend and the created species made their own way on either side of The Veil, those roles have been unchanged.

We women of Sekhmet's Pride recognize each other as lionesses, the hunters, the defenders of our family, which has evolved into a nation. We call the men of our society males, because we as a people don't consider them lions. Lions would take command, would dominate in the field, and in the home. In our culture, the very idea of men being in control of anything except for when they choose to brush their teeth is more than just ludicrous. If we had a national religion, the idea of men taking a leading role would be considered blasphemous, and whoever suggested it might end up getting burned at the stake."

Megan nodded slowly. "That's more than a little intense, Della, but I think I see it. If you called a man a lion, you'd be acknowledging something your race hasn't done in, wow, forty thousand years? A man running his home and family? In charge of a lioness? Yeah, I get it. There's no way you would accept a man running anything in your society."

Trini leaned forward, looked Della in the eye. "Unless that male proved he was a Lion for real. Then, because of those genetic codes built inside you all, you'd have no choice but to follow him!"

Della nodded. "Yeah. And here we are today. Even if I wasn't Lee's Guardian, there is this thing in me—it calls to me to follow where he leads. It would be easy to resist if he was a schmuck, looked like a naked mole rat and smelled like a warthog's behind. But he doesn't, and I...I..."

"Enough," Chief Sykes demanded in a calmer tone than usual. "This has gone way beyond table talk. I understand, Della. We all get it. Anyway, I'm staying, and I'm going to avail myself of all this exercise gear, and the big whirlpool and sauna, and treat this like a paid vacation." He looked nervously at Melene. You think, maybe, I could have my old lady visit? Once or twice?"

"You?" spluttered Ben. "Acting like a grizzly bear with a sore tooth? You have an old lady?"

"Sure, Gregg. It should be safe enough, and there's plenty of room. Just make sure that you never leave or come without an agent of The Cadre escorting you. And if any of them have magic Talent, they must be thoroughly scanned to make sure whatever this thing is isn't coming along for a ride."

We continued discussing things, like how the females of The Pride became so dominant, how many other Matriarchal societies there were on Lyrodrylle, which friends or family members to invite over to stay, things of that nature, Della was mostly quiet.

She said her piece. She made her case. And she was leaving it with me.

She looked at me. I smiled, and nodded. She smiled her half-smile, the left side of her face frozen and unresponsive. Half of her smile was more than enough for me. We'd work out the details later.

Chapter 18. The One, but why not The Only?

I really shouldn't have been surprised by Trini's question.

But I was. It was as if she could see the wheels spinning in my head. Perhaps it was the timing. I mean, the three of us did spend the last ninety or so minutes wrecking another set of furniture (A very good thing we had so much stuff in storage). But no, Trini wasn't the type to not face issues head on.

"This Della, or Tilsa, whatever her name. Is she that chick you were talkin' about? Fight by your side? Ride or die? Hand you the bullets while you're shootin'?"

Megan had turned over, wanting to see my reaction, hear my response.

In the short time we'd known each other, we didn't play useless games. I wouldn't start now.

"I don't know," I replied slowly. "She might be. I've had these dreams, fantasies. I had these imaginary friends, Trini. Two girls, twins. They seemed so real to me, but not clear most of the time. There were those rare times when I could see them clearly. They didn't look anything like Della. Darker skin, darker, curlier hair. Those times were rare, but they always seemed to mean so much to me. Like we would be best friends for life. Maybe more than best friends."

I looked at the precious women in my bed as I described other females. They looked more interested, more curious, than jealous. I guess that was just the way they were built, maybe being up front from the start led to the kind of relationship we seemed to already have. Whatever the cause, I felt blessed that we seemed to be able to talk about anything.

"I'm talking about these twins, Trini, because recently, Melene told me that they weren't just my imaginary friends from childhood. They were, are real, they exist. She said it would all be explained to me very soon, but in the meantime, I'm stuck on knowing I wasn't just making stuff up to deal with my loneliness, and I'm not sure how I feel about that.

"And now, here comes Della. I do feel like she could be my Right Hand for Life. She seems to want to be. But I really don't know that much about her. And what of these twins I'm going to learn about? Whatever kind of relationship we might have had, which I seemed to have forgotten completely, how would they fit into my life? Would they even want to fit into my life?

"I'm just very confused right now."

Trini laid back on the pillows and sighed. "I forget sometimes that me and Megs are older than you, Lee. I mean, I only got you by a year, but I've been out in the world while you been cooped up, building these tasty muscles of yours. Point is, there's so much about living that you ain't learned yet. I wish I could be the one to teach you, but like you said, way different roads."

"Yeah," Meg nodded. "You're a fighter, Lee. A warrior. But the madness you gotta deal with in just living—that can take it out of even a big bad warrior type."

She smiled sweetly. "But I get a vibe from this chick, Lee. I get that feeling, when she commits, it ends only after she's dead and buried, and even then there might be issues. I'm thinking, I'm feeling, that she might really be the One, but she probably won't be the only one."

"Huh?"

"Such a boy. I don't know the terminology on the other side of The Veil, but in most English-speaking cultures, it's called a harem."

"A harem? But I...but I didn't, um..."

"¡Idioto! What you think is happenin' right the Hell now?" Trini giggled. "You think I'm lookin' forward to a different man, after being turned out by you?" She snickered. "I'm telling you for real, Bruh, you need to be careful about where you lay the pipe, if you don't want an army of hoes tracking you down everywhere you go!"

"Preach, Sistah!" Megan howled. "Please, Lee, please, please, PLEASE be selective about that sort of thing. I'm having enough trouble letting you go out there. With everything we all got going, this is probably the last time me and Trini will have with you. I truly feel sorry for the men that'll come after you."

"Verdad, Mami, I'm holdin' straight-up auditions from now on," Trini announced. "No scrubs allowed to apply, finalists better have a Superman cape around they necks!"

I laughed and kissed her throat. "You do deserve the very best, Mi Reina."

"Now see? That's exactly what I'm talkin' about!" With that, the little minx climbed back into her saddle. "I got enough gas for one more ride, Lee, and this time, I want to feel you let go of everything inside of me."

"But…"

"I know, can't have no babies. I showed you my Meter. Let's go! Giddyap!"

I relaxed and let her have her way. Yet another needed innovation from Lyrodrylle, the Contraceptive Meter, or simply The Meter or The Disc, was a flat disc full of microcircuitry that was placed carefully in the pelvic region, and then it essentially faded from sight unless the wearer wanted to adjust the settings or perform minor maintenance. The device adjusted the hormonal balance of women, preventing them from producing fertile eggs without jacking up their internal organs. It wasn't invasive, barely noticeable, and when in use, one hundred percent safe and effective. Those cultures on Earth that still preferred their women barefoot and pregnant were the only ones displeased with this particular innovation being introduced to humans.

There really wasn't a legitimate reason for my caution in letting myself go, since both Trini and Meg made sure their Meters were operating properly, but it was hammered into my head by Melene, for as long as I could remember, that I had to be painstakingly careful with my seed, even in the midst of an orgy or participating in a bedroom gymnastics marathon. The males of The Pride may have been treated like second-class citizens, but the use of their seed was closely monitored. The lionesses were not with the idea of there being an emergence of people with the same gifts of The Pride who had not sworn allegiance to them. The Children of The Pride were not at all interested in potential rivals to their preeminence.

I was thinking too much again, so I stopped and gave myself over to Trini's delightful efforts. I'd like to think I showed her and Megan some things in our time together. It certainly seemed so that night, as I handed over the reins and allowed myself to be lovingly abused.

***

It was three o'clock in the morning, and I couldn't sleep. I think I knew why.

I quietly left the two, allowed them to sleep and recover from their ministrations. Meg and Trini were truly hard-working ladies who never half-stepped in any field of endeavor. By The Gods!

I made my way down the stairs, down to the main floor, and walked through the hallway to the training salon. I sat on the mats and looked around the darkened space. After a few minutes, I detected a very slight disturbance at the far corner of the room. I focused on it, and soon the almost unnoticed divergence of flow in that corner slowly grew, became more apparent, then finally coalesced into a tall, magnificent vision of feminine splendor in grey gym shorts and a blue tank top. Her ability to fade out of view, another genetic trait generously bestowed on the people of The Pride by our Atlantean originators, was an ability all those of The Pride could do, but it took meticulous training to fade so completely in plain sight. She didn't have to say it. We both knew she was in the room before me, and that she allowed me to see some bit of her before she released her Fade completely. And we both knew that only in direct sunlight might she be detected when on the hunt.

And we both knew that she was, indeed, on the hunt.

She slowly made her way to me, and then sat down before me. Close enough to touch, we kept apart, only through our eyes was there contact.

"I see you," I intoned calmly.

"Do you?" she challenged. "Do you see me?"

"I do."

"How much of me do you see?"

160

"As much as you allow. There are depths to you, Della. Layers. Stories. When you choose, I will see them as well. Then I will see all of you."

She took in a breath, then another. "Who do you see?" she asked, a touch of tension, of hesitancy in her voice.

I didn't keep her waiting. "I see mine. I see she who belongs to me."

She released a breath she didn't know she was holding, and nodded. "I see you. As much as I can see of you."

"And who do you see, Della?" I asked. She bit her lip.

"My lion," she confessed. "I see my lion before me."

I nodded to her response. "Are you ready?"

"Yes. Are you?"

"I hope so. This is my first time."

She smiled. "You can't do it the wrong way. Just with the wrong people."

"Okay."

I closed my eyes and released my essence, my scent. And she released hers.

Those of The Pride considered the releasing of our pheromones deliberately as an extreme act of seduction when both parties are willing, and an act of rape if unwilling. I didn't do this consciously with Trini or Megan, though they could feel something about me that was different than other men. Basically, if a man or woman was exposed to the pheromones of a Child of The Pride by force, then choice is no longer possible. In numerous battles of the distant past, enemies of The Pride were lured to their deaths by the female warriors releasing their pheromones as one, causing the enemy to drop their weapons and run to their doom. This particular battle field tactic was eventually banned by The Pentagram as a completely unfair advantage. This almost caused The Pride to go to war with all the other forces of The Pentagram, but cooler heads prevailed.

We sat there, untouching, wrapped in each other's essence. It felt far more intimate than the sex I shared with Trini and Meg hours ago. I opened myself to her scent, she filled me. I felt the burning heat of the sands beneath the noon sun. The green leaves of the forest. The caressing breeze of the wind flowing through the tall grass. A multitude of flavors: sweet, pungent, tangy, delicious, and all her. All Della. My Della. Mine.

I felt the sweat trickling under my shirt, my breath shortening. The tingling sensation in my groin as I began to harden. I smoothed out my breathing. It wasn't about that. Not yet.

After hours, or seconds, we opened our eyes and looked at each other. Into each other.

"That was my first time too," she admitted. I quirked an eyebrow in inquiry. She snorted. "I'm no virgin, Lee. I never needed to release my essence. Before the scar, if I wanted to engage, all I ever needed to do is show up and show willingness. After the first couple of times, I did neither. I found myself wondering what all the fuss over sex was all about. I rarely found myself truly aroused by a man, or woman."

She brushed her hand across her scar. "And the one time I did feel something like arousal, I was given this memento from a higher ranked lioness with a poisoned blade. A poison specifically geared toward affecting those of The Pride. I couldn't heal from this. Not completely. She's an evil scrag, and I was a newly minted officer of the Defense Forces. She baited me in; she was intent on taking my life, but I was faster than she expected. Her seniority in rank and her connections were the only reasons she wasn't brought up on charges for having such a weapon and using it on a fellow lioness."

I nodded. "Thank you, Della. I see more of you, I see you more clearly. I see your scars. The one on your face and the ones inside you. I will never turn away, never stop seeing you."

We made our way to our feet. I reached out for her, took her in my arms, and held her. I felt her relax and wrap me tenderly. We stayed that way for a while.

"We're not gonna screw like rabbits, are we?" she murmured into my neck. I chuckled.

"Not here. Not yet."

"Dammit. The first time in my life that I understand the madness of real passion, and I get clam-jammed by a pair of humans!"

"I care about them, Della," I replied, though laughing too. "Deeply."

"I know, Lee. I hope I can receive that kind of care and fidelity in the near future?"

I leaned back to look at her. "I've had sex before with other people, Della. I've never shared essences with anyone but you. And I think the list of others I share my essence with will be rather short. You'll make sure of that."

"Me?"

"You're my lioness, Della. Maybe not my only, but you are my first. That means everything to me."

"Oh, Maahes," she purred. "My lion. It's as if you answered a prayer I was too afraid to consider praying for."

"Yeah, I get that a lot," I snickered playfully.

"Watch it with the ego, buster," she giggled. "Don't make me have to deflate it too often!"

We hugged again, and we parted. I was afraid to kiss her. If I did, I knew all care and consideration of Trini and Meg would swiftly evaporate. She knew it, and gave me her half-smile. "So, what now, my lion?"

I smiled. "It'll be dawn soon. How about a run?"

She nodded happily. "A morning run through the urban jungle with my lion? Sounds perfect."

"Well, suburban jungle, but—"

"I'll meet you out front, you idiot!"

Interlude: Five Years Ago.

They were attacked without warning.

THOSE GUARDING THE FACILITY, located on one of a dozen unnamed islands near the frozen lands of Lyrodrylle's southern pole, were the best of their breed, and that was saying something. And there were quite a few of them swarming what was essentially an unobtrusive hill with a massive laboratory jammed on top of it, sitting in the middle of the seas. They kept a sharp eye out in all directions, but there was nothing to see, except for the many icebergs that drifted past the island. Some came closer than others, but that wasn't unusual. Icebergs drift where they will. If one drifted too close, they'd blast it to pieces if it was small, treat it like unscheduled target practice, or one of the Talents present would send out shields to shift its course. The warlock, or group of warlocks and hags, would be virtually useless for a day or two after, but it wasn't like they had anything else to do.

But what might happen, if a particularly huge iceberg drifted much closer than normal to the island, needing seven of the ten Talents on the island to push it aside? An iceberg that had an industrial-sized anti-grav unit attached below its surface, coupled with a marine outboard motor, with nowhere near enough power to move an iceberg, unless the iceberg was unexpectedly a quarter of its actual weight?

Combine the two, with a rage and unflinching resolve that could shatter mountains, and you ended up with an iceberg that passed within two hundred yards of the island before being pushed to the side. Too close, almost disastrously close. But not that out of the ordinary. One of the watchers remarked that that particular floating ice castle seemed determined to draw close to the island, and its pattern of drift seemed to occasionally go against the current, but she was amongst the younger of their breed, and went mostly unheard, as was often the case for the young in their culture.

The crisis ended about three hours before dawn. The flood lights surrounding the lab were at their brightest, but the guards were not. Though armed forces are trained for battle at all hours of the day, no soldier truly looks forward to combat in the wee hours of the morning.

Unless you are vastly outnumbered, and needing every edge you can find.

There were forty guards surrounding the exterior of the facility. It wasn't until half of them missed their checkpoints before someone noticed, it happened so swiftly. Another ten had to seemingly disappear before the alarm was sounded, but by then it was far too late. The position of the remaining ten were zeroed in, and the noise-suppressed rifle wielded by a deadly marksman sent them into oblivion in less than ten seconds. The remaining fifty guard units made their way out of their barracks, and were wiped out in their entirety by a pair of modified Browning M2 machine guns. Say what you will about humans, they put together rather impressive firearms, and the Ma Deuce still retained its position as bully of the yard.

Hal Bergen, despite the brilliantly insulated wetsuit from Eliondra, was still chilled from the swim from the iceberg, Well, the drag, to be honest. Bezine did all the swimming. But he sucked it up. The time had finally come and neither he nor Bezine would be denied. The Elves thought the two were long dead from the ambush. They couldn't know the sneaky genius that was Lionel Seckett. Lionel didn't let anyone outside of His family know his strength in Psychomancy. The last remaining Ellovysian on that rock saw two shattered bodies and a wreckage that was once a modified salvage tug. He left with his prizes, and Hal spent two months waiting for Bezine to heal from the bullet that entered the side of her skull at an angle, instead of plowing into her brain, because of her superhuman reflexes.

The level of planning the Elves used in their plan to trap and contain The Secketts, then disappearing without a trace, was near flawless. The only fly in their ointment was that Bezine Seckett, Lionel Seckett's guardian and mate, had been exposed to his essence in countless times of passion and in the middle of the fiercest firefights. If Lionel was alive, and not in outer space, Bezine could and would find him.

It took three and a half years, the draining of most of the hidden funds and resources the family had cached away throughout Lyrodrylle in case of emergencies, and an inhuman defiance of the odds from the two, but the facility's location was discovered. It took another year and a half to plan and gather the required devices and tools. It was Hal's idea to use an iceberg to approach the island, close enough for Bezine to swim the rest of the way and tow Hal and their equipment along. If she had to drag a naval destroyer along, Bezine would have gotten it done. After they made an undetected landfall, Bezine stripped down to her briefs, unsheathed her twin short swords, and went on the hunt, while Hal followed in her wake, toting his high-powered sniper rifle to the highest level he could find, and contributed to her efforts.

When the last trooper fell, Hal put a hand gently on the lioness' tensed shoulders. "Take care of the active Talents first, B., I'll handle the exhausted ones."

Her nostrils flared in frustration. All she wanted to do was smash her way to the labs, but it was unprofessional, and extremely dangerous, to leave living enemies behind you.

They went to work. Those Talents not washed out from shifting the iceberg rained a multitude of spells on Bezine. Her immunity to Mystical Energies allowed her to walk through the onslaught as if taking a stroll through the park. The Talents whose energies were already exhausted died a cleaner death from the .45 slugs of Hal's semi-automatics. The others were messily shredded.

They moved further into the facilities, dispatching the scientists that crossed their paths, until they reached the main lab, and were confronted by an Elder Elf, standing before two small lab subject pods and holding a device in his hand.

"Stop this now! If we can't have them, then no one will! All I need to do is press-"

That was the info Hal wanted. He wasn't holding a Deadman's switch. Good.

The device flew from the Elder's hand as Hal's bullet plowed through his brain. Bezine sped forward and caught it before it could land.

The two walked toward, and then around the pods, made their way to the front of the being-sized containers, and beheld the efforts of the Elves over five years of horror.

Hal spewed forward everything that ever entered his stomach. Bezine fell to her knees, weeping, something Hal could barely notice in his misery. But did notice, because in the twenty-plus years of close friendship with the family, he only saw Bezine weep once in all that time: When Belinda gave birth to their precious Maahes.

The true horror of the Elves' malicious, malignant experiments wasn't that both bodies had been shaved and placed with electrodes sticking out of their heads. It wasn't the missing arms and legs, or missing everything from the waist down, with some device attached to the dangling end tip of their spines. It wasn't the open cavity with their still functioning internal organs on display. The truest depth of depravity to the desecration enacted on them was their eyes. The darting, blinking, fully aware eyes that made it clear that they were kept nightmarishly awake and alert for the full five years of violation. They knew what was being done to them. They could see it happening, and they were utterly helpless to stop it.

Just before Bezine smashed her way through the monitors, devices and flexible tubing, she felt Hal hugging her from behind, his words stopping her from flinging him away.

"Bezine, my love. Don't! Don't smash your way to them. These machines are keeping them alive. Don't destroy them before we better understand what they do!"

She paused and reengaged her brain. She nodded, and they began their study. The first move was to identify and remove the devices that were inhibiting their Talent. It took a couple of days to clearly identify those devices that focused on life support, and they proceeded to remove the rest. Hal was busy reading and translating the notes of the Elven scientists when Bezine came in from her exploration of the facility.

"These Hellspawns have a Regen device on the lower level, and the gear needed to make it mobile. We should move it and the two onto the iceberg when it returns, so we can get out of here ASAP. You did remember to set the iceberg to return?"

"Yes," Hal answered, still translating the notes. He spent three months creating the living area in the middle of the bloody thing, programmed and placed the anti-grav unit and outboard motor, made sure the remote steering device was functioning and correctly dialed in. Of course he set it to return!

He took a breath. They were all furious, in serious lack of sleep and rest. Tempers were frayed.

He looked up at Bezine, who was staring at him curiously.

"My love?"

Oh, damn. She wasn't so caught up in rage after all.

"I was afraid for Lionel and Bezine. Under a great deal of stress. Forget I said that!"

"I can't forget it, Hal."

"But I, but, well, nothing, I guess."

"Hal, you know Lionel and I, we, well…"

"I know, B. I know. I respect that, and love you both. Deeply. I never would have said anything, I was just so afraid for them."

Bezine looked at him, her face still. "How long, Hal?"

He sighed. "The moment I met you all."

"That long, Hal?"

"I'm probably going to feel this way for the rest of my life, B, so who cares when it began?"

"You're impossible," She told him, then wrapped him up in a deeply affectionate hug. He sighed into her shoulder as he hugged her back.

"Hal?"

"Yes, Bezine?"

"That's highly inappropriate."

"I know. I'm sorry."

"It's alright. We're going to have to talk about this when my family is safely moved to a secure location and we're not in danger of incoming enemies. But we will talk about this."

He nodded solemnly. Not looking forward that chat. "I've been thinking about that," Hal offered.

"What are your thoughts?" She watched Hal slowly begin to pace as he replied.

"Even with the Regeneration Unit, it's going to take years for those two to recover fully, if they ever do. We just have to accept that. If the Elves are intent on getting them back, they'll probably have forces near as many of The Veil Waypoints as they can muster. I personally think there's a mole somewhere, or else we wouldn't have gotten so thoroughly mouse-trapped. I'd like to think we would have noticed the Elves rebuilding, unless there's a cover up. But shelve that for now. Our going to any of the allied states of The Pentagram might precipitate a war nobody is ready for, except possibly these covert Elves. I'm thinking, we need to find a place on this side of The Veil- someplace completely remote, completely unexpected, and completely capable of fending off uninvited guests, if necessary."

"I can go with that," Bezine nodded. "But there is no place like that. In the final analysis, anybody can be bought or coerced, and any location invaded."

Hal smiled. "Not New Israel."

Bezine nearly collapsed to the floor on lifeless legs. "Menchit's Bones!" She whispered in a strangled voice. "You're talking about the Yeshua Revealed Collective!"

"Yep. The very same devout fanatics who told Lionel, after he helped them to find a few of their sacred relics, that if he was ever in need, he could call on them for assistance."

"How could I have forgotten about that?" She wondered. "This was a good ten years before we came to your office at Sturm, Ruger and Co. The only reason you know about that is because we told you about it!"

"It stuck out to me. A community of hard-core worshippers of Jesus, planted in an out-of-the-way island in the middle of the Aeolian Sea, chock full of high-powered Battle Mages and bursting with the latest in most known forms of warfare, just to make sure nobody gets their grubby paws on the true cross of the Messiah again?"

Bezine smiled. "Yeah. They'd be perfect. If we can get there."

"Icebergs melt rather slowly, and we can dial up the anti-grav unit a bit more. It'll take a lot of strain off the motor, and we can probably cannibalize some of the equipment these worthless pieces of scum have here, so we'll be able to move much faster. We'll make it!"

"I believe you, Hal." She smiled warmly. "I believe in you."

Hal blushed and ducked away from her gaze. It was her intensity that called to him so deeply. "Let's go to Belinda and Lionel. They might worry something happened to us. I don't want them to ever feel abandoned again!"

"Yes! Let's go!"

Book II.

Chapter 19. Crewed Up

We cleared out three days later.

IT WOULD'VE BEEN THE NEXT DAY, but there were complications. The first being the Feds, and the D.I.A. deciding to play silly buggers before we could leave (I confess to be a closet Anglophile. The British have brilliant ways of calling you Cat-Scat). Their interference was thoroughly annoying, but not the only reason for the delay that day. More later.

The small squad of Cadre personnel and family members of those staying in my home came that morning and told us that a detachment of Federal agents and Director Dellums, fronting a squad of his agents were standing at the top of the block looking all threatening and stuff. They seemed to require my presence.

Oh Joy.

Happily, my boss was on his way, so I wouldn't be left swinging in the breeze. Melene and Della decided to suit up for the occasion, and soon, two magnificent women, dressed in combat boots and armored, reinforced leather combat suits in gunmetal grey, escorted me through the gates, down the block, and to the entrance to the street, where four suited Feds, five agents in fatigues and their Director were standing in front of a S.W.A.T. van and the appropriately garbed police unit.

"What is it?" I asked. One of the Feds stepped up. He looked grim enough. He held up a folded set of papers.

"I am addressing a Mr. Lyam Seckett?" When I nodded, he tried to hand me paperwork.

"This is a federal warrant to search your premises, to establish that a Ms. Trinidad Flores, United States Citizen, is not being held against her will in said premises, and if so, to arrest you on the charge of kidnapping. This is also a subpoena, requiring you to appear before the Federal Court at 1 Federal Plaza, this morning, to establish whether pending charges of kidnapping, rape and coercion may be applied to you. Will you comply?"

I sighed. They wanted to flex. Okay then. I began reaching into one of the pockets on the inside of my coat, and the feds and police whipped their guns out. Pretty good reaction time. For humans. I looked at the lead Fed. "If you all don't want to meet your Maker a lot sooner than expected, you will put the firearms away and let me get my badge."

The guy actually sneered. "You're threatening federal and local agents of the law?"

I turned to Dellums. "This is pretty scraggin' low and petty, Director. Even for a scat-dump like you."

The director turned a bright red. "Your high-handedness has caused this! It's time you were put in your place!"

I turned back to the Fed and his gun. "I'm pulling out my badge of office. I am clearly stating my intentions. If I pull anything else out, not only will you be justified in filling me with holes, I clearly tell my friends here to not wipe you out of existence before my body hits the ground. Take that any way you want, Agent."

I finished reaching, and slowly pulled out my Nemesene Badge. Then showed it to the agent. His eyes bulged alarmingly.

"You're familiar with this?"

"Yes."

"You understand why I can't hand it to you?"

He nodded. "When the link is established, you're the only one who can touch it."

"Were you made aware that I was a Deputy of The Cadre before all this was arranged?"

"No."

"Well, Agent...?"

"Sawyer, Deputy. Hamilton Sawyer. Special Agent in Charge, kidnapping, F.B.I."

"Thank you. As I was saying, I find your lack of awareness strange. Director Dellums was fully aware of my position. Ah! My boss, Chief Nemesene of The Americas, has just arrived. Maybe he could add some clarification?"

The agents wilted visibly when they saw Digby in his three-piece charcoal grey suit, a slightly lighter grey complexion, and a thunderous expression on his face.

"What is the meaning of this, Deputy Seckett!" Digby barked, making Della take a step back. She hadn't had much time with Digby yet. "I expected you to be on the road by now!" He jerked a thumb at the two agents behind him. "These two were expecting to have to catch up to you on the road! Explain the delay!"

"Well, Sir, Agent Sawyer here,"

"I know Special Agent Sawyer!" Digby roared. "He served as a liaison to The Cadre two years back. He knows how we operate."

"I'm suspecting, sir, that he wasn't informed that The Cadre had taken over the Flores Case."

"How could he not?" Digby looked thoroughly baffled. "I sent over all the paperwork to The D.I.A., and as they are directly connected to every Government on this planet, they inform all potentially involved federal and local agencies that we're taking over a case and why! That way, nobody feels that we're just throwing our weight around!"

He turned his sulfurous gaze on the agent. "Didn't your Bureau Chiefs get the paperwork?"

"Um, I'm going to have to say no, Chief Crusher. I don't believe they received any official notification of your involvement on this case, much less The Cadre taking it over."

My chief slowly turned, and looked up to Dellums, who had gone an ashen shade. "Why does the F.B.I. not know all this already, Director Dellums?" he ground out in a voice that could crumble boulders.

"Well, I'm really not sure, Chief Crusher. We had a rather destructive incident at our headquarters recently, you see, and, perhaps … the files … got … lost?"

Like a mouse before a hooded cobra, Dellums couldn't tear his eyes from Digby's 'Impending Violence' stare. It took Digby turning his gaze to me that allowed the man to start breathing again.

"Who is this next to Deputy Alabato?"

"Della Manville, Chief. Guardian Division, Sekhmet's Pride. The Lioness sent her. I'm her assignment."

A smile flickered across Digby's face, and then he shook his head.

"Here we go again," He sighed mournfully.

"We didn't turn out too badly, Chief," Melene interjected impishly.

"My hair didn't turn all white until your team hit the field!" He moved and stood before Della, who looked right back. "What say you, lioness?" He asked abruptly.

"He's my Lion." Della shot right back.

"Figured. Heard you were coming, wondered what kept you. Don't bother explaining. Just curious. You two vouch for her?"

"She's a monster, boss." I responded firmly. "My monster now, sir."

"I concur." Melene answered.

"Hmph. Good." He fished in his jacket pocket, then pulled out a Cadre badge and handed it to me. It was slightly smaller than mine, with a silver finish instead of the old gold finish of the Deputy.

"Being demoted from Lieutenant in the Guardians to Companion in The Cadre okay with you, lass?"

Della smiled. "I'm exactly where I want and need to be, Chief!"

"Good. Make sure you walk him through getting her on board, Melene." He turned his attention back to Agent Sawyer. "My Deputy will not be accompanying you to Federal Court. I will be going to Federal Court, and I am going to have a lengthy conversation with all parties associated with this subpoena, this warrant, and the current status of this case. I would strongly advise you to inform your chiefs that I am on my way. As for you, Director-"

"Lee? What's going on?" Trini came through the protective barrier across the street. "The new guys said-"

As she was speaking, I caught the slightest glint. I don't know where, or how. I simply formed a shield as fast as I could and threw it, and myself, over Trini.

It felt like a cement truck slammed into my back and crushed me to the ground, with Trini below me. I could hardly move, but my hearing was working well enough.

"You two! Find that shooter and take him down. Move!" Digby barked. "Melene, Della, get those two back to the house, and get Lee into the Regen unit. What the bloody hell are you idiots doing? Secure the damned perimeter! And you, Dellums. You set this all up! Just to get Ms. Flores exposed and unprotected. And it's only Seckett's instincts that had him wounded instead of her dead. Was that the plan all along?"

"Digby, no! How can you…" It was about that time that I fell into unconsciousness.

***

I swam my way back to consciousness. When my eyes opened I saw myself surrounded by beauty. Melene and Megan looked worried, Trini was quietly crying, and Della had her arm around Trini's shoulder. I sighed, realizing I was back in the contraption.

"All, right. I'm here. Catch me up."

The others deferred to Melene. "The bullet was a .50 cal. from a Barrett. The bullet was coated with spell breaker runes, so it went through your shield. You wearing your duster saved you from worse damage. As it is, your T6 vertebrae was concussed, you have severe bruising and swelling. You should be able to get out of the unit by tonight."

"Good. The shooter?"

Melene grimaced. "Digby's companions got him. Wasn't a Maenad. At least we don't think so. Looks like a twisted copycat. Agreed with the crazy women trying to stop that 'jungle bunny music'. Once again, humans and their racist attitudes create unnecessary issues. The internet's pretty much located the general area of our home and promptly shared it with the world." Melene

176

sighed. "However this shakes out, Lee, I think we're gonna have to move. Digby's offered his old house—well, fortress—but well, there's so many happy memories for me here." She sighed, shook her head to clear the memories away, and continued. "Digby went downtown, raised Hell, a bunch of federal agency chiefs are running for cover, and Director Dellums currently finds himself in a world of hurt with no one looking to bail him out. He's well connected, so he'll probably survive, but this sector of the D.I.A. has a major black eye, and hearings regarding the efficacy of the D.I.A. as a whole are being considered in the U.N.'s General Assembly."

"The whole damned Division?" I gulped. "They do good work! And The Cadre can't be everywhere!"

"They should have just made themselves an affiliate of The Cadre, like it was suggested to them from the beginning!" Melene snapped. "They only formed the Division as a response to The Cadre, wanting the same investigative scope, the same types of agents, but with little of the scrutiny and processing!"

"Scrutiny? Megan asked.

"It's part of the discernment process, Megan. The badges we carry are imbued with an essence of the Goddess of Justice, Nemesis. Later tonight, Lee is going to place a badge into Della's hand and ask her a series of questions. If she is deceitful, or lacking in her zeal for justice, the badge just might burn her hand off."

Trini looked up at that. "Are you nuts? Burn her hand clean off?" She looked up at Della. "You wanna do this?"

Della smiled grimly and nodded. "My personal experiences have made me a fanatic of the legal quote you humans regarding speedy trials: 'Justice Delayed is Justice Denied'. I'm very much in favor in helping along the process of meting out 'Divine Retribution' to those who deserve it."

Trini looked at her, then down at me. "You two should get along great. She's straight Cray-Cray too!"

As was expected, I was released from the device late in the afternoon. Melene walked me through the commissioning process with Della, and it was indeed a lot less intense than my own, or it seemed that way from Della's description. She felt the acute burning sensation, but received no visions, and it seemed to move along faster. I was finally reintroduced to Kallan Drenner, a native of Gerovitavia, one of the city-states founded by a Lyrodryllian that was worshipped as a god by humans, and then chased out of Earth by The Cadre. The folks had a well-earned reputation for enhanced strength and keen martial abilities. With him was Lisbeth Ridder, a native of Eliondra and a 4th Degree Sorceress. I say reintroduced because these were the two that put me through my Nemesene Trials, and happily, they bore no grudges.

"Not the first time I got burnt to a crisp," Kallan chuckled. "First time Lizzie did it though!"

"You looked pretty good deep fried!" Lisbeth retorted with a smile. "Any idea where we're headed, Deputy?"

"I haven't been informed yet," I replied.

Lisbeth frowned. "Shouldn't the agent in charge know where we're going already?"

I was confused. "Melene's in charge." I looked at their expressions. "Isn't she?"

"Not what we were told," Kallan answered.

Wait one damned minute! "Melene!" I shouted.

"Coming!" she replied from close by, in that over-sweet voice that always meant unexpected trouble for me. She swept into the salon, closely followed by Della. "Why the shouting, dear?"

"I've just been informed by these two that I'm in charge of this expedition!"

"Oh? You didn't know?" Melene screwed her face in a patently false 'puzzled' look. "I didn't already tell you?"

"You know you didn't, Aunt!"

"Well, Lyam, you were the agent heading up the investigation when The Cadre took over the case. Why would you assume that someone else would take over when the case moved into different territory?"

"Possibly because I'm only a two weeks or so in The Cadre and don't have clue as to procedures? Or maybe, since I've never conducted field work, it might be wise to put a veteran Deputy with field experience in charge? No, I like choice A better: How the Hells would anybody assume that I'd know what the Gods-cursed procedure was?!"

"Alright then, Lyam. Your work on this case was rated Very Well Done before and after you joined The Cadre. The Chief saw no reason to relieve you of command of this case, and requested that I assist you in the role of advisor and senior companion for your team. Clear enough?"

I could have went at it longer, but I was beginning to feel petty and childish. "Clear. Thank you. Were you informed as to where we would be going, Melene?"

"Yes." Her tone sobered up quick. "Pretty much 'worst-case scenario.' Alistra finally got a strong bead on which direction the possessing entity returned. South and east. Whatever this thing is, it's either on an island near Decados, or in the middle region of the continent."

I felt gut-punched. Lyrodrylle had three continent-sized land masses and the final count on islands and atolls, large and small, habitable or not, still hadn't been completed. Pangaea was the largest of the three. (Before you holler, look at the history books. The humans stole the name from Lyrodryllian cartographers, when they got a look at those maps and saw the size of the continent. So there!) Aldemeron was in the middle in terms of size. Then, there was Decados. Just large enough to be considered a continent, the name originates from a descriptive term from another super-ancient Lyrodryllian language no longer in use. It basically translates to 'Wasteland'. There were no recognized nations, city-states or any type of organized municipalities on Decados. The very few sentients on the continent, towards the far north and south, were all informally sectioned off into tribes, conquered territory by a few warlords, or lands where most beings moved through as swiftly and quietly as possible, due to the savage beasts within. There was a time when other societies crammed sailing vessels full of their criminals and malcontents and shipped them off to Decados. That practice was ended, but the damage was done.

To get there, you had to get to the southern coast of Aldemeron, get on something that floated and was as sturdy as possible, and sailed southeast. One could not fly an airship to Decados. The winds weren't particularly fast, but there were no consistent airstreams overhead. Wind directions went mad in the airspace above; it was as if The Creator discouraged even birds to fly anywhere near the place.

To take a challenging situation straight into, 'Ya gotta be kidding!', Decados is the only large land mass without even one Veil Waypoint. Even a bunch of the islands of Lyrodrylle and Earth have at least one waypoint. Three of the larger islands have two! Not Decados. Even The Veil wanted no parts of the place!

In short, Decados was pretty much the foulest of cat-scat hoagies, and my team was gonna have to take a big friggin' bite!

We thought we'd get on the road the next day. We were wrong. My Maestra, Alistra, and Dr. Delphine Mendenhall, my family's chief medical doctor and someone I hadn't seen for a year or so, ambushed us early the following morning. It was good seeing them both. My Maestra looked fully healed, and, as always, Dr Delphine looked her usual short, Hot-Soccer-Mom self. From the time I was born, she was there. Watching my growth, using her advanced medical knowledge as a graduate of the Cremon Eft School of Medicine to further assist my body's healing abilities and structuring the exercises I needed to do to convince my genetic immunity to magic to lower itself enough for me to use my Talent. She helped me through the internal crisis my body underwent with the two genetic opposites fighting for dominance in one body. She is truly one of the jewels in my life.

"I worked too hard on you to have you getting shot, stabbed, or broken every couple of days!"

The rest of her tirade was muffled into my chest as I swept her up into a hug. I hadn't seen Dr. Del for nearly two years. Some emergency or something across the two planets always required her skills, but I think part of it was that she was finding it increasingly difficult to be around Melene and me. She missed my parents about as much as we did.

She patted my shoulder with affection. "Let me go you big grizzly! I'm bruising!"

"I missed you, Doctor Del."

"I missed you, Maahes. We'll talk later. I need to make sure you and your team are as ready for this mission as possible. From what Ali's told me, there's a potentially dangerous mental component involved. Working with her Psychomancy and my

Mundane Mindscape Techniques, we should be able to be helpful."

I smiled at her upbeat, energetic face. She was always lifting my spirits when I was younger. Sometimes by just being around. She seemed to take my parents' disappearance harder than anybody outside of Melene and me. I have a memory of a long talk I had with her a year before my parents left, but I can't remember it clearly.

"Just seeing you again has been helpful enough."

"Enough of that, naughty! I swore I wouldn't go the cougar route when you got older. Don't be tempting me to reconsider with those big brown eyes and all those muscles. Sit down and let me check you out!"

"Me first, Del," my Maestra insisted. She wanted a rundown on everything that occurred while she was recovering. Then she wanted to look through my mind to see what developments I'd managed to add to my Sorcerer growth, which really wasn't much, to be honest. Finally, she and Dr. Del spent the rest of the afternoon and night working me and my team over. Physicals, Emotional Stability adjustments, but they went hard on Mental Health, hours on meditation, mental mapping, a half dozen other exercises, techniques and disciplines, pretty much stuffing our heads with some mnemonic constructs that might help in the mission.

"Trust me, you're going to thank us when you get back," Alistra assured us repeatedly. It seemed her insistence was more for her benefit; it wasn't like any of us complained. Well, Kal complained that he wasn't getting more attention from Dr. Delphine, but she was pretty hot for an elder lady (Yes, I dated a 200-year-old werewolf. In my defense, she didn't look like she'd hit thirty yet, much less forties). As we broke for the night, I heard a brief exchange between Dr. Del and Melene that had me a little confused. Actually, a lot.

"It's still in place, Mel, but it's starting to fall apart."

"There will be no need for it very soon."

"Good. I still feel like a bloody traitor for doing it!"

"It was needed, more than even you can understand."

"Will I be forgiven?"

"Of course, Del. But you must forgive yourself as well. You know how grateful I've always felt."

"I know, thanks. Soon?"

"Less than a month."

"Then I'll clear the schedule. I'll be here."

Don't you just hate when you eavesdrop on people who know what, or who, they are talking about, so they don't bother with topic sentences? Might as well have saved my sneakiness for a more juicy bit of gossip!

Ah well. It was late, and I was tired, so, off to sleep.

Chapter 20. First Impressions
I stood before the Waypoint in awe.

IT WOULD BE A WHILE BEFORE I BECAME JADED with traveling through The Veil Waypoints. Actually moving from one planet to another, simply by walking about fifty yards through a specific space in one planet into the space of another. It was exhilarating. And frightening.

This was my third trip through The Veil, The Mystical Barrier/Umbilical Cord that separated Earth and The Mystic Lands, as the more fanciful humans have come to call Lyrodrylle. Their myths and fairy tales have innumerable tales and even explorative accounts of times when humans found themselves in an entirely different reality. Lands of fairies and trolls, witches and dragons. Those who told or wrote of these encounters were considered story tellers of great imagination, or insane (temporarily or permanently). None would believe they were simply eye witness accounts, albeit slightly inaccurate and a bit exaggerated. Others shared accounts of mythic creatures they followed through the woods, only for them to vanish before their eyes. If these people who were laughed at only knew that the Bigfoot they saw was finished visiting friends, and had simply hopped through the nearest Waypoint just in time for dinner.

The Sundering ended the luxury of disbelief. Through the purposeful actions of an insane cult merging with the unchecked damage to the magnetic field of Earth by the multitudes of nuclear testing for nearly thirty years, The Veil collapsed, and for over two years, the two planets were forced to mostly merge into the same space in this corner of the universe. If there were any miracles to be had at the time, one might have been that Lyrodrylle was a slightly smaller planet, had only three continents, and was more of watery planet than Earth. Another might be that The Veil was merely collapsed, not destroyed entirely, which would have caused the total annihilation of both planets within hours of the partial merging.

It was still a time of unimaginable death and atrocity. So much so, even those Talents that practiced The Dark Arts sacrificed their lives in combating the continuous natural disasters that exploded throughout the merged planets. (Thank The Creator for the forty Talents that died stopping Yellowstone and Italy's Campi Flegrei from erupting, and for Vesuvius and Krakatoa deciding to wait till another time. Mts. Rainier and Merapi in Indonesia, amongst others, were horrific enough.)

Those that were not racing from one scene of destruction to another joined together as one with all the most brilliant scientists left alive and constructed the healing spell/process/prayer that brought The Veil back into its proper function. In the end, sixty years later, it was estimated that two thirds of the Earth's population and half of Lyrodrylle's was lost due to the effects of The Sundering.

So many deaths. You'd think all beings on either side of The Veil would be tired of bringing violent death to each other. But that's just wishful thinking.

We had to fly to Tuxtla Gutierrez, Mexico, then drive through Chiapas to reach the Veil Waypoint located in the Lacandon Jungle, not too far from The Palenque, a Mayan city that was destroyed somewhere around the human's 7th Century. The trip was smoothed out immensely with The Cadre's Diplomatic Status, but it still took most of a day until we stood before the barely discernable Waypoint. It was no wonder Earth folk stumbled into and through the passages so often. They still do. There are more than a few Waypoints in the Pacific, and in caves and in the air and sea that still haven't been properly located and categorized.

This particular Waypoint led into La Pleasaunce, a medium-sized city 500 miles south of the Tellerman Border. There were no waypoints further south on Aldemeron. Aside from Tellerman and La Pleasaunce, there wasn't a whole lot of keen interest regarding Aldemeron. A ton of mid-sized principalities and sleepy duchies, and at least three dozen smaller nation-states still pulling themselves together from The Sundering. Aldemeron, to most Lyrodryllians, was considered a relatively stable, reassuringly dull land mass. All concerned were in full agreement that there had been entirely too much excitement these last seventy years.

It was tempting to head north first. I'd never visited Tellerman, a country that was essentially a conveniently minimal state governance model for the cities centered around specialist contractors and custom design markets. Imagine a country having in its borders a city like Weaver's Rest, a whole city of artisans churning out the specific designs and signature pieces of the fashion houses on either side of The Veil.

(Yes, sixty years later, the worlds had indeed recovered enough for High Fashion to be in astronomical demand. Tellerman had at least one whole city to cater to this market, and the market was booming.)

Yeah, it would have been a good visit. I had some ideas of my own in regard to armored gear. But we were more than adequately prepped for the mission, and the clock was ticking.

La Pleasaunce had a reputation for being a Party City. Like The Grand Canyon was known as a gap in the Earth's surface. Those in desperate need to forget their troubles (And their names, where they live, date of birth, etc.,) were advised to find their way to La Pleasaunce, which has been described conservatively as a mix of Las Vegas, Ibiza, Berlin, Buenos Aires, and a cocaine speedball.

I took a moment to look my team over. I followed the advice of Kallan, who suggested we should appear casual, not warlike, and have all our gear stowed in our PDPs. As agents of The Cadre, we all had one of our own, and we all loaded a ton of stuff in them. I had my Staff in my skin sheath, and Lisbeth had hers on a reinforced band on her arm, with long sleeves covering it. She and Kallan were the only ones wearing any kind of jewelry, and their matching pendants with a thumb sized cabochon sapphire. They got a few wicked comments from Melene, but since their response to the kidding was that Chief Crusher told them to wear them and not take them off, ever, we pretty much forgot they were there. It was a Cadre thing, one above even Auntie's pay grade, I supposed—so, whatever.

Expensive jewelry aside, the plan was to attract as little attention as possible as we went about our business. We were just passing through, after all.

That didn't work out too well.

I nodded Melene forward. Even if we didn't look it, we were on a mission, and I couldn't think of anyone I would prefer over Melene to take the point. I followed Kallan in, and tried to keep my focus as I passed through the twinkling, cascading lightshow that was the Waypoint interior. There was so much more happening in the roundish tunnel of lights than my mortal senses could comprehend, but it was like a semicircle of swirling, ever-shifting kaleidoscopes of light. I always feel just a bit disappointed with reality after spending the merest moment walking through what felt to me like a few breaths after The Big Bang. Like watching all reality bow in obedience after The Creator said, 'Let There Be Light'.

When I cleared the passage, I saw something quite unexpected; Melene and Kallan were being confronted by a platoon of women. They wore black fatigues, carried large caliber rifles and handguns, and looked strikingly similar to Melene in size and build. The military gear did little to conceal the fact that these women were all scary good-lookin' and built like voluptuous Valkyries.

Sadly, there was a decided lack of smiling on their faces.

I strode up to Melene, who was explaining in a low voice to the woman with the most metal on her shoulders, that the leader of her group was just emerging from the Waypoint.

"What's the situation, Melene?" I asked when I reached her side.

"We're talking, Boy!" The officer snapped. "Stay in your place and stay silent!"

The beginnings of a swell friendship.

"Major, he is the leader of our group," Melene explained in an even tone.

"Him? You can't be serious!" she scoffed. "What foolishness is this?"

I placed my hands behind my back. Just to be sure. "May I ask your name, Major?"

"No you may not! What you can do, male, is be quick with the reason why we don't escort you to our headquarters and put you in chains!"

Della stepped forward, but I held up a hand, so she stayed in place. I noted that a few locals not completely drunk out their necks were starting to close in for the latest piece of street theater. "Major, this is not something we should discuss in the open. It might indeed be a good idea for you to bring us to your headquarters, so we can discuss this in more privacy."

My response threw her a curve she didn't see coming. These women were obviously lionesses, probably soldiers of The Pride's Expeditionary Forces, since we were not on their homeland.

"Well, you've got a pair. I'll give you that. Sure, boy, let's go to the HQ and have a chat. Sergeant, you and your squad escort. Lieutenant, take over monitoring the Waypoint."

We soon found ourselves walking silently along. Even on the outskirts of the city, we could see the festivities were just getting into high gear. The streets were crowded with revelers, instinctively shuffling to the side, melting out of our way as we passed. Seems the lionesses had already made an impression. Most of the brick and stone buildings we passed were no more than four stories high, so we could easily see the fireworks exploding high above us. Spectacular, especially since it was three hours past noon and the sun was beaming down in a clear blue sky. 'Moderation' was a curse word in La Pleasaunce.

When I wasn't staring up at the sky, I noticed that I was getting more than a few surreptitious looks from the lionesses escorting us. I wondered, what did they see when they looked at me? Most males of The Pride rarely walked in full stride: head up, shoulders back, honestly not giving a damn who was surrounding me. My aunt would have beaten me like a dog if I ducked my head or minced my steps, and I would have been too embarrassed with my actions to consider debating the issue. I was aware that even men of other races and cultures tended to walk small when lionesses were on the prowl. I didn't miss the 'keep it meek' memo. I burnt it to ash and left it in the toilet where it belonged.

I was a Seckett. We Secketts don't say 'go big or go home,' because we don't recognize the need for 'Or go home'.

Neither the Major nor her troop made a comment that I chose to walk next to her instead of behind, but I knew they were irritated, and might have even been considering some form of retribution for my perceived lack of respect. Oh well. Start as you mean to go on, and all that.

"Right, then," the Major snapped as we made our way into the three-story building, then a nearby office. It looked like a well-appointed hotel that the Lionesses probably took over for their HQ. "Now, what is it you've got to talk about that needed so much privacy?"

"If I may reach into my coat pocket?"

"Go on, we haven't all blasted day!"

I did so, and soon I was displaying my Nemesene Badge, as was the rest of my team. "We are in active pursuit of an entity that we believe may be located in Decados. The fastest way to get there, as you know, is to ship out from the southern edge of Aldemeron's coast. We must move as swiftly, and as unnoticed, as possible, Major."

She fell into the chair behind the desk she was standing behind. "You? A Deputy Nemesene?" She shook her head. "The world has truly gone mad. And to Decados? Just the five of you? Is The Cadre so desperate, that they now send field agents off on suicide runs, and put a pre-school aged male in charge? So be it, then, man-cub! It would be a good idea to get out of town as fast as possible. I wouldn't want to watch you lead this bunch to shallow graves."

So much could be said. None was. We had a job to do.

"Thank you, Major. We'll be on our way, then."

"After I get names to put in my report."

I nodded. "Deputy Melene Alabato, Companions Kallan Drenner, Lisbeth Ridder and Della Manville. I am Maahes Seckett."

The Major froze. "Seckett? You said Seckett?"

"I did."

"Would it be possible that you would be in anyway related to the heathen traitor, Lionel Seckett?"

"He's my father."

"I should have known." She slowly rose out of chair, leaned over the desk. "I should have scattin'-well known! Another psychotic, maladjusted male that scorned the sacred traditions of The Pride, maliciously shoved himself into a role reserved for deserving lionesses, and capped it all off with turning his back on his home nation. I. Should. Have. Known!"

By the time she was done with her rant, her face was inches from mine, and I had to deal with the spray impacting with my face. I took the piece of cloth Della was holding out to me, wiped my face of her spittle, and looked the woman in the eye. "If that is all, Major, we'll be on our way. Let's move people."

"I didn't dismiss you!" the Major snarled. That was bad. When we turned to the door, she slapped her hand down on my shoulder. That, lady, was suicidal. "I'm not done with you!"

I turned back to her, so swiftly that her hand flew off my shoulder. "Yes, Major. You are."

I didn't raise my voice. Didn't need to. Even in her excited state, she was a lioness, a commanding officer of highly trained, highly professional warriors. She was well aware of The Cadre's Ascendancy Protocols, and any being with three working brain cells could recognize that the look on my face told her she was seconds away from imminent mayhem and carnage.

She didn't want to take a step back from me, but she couldn't stop herself from doing so. I nodded to my team, and we stepped.

We didn't speak until we made our way to a bistro about two miles away from the Lioness HQ. We were all starving, and we needed to save our trail rations for when we hit Decados. We ordered quite a few courses. Lisbeth and Kallan were healthy eaters, and the amount of food we of The Pride can put away bordered on obscene. It took a while for me to work through some things in my head, and my team waited on me. Bless 'em.

"Melene," I asked. "Do all the People of The Pride feel that way about Dad?"

She sighed, and nodded slowly. "Many. Not all. Too many."

"I never did." Della offered fiercely. "I have an aunt and three elder cousins who were there at The Heights! Lionel Seckett saved them from being dinner for a horde of the undead! We cherish his memory in our family!"

"Thank you for that, Della." I sighed. "Guess I won't ever get the chance to go to my homeland."

"That day will come, Lee," Melene vowed. "It must. We'll discuss why very soon. But I know in my heart that the day will come when they wholeheartedly embrace a Lion of The Pride!"

"I've read about The Battle of Tandora Heights," Lisbeth interjected. "You were there, Melene. Was it as awful as it seemed from the text?"

"Worse. No written record could fully describe it, watching the seemingly endless waves of bogarts, ogres, ghouls and other foul creatures, eating the flesh of vibrant, valiant warriors before your eyes. Watching the sky above you exploding with countless spells. The air filled with stones and boulders crashing into the lioness' positions. It was beyond words."

I had heard the battle described before, numerous times. The talk at the table faded as I thought about the confrontation, and possible repercussions. I also did some hard thinking about why a company of lionesses were garrisoned in La Pleasaunce. The City was considered a Friend of Sekhmet's Pride, but from what I was taught, it was the last place The Pride, or The Pentagram, would consider needed to be garrisoned. And they were too far away from possible enemy municipalities to feel the need for on-the-scene protection. What was going on that might have an impact on our mission?

✳✳✳

The food was excellent, the atmosphere festive but relaxing, and the live music being played by the jazz trio was worth listening to. But the sun was still high enough in the sky that we could get another 500 miles closer to the Aldemeron coast before calling it a night. Before I could call for the bill, I saw that the entrance to the club was full of lionesses. Swaggering, talking loud, and heading in our direction.

"Oh, well, damn!" Melene murmured.

"There's always one in every bunch," Kallan chuckled. "At least."

"We don't have the time for this Cat-scat!" I snarled as the four soldiers made their way to our table.

"Seems we'll have to make time, My Lion," Della snickered.

"So not helping,"

The one leading the pack wasted little time when they arrived.

"You the burnt-skinned male that forgot his place and disrespected my Major?"

Big voice, big attitude, and at 6'7" or so, big lioness.

"You're out of line, soldier," I tried to keep my voice cool, nonthreatening. "I am a Deputy of The Cadre. My team is on assignment, and as you already know, impeding the progress of a Deputy on an active assignment can result on you and your commanding officer being brought up on charges with The Pentagram."

"What I know is that you're the useless son of a renegade and deserter to The Pride! And I know that no weakling male of The Pride has the brains or balls to lead anyone to the toilet, much less on a mission! And I'm very sure that either you're a lying sack of Cat-Scat who needs to be taught a lesson on how to behave when in the presence of your betters, or the standards of The Cadre have fallen so low, we all might as well kill ourselves now and be done with it!"

She smirked as the other women nodded and murmured in agreement.

"I also know that I'm going over to The Ring, a few blocks over from here. And I know that if you're not there in a half hour to receive your proper chastisement, I'll come find you and drag you there, and if you run, we'll be spreading the word that the son of the traitor is spineless, as well as an oversized sack of steaming uselessness!"

I sighed as we watched them troop out. Should have expected it, and just left instead of getting something to eat. Even La Pleasaunce had people who have problems with their aggression. The City, in response to the need of visitors and locals needing to let off some steam, built a number of mini-arenas in various locations throughout the city. The concept was for combatants to deal with each other's issues within the walls of the space, and once they were done, one way or another, the matter was closed. No revenge, no charges, no taking the matter to the authorities. If I walked into that space, I went in as myself, not a representative of The Cadre. Them's the rules.

At that particular moment, I was pissed enough to go there and burn the whole damn place down! "Do I really have to do this?" I sighed, suddenly feeling weary, all the way to my bones.

"Yes," Lisbeth answered firmly. You were challenged in a public setting. According to this City's Ordinances, you have a grievance that must be settled, or you must leave the city. Beyond that, the honor of The Cadre and its authority have been questioned, and your ignoring that would cause all agents to take a big hit. We can't afford anyone, even lionesses, to think they can disregard or flout our mandates."

"And besides that," Melene interjected. "You are your father's son. You are a Seckett. And Secketts don't take scat from anyone, anytime, anywhere."

"By the way," Della added. "Two rather scurvy types just scuttled out the rear entrance. I'm curious as to whether they have a crew they are running to, and who they might be interested in."

I nodded, then turned to Kallan, who smiled grimly.

"Smoke the biddy, we buy a transport like we planned, and we leave this joint in the dust."

"Alright. Let's get to it."

Chapter 21. Making a Point

The whole scraggin' thing was so blasted unnecessary, but nobody asked my opinion.

THE LIGHTING INSIDE THE RING was bright enough to see clearly, but there were a lot of shadowy spaces. The tiered seating surrounding the matted space looked like it could accommodate two hundred or so. There were few seats available.

It seemed that nearly half of the company of lionesses decided to bear witness to my deserved punishment. I was saddened. With Melene and Bezine as my very few examples, I always held the lionesses of The Pride on a high shelf in my heart. I knew my estimation of these warrior women was unfairly elevated, but seeing so many acting with the same petty vindictiveness as any other race of sapient beings might broke my heart a little.

My opponent was standing on the elevated space, talking and laughing with two others. She had stripped off her uniform blouse, and wore a well-constructed sports bra under a sleeveless tee shirt. Her shoulders and arms were covered in firm, chiseled muscles. Overall, she was long, sculpted, and confident. Why shouldn't she be? I was just a weakling male, after all.

My sadness was wiped away by the presence of their Major, sitting up front with a cheese-eating grin plastered on her face. It might not have been a set up, but it sure tasted like it.

So be it.

"Well! The piss-ant at least showed up for his ass whipping!" the warrior roared. "Saves me the trouble dragging you here. C'mon up," she guffawed. "And take it like males are supposed to!"

I wasted no time on the short flight of steps, ignoring the laughs and rude chatter from the crowd. The laughs faded some when I handed my duster to Della, and then tailed off completely when I took off my loose-fitting, long-sleeved Henley, leaving me in my black tank top, black khakis and boots.

My opponent closed her mouth soon enough. "You're pretty enough. Maybe when I'm done beating some sense into you, I can show you how to treat a woman."

I smiled. "You got a lot of turds comin' out your pie-hole. Put a clamp on it, and let's get this done."

She snarled, and then walked in guarded. Confident but careful.

I placed myself in a mix of a Muy Thai/boxing stance. Light on my feet, arms forward, body angled, fists clenched but loosely—ready.

She started with a jab, which I slapped to the side. She put some weight into it, and was surprised to see it deflected with so little effort. She moved in closer, threw a left jab/right hook combo. I was no longer in front of her by the time she was finished with the second punch. She was no longer smiling. She threw another hard jab, planning to hammer her way through my defense. I ducked under the punch, moved closer to her body, and unleashed three hooks. Two to the ribs, one to the side of her head.

Respect due, she stayed on her feet, though I could tell her body was considering a nice lie down. She shook her head, refocused her eyes and came back in.

She reached out to grapple. I grabbed her forearms and slammed a knee into her rock-hard abdomen. She pitched forward, driving her face into the uppercut that was blasting its way up to meet it. Never punch at. Punch through, or don't bother. She slammed hard unto the mats.

I stepped back. She wasn't moving. She was down.

My instincts and a barely noticed movement out of the corner of my eye allowed me to drop under the roundhouse kick that was speeding towards my head. I didn't think, just let the nearly twenty years of learned behavior kick in, sending a sweeping leg towards whoever launched the kick, swiveled up towards a body that seemed suspended in the air, focused all my torque, and drove a pile driver into, then through the body of the lioness that tried to catch me when I wasn't looking, and kept driving until her body and my fist, impacted with the floor. She'd have to relearn how to breathe before she tried some crap like that again.

I turned, moved back towards where my people were waiting, keeping everyone else in sight. Another of my challenger's allies snarled, then stripped off her blouse.

"My challenge was with her," I pointed to where the first was still unmoving. "This is not honorable."

"You're a piece of scat, male, unworthy of honor!"

With that she ran forward and leaped into a flying side kick. Must have been new to this, or too enraged to think clearly.

In response, I grabbed her ankle with both hands, swept her around in a screaming arc that lifted her higher into the air, then used her momentum, and every muscle I could beg, borrow or steal, to smash her back into the mat. I looked down at her. She looked in agony, then terrified when she realized that I still had her leg in my hands. I allowed her to see all that could happen to her in my eyes, then I released her ankle from my grasp. Her healing factor would have to kick into overtime before she was getting up on her own.

I stepped back, surveyed the devastation, then the other lionesses standing off to the side.

"Anybody else?"

The three stepped back.

Della stepped forward, handed me my shirt. I nodded my thanks, put the shirt on, then made my way down the stairs. I stopped before the stunned garrison commander.

"Your soldiers violated the rules of The Ring. With malice and forethought. Whether you ever admit that they did so under your bidding or permission, this will be reported to my Chief, Digby Crusher. I will leave it up to him as to what happens next." I leaned into her face. "I am the son of Lionel Seckett, Major. The next time you speak of him, you better put some scraggin' respect on his name, or I will tuck my shiny little badge away, again, and come looking for you!"

I looked up from her, sent my glare to all her soldiers around her. None would meet my look.

Not quite the wondrous, faultless paragons I spent most of my life fantasizing over. Well physically speaking, they were still lightyears beyond stunning. But in what truly mattered? This bunch at least came up short. Sad.

I didn't do a good job concealing the contempt I felt for them at that moment. A few had the grace to wince and turn their heads away as I walked out with my team.

"There's a transport dealership two miles away that's reasonably trustworthy, from what I've heard." Lisbeth noted as we passed through the stunned crowd, then the entrance.

"Let's go there now." I replied. "Might be a good idea to put some distance between us and La Pleasaunce."

"I've heard some things, Lyam," Melene offered. "There has been some disappearance of some lionesses on foreign soil. A lot of unease at The Pride. In addition, there's been an upsurge in transients these past few years. Not here for partying or any fun at all. Hanging around the city, closest to the Waypoint, like they were keeping an eye on who may use it, or come through it."

"Lionesses missing? Unknowns taking up space for the past three years?" I considered that, felt a frown forming. "That's a lot of stuff happening at the same time. Could it be connected to us?"

"I won't rule it out. Not yet. By the way, the presence of the lionesses was the response to the request of assistance made to The Pentagram by the City Leaders."

I thought about it some more, then shook my head.

"Let's focus on the task at hand. A bunch of roughnecks stooging around a Waypoint can't concern us."

"Unless they decide to stop watching the gate and follow us south?" Lisbeth teased wickedly.

"Don't even joke like that, Liz," I replied worriedly. "We've got enough to deal with!"

"Yes, boss! Um, I was wondering, Lee. Were you holding back when we were testing you?"

"I don't think so. Why?"

"Why?" Kallan snorted. "You wiped those broads out in less than two minutes, without taking a single shot! No way we're in their league, to be honest."

"Oh." I thought about it. "Neither of you pissed me off first. Didn't disrespect my father."

"Note to self," Kallan intoned. " 'Deputy touchy about his dad and has respect issues. Be careful. Might die.' Got it. Thanks for the heads-up, oh great and glorious leader!"

"Kal, did you wanna go back in the ring back there?"

"Oh, look! Here's the dealership already. Let's go, kids!"

I looked at the man jogging away. "He is kidding, right?"

"Some." Lisbeth answered. "But Lee, you couldn't see the expression on your face. From the moment you walked into the arena, your face was cold, still. Like a relief chipped out of Ebony Heartwood. You looked like the whole business meant nothing more than taking out the garbage. Just an unpleasant chore that needed doing."

"Only until the fights were done though," Della added. "Then, you looked...well, frightening, Lee. You looked like you were about to rain fire down on the whole place!"

"He looked magnificent, as his father did," Melene declared, pride ringing in her voice. "Why do you think a whole island of Warriors are still so afraid of my lions?"

I looked to her, saw her eyes shimmering, and smiled with her. I reflected on the years after years of training, of bones broken, blood spilled. Of tears shed. And I better understood what all the pain and sacrifices we shared were for. She knew this day would come, and that there would be many more days like this in the future. Nothing would be given. It had to be earned.

I understood that much better now. I wasn't shaped to survive. But to win.

To destroy all opposition. To conquer.

To be a Lion.

So let it be.

The transport we settled on looked eerily like one of those bus-like RV's that were so popular before humans were finally weaned off fossil fuels completely. The dealer explained the similarity.

"This high-roller fellah liked their style, bought one, then blew through two hundred grand in Eliondrian credits to convert the engine over into electric, added the driverless option, added some armored Invisi-steel to the exterior and reinforced the suspension. Upgraded the communications suite, too."

"Near-on a million dollars?" Lisbeth gasped. "Just for a comfy ride?"

Shook me up, too. The current rate of exchange on both planets was four American dollars to the Eliondrian equivalent. Spending 500 grand American currency was a lot. Somebody pending that much in Eliondrian currency, which translated to two million AC on little more than a rolling penthouse must have been rolling in bucks, or bug-eyed nuts.

"What happened to this high-roller?" Kallan asked.

"La Pleasaunce happened," The dealer shrugged. "Got hooked into a game of five-card stud with a couple of professionals. Went all-in, and got wiped out on the river card. Ended up hooked on the dust. OD'd in a low-rent shack on the outskirts, where the poor and homeless hang.

"He didn't have much family, and what there was had no use for the damned thing, so I took possession." He shrugged again. "Makes no sense to sell it for under 230 grand."

"We'll take it!" Melene announced.

"We'll what?" I couldn't believe my ears were working.

"I can't count how many times a vehicle like this would have come in handy when we were on the road, before you came along." Melene was almost vibrating. "Sleeping outside in the rain, going to the bathroom in the woods. Eating cold hardtack instead of whipping up a home-cooked meal while on the road? You'll love it, Lyam!" She stared at the suddenly nervous dealer. "Especially since it's going for only 240 grand in U.S. currency?"

The dealer swallowed hard, backed up a step, then nodded in defeat.

"Whaddya mean I'll love it?"

"Yes, dear. Your birthday is less than a month away." She smiled brightly. "Happy birthday!"

I stared at her. "You're serious! All this money? Just for a bus with a bed?"

"And restroom and shower," the dealer reminded. "And stove and refrigerator!"

"But Melene. It makes no sense! We're on Aldemeron. You expect me to dish out shipping fees whenever I might need this whale on Pangea, for instance? Or one of the other nations? How would I get it back to the other side of The Veil?"

"Silly cub," my aunt gurgled. "How do you carry anything you wish to bring with you on the road?"

My eyes fell out of my head. "You can't be serious?"

"Give it a try."

She knew I couldn't pass up a dare like that. I stared at the behemoth. It stared back. I walked around it. Looking for an edge. Finally, I looked up at the left rear-view mirror. If it was even possible, the mirror would do. I pulled out my PDP, opened the flap, reached up to the mirror and started sliding it into the opening.

Then nearly slammed my face into the pavement.

"What in all Seven Hells did you do with my property?" the dealer screamed hysterically.

Damn good question. The blasted monstrosity disappeared into another dimension. Now for the big finish.

"Y'all might want to back up a bit," I made sure there was a lot of space around me, then reached into the PDP, and thought about the tires of the vehicle. I imagined as clearly as I could my hand on the left front tire, gripping it from the side, near the rim. And then, I felt it. The smooth, hard surface. The treads digging into my arm. Just to be safe, I laid myself flat on the ground before I began pulling on what I prayed was actually the tire.

And I watched the opening of the PDP spread. Wider, wider, until I could see some of the tread emerging...

Then, the vehicle suddenly came back in existence. Sitting over me. Much better than on me, but still not great.

"Um, Della? A little help?"

She laughed her tail off, the wretch, but she did grab me by my shoulders and hauled me out from underneath.

"I think you're gonna have to work on that one," the fiend giggled.

"See?" Melene crowed. "It worked! Just as I knew it would."

"You knew?" Kallan sounded quite skeptical.

"Yes! Well, maybe not quite knew, per se, but the theory was sound, and well..."

"Maybe you were hoping that if this beast actually landed on him, he'd be strong enough to hold it up?"

"Now Kallan, I'd expect a more optimistic attitude out of you, you know."

"This has been so much fun already!" Lisbeth chortled in glee. "Everyone always said the Seckett Clan does things with Style!"

Chapter 22. Blood in The Tall Grass

We were an hour out of La Pleasaunce when Lisbeth called out from the front of transport.

"Hey, Lyam, you know how I was kidding about those transients comin' after us?"

"Yeah."

"Sorry!"

I groaned my way up from the rather comfortable couth towards the front of our new ride.

"Oh, you gotta be friggin' kidding me!"

About a mile ahead of us, all four lanes of the thruway were blocked off with transports and two dozen intimidating types. By the show of guns, there seemed to be little interest in a friendly discussion of the weather.

"Who are these scummers?" Kallan asked. "How did they get in front of us?"

"They probably came out of Haylen Springs," Melene replied. "It's the next town down from La Pleasaunce."

"Okay. But who are they?"

"No clue, Lee. They likely have some connections with bandits we left behind."

"Well, screw this," I looked to Lisbeth. "Turn this damned thing around. Put some distance between us and that bunch. Fast as you can."

"Thoughts, boss?" Kallan asked.

"This whale isn't armor plated enough to withstand heavy gunfire, so it's just a liability. It's less than an hour to dark. I'm thinking we get as far out of eyesight as possible, drop the ride into a PDP. Then we get locked and loaded and go ask the jerkwads why they're blocking the road."

"You think they'll just tell us?" Lisbeth asked as she finished were wide turn.

"No, but Della and Melene can be persuasive. Somebody'll say something. Them, or the group coming down from La Pleasaunce."

"How do you know there is a group coming from there?"

"Don't know, Liz, but if I was setting up a trap, I'd prefer my target to be pinched from behind as well as ahead." I smiled grimly. "The only nasty bit would be if they got bogies to the side as well."

"I don't think there are any," Melene noted. "They didn't have a lot of time to put this together. They couldn't know we were heading out the same day we got in, nor which direction we were going in."

"That's the hope," I answered. "This is good, Liz, we should be out of sight by now. Pull over."

When our RV came to a stop, we wasted little time hopping off, then I carefully reached up and out with my PDP and once again, the multi-ton monster disappeared. Those Eliondrian Technomancers do some hella good work! I loped to the side of the road and took in the sights. There wasn't a lot to see in this section of Aldemeron. The continent has an extensive throughway system towards the middle and northern territories, but the roads taper down to one massive roadway the further south you go. For us to get to Pilgrim's Cove, we had to use this path. We all took a good look around, but there was nothing out there to see. Just the road and open space. The land was flat, without much undulation. There were hills and other rises in the landscape, but they were miles away in the distance. The only vegetation was the tall grass on the sides of the road.

I lead the team deeper into the slowly waving blades, which came up to our shoulders in some places. Good.

"Della, take point. Lead us to the bandits ahead. Melene, listen for anything coming from where we came in. Liz, Shield yourself and Kal, try to match the space around you as best you can."

"And you, Lee?" Kallan asked.

"I'm ghosting," I answered. It took a long time for me to get proficient with Fade, and I wasn't as good as Melene, or Della it seemed, but I did well enough. Especially when surrounded by tall grass and the shadows were getting longer.

We were on the path Della set for about an hour before three vehicles came blasting down the road. Kallan looked to my outline in the grass, smiled and nodded. I appreciated him giving me credit, but it only made sense to look for a hammer if the anvil was right in front of you.

We travelled another half hour before Della faded back into view, kneeling down, one hand up.

"I'm starting to hear them," she breathed. "They've got crew up the road and in the grass."

I nodded. "Blades out. You two, hunker down. Stay shielded. Kallan, if it's one or two sitting on top of you, take 'em out. Silently. Liz, can you do Air Snatch?"

She smiled and nodded. The Air Snatch spell, fully applied, can pull all the air out of body and collapse the lungs. Death was horrific, painful, but silent. Light Arts Laws say I was telling Liz to commit murder with her Talent, basically a death sentence violation. The Nemesene Protocols say different, though. I somehow knew our Celestial patroness would let us know when we crossed the line.

"Good. I can't, not yet—I gotta use Ice Pick and a blade. It's dark now, so we three will hunt."

I wasn't happy with leaving those two stationary, but they made less noise that way. And they couldn't Fade. I could see by the way he moved that Kallan was a great hunter. But we needed to go beyond a great hunter, We had to go into ghosting through the grass without a rustle, unseen, unheard, and bring death without a rattle or moan. We three spread out and went to work.

My first was the easiest. Probably still acclimating to the dark. I went still, felt him pass to my left. I rose up, clamped his mouth shut, slashed the carotid, and then gently lowered him to rest. Then continued on. The second was louder, but it wasn't my fault. She tripped over the body of one of her fellow bandits, and cried out when she hit the ground.

"What is it?" A voice called out from nearby.

"Felton's dead." She replied.

Her teammate's answer was suddenly shut off. When she tried to call out to him again, she found a hand over mouth, and she was rapidly bleeding out.

"My bad," Della whispered in my ear. I shrugged. It wasn't like we were going to bury them. I decided, for some reason, that that was the perfect time for a kiss, so I kissed her. She smiled, kissed me back, and said, "I don't think anyone was close enough to hear them." Then she winked, and faded away again.

Periodically, we'd circle back to make sure Liz and Kal were good. The third time I did this, I saw Liz opening the ground around her and Kal dropping a body in the hole. And I smacked my head. I'm stronger than Liz in Earth magic, but I didn't even think of using it as she did. I faded up into view in front of Liz, pointed to the ground, and gave her a thumbs-up. She smiled and nodded, and then I faded away again. I went back on the hunt, this time quietly burying bodies as I went along, or dispatching, then burying the body when I ran across a bandit still breathing, which was becoming rare.

After another half hour, Melene faded up in front of me, and pointed to the area on the other side of the road. I nodded, and we crossed the lanes and continued. One target was walking through with a shield spell activated. I considered using Ice Pick to shatter her shield, but chose instead to leave her to Melene. Because of all the work I had done to build my Talent, my immunity to magic was lower than hers. My aunt should have no trouble ignoring her shield; she'd probably strangle that one.

I was approaching another target when a shot rang out, followed by another. My target began moving towards the shots, but I surged forward, grabbed him from behind and snapped his neck. Then I moved quickly to where I heard talking. When I drew close enough, I saw two tall, long-haired men with guns out, standing over Della. She was lying on her back, and the two were pointing their massive revolvers at her.

"Yes, she'll make an excellent candidate for our procedures," One of the men noted in a voice that was strange to my ear. Melodious, but revolting. Pleasing to the ear, but sickening to the soul.

"Indeed," The other agreed. "It has grown more of a challenge to gather more subjects. What with that, and the loss of The Secketts, The Hierarchy is beginning to make troubling sounds."

I was about to rise up and begin slicing off the limbs, but a hand rested gently on my arm. Melene was there, she wanted to hear more.

"Has anyone found out how they were lost to us?"

"No. By the time the relief group arrived, the facilities were smashed to pieces, all samples and notes on site were missing, as were all the bodies of guards, scientists, Talents, and The Secketts. We currently believe a renegade clan of our people wanted control, and took it.

"It doesn't matter, though. Even if we do recover them, I believe we've learned all there was to discover of them. But their child? A mix of both of them in one body? That is a treasure we must secure! Where are the searchers?"

"Out in the field. They should be returning shortly."

"It's been hours! How long could it take? There's only five of them, and only three are of any value. Instruct the rest to simply kill the two others, and wound the other three if they must."

He laughed, and it felt like I would never smile again in this life.

"I mean, they do heal from anything, Isn't that right, my dear lioness?"

I was only a half second behind Melene. Her long blade went into the base of funny guy's skull and drove upward. That half second was enough for my target to activate a shield, and he only stumbled when my attack battered into him. He turned, and his eyes widened.

He attacked with a laser of light, it impacted against my shield as I drove a ripple of Ice Picks, then a Solar Lance when I felt it weaken. He returned spells, but they were at a slightly lower intensity, slightly slower rate than mine. I threw another Ice Pick, his shield shattered, then I sent all my energy into a Chained Lightning spell that flash-fried his body into a blackened corpse.

After that, it was a bit of a blur. I think there were about ten left alive. They did not remain alive long. There were two more Dark Talents. I emptied a clip of .50 cal. bullets into their shields, then hammered them with Solar Lances. I felt a slug hammer into my shoulder. I spun out of the path of the follow-up bullets and slammed a new clip into my Desert Eagle. The gunner was switching out clips when I put a bullet through his throat. Then I was done, because Liz and Kal had swept in and took out whoever was left standing.

I took many deep breaths, working hard to reengage my brain. It took a bit. I walked over to where Melene was hovering over Della. She didn't look all that wounded, and was even smiling.

"What the Hell, Lee?" Della snorted. "I thought I'd have to lie here all night listening to them dialoguing!"

"Are you okay?"

"Very," Melene answered. "The gear we got for the team is very effective. Bruising on her lower back and upper chest. The bullets didn't penetrate."

"I shook my head. "And you figured their shooting and what they were saying identified them as bosses, so you laid here like you were taken out to let us find them easier. You are absolutely brilliant, Della. Freakin' brilliant!"

Thank you, Kind Sir," She purred. "But if you don't mind, my back does hurt like Freeze-Dried Scat, so if I could lie down on a bed instead of the ground?"

"Of course,"

I began walking to the road, then I stopped and began shaking uncontrollably. I couldn't stop. Then I felt arms wrap me from behind, and the arms seemed to have given me permission to cry. So I did. I collapsed to my knees and cried, and my aunt held me and shed tears as well.

"What happened?" Kallan cried out. "What's wrong with him? Is he going to be—Holy Hells! Is that an Elf?!"

"Elf?" Liz asked. I heard her move. "By the Divine! That is an Elf. The crispy one, too! Look at the ears. What did we stumble into now?"

It took a bit, but I pulled myself together. It took some time to get the vehicles off to the sides of the road, confiscate any gear that might prove useful, and then pull the RV back into this dimension. After we all had our turns in the shower and facilities, we made sure Della was taken care of and comfortably situated, which for her meant snuggled up on my side. She felt like a perfect fit to me, I will say. After that, we set up the RV's advanced comm system and put in a holo-call to The Cadre's Headquarters, located in a massive, ten-story tower close by the mountain-sized citadel that was The Pentagram.

After the connection was made, we watched as Pietor Higby, The Cadre's Director of Information, came into holographic view.

"Yes, Deputy Seckett. I was just leaving the offices when your call came in." He frowned. "I'm assuming that the person wrapped around you was wounded in action?"

"Yes Sir. I apologize for our looking so casual, but we just finished dealing with an ambush, discovered some potentially critical information, and decided we needed to call in ASAP."

"I figured that would be the case, which was why I decided to take the call instead of wait for a summary." He smiled grimly. "We in The Tower have been trained to accept that Secketts only call into the HQ when a routine situation has blossomed into a crisis of epic proportions."

"Director," Melene interjected. "If I may, we believe that the Chief Director may need to be on this call as well, and our Chief Digby, if the conduit to Earth is active."

"Do you now?" The Director sounded skeptical.

"Yes, sir. It involves Ellovysians."

His jaw dropped. "Rumors of Elves?" he whispered, almost like a prayer.

Melene smashed those prayers. "No, sir. Confirmation. Death of Elves. Two of them."

"Gods, no!" he wheezed. "Alright, Deputies, hold for one."

His image froze. We waited. In a few brief seconds, a frozen image of a woman sitting at a desk appeared, and a minute later, Digby's Image came up. With that, all three images unfroze.

"Is Della wounded?" Digby rumbled.

"Bruised badly, Chief," Della answered. "Fine to continue on mission."

"Glad to hear it."

"As am I," spoke the serene-seeming woman sitting at the desk. "Director Higby mentioned something about Ellovysians?"

"Yes, ma'am," I swallowed. "We've only been in the field for a day, but it's been a helluva day. Or maybe me being a rookie, it felt that way."

"No, it was a helluva day, Lee," Liz, replied. "And I ain't no rookie!"

"Thanks Liz. Ma'am, sirs, would you prefer the full report I will be submitting or the highlights?"

"Make it full," The Chief Director sighed. "We might have a different perspective, and additional information that may shed light on something that may seem obscure to you."

"Yes, ma'am. I hope you do."

***

"This explains The Pride sending out Expedition Forces before the call from La Pleasaunce came in!"

The Chief Director no longer looked so serene. A worry line was firmly etched into her forehead.

"Yes," Digby frowned. "And to four other locations, at last count. Women of The Pride have not simply disappeared. They've been purposely targeted and abducted."

"Indeed, and we now know by whom." Alons Ginley, Director of Operations, was pulled into the call shortly after I began my report. "A pity the Elves couldn't be taken into custody instead of summarily executed. Any thoughts, Deputies?"

I looked away from the smug face of a classic armchair quarterback. Melene answered for us. "We were under emotional duress and in fear for the life of our comrade, Director. Not an excuse. Simply an explanation."

"Yes, I'll make a note of that,"

"You make a note of any of that, Alons, and we will have words!" snapped our Chief Director. "Instead of taking the time to grieve, they are supplying us with the first actual proof that the

Elves are back in play, instead of hints and speculation! Now that we know there's meat on those bones, the rest of The Cadre can get out there and do their jobs, instead of relying on a Deputy that's been on sabbatical all this time and another who's on his Maiden Run! And I would dearly love to hear how all our agents in the field never bothered to check out this 'transient' situation in La Pleasaunce, on the off-chance that it might be connected to something more critical?" Her image leaned forward at the desk. "Maybe then we might have suggested a different Waypoint, instead of allowing the target the Elves were seeking to walk himself into their waiting laps?

Sufficiently slapped down, the D.O. nodded humbly, and the Chief Director continued.

"Regarding the Seckett disappearance, Deputies, I would advise you both to hold off on preparing the funeral rites just a bit longer. There have been rumblings, unsubstantiated at this time. But as they say, a rumor that refuses to die may not be just a rumor after all. And there's been a lot of noise on this side of The Veil. I hope I'm not being cruel, but I would ask you to not give up hope. Not yet.

"In regard to your present case, we believe you are on the right track, heading in the right direction. Chief Digby did not give you this assignment on a whim. He believes your team can succeed, even if a whole continent is pitted against you. Your Chief has arranged for a reliable ocean charter to meet you at Pilgrim's Cove, since it's unlikely that you'll be able to secure a way to Decados on your own. The Captain will be waiting to hear from your team. She's been paid in advance, so there is no time pressure, but don't dally. We need this case closed soonest.

"As for the incident in La Pleasaunce, the Secretary of Defense for Sekhmet's Pride and I will be having words. You upheld the Honor of The Cadre admirably, Deputy. Now, we require certain parties to relearn the lesson of what happens when one offers disrespect to those chosen to mete out Justice to All Peoples!"

Definitely no joke, I thought, as I noted the fire in the Chief Director's eyes, even though it was a holographic image.

"Was there anything else?" The elder woman asked to all.

"Yes." Digby responded. "I'm proud of your team's efforts so far, Deputy Seckett. All of you. Now, get that lazy cat back on her feet and all of you get back to work!" He nodded to the Chief Director. "Milady, we need to talk. About this, and other matters."

"I will make sure to have space for you tomorrow afternoon, Digby. Alons, Pietor, meet me in the strategy room in ten minutes. Deputies, Companions, get some rest. You earned it."

With that, the images faded away. We sat there, quiet, reflecting.

I broke the silence. "I felt a little out of control for a minute out there, guys. I apologize."

Kallan nodded, his face serious. "On the one side, everyone has buttons, Lee. Yours are more exposed at the moment, easier to push. Your actions did not lead to any of us being wounded or compromised—so you learn, you grow, and you move on.

"On the other side, you've fought twice in one day against multiple enemies. Once by yourself, once with your team. In both instances, you developed well thought winning strategies, you included the advice of your teammates as you formed these strategies, you learned and adapted on the fly, and you concluded each confrontation with success, with minimal harm to yourself and your team. In all, I am personally very confident in your leading this team, and will be very annoyed if you spend the rest of the night second-guessing yourself. With that, I'm finding something to eat!"

As Kal walked to the kitchen area, I felt Della tapping me on the shoulder. She pointed to Kallan.

"What he said." Then she closed her eyes and snuggled again. I looked over to Lisbeth, who was tapping her chin in thought.

"What? Oh, yeah, you're doing fine, Lee. But what you heard the Elves saying got me thinking. They can't figure out why all the stuff was smashed and the bodies missing. Now, if they were near a large body of water, then the bodies could just be tossed. Or maybe they're still alive somewhere. It could indeed be a rival Clan. What little we really know about the Ellovysians is that they have a ton of clans within their race, and the clans hate each other as much as they hate us! That could be the case.

"But, listen. What if you were trying to break out of the place, and the last thing you would want is to leave behind anything that might be a clue to what happened, or who did it, or where you might go? Wouldn't it slow down the Elves trying to find you if first they have to figure out what actually happened?"

I thought hard on what she said, then I heard Melene chuckle.

"Lionel, not so much. But Belinda and Bezine? Those are some truly twisted kitties. That kind of attention to detail and misdirection is the kind of thing they'd love to pull off!"

She smiled at me. "I feel it. Maahes, I do. The Elves weren't done with them, and now they can't find them! I feel it. I feel their hands in this! And this is the best I've felt in years!"

"Yeah. Me too." I felt Della wiping my tears away. "Me too."

Chapter 23. A Severe Lack of Pilgrims
We spent little time in Haylen Springs.

WE WERE ONLY ABOUT AN HOUR OUT, so we pulled into one of their designated camping grounds and called it a night. The next morning, we rolled into the medium-sized burg, recharged the RV's energy packs and the four extra fuel cells that came with the vehicle, and then we went shopping. Items placed in a PDP basically go into a form of stasis, so the food we stored didn't go bad or come out tasting funny. Considering that three of the five on our team could each eat as much as four mundane humans, food supply was pretty critical. For those other than of The Pride that are fascinated by the topic, they are pretty shocked by how diminutive the amount of waste we excrete is. Again, genetics. Our internal organs and various bodily functions break down just about anything that makes it to our digestive system. I will say, in all honesty, that standing downwind of us while we're letting go of excess gas can be pretty fatal, but what little doesn't get shredded and sent somewhere in our bodies is eliminated. You'll never here about People of the Pride complain of storing waste in the intestines or bloating. The Atlanteans were exceeding focused on creating the most optimal organic machines possible.

One can argue that they did their jobs too well. For People of The Pride, our metabolisms are such that if we don't have an adequate amount of food, we soon begin to eat ourselves. This is true of most organic digestive systems, but as is usually the case, the situation for my race is beyond extreme. Melene shared with me a time when she was in the field and was unable to eat for three days. She ended up losing close to thirty pounds of muscle in those mere three days, because she carried so little stored fat on her body.

When we finished picking up enough groceries to make the local shopkeepers nervous, we loaded, pulled out, and made our way further south. There were a few small towns and villages we would pass on our way to Pilgrim's Cove, but we decided that since we had another 900-plus miles to go, we might as well just set the auto driver and keep it moving. The retrofitted RV zoomed along, and we spent the time trying to make plans with little information, and when that grew too annoying, we'd take out our gear and organize, clean, polish, or just look at it.

I couldn't help but feel a little annoyed when it came to my weaponry. I had plenty of ammo, I had acclimated to the Desert Eagle handgun Melene insisted on me using as primary with my beloved S&W 500 as backup, and my 'twins', two custom built 24" Bowie knives were ready and waiting. I didn't feel the need for a rifle or shotgun. My spells and handguns were all I believed I needed for taking out an enemy at a distance, and I really didn't like using a weapon that needed both hands.

(Of course, it didn't take me long to get over that bit of idiocy—but please remember, it was my maiden run on an extended field operation, and as a Deputy of The Cadre. You live, hopefully, and you learn.)

Anyway, I didn't have a sword I was comfortable with, though, and I felt the lack. My Bowies were like short swords, but I had trained extensively with longer blades as well. I brought along a falchion-modeled sword, but it felt a touch flimsy, and the blade was only 28".

Whenever the subject came up in conversation, and it did often, Melene would simply smile and say, "Your sword will arrive when the blade is ready, stop fussing." With a heavy emphasis on 'your'. It was a part of an extended, annoying mystery, which included her recording me and her going full-out with swords, her meticulously measuring every inch of my body (not every inch, pervs!), And having a mold created of my hands gripping a hilt made of modeling clay. Sounds not too freaky, right? How about the part where she collects a small sample of my blood? We're talking about seriously stretching the bond of trust there. Everyone knows just how hosed you can be if an enemy gets a viable sample of your blood, hair, fingernails, saliva, any of that stuff! All of this packaged and sent off a year ago. Since then, when I suggested, requested or begged that we go shopping for a blade, her response would always be "Your blade will get here when your blade is ready. Not before. Don't waste money buying a weapon you will not use."

This, from the same one that happily blows through wads of money on a RV that could comfortably transport ten or so people for one damned mission, but gets fiscally responsible on a blade I needed ASAP?

Unlike other negotiable topics, Melene was a solid wall on this one. I didn't really get it. Some blades are better than others, better quality, more craftsmanship, but a blade is a blade, right? But, I trusted her, so that was that. As I had done for most of my short life, I had to put up with 'good enough' until 'mine' arrived.

Well, so far so good with Della—so, yeah, I'll wait.

The others, with their years of experience in the field, seemed quite content with their weaponry. I was worried a bit for Lisbeth. She seemed familiar with the single-edged short sword with a knuckle duster covering her hand, and the 1911 .45 automatic that she took out often to clean and inspect, but most Talents were just not that helpful in a fight that didn't include casting spells. I kept in mind, though, that Digby wouldn't have placed her on my team if she could be a potential weak link. He knew I needed all the help I could get!

With all the weapons Kallan pulled out of his PDP, and the joy he seemed to get out of handling them, I felt no concern with him at my back when it dropped into the pot. The Queen of his Set seemed to be the .50 cal. BMG Bull Pup. It was a monster, even if it was built to be fired without a bi- or tripod. He let me fire it off a few times in the range we had behind the house. I felt the kick, even with my physical gifts. I flirted with an 'Expert' rating with a rifle, according to the way the USMC rated marksmanship. As far as I was concerned, Kallan with that gun rated 'Death,' plain and simple.

And there was Melene, and her lethal assortment, which included two Desert Eagles and her personal favorite: an automatic shotgun designed specifically for her by 'Uncle Hal,' Hal Bergen. Rifled barrel, pistol stock, drum loading, with a multitude of sabot rounds, HEAP and HEFA rounds, filled with silver, cold iron, or simply lead, depending on the enemy.

Della's gear was less in terms of variety, but included throwing blades of silver-coated steel. Her hand-cannon and saber were of good quality, but I decided that if she was going to be with me pretty much for life, she would be in for an upgrade when this mission was done.

She smiled when I mentioned my intentions. "I'll hold you to that, my lion. But I am a Guardian. As Melene might have told you in the past, I am my best weapon. Anything else is simply an extension of my will." Then, she smiled.

Have to say, the little half-smile, and the frozen half of her face, made for nervous thoughts.

One of the byproducts of the Mystical link between Earth and Lyrodrylle is that both planets rotated around the sun at pretty much the same speed, though in different dimensions and Lyrodrylle was a smaller planet. So a Lyrodryllian day was the same 24 hours and change. The human astrophysicists collectively huddled into a corner and shuddered when they contemplated how impossible that should have been, but the Lyrodryllians simply shrugged their shoulders, noted that it was an 'Arcane' thing, and kept it movin'.

All that to say that we left out of Haylen Springs around nine in the morning and arrived in Pilgrim's Cove around midnight. The coastal town was of good size, and a lot of it was in the dark when we hit town. Not the dark of a town at rest, but in disrepair. We set the speed of our vehicle to 5 MPH and took in the sights, such as they were.

Many of the buildings we passed as we entered from the road looked deep in neglect, or unoccupied, or just straight nasty. Some of the windows had glass, but more were open to the elements or had been boarded up. Sad.

As we went further in, there seemed to be more signs of life. Buildings looked like they were being used, more glass intact in windows, and there were people on the streets. They didn't look all that steady, but they existed.

"This doesn't look right." Della murmured. "Doesn't feel right."

"My internal itchies are starting to wake up," Lisbeth added. "I can't put my finger on it, but something ain't kosher."

I did not have a team of alarmists. I paid heed to their vibes.

"Liz, take the wheel. Turn at the next corner, and take it back to the northern entrance."

"What are you thinking, Lee?"

"Smaller profile. Less noticeable. We can hear and see what's happening on foot as well."

"Walk it in?" Kallan nodded. "Sounds like a plan."

After we packed up our ride, we strode in quietly, keeping to the shadows. It took about a half hour of walking before we saw anyone to hide from, and as before, we seemed to have gone unnoticed.

"Now, that's way wrong!" Kal muttered quietly. "It's not like we're exactly hiding here. If I saw three hot chicks out at night, I'd at least turn my head!"

"Why, thanks, Kal," Lisbeth answered. "But it's like they don't even see us."

I agreed. The group ahead of us consisted of four men, and seemed to be staggering. We followed them from about a hundred yards back. As they continued on, we saw another group of two, another of three. And others, all heading in the same direction. They didn't talk much with each other—they just kept going. After another ten or so minutes, we saw them heading towards a building that might have served as a town hall at some time in Pilgrim's Cove's past, but it looked too ramshackle for that to still be the case.

We stopped and moved deeper into nearby shadows. "Tell me again, what little we know about this place." I asked Melene.

"About five hundred years back, there was a quasi-religious movement to bring civilization to Decados. Those that were a part of this madness built this town. The idea was to use the town as a launch point to those travelling to Decados as part of the effort. Ships left out full of volunteers, came back mostly empty. Soldier types went over to save those on the continent. None returned. The movement lost steam pretty fast after that. They tried to flip the town into a fishing and shipping economy. Didn't work. The marine life in these parts were just barely edible, and nobody needed anything freighted near this part of the planet. So the town mostly withered on the vine."

"So, these zombie look-alikes are either hard-core denizens of the ultimate skid row destination," Kal opined, "Or something real sideways is happening."

"Ya think?" Lisbeth chuckled. "Should we move in closer, Lee? The traffic seems to be done."

"Wait, let's pull back for a sec."

I waited until we were gathered closer. "I feel something off here, as do you folks too. Frankly, that doesn't have to mean anything to us. This place is just a jump-off. We can call in the charter, meet them on some available shore near the coastline, and be out. Or we could investigate what's going on here.

"Personally, I'm for investigating, and I'll tell you why. If we're right about the source of the crazy women attacks is somewhere in Decados, then those women have to get out there somehow! And get back. This is the only likely place, and—"

"Stop," Lisbeth giggled. "You had me at hello."

"Huh?"

"Some low-budget human movie. Wasn't that great, but had good lines. Point is, boss, I think we were all already there, and wondering if we would be able to convince you."

"Della punched me lightly on the arm. "We've all been around the block a few times already, My Lion. But we are very happy your brain works so well."

I grumped, a little embarrassed. "I swear, I have no idea why I was put in charge sometimes."

"There are a few reasons you don't really need to know about right now," Kallan answered. "But they are good reasons. All you

217

need to accept now is that we trust you to lead us, your Chief trusts you, and you've done very well so far. Better than more than a few veteran Deputies I've had to deal with. You seek the opinion of those who have more experience, but the final word comes from you, Lee. That's as it should be. As long as you keep doing as you've done so far, none of us will have any issues following you, boss."

"And of course, there's the simple fact that all four us together would have a very hard time defeating you, Maahes," My aunt pointed out. "In The Cadre, someone that powerful tends to be placed in leadership roles. It's just a very happy coincidence that your ability to walk and chew gum at the same time is nearly as impressive as your physical abilities and Talent."

I smirked. "Nearly?"

"Yes. I wasn't surprised, but then, I've been watching you all your life. You've always been a scheming little squint!"

"Game, set, match!" Lisbeth announced quietly. "Do you ever win an argument with her?"

"Not that I recall," I grinned, chucked my aunt on her arm. "Okay, thanks, folks. Now, stroll in? Recon? Infiltrate?"

"It might be important to mention," Lisbeth noted. "That with all these shufflers, I didn't see one female."

"Hmm. Maybe you three should stay on the DL. There's a stand of trees not too far from the entrance. You ladies hang there, Kal and I will move in closer. Let's go."

We separated and went into action. Kallan and I adopted the shuffling gait and moved towards the large, dilapidated structure. As we neared the door, we used our superior sight to see as far in as possible. It seemed the main floor was opened up, with crude, mismatched tables and chairs jammed into the space, and our shamblers packed in at the tables. All sitting, eating, and not talking. At all. We shuffled through the entrance, brushed the wall on our left. If we were noticed, hopefully they would think we were looking for a place to sit.

Kallan was right behind me, so I was reasonably sure no one else in the place heard him quietly throw up in his mouth. I couldn't fault him. We were close enough to see what the men were eating.

It might have begun its existence as 'food'. On the plates, it better resembled month-old roadkill. Including the green streaks of rot, the runnels of slime, the sickly yellow globules that burst on contact into rancid pus trails. And maggots…endless maggots. Crawling on the plates, being chewed and swallowed. Wriggling out of the mouths and beards of the diners.

In all, considering the visual, the sounds of the non-stop gorging on putrid filth, and did I mention the smell? No mortal words could come close to describing the effect.

Then it got really bad.

"Yes! Eat your fill. No one goes hungry in my banquet hall!"

The voice, akin to nails on an old-school blackboard, came from a tall, cloaked figure standing on a platform at the head of the space. It was vaguely male, judging by the voice; the hooded cloak it wore, a damned impressive one, concealed everything else.

Except the red eyes that flashed briefly in our direction. Red, glowing eyes.

I felt Kallan stumble into me in a clumsy way, in keeping with our pretense of being a part of the club.

"We need to go," he breathed into my ear. "Now!"

I didn't question. I just turned to a break in the wall that was close to where we stumbled, and then crawled inanely into then through the opening, with Kallan stumbling through behind me.

"We've got to get back to the team!" He hissed. "Vampires don't usually run solo!"

Damn. It officially went pear-shaped.

In my defense, I've trained to fight vampires, but Ms. Lucy was the only vampire I had ever actually seen, and her eyes didn't glow red. Unless she wanted them to.

"Those aren't zombies," Kal continued as we moved through the deserted side hall back to the main door. "They're thralls!"

Behind us, we heard the offensive voice ring out, "Get them, my children! Bring them back to our embrace. We will suffer no outsiders to live!"

"Shit." Kal let go of the pretense and began hoofing. I kept pace. We both took out our handguns and blades. Both my Bowies had silver mixed into the blades, which was toxic to the undead.

We had just made it to the entrance when an explosion of small artillery roared into the air. Time to haul ass!

As we cleared the entrance, we saw a small horde of humanoid monsters streaking to and around the small grove of trees where the ladies were waiting. From the bodies either laying still or flipping backwards and smashing into the ground, one could assume our teammates weren't taken completely by surprise. I put my bowie back in its sheath and tapped into the power of the Staff sheathed in my arm.

"I'm makin' a hole, Kal."

"Get at it, then!"

Instead of using my go-to Solar Lance, I dialed up the Fire Storm spell and hoped Liz's shield was reinforced. I released it in a straight line from where we were to our team's location, and put a lot of Mana fuel into it. Everything in the spell's path was immediately reduced to cinders. We dashed through the newly made corridor, feeling the heat of the ground through the soles of my boots.

"Comin' through!" Kal called out, and we didn't hesitate to run head on into a shield that was no longer before us. We didn't stop until we stood next to our team, and we watched when a red-eyed sucker got sliced in half as Liz resealed her shield.

"Was all the pyro necessary?" She grimaced with effort. "Your spell weakened my shield a lot!"

"I'll take over," I replied, then slammed a larger shield over hers. "Fire 'em up!"

Immature, I know, but I was rather proud of my shields. Especially when I was finally able to form them into One-Way Constructs, allowing me or mine to shoot out from the shield without allowing anything from the outside to penetrate. There were times when I thought strong, highly trained Talents had way too many unfair advantages, even if I was one.

This was not one of those times.

"Scraggin' bloodsuckers!" Della surprised me with the venom in her voice. "Makes sense. If something scummy is happening, they have to be involved somehow!"

"Focus!" Melene snapped as she reloaded. "The next wave is coming. The suck-heads are pulling back, these look like the zombie-types!"

"Thralls," Kallan confirmed. "A whole friggin' town hall of them. What's the ROE, boss?"

Rules of engagement? Damn good question. Simple answer.

"They're done. Take 'em down. All of them."

So we did. Good thing we had a scrag-ton of ammo in our PDPs. There was a moment of disquiet in my heart as we mowed down the mind-warped men. They were just puppets. The vampires, like the one that leapt on top of the barrier and began hammering away with a full-sized battle axe until Kal put a .50 cal. silver slug through its head, they were the true enemy. But this wasn't the time for mercy or choosing more deserving targets. The vampires were using them as cannon fodder, expecting our ammo to run dry or the shields to weaken under the constant pressure.

They didn't get the memo. The one that would tell them they were no longer the Apex Predators in the vicinity.

It took a half hour, but the flood of puppets crawling over the growing mound of dead bodies surrounding our position tapered down to an insignificant trickle. Then, to nothing. My team stood tall, facing outward in all directions, looking for stragglers.

"Dawn's close," Lisbeth noted.

"Yeah, the vamps are going underground." Kal checked the load of his shotgun. "Good thing you and Lee insisted on that extra two dozen boxes of ammo for each of us!"

"It's not like we couldn't afford it, or it would be a burden to tuck away in our PDPs." Melene shrugged. "And we don't have access to a supply depot."

"True. What we doin' about the bodies, Lee?"

"Torch 'em. Clear this garbage out of here, and then we sit down and figure this mess out."

Chapter 24. En Garde

None of us were all that hungry or tired, but we ate and rested anyway.

WITH ALL THE THRALLS NOTHING MORE THAN DUST after Liz and I used our strongest fire spells on them, and their former masters keeping away from daylight, we brought out the RV, encircled it in runes and wards of protection, then chewed on some trail rations while we sat and tied to figure out the latest buzzsaw we stumbled into.

"All right." Melene looked to see if we were all paying attention. "Let's step back and look at this. Two things to consider off the top. Pilgrim's Cove is the route to take if you're going to Decados, which makes this the only place to come to if you're leaving Decados."

"That is not beyond debate, Melene," Della noted. "'Most likely' and 'most convenient' does not immediately translate into 'only'."

"True. But let us then consider the presence of vampires. Why have they created an operation here, of all places?"

"Seems to me," Kallan put his slice of ham down and leaned forward in his chair, "that these blood suckers are somehow mixed up in our mission. That's probably where you were heading, Melene. My experiences tell me that vamps don't populate a garbage dump like this place unless there was a scheme with a massive potential payout involved."

"Some more fuel to the fire," Liz offered. "We only saw males as their thralls. Is it likely that there would be no women? At all? Why only men?"

"Maybe," I considered. "Maybe the real question is, where are the women?"

I shook my head in frustration. "Whole lotta questions. Not enough answers."

"One thing we can consider real is that the vamps can't be higher than 3rd Generation, or else they wouldn't have scattered when the sun came up." Kal went back to eating after that offering.

"We'll have to assume it, for now." I looked at my team. "Obviously, we have to find their lairs. Or their boss's lair. We need to confirm why they're here and, if they have anything to do with our mission, find out how, before we take them out. This nest will be taken out. They have treated us like enemies, and my Auntie taught me to not leave enemies on my back trail."

"Spread out?" Liz asked.

"No, I'd prefer us to go as a unit. We should probably set up our comm units in our ears, anyway, but I think it best we don't get separated. We'll take more time and cover less ground, but we'll be safer, more powerful together, and we're not on a deadline. I think."

"I can sign up for that!" Lisbeth smiled. "I like my boss being so worried about me. Can I snuggle up with you next time we go to bed?"

I chuckled. "That's up to Della, Liz."

So, that's a no," She sighed.

"Maybe in a couple of decades," My Lioness assured her with a grin.

***

We started with the big Town Hall building, ghosting up the stairs to the rooms on the upper floors. Methodically, we would enter a room, sweep it clear, then head to the next. There was nothing on the top floor. The next floor down was more productive.

The second door we opened revealed a room with the windows covered in heavy drapes, and two bodies lying flat on their backs and unnaturally still. They didn't look like in-charge types, so Della plunged her silver-coated blades into their chests, through their hearts, and the bodies crumpled into dust. We moved on. There were two more rooms on that floor being occupied, and five more were dusted.

As Kallan led us to the stairway for the next floor down, he was suddenly smashed into the stairs by a vampire not in a coma state. A 3rd Gen, at least. The fiend's mouth flashed to his throat, but was balked by Lisbeth's shield breaking his teeth. Before he could retreat, Melene had her hand around his throat and her dagger at his eye.

"Why have you taken over this place?" She growled. "Silver to the heart kills immediately. Everywhere else is just agony and slow death because of poisoning. You're going to die, monster, you have five seconds to decide how!"

He struggled, but 3rd Gen vamps were no match for warriors of The Pride, one-on-one. "I don't know," he finally admitted. "All I can tell you is that we are sent out all over the continent to gather subjects and bring them here. After enough have been gathered, we send them off."

"To where?" It was as if the warm, nurturing woman I knew my aunt to be was nothing but a mask, and the cold, hard vision of implacable justice was her true self revealed. Very scary.

"To the shrine on Decados," The vampire supplied, his red eyes widening in fear, and resignation. "In the middle of some old ruins there."

"You've been helpful," Melene nodded, and then plunged her blade into his heart, and seconds later, her hand grasped nothing but dust and air.

"You didn't ask about the women," Lisbeth hissed.

"He's only the first," My aunt replied grimly.

She was right.

We found another half dozen scattered around the offices of the main floor. But they didn't know any more that what we were already told. We continued on.

We entered the 'Dining Hall' that revolted Kal and I so violently. Empty of beings, we made our way up to the platform where the vampire stood. On the elevated space was a table, and on the table sat a massive, curled horn. It was filthy, tarnished almost black, and smelled like a legion of gangrenous wounds.

"By the Gods!" Melene snarled heatedly. "The Cadre needs to get this to the labs!"

"What is it?" Della asked nervously.

"What do you think, Girl? It's a corrupted Cornucopia!"

"A Horn of Plenty?" Lisbeth stuttered.

"A Corrupted one!" Melene insisted heatedly. "It was believed amongst our best researchers that only a true demonic could corrupt such a blessed artifact. I hope this means that they are wrong, or else we will have to abort this mission and call in at least a platoon of Battle Mages!"

We watched as she dug into her PDP for half a minute, and then pulled out a large, shimmering sack that had a secure cinch tie at the mouth.

"Do you normally carry around a collector's satchel?" Kallan asked, his tone on edge.

"When you've had the experiences I had with my Lion and our FAST Unit," Melene replied. "You learn that 'worst-case scenario' is frighteningly synonymous with 'most likely outcome'."

Carefully, she placed the bag at the rear end of the horn, then carefully moved it forward until the whole fouled artifact was covered. She pulled the satchel closed and secured the straps, with a sudden spark of blue and green stars erupting from the fastened cap. After making sure it was secured, she placed the smaller end into her PDP, and the whole thing disappeared.

"I don't think the thing could affect my gear in that dimensional space, but better safe than sorry."

"Just, wow," I stuttered. Melene smiled in response.

"Us old ladies can still astound you young cubs, eh?"

"Cubs, my butt!" Lisbeth snorted. "Kal's 72, and I just turned 65, and we're both gob-smacked!"

"When this is over, I'm really gonna look forward to you telling us about some of those missions, Melene!" Kal was almost drooling at the prospect.

"Later, if you're good. For now, I think we'll find more nests below this building. Vampires are possessive, and creatures of habit. Whoever's in charge of this cesspool wouldn't go too far from such a prized possession."

"I agree." I pointed towards the rear of the makeshift stage. "I feel a breeze coming from there. Let's check it out."

As I moved towards the moving air, Kal's head whipped around, back to the hall's entry. "I thought I saw something moving back there."

"You want to check it out?"

"Yeah, Lee. I don't like the idea of something creeping up from behind."

"I'll go with," Lisbeth offered.

"Good. We shouldn't be isolated in hostile territory."

Liz smirked. "You'd make a good Boy Scout, Lee, or whatever the humans are calling them these days."

The two trotted off, as I moved deeper into the dimly lit space. There was indeed a sizable gap in the rear wall. I opened the space up some so I could fit through it, wrapped a heavy shield around my body, and then slid in the space, falling into a shaft of darkness for ten or so feet. I activated a small fireball and cupped it with my hand.

"Looks clear." I called up. "This isn't a part of the original floor design. It's been tunneled out."

"Move over," When I did, Della landed beside me, and Melene followed. Then we waited.

Melene noted my fidgeting and tapped my shoulder. "They're grownups, and veterans. It's probably some vamps or thralls we didn't catch in the sweep."

"We didn't check out the other buildings in town," Della reminded.

I nodded, relaxed some, and we waited. It was another five minutes before Kal and Liz hopped down into the space.

"There you are!" Kal chuckled. "Saw the big hole back here, figured you'd jump in."

"Everything good?" I noted the two looked a little disheveled. Like they hurried to get dressed? Oh no they didn't!

"A small squad of bogies lurking by the next building over," Liz explained in a tone that was very casual, even for her. "Just wanted to make sure they were the only enemies close by. We should be good."

"That's good work, then." I nodded. They knew what they were doing, after all. Better than I did, in my opinion. I was tempted to take a good look at their auras, but focused types like Cadre agents can detect when someone's giving them an Arcane once-over, and doing that sort of thing without permission is considered very rude, so I kept my vision in the 'normal' parameters. I was just being paranoid.

Soon, we were all making our way through the tunnel. It seemed to stretch a good thirty feet, then led further down, into the bedrock under the town, and finally opened into a large natural cave system. We could hear the roar of the seas nearby, though the cavern itself seemed quite dry.

It took us a bit to acclimate to the surroundings, but the torches that were punched into the cavern walls were helpful. It helped us to see the platoon of vampires that were crawling along the walls and ceilings towards our position.

"New blood!" A rather limber vamp dropped from the ceiling to stand before us. "This is delightful. Fresh new blood from strong, healthy bodies."

"Really?" I couldn't stop from sucking my teeth. "Isn't that just a little too cliché?"

The vampiress shrugged as she pulled out a short, curved sword. "They do say the old lines are the best lines. And I am pretty old."

I shook my head, sadly. "Shame you're not getting any older."

"Is that so?"

Her speed was blinding, and her slash to my neck showed great skill. If my neck was still there, I'd have been toast. I saw the terrified shock on her face when she felt my left-hand Bowie pierce her heart, then she dusted away.

The other undead swarmed in. About a dozen, all 3rd Gen., and old as hell at that. I knew this because only 3rd Generation or higher could be fully active during the day, even underground. And, unlike most of those at their level, this bunch had a whisker of an edge in speed, though still not even close to as strong as a Child of The Pride.

I watched as Kallan and Lisbeth went back-to-back. Neither were as fast as the vampires, and Kal was equal in strength, but the two worked as a skilled, experienced unit while the vampires fought in solo mode. Watching Lisbeth flickering her shield on and off, stunning incoming foes while Kal sliced up those trying to recover from being stunned. It was like they were old partners that danced together for decades!

Melene and Della, they were just Goddesses of War that demanded bloody tribute. I knew I bested them both in strength and endurance, but they had me in agility and speed, and they used all their gifts to dance by, around, and through the enemy. Punching a dagger through the jaws of one, slashing the Achilles tendons of another, ducking under a thrusting blade and returning a blurry riposte to the heart. They were beautiful.

As I dusted my third enemy, I detected movement yards deeper into the cavern, which turned out to be the tall, thin figure enveloped in the midnight hooded cloak. The glowing red eyes were more pronounced in the gloom. So was the flame-wrapped longsword he carried. I made my way to him. Bladework, then.

The lack of confidence I had in my blade worried me, but I'd deal with it.

"Has she decided to renegotiate the deal, then?" His voice still irritated the Hells out of me, and the echoes in the cave made it worse.

"Who's she?" I asked. "And what deal?"

"Ah, just a sad coincidence for a pack of blundering fools. Good for me, a shame for you."

"I wouldn't mind you telling me what all this is about."

"Oh! Explain my dastardly plan?" His chuckle sent icicles through my brain. "I've seen some of those movies, when I was much younger. Sorry, young fool, wrong melodrama. You'll just have to go to your death as clueless as you came into this world."

He settled into a High Line position. "Shall we?"

I was barely braced before he sped forward. I just got my sword in position to block before he slammed down into my guard. He was stronger than the others, must have been at least two centuries old, maybe three. Faster. Obviously skilled. Possibly Master level.

He quirked an eyebrow at the fact that I was still standing, and he had no hit. He remedied that deficiency on our next pass. It was a blurred exchange. I was going on instinct and conditioned reflexes. At the end of the exchange. I felt a tug at my left shoulder. I stepped back and felt the space. I went cold. There was a three-inch tear in my duster. There shouldn't have been.

"As you noticed, My Oldest Friend has more than a simple flame enchantment," The Vampire grinned. "I hope your flesh is more resistant."

The spells on the sword were obviously stronger than the ones on my duster. Nuts.

He upped the tempo of our next pass. I kept with him, sliding, blocking, but it was a struggle. A struggle he took advantage of when I felt his blade slice through my coat sleeve then the slightest hint of cut into my left arm. First, there was nothing, then a burning sensation. Worse, the arm felt heavy, unresponsive.

Scrag this.

I tapped into my Staff, sheathed just under the cut in my arm. I pulled Mana, pushed it through the arm, refusing to allow it to go completely numb.

Then, I reengaged.

The next pass was even faster. He used a two handed style mostly; Not because the nearly four foot blade was hard to move, it just seemed to be his forte. Worked well enough so far. The honors were even mostly, but I didn't misdirect his last side slash enough, and he scored a miniscule slice on my right thigh. I had to stumble back, the leg almost buckled under me. I increased the flow of Mana through my system.

He blinked at the mark he left on my leg and smirked. I felt my lips pulling into a snarl as I hurdled back into battle.

He met each attack with ease and riposted immediately. I gave ground before him. Had to. His sword was longer, nearly as wide as mine, and the damned thing was flaming! I just dodged a thrust to my abdomen, but his follow-on knee into my ribs sent me back a few yards. And I could feel my Talent battling against the effects of the blade. My leg so wanted to fold, but I refused to allow it to. His technique was archaic, I could recognize it. Didn't mean it wasn't kickin' my ass—just that it was specific, an unblended mode that he executed masterfully.

But I held my own. I'm very sure he didn't expect to hit the five-minute mark with me. His long, emaciated face lost its confident sneer, and he snarled into a deeper focus, as he attacked with rapid-fire slashes, using his two-handed style to bring his sword blurring in continuous arcs of flame swarming through the gloomy space.

"Impressive," The undead sneered. "Wouldn't have expected a savage such as you to have enough of brain to learn the forms. But you must know you are sadly outclassed!"

Savage?

Really?

I got your savage, you wannabe Bela Lugosi!

I dug deeper, called on even more of the Mystic energy stored in my Staff, and within me, impelled it to flood through my body, pushing my internal system to build faster, repair faster, react faster. Then I forced the pace, gave myself over to my aggressive nature. My blows weren't as polished, but I hammered them in, forcing him to reset his feet and hesitate in returning a response. I began to match his speed, and then slowly, slowly, surpass it.

I came in hard, let loose with an arcing slash that would slam his blade out of position so I could reverse slash into his head. Good plan. Really good execution.

And my Gods-Cursed blade shattered all over his guard.

The fact that we both paused to look at the broken piece of shit saved my life. His moment of surprise allowed me to roll backwards, away from the side slash that should have split me in two. He laughed when I reached under my duster and pulled out my twin Bowie knives.

He laughed. Then he died.

His style of swordplay was brilliant, and yes, he was a master of that style. Only that style.

I on the other hand, may not have a 'Master' rating quite yet. But I was 'Hella-Great' at making do with what I had to work with.

I blocked his much longer blade with one blade as I sped an attack to his face with the other. He flinched, ducked out of the way. I came in, relentless, swallowing up the space between us. He needed more room to move his pig-sticker more effectively. I refused him that room. I was inches from him, and stayed there as I rapid-fired blades, fists, cross guards, elbows, even a head butt or two. He dipped a step back. I let him have the space he so desperately wanted. He put his all into driving his sword to my throat. I dodged the thrust, drove my shoulder into his chest. A twist so my shoulder stayed in his chest allowed me to slash down on his dominant wrist, causing him to lose a strong grip on his sword. The damned thing was burning my clothes and was on the way to burning me, but that was the price of admission. While he was focused on adjusting his grip, I smashed into his arm, causing him to swing it wide. Away from protecting his chest. I moved my hand within the cloak as it flared open, exposing his trunk. I exploited the small opening, and hammered my right-hand Bowie into the side of his chest, then jammed the blade deeper into that vulnerable space. I split his heart with that blow, and stood over a pile of dust, a flaming blade, and a big, cool-looking hooded cloak.

Della was by my side in a heartbeat. "That was close, Lion. I thought I would have to shoot him."

"Would have been a waste of bullets," Melene chuckled as she stood over the Vampire's cloak and sword. "Unless you got him from the front, that is. Look at the inside lining, this is one of the War Cloaks weaved by Minerva."

Della picked up the garment. The black exterior seemed to absorb what little light there was in the cavern. The interior was lined in burnished, antique gold. In the center of the lining, an olive tree was woven in.

"I never heard of a war cloak." Lisbeth came over and ran her hand along the black exterior. "How does it feel like a hardened shield and flap around like cloth?"

"And when you say, 'Minerva', it feels like you're making a distinction." Kal noted.

"I am, Kal. It's one of those treats you get when you offer the Elders of The Cadre an all-night bender." She smiled. "You know the ones. They don't go in the field anymore, always critical and ornery. All they need is to be treated with the respect they earned and allowed to feel that they still have a lot to contribute. Just sit them down in a cozy watering hole and keep the drinks coming.

That's when you hear the real good stories. The ones that don't get recorded, the stories the bosses hope will fade to the point nobody remembers them." Her brow wrinkled. "But you know this, Kal. You sat in on a few of those 'Improvised Training Sessions' yourself!"

Kal shrugged. "You were there getting an education. I was there to get hammered!"

"I'm guessing you were successful." My aunt chuckled at Kal's rueful expression.

"They had a story about Minerva and big capes?"

"Sure did, Della. Seems, about a few hundred years before The Cadre made their big push against all the Wannabe Deities, there was an undeclared war going on between Athena, the Greek Goddess, Minerva for the Romans and Menrva for the Rasenna, or Etruscans. All three claimed to be the Goddess or War, Weaving and Wisdom. Their three-way Catfight was a perfect example of the reasons Nemesis decided on creating The Cadre and begin regulating the behavior of all the Playacting Lyrodryllians, eventually deciding that they needed to be cleared out of Earth. Humans had enough issues with the real Powers and Principalities acting screwy, and the wannabes from Lyrodrylle were just making the whole thing impossible to deal with.

"According to the old heads, the humans in and around the Mediterranean were getting wiped out in constant undeclared wars. Not amongst nations, but amongst disciples. You know religious wars are the most vicious wars to fight! Athena made up an elite unit sporting her Aegis shields; light as a feather and damn near indestructible. Menrva retaliated by putting together her own elites, wearing suits made out of Derilium metal shipped out of Lyrodrylle. Not to be outdone, but Minerva proved herself to be the better weaver of the three by crafting a cloak. Somehow, she found a way to interweave Dejebelian silk with Derilium metal, dropped a ton of protective sigils between the outer weave and the lining, and made these cloaks, Dyed the outside black and lined it in gold."

She took the cloak and smiled. "Here's where the chick really kicked their butts in Style Points!" We watched as she reached into

232

the cloak and pushed. As she did, a sleeve emerged, covering her whole arm.

"It can convert into a coat?" Kal's jaw dropped. "A hooded, overpowered gambeson that protects the whole body? Dammit, Lyam. You hit the jackpot!"

"What?" I was confused.

"SOP for Cadre field agents," Melene explained. "'Spoils of War' is definitely still an active policy in The Cadre. We all share in the spoils of melees, but an agent doesn't share out in a duel, unless he or she chooses to."

"Well, that's fine. Who wants it? I don't need it."

Lisbeth was about to raise her hand, but was cut off by my Lioness.

"Um, yes you do," Della put two fingers through the hole in my duster. "This isn't the only blade around that's been enchanted to go through even augmented armor like a knife through butter. But the protection weaved and enchanted into this garment is far superior to anything being crafted today, except possibly those working with the knights of The Order of The Crescent Moon. This, combined with you being a child of The Pride, brings you even closer to full Juggernaut levels. This blade wouldn't have penetrated the War Cloak. And somehow, I think you'll be squaring off against these types of blades more often than the rest of us will."

I noted Kal and Liz nodding with Della's assessment, grudgingly. I looked at my aunt, who gifted me with the duster I loved so much. She smiled broadly.

"Oh, don't worry so, Maahes. Your duster can be repaired. But I would easier in my mind if I knew you were wrapped up in gear that would never need repairing when you're in the field."

As she handed the cloak to me, I reached down for the longsword. I grabbed it by the blade, since the flames had finally gone out. I held it out to Della, as I heard a sudden intake of air from Kallan.

"Here, take this. The blade being built for me is supposed to be ready soon, and this type of blade isn't my style anyway. Consider this the first of the upgrades I promised."

The flash of almost lust in her eyes as she looked to the sword informed that I chose wisely.

"Wait!" Melene stopped me from handing it over. "It's good you picked it up from the blade, Lee. Let me see the grips." She looked it over when I raised it closer to her. "Thought so. There's a small hole in the cross-guard. I'm betting a needle comes out to puncture a hole, draw blood when someone's gripping it. Its old bearer is dead, so Della, I think it's going to want a sample of your blood. You sure about this?"

"Quite sure." Without the least hesitation, Della took the sword from my hand. She hissed for a moment, then took a breath. We saw the trail of blood flow from her hand, then slide through her fingers to soak into the leathered grips. My Lioness smiled at us, then she narrowed her eyes in focus, and the flames returned to the blade.

She focused again, and the flames subsided, and then ignited again in her eyes when she looked at me. "No need for me to have access to Talent." She cried in delight. "The blade must already be infused with Mana. The blood being drawn is just the artifact recalibrating itself to the new owner. Now, it'll only respond to me. She turned her eyes to me. "You know what's gonna happen when we have at least ten minutes of downtime, don't you?"

I'll admit it. I was intimidated. Turned on, but a little afraid. This was the Lioness of my daydreams. A Warrior Goddess, worthy of worship, spawning fear with the raising of an eyebrow.

"Um, well, we need to look the rest of this place over. Er, let's go."

I don't think anyone laughed as I scuttled away, but I'm sure they considered it.

Chapter 25. Treasures and Tragedies

A few hours later, we had to make another call to The Tower.

THIS TIME, THE CALL WAS SENT DIRECTLY to the Chief Director. The stress was plain to see on her face. Mainly because she didn't bother trying to hide it.

"Have you and your team bashed in another hornet's nest, Deputy?"

"I believe so, ma'am. We've got to proceed on to Decados—but, well, we can't. Not until someone can get to Pilgrim's Cove and take care of these victims."

"Victims, Maahes?" Her lips thinned out as she tried to stay unmoved.

"The women," I had to wipe my forehead, resettle my stomach. Never had a case of the nerves before. Not this bad, I mean. "We found the women. We believe they were going to be sent to Decados. The next batch of Maenads, or whatever they would be programmed to do."

She blinked, twice. I saw the grip she had on her hands tighten on top of her desk. "How many?"

"Four hundred women." I gulped. "A hundred or so are dead, milady. The rest, the rest…it's bad, boss. It's real bad."

My mind couldn't stop itself from the loop I was stuck on as I reported to the leader of The Cadre.

We left the first main section of the cave system. Two openings led to deeper, darker spaces. One of them led to where the vampires created a lair. Three dozen beds scattered around, ornate chests and cabinets stored their gear. A lot of it looked like high-quality stuff, so we spent some time looking it over and shoving the best of it in our PDPs to share out later, the rest we either left or burned to ash if it was potentially dangerous to others. We wondered why the vampires weren't wearing the frankly superior sets of enchanted leather armor when they did the meet-and-greet with us, but Lisbeth and Kallan appreciated the upgrades, not even hesitating to strip down to their underwear and change gear as we stood and watched. I noted some interesting bruises on them, just under the oxidized chains of the pendants around their necks, but they probably got them in the scrimmage with the vamps.

They were initially worried as the gambesons and close-fitting trousers shifted on their own, fitting themselves to their new owners' shapes and sizes, but after that, it would probably take more money than most banks had in their vaults to convince those two to take them off. There were more sets of the same quality and enchantments, but Melene convinced me to hold them aside for the rest of my team. She just smiled at my momentary confusion.

"Maahes, think. I already belong to a Unit, and I outrank you at the moment. Lisbeth and Kallan are loaners from Digby's Command Unit. Your actual team consists of you, and Della." She chuckled as the whole picture became clearer to me. "Trust me, when the eventual 'Success' rating on this mission makes its way through The Cadre, you'll have to beat the volunteers back with a club, so don't worry about it now."

She's expecting 'Success'. I'm praying for, 'Still Breathing'!

After we finished sorting through our plunder, we continued deeper into the dimly lit space, and stumbled over another set of large chests and bins. These were filled to overflowing with coins, paper currency of all the different nations of Lyrodrylle, a substantial load of Earth currencies, and watches, jewelry, unmounted jewels of varying sizes, and a vast assortment of gear; clothing and either leather or metal armor the vampires decided were worth keeping as loot for themselves. If I wasn't already swimming in wealth, I would'a been set for five lifetimes from this haul. Now, it was all up to the 'Living to spend it' part of the equation. Some of it looked recent, most looked like styles from decades in the past or even beyond.

"Hey, Liz!" Della called out. "Think there's any pendants like you and Kal's here? Maybe we can all have matching sets now!"

Liz gave a weak smile and grunted something in response, clearly distracted by all the glittering stones before us. Sure distracted the scat out of me!

"Lee, come, you must gather these, now!"

I rushed over to my aunt, who was standing before a large chest. Its lid was flung open, and inside was four sets of glistening, finely crafted black chainmail hauberks, and four swords of varying sizes and styles. One was as long as a Claymore, but only one side was sharpened. Another was a rapier that was slightly wider than most in that style. The last two was an exquisite katana and a for-real Chinese 9-Ring sword.

"You probably won't be able to keep them, but we must bring them out of this cesspool!" She snarled as she spoke, her fury barely contained. "Those are the armor and swords of Knights of The Crescent Moon!"

My throat went dry. Unable to even swallow, I just nodded and followed my aunt's directions.

"I never met a Knight of the Crescent Moon," Della looked shook as well as she lifted one of the long sleeved metal shirts. Even with her height, the armor looked as if it would cover her from shoulder to knee, and the shimmer of the black links was breath taking. "Menchit's Bones! It feels as light as a feather!"

"Yes. Those hauberks aren't painted black, Della. That's real enchanted Galvornium. Those and the swords have runes and sigils built into them as they were crafted. Nothing and no one of Evil intent can even touch them, much less put them to use!"

I looked up at the hitch in her voice, saw the tears on her face. "Aunt?"

"Don't mind me, Maahes. I just weep for those valiant beings who were somehow killed by these eternally damned monsters! To be of such noble character, such matchless warriors for The Pentagram, but to end their lives as food for those they swore to destroy. It had to have damaged their souls before they passed on. I pray to The Creator that their spirits found the way to Paradise."

"They had to have been tricked somehow," Liz offered, with respect. "Crescent Moon Knights are a lot like you, Lee. With the armor, skills and enchantments, they were each the equivalent of a short battalion!" I noted that she and Kallan had moved themselves further away from us. Or was it further away from the knightly treasures? I was too caught up to think too hard about it.

"Either way, we'll get in contact with The Pentagram. They may know who the owners of this gear were, and can officially lay their names to rest."

My decision made me feel good, for some reason, and resolved to make sure we did that before we went over to Decados. My aunt and my teachers all agreed when they spoke of the Order. The Knights of The Crescent Moon were the absolute worst enemies to have in this life. They were mostly solitary, but only Nemesenes, ranked much higher than Deputy, could match a Knight Protector's authority to command even whole cities if necessary. Knights didn't have specific assignments; they went wherever the Hells they wanted, often alone, and could choose to answer or ignore a request for assistance, even from The Pentagram hierarchy.

I was deep in thought about the fates of the knights as we collected the rest of the vampires' loot and backtracked to the previous cave space, then travelled down the other passage. All thoughts were snatched away by the smell that hit my nose as we continued through the dimly lit tunnel.

"What the? ... Oh! Gods!" gagged Kal. Liz actually started heaving, swiftly followed by Della. There was no way I wasn't heaving as well.

"I've never smelled anything this foul in my life!" Liz whimpered, needing an ill Melene to help her back to her feet.

"What could this be?" Melene moaned as we staggered on, finding cloths to wrap around our mouths and noses. It didn't help much.

"I don't—" Kal began, but was cut off by Della.

"Quiet! Listen. Hear it?"

I did, after we quieted. The sounds trickled forward, varying in pitch and constancy, but always the same emotions. Moans of despair, shrieks of agony, sobbing cries of complete, abject misery. The sounds of lost, desolate souls so deep in all Seven Hells that hope was nothing but a myth told to gullible fools.

We felt that all-consuming sense of hopelessness seep into our internal organs as we continued forward. We had to. If we did nothing else, we had to put those multitudes of lost voices to rest.

The visual was almost as bad as the stench, but much worse than the sound.

Under a swath of primitive torches, we saw the whole, wide cavern was full of chained, filthy, miserable women. Chained to walls, floors and each other, dressed in remnants of rags, forced to sit in horrific mounds of their own waste. Their bodies and faces, what could be seen under the straggling ropes of matted hair, were gaunt, sickly, covered with sores, and difficult to observe clearly due to the insects and other vermin crawling on, over and around them. None of them were standing. It didn't look like they could. Some were laid out, many were even buried under the filth, the vermin, and other prone bodies.

But the eyes looked out, those that retained enough of a mind to notice our presence. It wasn't just the misery and horror that reflected out of their gazes. There was also accusation mixed in with the profound hopelessness. Was it us that were accused of allowing this to happen to another living being? Was it the gods and goddesses? Was it The Creator? It didn't matter. I felt guilty, and ashamed, that I did not protect them from this fate. That I was standing there, hale and free, instead of chained into the filth and waking nightmare with them. That I could still remember that hope and joy actually existed in the land of the living.

I felt a hand on my arm. "My Lion," Della stumbled over her words. "Many of them are dead or dying. We must get them out of here."

"I can rust the chains down, weaken them to where it's easy to break 'em off," Liz gasped.

"Show me how," I replied. "We'll do that, and then you three help them. It might be better for Kal and me to stand aside."

"I'm sure their trauma has little to do with men, but it could help." Melene gagged again. "Whatever we do, let's get moving, before we pass out ourselves."

It was beyond what could fit into mortal words. More than a few of them fell face-first into the offal when they no longer had the chains to hold them up. None of them could walk on their own, so Kal and I carried the unconscious ones while the females handled the ones whose eyes were open. I believed they were too deep in their personal Hells to actually be able to see us, but we did it that way anyway. It took hours. We had to move those still living gently, and even with levitation spells, we had to do multiple trips. We all cried countless times when we picked up a body that was light, still, and stiff. We would continue on, like we were serving penance for all the sapient beings on both sides of The Veil. Accepting the consequence of not discovering a way to find these desperate souls before they could lose their souls in a dark, lonely chamber of living death.

We finally brought them all to the large assembly space in the Town Hall building. We shared what little medicine we had, while I near-on drained myself dry as Liz and I used the few health spells we knew to pull back those too close to death to survive on their own for a few more hours. We gathered water in all the containers we could find or contrive, and those victims that could survive the process were washed clean for the first time in years, possibly. Those too frail were gently bathed, wiping away as many layers of dirt and filth as was possible without causing them further damage.

It was horrible. None of us felt better for rescuing them. We all felt filthy. Ashamed. And profoundly wretched that we couldn't do more.

"Is there any actual food in this cesspool?"

"No, Lee. Only our supplies, and it's not enough for so many."

"They can't eat more than a bite, Melene. Pull our food, let them start the process of reintroducing food to their systems. They probably need water more, anyway."

"What about the mission?"

"These women are the mission, Melene! You know why they were all collected and chained up down there!"

"We all know, Maahes! But we must complete the mission, so this never happens again!"

I sighed. Of course she was right. But there was no way these victims would be left on their own.

"We need to call HQ. They need to get some resources down here now!"

***

Her head was bowed toward her desk when I finished the report. "By the Gods!" She whispered. "That this has been happening on our watch. For decades? Centuries?"

She looked up, a mask of contained rage on her face. "We are not perfect, Deputy. We can't be everywhere, see everything. But when our faces are shoved into the pile, we can damn well act!

"One of our airships will be diverted back here. It will be loaded with medicines, food, healing Talents and companion agents headed up by Director Ginley. They will arrive before midnight. Do the best you can until then. Anything else?"

"It might be best to send our charter to this location. If she could be loaded with a supply of food and other needs for us, we can continue the mission." I looked away from her Hologram. "I'm sorry, ma'am. We couldn't leave these poor souls without help or hope. We'll get right to work as soon as the director arrives."

"Look at me, Deputy," I followed her directive. "We knew putting you in charge of this mission would be challenging to you. We had no idea it would grow into a maelstrom of madness, with a crisis around every bend of the road. Sixty years after The Sundering, we'd hoped such acts of utter depravity might have died down. We all were very naïve.

"We would accept your choosing to step down as Lead Deputy, allowing you to follow Melene's lead. No penalties, no repercussions. You've done enough to warrant that level of consideration."

I was tempted. So very tempted.

"No, ma'am. I'll finish what I started. If I wanted a smooth road, I wouldn't have taken the badge. My team's got my back. I'll stick with it."

"Well, that's it then!" She smiled. "Stubborn, just like your parents! Nobody can say I didn't offer you an out. But you have my thanks, young man. You've done The Cadre proud.

241

"Now, if you wish, I can direct your call to the office of The Grandmaster of The Sacred Order of The Crescent Moon. I'm sure they would appreciate hearing from you."

"Thank you, Milady."

After a minute of static, the holographic image resolved into a man standing at parade rest. The thirty-inch image still gave the impression of a tall, massive man in a dark military-styled tunic, trousers and calf-high boots. He was fully bald, with a full beard and mustache with a heavy set of eyebrows sitting on a pale-complexioned face. Sitting on his chest was a huge crescent moon pendant.

"You are Deputy Maahes Seckett. Son of Lionel Seckett and Belinda Seckett. Your Chief informs me that you are currently on a field mission but needed to contact our order for some sort of assistance?"

"Not quite, Milord. While on mission we discovered certain artifacts and decided that your order needed to be contacted."

"Artifacts? Go on, then."

I went through the story, then again, then pulled the swords out of my PDP and showed him. He sagged for a moment, and then firmed himself back into straightened posture.

"Those are the swords of Companion Durolan, Knights Protector Triste, Himiko and Knight Commander Minsheng. We lost contact with them more than a hundred years ago. Your contacting us allows us to mourn them properly. That is appreciated. More than I can express in words. A member of our Order is currently in Halston, the town north of La Pleasaunce. She will be sent to Pilgrim's Cove immediately to collect the swords of our Companions."

"Yes, milord. We must continue with our mission, but Director Alons Ginley of The Cadre will be on sight if we must leave before your representative arrives."

"I know him well. That is acceptable."

"But Sir, do you wish to collect their hauberks as well?"

His smile was grim. "That depends, Deputy. Do you think you could put them to worthy use?"

I gaped at him. Couldn't help it. "Milord, I swear by The Creator that neither I nor my team would ever tarnish the honor of your Order, or your deceased Knights! If I cannot find warriors worthy of their service, I will walk this mail to your Temple myself!"

"Well said, Deputy Seckett, who by my decree will be known by word and documentation as a formerly recognized Friend to The Sacred Order of The Crescent Moon!" The image leaned forward. "You do understand, I hope, that we would prefer this beneficence to not be bestowed posthumously? You and your team will be expected to succeed on your mission and return so that you all can be properly invested."

I smiled. "That's pretty much the plan, Milord."

"Good." He stared silently for a minute. "Nothing troubling, Deputy. I just wanted to see if you were worthy of your parents' choice."

"Choice, sir?"

"Indeed. Your parents were approached by me personally, nearly thirty years ago. They were chosen by The Order to be invested as Knights Protector, but they turned us down. They said that they were tired of the madness, and wanted to begin their family. Meaning you, I surmise."

I thought I was done with being thoroughly mind-wrecked. I was wrong. A Knight Protector had the authority to command Knight Companions, and pretty much anyone they damned well pleased! Only Knight Commanders were of a higher rank, of all the military organizations on Lyrodrylle. Even rulers of nations had to toe the line when a Knight Protector or Commander was flexing. Of course, a request going out for the presence of a Knight Protector generally meant that at least one nation was about to be destroyed, sometimes more than one.

Yeah, makes sense The Order would want to give my parents the 'Official' authority to cause the level of mayhem and upheaval they were about to do anyway.

"Just know, Deputy Seckett, that we are careful about who we formerly recognize as Friends. We will be keeping an eye on you and the other members of your present team, in hope that you will continue to be a shining light in the midst of Darkness."

"I'll do my best, Sir." I replied, and bowed to his image. When the image was gone, I turned to Melene, who sitting with the rest of my team. "You never mentioned that bit, Aunt."

"I didn't know it. Belinda and Lionel kept that one to themselves." She shrugged. "Makes sense, though. Before we slowed down, our team was being called for nation-level issues pretty often. It was becoming insane. As if people needed them for reassurance more than they needed help in solving their problems. It was too much."

"Friend to The Order." Kal snarked. "Well, that's that, then."

Della noted his moody tone. "What do you mean?"

"Well, Della, the only reason Kal and me are companions and not deputies at least is because we really didn't want to be bothered with Command issues," Lisbeth explained. "Forming teams, running missions, reporting in every two minutes. Well, now that we're going to be closely associated with someone on the direct path to eventual Knighthood, more sooner than later, then our Chief Director will probably demand that we be promoted ASAP."

"You two are funny," Melene noted wryly. "Digby's got about thirty companions on the North American section of his Sector alone. Why do you think he chose you two specifically to test Lyam, then become members of his team on his maiden run? You two were coming out of the shadows, whether he gets dubbed by The Order or not!"

"Yeah, I guess," Kal admitted. "Gonna miss letting someone else make the big decisions."

"Sucks to be us," Liz pouted.

Chapter 26. A Tigerfish, of Sorts

We were hoping that the vessel that would take us to Decados was sturdy with some room.

OUR HOPES WERE FULFILLED, but not quite the way we expected.

The airship came first. I was a little disappointed that I couldn't see massive vessel clearly, it was so high up in the midnight sky. The Talents didn't bother with shuttles or skiffs; they simply translocated load after load of supplies to the open space before the Town Hall, then themselves. I was envious. I wasn't quite confident in my translocation skills to use the spell on myself yet, much less bring five or so others at the same time. Well, I was still a growing lad. It would come.

We watched Director Ginley stride forward, hand out for a shake.

"Deputy Seckett! We're here now, where are the patients?" His handshake was firm, and the look in his seemed a bit disappointed there were no more vampires to shred into pieces.

"They're right inside the big structure behind us, Sir. We're grateful you folks got here so quick!"

"We'd have been here sooner, but the Chief didn't want the teams to translocate to a location none of us have been to before. Yes, that's right, Seckett. None of us have found it necessary to come this close to Aldemeron's southern coast. Truth be known, a few of us are a little jealous of your team. If we weren't ordered by the boss lady to secure Pilgrim's Cove and begin preparations to develop it into an outpost for The Cadre, there'd be a few hitching a ride to Decados with you. Me included."

I chuckled. "Actually, knowing some hardcore Warriors are no more than a boat ride away from saving our tails makes me feel a helluva lot better about having to go there!"

"I'll bet it does!"

I looked at the being who spoke as he moved to the director's shoulder. A bit taller than me, massive shoulders on a bulky build, dressed all in black leather and silver-toned plates spaced strategically along his frame. The sneer on his lightly tinted green skin matched the depth of the sneer in his words.

"Deputy Talos Korr, my Aide on this assignment." Director Ginley made the introductions. Korr just kept sneering. I just nodded my head. I had no time for a T.A. (typical asshat) desperately in search of his manhood.

"Well, my team is basically ready to go. Any idea when our ship might arrive?"

Ginley smiled. "For one, Seckett, according to the Captain, she's been on location for the past two hours, basically waiting for us to arrive. Secondly, well, it's not quite a ship. Let's go to the dock."

I nodded to my crew, who were hanging back in respect. They followed us as we made our way through the remainder of the wrecked town. This Korr joker tagged along, which would have been no big deal, if he could keep his mouth shut. He didn't.

"Shame you being demoted like this, Meli," he sniped at my aunt.

"As was always the case, Korr, you have no clue as to what's going on, so your insult carries little weight. And it's Alabato. Only my friends address me as Meli, and we were never friends."

"Well, I thought that might change, since your Mister Perfect has been MIA for so long. Wouldn't want any rust to build up in the pipes, now would we?"

"Is this guy always such a Tool?" Della asked Melene in a conversational tone.

"No, he's relying on Director Ginley intervening before I rip his throat open and shove his tonsils up his crack."

She continued, ignoring the snorts of building attitude from the guy.

"Korr's a good enough field agent, in his way. But for quite some time, he's been suffering under the misguided notion that he was in competition with Lyam's father. Whether it was the missions, the success rates, or even the members of Lionel's team, he often felt that he had to surpass his achievements. Sad, really, because while he was focused on attempting to top Lionel in some way, Lionel, on the other hand, often forgot that Korr even existed. Why someone would deliberately put themselves in somebody else's shadow is beyond me, but then, I don't suffer from terminal male-ness."

I could feel the waves of rage flowing off the Deputy as the two discussed his issues with the same passion as one choosing whole wheat instead of pumpernickel. Kal and Liz weren't in the least successful in covering their snorts. The Director didn't say anything, but I saw a small smirk on his face.

"By the way, Seckett, I do wish to apologize for my comments from before. I was mostly in shock that there was evidence of Elves back on the scene that I forgot the general rule in The Cadre regarding Ellovysians. Which is: Kill them, make sure they're dead, then raise their ghosts and ask them any questions you might have. Elves are amongst the most dangerous foes one can have. Almost as impressive as the Warriors of The Pride in their physicality, and able to wield magic at high levels of Talent. The whole race of them would make great Battle Mages, if only they weren't bug-eyed crazy and totally evil with it!"

"You got that right, sir!" Korr jammed himself into the conversation. "Took me nearly thirty minutes to take out that Elf I caught up with four decades back." His sneer returned. How about you, kid? How long? Or did you need help?"

"Oh, I took care of him myself," I replied mildly. "Must have been about, oh, forty."

"Forty minutes!" the greenish agent snorted in glee.

"No," Melene corrected. "Forty seconds."

"Seconds!" His eyes bugged, which looked good on him. His whole face was too squinty to me.

"Melene took care of her Elf in about three seconds," I added. "But he never saw her coming."

"Oh,"

We continued in silence, past the shacks that leaned on each other for support, through the cobbled streets that gave way to warped wooden planking as we neared the long pier that stretched over the water. I saw no ship, but there was a thick pole standing up from the water. As we went further down the pier, the pole began to rise, and soon a glint of metal showed through the depths. That glint grew into a hull, and soon I was staring at a good-sized submarine sitting by the end of the wooden platform. In less than a minute after emergence, a figure was making her way from the conning tower, climbing down a ladder on the side of the vessel, and then lightly skipping from the ladder to the pier. She was dressed in a somewhat florid outfit, reminiscent to naval uniforms of the early nineteenth century on Earth. The wardrobe did little to hide her tall, curvy shape, or the triangular furred ears that sat near the top of her head and the long, orange tail with a black tip that swayed slowly behind her. I'd not met many beastkin. She was my first female of that Society of beings. And she made an outstanding intro!

Straightening her shoulders, and placing a hand on the hilt of a saber at her hip, she dipped her head to the director briefly.

"Lettie Templeton, Captain of Tsunami, at your service,"

"We've met, Captain, and I thank you again for your prompt arrival. This is Deputy Lyam Seckett, lead agent of the team you will be taking to Decados."

She reached out a hand, and I gripped it firmly, but with care, and bowed a bit over her hand.

"I'm honored to meet you, Captain. My hopes of arriving at Decados undetected just skyrocketed."

"Hmm. Young, but respectful. I like that!" she growled. "We heard reports of Vampires on the scene, and decided to stay buttoned up until the Director showed up. I hope you don't take offense."

"It was the smart play, Captain. Another indicator that we will be in good hands." I smiled. "Now, if you have any small torpedoes we could carry when we leave the vessel, that would really be helpful!"

"No can do," She chuckled. "But you know, we just might be able to rig up some portable explosives. I'll have my first mate look into it." Her grin widened. "Of course, that's an extra service beyond the charter, so…"

I thought about all the loot we collected from the lair under the Town Hall. "Trust me, Captain. If you can build it, we can afford it!"

"Oh we're gonna get along just fine! You ready to sail?"

"We are." I turned to the director. "Sir, the chest with the Knights' swords and the secure container holding the twisted Cornucopia are sitting on the platform in the room where we were helping the women. Also, that building was the only one we actually cleared. I know your people will be careful. I just wanted to make sure you were fully informed of the situation here before you made the assignments."

"We were sweeping towns before you were born, Boy!"

One more sneer from the T.A. section.

"Enough, Korr!" Ginley snapped. "He's looking out for fellow agents! Respect that!

"Thank you for the heads up, Deputy. It is appreciated. You should get a move on. Sooner started, sooner done!"

He shook hands with us, and we followed the Captain as she leapt to the ladder and made her way up to the hatch.

"You're starin' at my butt, mister," she snarled at Kal, who was directly behind her on the ladder.

"It stared at me first!" he snapped back.

"Yeah," she snorted. "That sounds about right."

***

"So, when these Russians came up from their deep-sea run, they had no idea they slipped through a Veil Waypoint, and were no longer on Earth. Worse, they found themselves smack in the middle of The Leviathan Straits!"

"Oh! By the Gods!" Della stuttered. We all felt the same way. The Straits was nothing but wet death, even for its typical inhabitants. Nothing ever actually 'lived' in The Leviathan Straits; they just survived a month, or a year, longer than anything else. A thousand miles long, two hundred miles wide, and filled to the brim with leviathans, which typically had the dimensions of one and a half football fields, a shark-like mouth, and tentacles springing out from around its maw. But the leviathans had company. Lots of company. Massive, armored squids, megalodons that survived from prehistoric Earth, schools of Mosasaurus that actually originated on Lyrodrylle before making an appearance on Earth millions of years ago, Countless pods of Killer whales that didn't take jack from anything, and so many others. Many researchers have asked why it is these creatures seem to refuse to migrate to more roomy and slightly less hostile waters. The growing theory is that the beasts there are more sapient than we know, and none of them would back down from the others. Maybe there's something about the quality of the water or the nearby reefs that seemed worth fighting for.

What we learned from the captain was that the Akula-class attack sub, on its second set of sea trials, found it impossible to surface. After the crew ran out of air, the sub slowly drifted to more peaceful waters. It was eventually discovered by a large family of beastkin that made their living through ocean salvage. Instead of selling the sub, they cleared it out, subcontracted a team of marine engineers, from Tellerman, of course, to reinforce the outer hull and give a significant upgrade to the propulsion system, then included it in their fleet. Captain Templeton, as one of the heirs of the family's salvage empire, took the opportunity to make herself the 10th Captain of the sub, and has led the family into branching out, networking with various government agencies that might prefer a more unnoticed approach when seeking information or inserting themselves into potentially hostile territory.

"Didn't the Russians want the submarine back?" Della asked.

"For one, it was legitimate salvage, top to bottom." The captain explained. "The crew was dead, all of 'em, and the boat was way beyond international waters. Besides, there was no way they would've been able to recover it themselves. Legal finders-keepers.

"For two, they sent a few of their best spies to get it back. It didn't go well for them. With extreme prejudice, it didn't go well. So they made a formal complaint that eventually made its way to The Pentagram. The whole Assembly basically told the Soviet reps to kick rocks and die, and they backed away."

I laughed at her smug attitude. "Outstanding, Captain. I really need to spend more time on this side of The Veil. Without being on a jacked-up mission, though."

"Speaking of the mission," Melene prompted gently.

"Yeah, the insertion." The Beastkin reached from behind her and placed a thin monitor on the mess table we were all sitting at together. She tapped the screen, and we saw a large display of Decados as seen from above. It looked sorta like an elongated human heart, without all the valves and vessels.

"Now, there's no way to come at the continent from the South. The entire coastline is filled with sheer cliffs. The North is manageable, but then you'd have to go through some seriously contested territory. It's virtually a land-based equivalent of The Leviathan Straits.

"And there's no need to go through all that, because I think I know exactly where the vamps land their humanoid cargo." She moved the curser two thirds of the way down from the northern coast, and to the East. "There's a crude but functional dock here. I've surveyed it. No way me and mine were leaving the sub, but we're a curious bunch by nature, and we had time on our hands." She shrugged. "It also helps the rep when you do something no one in their right mind would even consider, like taking a sightseeing cruise of Decados' coastlands!"

A uniformed male with the rounded ears and coloration that reminded me of a cougar walked up to the table. "Ma'am, we're pickin' up a signal. It's intermittent. We think it's a tracking device of some kind. Thing is, we checked out everywhere. We can't locate it anywhere in the hull."

Captain Templeton's eyes narrowed, and then flicked towards us. "You folks have anything you can tell me?"

"Can tracking devices work even when they're in a PDP?" I asked Melene.

"I don't believe so. If something is in there, they are virtually no longer in this particular state of being."

I looked around, received no responses and shrugs. I slid my Staff out of the flesh sheathe in my arm. "This is the only thing I'm not carrying in my PDP, Captain. Could this be it?"

The crewman shook his head. "Begging your pardon, sir, but we already ran three passive scans on you and your team. Nothing was detected." He looked at me nervously, worried about how I'd react to being scoped out.

I chuckled. "What did that Governor from California say that became famous?"

"You mean that Reagan wacko from the 1980's?" Melene snorted. "He wasn't the first to say 'Trust, but Verify', but yes, a lot of people attributed it to him."

The Captain asked, "Who's Reagan? By the way, the Russians have been saying that a damned long time before forty years ago. 'Doveryay no Proveryay,' in their language.

"Well, she continued, "We must have picked up a bug somehow. Maybe one of the agents in Pilgrim's Cove planted it on the hull for some underhanded reason. Wouldn't expect something like that out of Director Ginley, though."

"Neither would I," Melene agreed, her face deep in thought.

"You might as well spit out whatever you're chewin' on, Deputy. We're gonna be taking up the same space for at least another five days!"

"Five?" Kallan asked, startled. "I thought it was eight days minimum from Aldemeron."

"With a surface vessel with a good motor." The Beastkin beamed. "Tsunami had a lot of upgrades put in place. We could get to Decados in eighty-six hours if we went all out." She turned back to Melene. "You were about to share?"

Melene sighed. "I suppose it's no great secret. There's been a consistent worry that The Cadre has been somewhat compromised. Information leaked. Communiques altered. Requests for aid going unanswered. And the question of how Belinda and Lionel Seckett, Bezine Alabato, and Hal Bergen could disappear off the face of both planets!"

She shot a burning gaze around the table. "There would never be a question of their loyalty to The Cadre, so one has to conclude that they were set up by unknown enemies to them or The Nemesenes. Enemies within The Cadre, somehow."

She'd never shared these thoughts with me. I considered them privately, but never speculated out loud. I thought the very idea of turned agents in The Cadre impossible.

Apparently not.

The Captain nodded. "Thank you for that, Deputy. Maybe we should surface and find this damned thing, if it's even there."

"If I may, Captain," Lisbeth offered. "Since your vessel can travel so swiftly, it might be best to take advantage of that and get to Decados as soon as possible. Once we arrive, we can disembark; you can inspect your hull and send out a call to our HQ, request reinforcement."

"Unless some black hat is sending a fleet, I'm in no need of reinforcement, Agent." The Captain snarled. "But it makes no sense to allow my boat to be tracked all the way to where we're going!"

"What do you think, boss?" Liz looked to me. "We've already been delayed on finishing this job. Hasn't Ms. Flores waited long enough to get back to her life?"

To be honest, I didn't quite understand why Liz was so insistent on her position. I shook my head. "I'm sorry, Liz. I'm thinking that however I feel is immaterial. I'm not in command on somebody else's vessel. I suppose that I could overrule her decisions, as the commanding agent on this mission, but it would have to be for a damned good reason. And I don't agree with your position enough to fight for it."

I hadn't ever seen the disgusted look that flitted across Liz's face expressed by her before. I worried about that over the following days, but I let it go. Too much to do.

"I appreciate the respect, Deputy." Captain Templeton bowed deeply from her seat, and then turned to her First Mate, who had stationed himself by her side throughout the discussion. "Armand, take us up. If something's latched on my hull, I want it found now!"

***

Soon, the Tsunami surfaced, and the scanners went to work. The device was found about forty feet away from the ladders. After it was deactivated, we submerged and were back on our way.

"Well, we found the little bugger, and we've increased the revolutions of our engines a bit." The Captain announced. "Not only will we make up the lost time, we'll get there an hour or so earlier than our projections. Not bad, I'd say."

"Thank you, Captain." I nodded. "And thank you for your courtesy before. We tend to talk things out in my team, but sometimes, like with this, there really isn't anything for us to decide."

"Call me Lettie, friend, and no need to apologize. I like your style."

"Thanks, Lettie. And my friends call me Lyam, or Lee."

"I thought your name was Maahes?"

"Well," I chuckled. "Maahes is my birth name. I took Lyam as the name I use outside of formal occasions. I always felt as if I had to grow into a name like 'Maahes'."

"I looked it up," She snickered. "I get your point. I kinda think you've grown enough to carry it, if you don't mind me saying."

"Yeah, maybe. But how do you shorten it, or make it feel familiar? Do I tell my friends, 'Hey, just call me Ma-a-a! Or maybe go with 'Heezy'?"

Lettie laughed. "Let's just go with Lee for now. The crew you build will come up with something eventually. They always do. They did for me!"

She laughed at my curious look. "Before you ask, Letivianca Jaline."

When I done laughing, I replied. "Your crew did us all a hella big favor, Lettie!"

Chapter 27. Social Dynamics

There was shift in our team that I could feel, as well as hear.

IT WASN'T AS IF WE WERE AT THE 'KNIVES OUT' POINT, but there was a sense of distance between, well, between those that had 'Pride' genetics and those that didn't. It wasn't overt, or particularly noticeable. But it was there. After a week of working so closely with this group, in gunfights and at sword point, waking and sleeping, the slight growth in tension felt like a ringing alarm in my head.

"I don't know what happened," I pondered, saddened. "I mean, how did we get here?"

"Well," Della replied, as she finished cooling her heated skin with a damp cloth. "A couple of days back, I locked you in this cabinet and wrecked your brains out, and you haven't told me to leave yet, soooo..."

I laughed with her, appreciating the release.

We were into our third day in the sub. According to Lettie, we were about thirty-two hours out from the dock she indicated. The meeting we held after the tracking device was found was, at best, stiff. It wasn't as if we could go into a lengthy planning session. None of us had a clue what to expect when we got there. But I thought that we had developed a good camaraderie amongst us. Respectful, but informal. But the vibe I felt from Kallan and Lisbeth indicated otherwise, and I was surprised. They didn't say or do anything provocative, but it was clear that they wished to be elsewhere, and were the first to seek out the sleeping cabinets that Captain Lettie had made available.

Since she carried a smaller crew than the previous owners, and upgrades to the sub resulted in more available interior space, she had expanded the size of the cabins to accommodate the larger members of the crew, like the grizzly Beastkin that can average 400 muscled pounds and close to 7 feet tall. Whatever plans Lettie might have made, Della made it clear that adjustments were required.

"I'm sleeping with him." She announced, pointing to me. "Well, sleep is optional. Either way, what's the best you can do?"

After she stopped laughing at the frightened expression on my face, Lettie replied, "Well, there's the cabin we reserve for The Sire of our Clan. He appreciates space. But, um,"

Della reached into her PDP and pulled out a ruby the size of a tangerine. "This'll cover the extra?"

"That'll do," the Beastkin gasped. "That'll do."

Standing a good four inches taller than me, Della stared into my eyes and growled.

Okay, she warned me what would happen if we had ten minutes alone time. That might be what she was used to, but she was gonna have to reset that timer.

One of Lettie's orderlies showed us to the cabin, and it seemed pretty big to me, to fit in a submarine where space came at a premium. The queen-sized bed was bolted to the wall, and the floor and the metal frame looked pretty sturdy. I was sure we would be testing how sturdy. Della closed and locked the door, then turned to me. And froze. I had to assume her previous experiences did not include her intended victim standing on his own two, fists on hips, daring her to pounce.

"I'm here, Della. I'm where I want to be. I'm not going anywhere."

The side of her face that wasn't frozen looked vulnerable. Uncertain. "I... I..."

"Come, here, my Lioness." I spoke gently, as to a nervous child, and opened my arms to her. "You're here with me, now. With your Lion. You're Home."

She crushed me into her arms, and I took it. I held her tight as she shuddered. Held her tight as she let go of the warrior, the grim stalker of prey. The bloody Goddess of War and Death. She let it all go, until she was nothing but Della Manville, the precious but damaged soul that allowed a careless moment to scar not only her face, but her spirit. She let it go, and I could feel her deep, happy breaths of release, knowing that I did see her, see all of her, and cherished her. Knowing that it wasn't me not seeing her scar, but seeing the brave, passionate soul that felt her insecurities, her fears, and still faced the world head-on, daring the world to give her their best shot.

But only letting me, finally someone in this life, see within; That with all her courage, all her strength, she was tired, and longed for someone to help her carry her insecurities and fears, or help her to let them go.

No more words were needed. We held each other, her hands pressing into my back as I gently stroked her hair. Then we kissed, crushed our lips, teeth, tongues into and around each other.

Finally breathless, I stepped back and took off my duster and tunic. Bare-chested, I stood before her, allowed her hands and lips to explore. Her touch was exquisite torture, but I closed my eyes and gave myself over to the sensation. When she was done, I undressed her, slowly, caressingly, kissing and gently nipping each newly exposed patch of skin. She was shuddering and groaning by the time the last article clothing was gone. She was perfect. Her luscious peaks and valleys sheathed in long, sculpted muscles; the impossibly narrow waist and washboard stomach, the entirety of her demanded a level of admiration that bordered on reverence. I needed no convincing; Della was the exemplar of the Lioness Ideal, and I would happily worship her form for the rest of my days.

I could see from her relaxed but eager stance that there was no fear or worry in her anymore. Only passion, barely contained.

"What would you have of me, Lioness?" I asked, holding my arms to my sides.

"I would have you pleased, My Lion," She purred, her tone raising the small hairs on my neck.

"Then please me,"

Well, she went right on ahead and did just that. It's not too often a man can say he was thoroughly ravished by his partner, but Della went to town and brought back groceries!

Following my lead, she undressed me slowly, touched me tenderly, and kissed me thoroughly. Then she picked me up, gently laid me out on the bed, and continued her explorations. Asking questions, testing theories, adjusting for new input, gauging reactions, and giggling happily when her ministrations resulted in hoped for responses.

We spent an hour or so in this, beginning to create the maps of each other's desires, reactions, sensitive zones, and even fantasies. The discoveries would continue, every day, every moment, and there would always be more to learn. But we were both soon overwhelmed to snarl, grasp, claw, bite, and find out just how reinforced this bed really was.

Playtime was indeed over for Della, and her beast came out, challenging me for dominance. To either bow to her will, or prove myself her Lion, in every phase of our growing relationship.

She had no idea how ready I was for the challenge.

Many Lyrodryllians had adapted the slang term 'Wreck' into their vocabulary. It originated out of the Lioness culture, and there wasn't anything the least bit subtle about it. The people of my ancestral culture made no bones about how much they indulged their sweet tooth for sex, as often as possible and with as many partners as was available. And they rarely made love. They Wrecked! Furniture, walls, clothing, and to some degree, their partners. Their preference was to treat the passionate act as a modified theater of war.

Whatever tenderness Della might feel towards me, she was a Lioness at her core, and her default setting was to dominate her partner, take control, set the pace, and bend him to her will.

Well, that was going to be a problem.

It became fairly obvious after a short span of time that she had never dealt with someone like me in the sheets. The master-class schooling under Trish's demanding tutorship came into its own with one such as Della. She grappled for dominance, I embraced compromise. She charged, I held my ground. She strived for possession, I retaliated with loving.

And as it was with Trini and Megs, Della's experiences trained her for sprinting. We were well into the second hour when she finally understood just what she was getting herself into. After the three-hour mark, she was done with the dominance games and simply gave herself over to Bliss. Somewhere around the fifth hour, the white flag was waving, and we could finally just enjoy the moment and each other. My Della let go of her fears and insecurities, laid her emotional baggage down, and embraced the truth that she was perfect in my eyes, heart and soul.

I made it all so clear to my Della. With words, with a touch, with a kiss. With fevered teeth sinking into her warm, vibrant flesh, desperately grasping hands leaving their mark, triumphant roars alternating with sobbing pleas. Nothing held in reserve, no holding back. She was My Lioness, my mortal goddess, now, ever, and always. And more than that, she was mine. She belonged to me, and she would have no other in this life.

There are those who might think such a state screams of objectification, sexism, chauvinism, and a few of the other nasty - isms. And I would tell you, again, we of The Pride are not human. From the very first purpose-built molecule, we were bioengineered through science and enchantments that no living being has been able to replicate for more than forty thousand years! A great many of the social causes other races and cultures champion are simply genetically incomprehensible to our kind. The genetic code in Della told her that someone had to be dominant in our relationship, and The Pride's history informed her that she would take the lead. After a whole quarter of a day full of ecstatic delirium, she found herself on the verge of total collapse, barely able to move an eyebrow, and more than willing to admit that she might've been misinformed.

We spent the rest of that first day, cuddling, kissing, caressing, and crying. She made me so very happy, I couldn't hold it in. I tried to explain it to her; the sensation of total, pure, bliss throughout my entire being. The feeling of completion, wholeness. How it felt unique, beyond anything I had ever known in my life. But, at the same time, it somehow felt familiar, as if I did feel this way some time in my life, but lost it, and was terrified that I'd never feel that way again. It was all so jumbled in my mind—but in my heart, there was no uncertainty. None.

"I love you, Della Manville. It feels like I've always loved you, and I always will."

"And I love you, Maahes Seckett. I've cried myself to sleep, many times, you know. Those were the times when I couldn't lie to myself, and admitted to myself that I needed to love, and be loved. Thank you, for finding me, seeing me, and loving me, my Lion."

"I will see you forever, with my eyes and my heart, my Lioness."

"I am content. Now, since you've pretty much paralyzed me from the chin down, could you get us something to eat? I'm so very hungry for food, now that I've over-stuffed my other appetites."

When she smiled, so sweetly, both sides of her mouth moved. I didn't comment on it; I didn't want her to feel self-conscious about it. But in my soul, I roared with joy, that I could have anything at all to do with that victory over her personal demons.

"For you, anything, my Lioness." As I creaked my way to my feet and searched for clothes tossed in every direction, I looked at her, still unmoving, and smiled.

"Did you really think ten minutes would be enough time for us?" I teased.

She blushed. "My bad."

***

We didn't spend all the time doing our best to warp metal, but between the lack of intel, the lack of space to properly work out, and the lack of warmth from Kallan and Lisbeth, we did spend a lot of hours of the day learning more about each other.

But the change in attitude from the two disturbed me more than I let on when we were with everybody. Only Della heard my concerns. Melene spent most of the last three days learning all she could about the submarine. I was starting to seriously wonder if she was weighing the pros and cons of The Secketts having one of their own. To be honest, from what I saw from the reports from my family lawyers, I could probably commission one, or purchase one from one of the nations on Earth and have it upgraded in Lyrodrylle, and do this even before I come into my full inheritance in—wow, my birthday was just under two weeks away! Hmm, maybe…

Consider it a disgusting indulgence of a spoiled and pampered rich kid if you want. When the Chronicles of The Secketts are finally unsealed and published, you'll think we should have had whole scraggin' fleets of submarines, surface vessels and airships! If we did, maybe a few of the friends and relatives you lost tragically over the years would still be alive! Screw it. We did the best we could. We all did.

Anyway, Melene kept herself happily occupied, Kallan and Lisbeth kept themselves apart, so Della and I kept growing a bond that already felt stronger than reinforced Battle Steel. I did lose track of time, so when Lettie came into the mess and told us we were about three hours out from her target, I was a little thrown off.

"Well then, time to get this done."

"Finally!"

I didn't step to Kallan's tone. Not verbally. But he ducked away from my glare quickly enough.

"Let's get ready to roll, people. We'll meet back here in two hours."

When we got back to the cabin, Della and I helped each other with our gear. We actually got dressed less efficiently that way, but it was fun, dammit! We put light, padded undershirts under the black chainmail hauberks, which reached down to just above the knees. Della layered with the smoke-grey enchanted gambeson and trousers we looted from the vampire lair. Since I was going with the war cloak, I had decided to take the sleeves off one of the leather zip-up jackets I brought and wear it like a jerkin. It felt weird as the trousers fitted themselves to me, but it felt real comfortable when they were done. Then we laced up our boots, I closed the clasp of the cloak around my throat, and we were good to go. We still hand another eighty minutes to burn, so we experimented on just how cuddly we could get wearing so much gear.

Not very, but so worth the effort.

We saw the other three were already waiting when we arrived. I also saw that Kallan and Lisbeth looked a little pale, and they leaned away from us slightly as we settled in. The scary thing was, it didn't seem to me that their bodies even noticed their leaning. What the Hells?

Before I could speak, Captain Lettie came bustling in.

"Our chronometers put us at about 3 P.M. Should we wait until it's dark?"

"No," I replied. "We're going in the dark already. It'll be best if we can see where we're going, at least."

"Alright. We'll have an inflatable ready to take you in. You have my frequency, so when you're ready for a pickup, give us a call."

I thought for a few seconds. "What's the range on your receiver?"

"We can hear you no problem up to a hundred miles away."

"Good. I want you to wait ninety-five miles away. We may have gotten rid of that tracking device, but it was on long enough for somebody to know the general direction we were going in. I don't want anyone to come sniffing around and find you."

"Yeah, but that might be a problem if you need a ride in a hurry!"

"Cap, if we need to run our tails off, that's a strong indicator that the mission has failed. And failure is not an option. Either way, we'll work it out. This team has had some pretty High-Powered results so far, so I like our chances."

***

All things considered, the ride to the ramshackle dock was anticlimactic. The sun was beaming down, and I could feel the heat of the day through the soles of my boots. Strangely, every part of my body covered by the cloak felt comfortably cool. I was rapidly falling deeper in love with my new garment. I pushed the sleeves into existence and settled my mailed arms more comfortably, then slid the hood into place.

262

We hurried off the dock, seeking any kind of sheltered space. There was none. From the dock, there was only a narrow dirt path that led into heavy forestation. I looked my crew over again. They were all wearing the newly found battle gear from the Vampire loot, but Della and I had the Order's chainmail as well. So be it.

"Della, take the lead. Kal, back her up with your Bull Pup. Liz, step behind Kal, be ready to shield them, Melene keep an eye out for Liz, I'll do Tail-End Charlie. I'll survive an ambush from the rear better than the rest of you.

"Let's move, low and slow."

Della nodded, noted the cleared narrow path into the forest, then stepped to the left of it and moved out in a crouched walk that was quiet and fluid. I would have preferred we fade out, but that wasn't possible for Kal and Liz, and if there were any predators nearby, two targets looked much more appealing than five.

Then again, if you can't count and are surrounded by like-minded predators, numbers don't really matter, do they?

"I see movement,"

Della's voice came quietly over the ear bud.

"Fall back, let's tighten up."

We had just enough time to drop a shielding spell before the first wave came in. I couldn't tell if the beasts were mutated in any way—just that there were a lot of them. Wolves, jaguars, bears, jackals, apes, the variety was countless. If they had teeth and/or claws, they attacked. Not each other. Us.

"They're cooperating," Della noted as she opened up with her handgun. "That sucks."

"Yep," I targeted a bear pinned against the shield by those behind it and stroked the trigger. The head exploded cooperatively. "Mundane rounds seem effective. Pick your shots. We've got plenty, but let's not waste it."

With the one-way Permeable Shield spells, it wasn't really that dangerous for us. The wildlife charged in, got popped, then was pulled out of the way or smashed down when the next beastie came in. Since I was the one on the team with the least field experience, I wasn't too worried about panic setting in.

I was, however, pretty scraggin' hot when Kallan suddenly turned and sent a bullet past my side in a downward trajectory, then casually commented, "You didn't extend your shield below us," Then went back to firing outward from us. I noted the hole about two feet away from me, and the head of a rather large mole sticking out of it. Yeah, prefer not to deal with those massive claws, and I paid heed to the advice, but still, that wasn't cool.

After an hour, I started feeling tired, and had Lisbeth take over.

"I can't shoot and shield as well as you can, Lyam. Our firepower will be reduced."

"If the shield stays in place, it doesn't matter how quickly they get popped, Lisbeth. Put up the shields. And remember to put one under us as well."

"I'm not the one on his Maiden Run!" She snapped.

"The way you're jaw-jacking in the middle of a firefight makes me wonder about that!" I snapped back.

Whatever she might have said after that was snuffed out when she saw my face. She put up her shields, and we continued on.

It took another half hour of waves for the numbers to decrease noticeably. We expended a lot of ammo, but we had plenty in our PDPs, and we didn't have to waste it on misses. The damned things just kept trying to push the shields down, not really giving us the chance to miss. After another quarter hour, the beast waves ended. We waited another half hour, eating, drinking water, and resting.

"Alright, I'm opening up a deep trench. Let's get these carcasses in the trench, and then we can cover it up."

"Why bother?" Lis asked. "They're dead."

"They can't be the only beasts on the continent, just the ones nearby." I replied. "Others might be on their way from further out. This pile could be a way of announcing where we are or are going, and it could be a chokepoint for us to deal with on the way back."

"Wait, before you bury them, they need to be harvested."

"Harvested, Melene?"

"A lot of medicines and Mystic Potions need the internal organs or claws, sometimes tongues of a number of these beasts. They all looked in prime condition, and-"

"Melene, no. We're in enemy territory, and the sun's just about all the way down. We bury the bodies, find a space that has rock under us, put up shields and wait for sunrise."

She sighed. "You're right. So much potential, though."

"We've only gone a mile in, Melene," Della offered. "I get the feeling there will be other opportunities."

"Yes, I get that feeling too."

"Well, I for one refuse to sleep on the ground in the middle of hostile territory if I don't have to!" Lisbeth announced. "Lyam, I'm sure your Maestra taught you the concealment runes and camouflage sigils?"

"Yes, but..." The light bulb went on. "Oh. Very good idea. Thanks, Lisbeth."

She simply nodded, a tight-lipped expression on her face.

We spent the next two hours burning away large swathes of trees and vegetation, until we cleared enough space to bring our RV out, then proceeded to cover the vehicle, including the tires, roof and undercarriage, with Mystic runes and sigils, connecting them back to a set of runes that assisted in collecting the ambient magic essences in the air and throughout the dense forestation around us. Once I activated the network of magic symbols and letters, the RV disappeared, and we had to be led by Della and Melene into the interior. I made sure to place one of my stronger shields around and below the vehicle, and then attached the shielding spell to my Staff, so I didn't need to keep constantly aware of it to keep it in place.

"We're as secure as is possible under these conditions," Lisbeth noted. She quirked an eyebrow at me. "It still surprises me some just how powerful and skilled you are with your Talent, Lyam. It seems that getting you into real life-threatening conditions, against opponents that you can attack with no restraint, has increased your speed of progression a great deal." She smiled. "Even now, with so much more for you to learn and add to your arsenal, you would prove to be an opponent very few beings would wish to face."

I bowed to her complimentary words, but I didn't really like the way she said them, and I definitely didn't like the smile that went with them.

"I blew through a lot of ammo, Lyam," Kal noted. "Can you pull some of my ammo out of your PDP?"

"Sure," I reached into my device and brought out a small case. "Saving up your supply for later?"

"Hmm? Oh, yeah. Figured to use up what you brought first."

"Makes sense."

"Thanks for your approval, sir."

Again. A flavor of snark that was completely alien to our established flow.

What the Unholy Hells happened to the cool vibe of my team?

The hair on my neck bristled when I began to consider the possibility that not all the enemies were on the far side of my shields!

Chapter 28. Of Scorched Earth and Pocket Dimensions

The shields worked as we hoped.

BETWEEN ROTATIONS ON WATCH, and the ill-defined discomfort I had growing within my mind, it wasn't all that restful a night, but I dealt with it.

Because of the nature of the enchanted gear, we smelled worse than what we were wearing, so we all spent the morning showering and putting the gear on again. I made a call to Captain Lettie, letting her know we were fine and moving further into the interior.

"And you might want to keep an eye out for wobbegong sharks," I made sure to add. "I heard there might be some in the area."

"I'll keep an eye out," Lettie chuckled. "If you could give me an idea of what the Hells they are!"

"Look it up in an encyclopedia somewhere. Fascinating creatures."

We signed off, and then after I put the RV back into the PDP, we moved out. Same formation as yesterday.

It was three hours of following the narrow but clear trail away from the eastern coast, putting down much reduced numbers of violent beasties, before the real fun started again. This time, we all watched flat-footed when a thick vine shot out of the ground by Della and wrapped itself around her leg. Just as the rest of the vine exploded out of the soil, Della was swinging her new sword. It took one slash to separate the heavy rope of vegetation from what we figured was the source, based on the screeching howl that resounded through the area, as well as the smashing sound of something heavy making its way through the shaded space. A lot of somethings, coming from different locations, coming at us.

Della fell back, and we shielded to better face…

Trees.

Weeping Willows from the Seventh Circle of Hell, it seemed to me.

They emerged around us, twenty or more feet high, massive trunks. Long, hanging branches that violently swept through the air like leafy whips of mayhem. And the pale, leafless cables that we realized were part of the exposed root systems of the trees.

"This is a really is a pretty violent continent," Melene snarled as she began blasting away. "Even the topiary comes after you!"

"We can't just shoot them down!" Kallan shouted as he pushed a new magazine into his Bull Pup. "They're too big!"

"And the roots are trying to drill holes in the shields!" Della noted, pointing to the thinner root segments pressing sharpened tips into the shield. And I'll be damned! The vibrating ends actually looked like they were drilling!

"Well, ain't that nothin'."

"I agree!" Lisbeth snapped. "What do we do? They'll get through!"

"Burn 'em."

"A flame spell in the shield? Are you insane?"

"No," I snapped back. "One, kill that 'tude, agent! Two, collapse your shield so I'm on the outside of it, and then reinforce it. As heavy as possible. Got it?"

So tired of this garbage.

She complied, and before the trees could adjust their attack, I released all my internal governors, and let the Hells loose!

There were two types of spells that Maestro von Brunner had me focus on in the brief time we had. Dueling spells that were specifically developed for maximum impact with minimum time needed for prep, designed explicitly for Ripple-dueling other Talents. The other spells were for large group settings; Area of

268

Effect spells. They took longer to prep, but these were the spells used when a Battle Mage was ridiculously outnumbered and neither retreat nor surrender was an option.

I never actually activated the Inferno spell, though I prepped it over and over until I had it perfectly aligned in my head. I didn't ever release it before, because, one - I had to be prepared for at least a half a day of recovery, if I survived it, and two, anything within a five-mile radius, not heavily shielded, would be utterly destroyed. Utterly.

Well, this seemed the perfect time and place. Lisbeth bloody well better do her part.

Just as the killer trees realized I wasn't behind a shield, I activated Inferno, and felt the spell itself wrap me in a shield as the white-hot, tsunami of flames raced outwards from me in a horrific circle of blazing devastation.

It took three minutes for the spell to be completed. When it was through, I stood in an expansive circumference of blackened earth. As far as I could see, there was nothing. No trees, no shrubs, no vegetation at all. No animals. Nothing flying overhead. Nothing, except my shield, and my team in another. In the distance, I could see and hear that the territory outside of the spell's foci was still blazing away. It seemed that a massive section of Decados' landscape would be undergoing some serious readjustment. Good thing the continent was lacking in 'innocent civilians'.

I looked to Liz's shield and saw it was thoroughly blackened, and there were very small but real cracks along its surface. She did her part. That was a good thing.

After another minute, the shield around me faded away. The ground still radiating massive amounts of heat, but it was just cool enough to not burn through my boots. That too was part of the spell. As Maestro said, "Its friggin' appalling how elegant a spell it is, when it's nothing more than an instrument of violent death written large."

I felt myself close to collapse. I held it together long enough to pull the RV back into this dimension.

"My Lion!" I heard Della's feet pounding towards me. "You're safe!"

"Yep," I had barely enough energy to speak. "Pretty drained. I'm gonna—"

I felt myself falling into Della's arms, and then felt nothing.

***

I woke up eventually. When I realized what was pillowing my head, I decided that there wasn't a burning need to get up. Really great pillows. Much better than memory foam.

"He's awake," Della announced in her warm, melodic tone.

"Is he?"

"Yes Melene. His pulse has increased. And he's making himself more at home."

I heard my aunt chuckling. "Yes, he and his father had very strong opinions when it came to preferred sleeping arrangements. I sometimes wondered how he ever got anything done, with him always trying to laze about, laying his rather heavy head on some part of our anatomy."

"Are you well, Lee?" Della's lips were very close to my ear as she spoke quietly.

"I think so. Nothing hurts, I guess. But I feel like I'd need a crane to stand up."

"From the conversations I overheard between you and the Maestro, this spell was only supposed to be used when there was no way to win, and the only option left was to kill as many of the enemy as you could before you died."

"Yeah, it's probably going to be a day or two before I can be strong enough to help much. Hopefully the fires still going will clear out any opposition close by. Where's the other two?"

"Outside," Melene answered. "On watch. They seemed very restless. Very agitated."

I didn't like the tone in her voice. "Melene?"

She sighed. "The thing is, they seemed more interested in the spell than your health. Maybe they just assumed you would recover."

"That's not it." That's all Della would say, and none of us wanted to continue the topic.

After a full day, and the consumption of vast quantities of food, I felt well enough physically, but I could feel the depletion of Mystic energy within myself and my Staff. I wasn't on 'E' anymore, but my capacity and that of my Staff was comparable to three of the five great lakes in America. It would take a while to fill up completely, and that wasn't going to happen while having to fight our way through this territory nearly every day. I'd have to make do.

We checked in with Lettie, told her about the latest issue and making sure she knew we were okay, mostly.

"Glad to hear. I've gotten word from Director Ginley. Pilgrim's Cove has been totally cleared. There were about twenty or so vamps that tried to sneak out or burrow deeper. No luck. They're gonna start moving equipment down there, turn it into an extreme training center as well as an outpost. He seemed very angry about how The Cadre could have ignored the whole southern coast of Aldemeron!

"By the Creator, he's pissed! 'Not even a patrol every couple of years?!'" The Beastkin was rather good at mimicking the director's hard-edged tone. "'What the burning Hell are we doing ignoring almost the whole southern third of a continent?' He was still ranting at somebody when they signed off."

"Wow. Okay. We're getting back on the road tomorrow. We'll keep checking in while there's no interference. This is going into day four, right? We should see some signs of something soon. You take care, and keep an eye out for those snake eels."

"Snake eels, now? I looked up your wobbegong sharks last time. Now I gotta look up—wait, I got my tablet out already. Yeah, I see 'em. Another Earth fish. Another...um, oh. I think, yeah, I will keep an eye out for 'em. They can be tricky. Thanks for the heads-up. You look out for them too, Deputy. Lookin' forward to having you on board again."

Della looked curiously on as we ended communications. "Snake eels? Wobbegong? Why the curiosity about Earthen marine animals?"

"Not just marine animals, Della," Melene answered. "Those two are amongst the best in the oceans in the role of ambush predators."

She looked confused for only a second. "Ah. Closer than you think, and you never see them coming until it's too late." She smiled as much as half a face could. "You were very thorough in his development, weren't you?"

Melene nodded grimly. "The only explanation for the disappearance of our family is treachery and ambush. I will do everything to ensure my Maahes does not fall to betrayal. If he must fall, it will be to the enemy before him, not to the blade in his back!"

Della nodded then turned back to me. "Lee?"

I shook my head. "Not now, my Lioness. Not yet. You know how I am thinking. Both of you do. That's all that's needed, for now."

***

We went back to the road the next morning. It took a bit for Della to find the trail, since so much was wiped out by the spell and the resulting fires that were still raging, thankfully miles away from our location. The subsequent three days were a bit eerie to me. It really wasn't that much territory, we could have covered the distance in a day and change if we drove instead of the deliberate creep. But we didn't have a deadline to make, it was smarter to let the forest fires clear our route, and only a complete idiot raced through completely alien territory, much less a territory with Decados' reputation.

Nothing attacked us as we continued deeper into Decados. Not only was there no attacks, there weren't even the expected sounds of a living forest. No birds making calls, no rustling in the undergrowth, no mating challenges. Nothing. Nothing moved. Nothing made a sound. Not too surprising, under the circumstances. But, unsettling, all the same.

"It's like whatever's nearby is standing still, holding its breath, and waiting for us to get far away." Kallan grunted. "Congratulations, Lyam. You've terrified a whole biosphere!"

"Whatever keeps us moving along, I really don't give a damn."

"It seems that Decados runs on the basis of predators constantly fighting to identify the Apex Predator." Della's voice

272

came in through the Ear-buds. "Perhaps that question has been answered for them, at least for now, and everything still alive is adjusting to the new reality."

"Perhaps," Lisbeth mused. "It's disturbing, if what you say is accurate, how intelligent these creatures must be. Non-sapient creatures are not supposed to be able to weigh options and make judgment calls. Strategic thinking is supposed to be impossible."

"Maybe that's been the key to dealing with Decados," I offered. "If you came here assuming these beings were as smart as you, possibly smarter, you'd be better prepared for whatever might happen."

"Most sapient beings carry around a massive load of preconceptions and misconceptions wherever they go," Melene replied. "They're rarely helpful, and make it difficult to shift your plans when things go horribly wrong."

"I see a stone pillar," Della reported. "It's sitting in a clearing that looks completely untouched by the fires, but the thing is unusually clear of any vegetation."

"Wait where you are, we're coming up."

Twenty minutes later, we all were standing before the ten-foot obelisk. It was indeed strange. Not the obelisk itself, which was covered in a strange set of writings along each of the four sides, but that there was about two feet of space all around it, and however long the object had been there, it looked more than preserved. It looked as if it was untouched by time, the elements, or even the surrounding conditions.

"Anybody recognize these writings?" I asked.

"Recognize what they say, no." Lisbeth replied. "But I think the one in front of me is in the Early Greek writing language. This over here looks like Egyptian Hieroglyphics, and this beside it looks like Germanic Runes. I have no idea about the fourth side."

"Earthen languages, old ones, sitting on an obelisk in the middle of a landmass on the other side of The Veil." Kallan shrugged wryly. "Sure, that's not in the least bit strange."

"Could it be a warning sign?" Della pondered. "A welcome? An esoteric sign-in sheet?"

"Whatever its purpose was," I replied, "I'm hoping it's an indicator that the ruins we're looking for are close by."

273

"How could that be?" Kallan pointed past the object. "Looks like the forestation gets even thicker up ahead."

"But look, Kallan," Della pointed towards the direction we've been travelling. "See the path? It's actually a real road now. It's wider, and you can see the stone used for paving. This object, and the change in the path, strongly indicates some attempt at civilization at some point in this continent's past."

"That road leads somewhere, People." I looked everyone in the eye. "If all we do is scratch this area off the list so we can look elsewhere, it's worth following. I mean, it's not like we got other directions to choose from, and the air's clear of smoke and stuff here.

"Close formation. Let's go."

We moved cautiously down the road. The trees and other forms of vegetation hung over the path, leaving us in a pervasive gloom that the sun high above couldn't penetrate. This area being so untouched, surrounded by fires still devastating the middle of Decados, had my internal warning system on full alert. There was only the sound of our footsteps around us, and I felt this particular silence had nothing to do with me.

"These trees look different," Kallan noted. "They look, normal. They don't look like the type to pull up their roots and move around."

"I see what you're saying," Melene noted. "Thoughts?"

"Anything living that might have been around here either left, or were killed."

"I can verify that," Della pointed to a patch of land a few yards to the left of the road. "There's a pile of bones over there. They look intact. Animals would have broken them down for the marrow, and the killer plants I heard about in other regions would have taken the bones too, dissolve them for nutrients. Aside from the foliage, and possibly grubs, this looks like a dead zone."

"The road is trending downward," Melene pointed out.

We kept a slow, measured pace, guns out and short blades in hand. There was the occasion patch where a sunbeam penetrated, but it was mostly shaded as we continued downward. It was after an hour of walking, passing a few more piles of whitened bones, before we reached what had to be an archway. It was wide enough for two modern-day sedans to pass through side by side, and stretched up a conservative twenty feet. We could see the white stone under the vines that had wrapped themselves around the whole thing.

"No walls attached." Kallan slowly reached forward and brushed some of the vines aside. "Stone looks in good condition. Just covered. There must have never been any walls to go with this thing, but it has to be some kind of gateway."

"But to what?" Lisbeth looked around worriedly. "There's nothing beyond it but more big bloody trees! Even the road ends at this thing!"

"The road ends at this gate." I could feel the wheels in my head creaking into overdrive. "Melene, a gate, sitting on top of a road. There's nothing beside it or around it. However much vegetation is wrapped around it, this archway seems pretty intact. Does that tell you what I think it's tellin' me?"

"I believe it is, dear one," she nodded. "Yes, I believe we're looking at another one of The Creator's little loopholes in the rules."

"Loopholes, in the…" Della frowned. "Are you talking about a pocket dimension?"

"A pocket dimension," Lisbeth murmured. "That would explain it. Part of the archway is in another dimension, so the entire structure would not be affected by the ravages of time and the surrounding flora."

The Lyrodryllian scientists of all disciplines, particularly the Astrophysicists, Mathematicians and Chaos Theorists, have spent close to fifty thousand years trying understand pocket dimensions, how they occur, where, how big they actually are on the inside. Even the philosophers and theologians lost their minds trying get a handle on the 'why' of their existence. The piece that truly fried a few million brain cells was that beings like lionesses of Sekhmet's Pride, who were immune to magic, could navigate pocket dimensions just like anyone one else, so the anomalies were not based on the Arcane, but on a form of science that was so very far beyond even the most advanced cultures, like the extinct Atlanteans and Lemurians. Not even they could crack the code of the pocket dimensions in their time, and they surely tried.

The best any could do were the Lyrodryllian Technomancers and engineers that found a way to design objects that could the replicate the behaviors of a pocket dimension, but asking them to explain completely how the PDPs they themselves 'crafted' actually worked led to objects being thrown and quiet weeping in corners. No one could deny the existence of pocket dimensions, and no one could explain how they existed, so sapient beings fell back to their default behavior, and exploited them as much, and as often as they could.

The most well-known PD was the Courts of the Fae, where those of the Seelie and Unseelie Courts resided. The few not of the Courts who were allowed to enter reported lands of impossible size, actual seas, lakes and rivers, mountains, valleys, even stars at night with more than one moon, and a sun that seemed closer but was not as hot to the skin. One Earth being who was allowed entrance actually wrote a series of books based on his visit, changing the names of those he encountered, creating a few characters out of his imagination, and renamed the whole space 'Middle Earth.' His stories were so brilliantly crafted, a whole new mythology was created amongst humans based on his stories.

I spent a healthy portion of my childhood hoping I would someday get the chance to meet Frodo Baggins, wherever he eventually ended up after his journeys.

The thing about these existential anomalies was, you generally had to be invited to enter them.

"Alright." Melene stood back from the archway. "If this is a pocket dimension, and if it behaves the same way most of these things do, then how do we get in?"

"Before we consider 'How', let's make sure we're all on the same page with, 'Why." Kallan frowned up at the archway. "The argument could be made that if whatever's in there needed the vampires to bring them victims, then it no longer poses a threat to anyone."

I shook my head. "I got a few problems with that, Kallan. First, we don't know what the threat is, how it works, when it got started, all of that.

"Second, whatever's in there reached out into this dimension and Earth's to affect the minds of Talents. What's to say whatever it is can't convince someone else to come here?

"Third, are we sure we got all the vampires involved in this operation? And there might be other races involved as well. Those three reasons alone tell me that innocent people may still be under threat, which means we didn't complete the mission. I'm not having that!

"Lastly, at least for me, is I don't like leaving an enemy behind me, one that can strike at a time I'm not ready or able to deal with them."

"I don't disagree," Lisbeth admitted. "But how do we get in?"

"We look for a token, and pray we don't need a phrase." Melene looked up at the archway. "Do you think you could burn the vegetation off of it, Lisbeth?"

The Talent shrugged, and invoked a controlled fire that soon had all the vines and leaves charred off the structure. As suggested, the arch looked almost pristine once cleared.

"That writing along the sides and the symbol on the keystone!" She pointed excitedly. "That's the Eye of Ra! Those are hieroglyphics!"

"Yes, it is!" Della giggled, delightedly. "That one was particularly eye-catching!" She laughed at her own pun. She was the only one, but we did smile some.

"Something, Della?"

"Yes, Melene!" With that, Della pulled out her PDP, dug into it for a few seconds, and then pulled out three pieces of jewelry that did indeed catch the eye. They were sunburst pendants, two on chains and one with a clasp on the rear section. All three had a large, blood-red ruby cabochon stone sitting on a gold sunburst. Along the edges of the sunburst, around the rubies, we saw hieroglyphic symbols that matched the symbols on the archway, and within the rubies was embedded the Eye of Ra, matching the style of the one on the keystone exactly.

"Good thing we took the time to loot the scat out of those suck-heads before we left!" Melene chuckled, and then caught herself. "Oh, I shouldn't have said that! Lucy hates it when I'm prejudiced against her kind."

"Those pieces of mobile road-kill were not her kind," I growled. "She'd be the first to take their heads, and you know it!"

"Yes, well, I don't like it when I'm being small-minded. Anyway, these might be exactly what we're looking for."

"Um, yeah," Kallan shuffled his feet. "But, um, who's gonna try them out?"

Really? Not even gonna act like you might volunteer? Wow. Just wow.

"I will," Della stepped before Melene could move. "I'm immune to magic, like Melene, and you mostly. I'm tough enough to deal with most threats, and we need Melene's experience and wisdom. I'm the most expendable."

But, you are mine! No scraggin' way, no...

I wanted to go in first.

The Warrior said, 'Let's go!'

The Leader of the team had to have the courage to say something different.

"Alright. Leave the other pieces with me. If you make it in, come right back out. Please. Just come back."

Della smiled her half smile, placed the jewelry in my hand, and looked at me. No words were needed. She knew I'd be in after her in a heartbeat. She knew which of us was making the bigger sacrifice. She winked merrily and strode to, then through the archway, and disappeared.

"It worked," Lisbeth breathed.

I growled. "It didn't work—"

Before I could say "Yet", Della came striding back to me. Um, us.

"Seems to work fine." Her eyes twinkled. "Miss me?"

I couldn't speak, I was so relieved. Just nodded.

"Nothing but more road, leading to a humungous temple thing," She reported. "I think it might be in the Egyptian style, but I didn't stick around to evaluate it. She smiled at me again. "I was under orders."

"Good, then," Melene clapped her hands briskly. "Now, let's see if we all need to wear the passkeys, or just one." She took Della by the hand and walked her back to the archway. They both disappeared, and then reappeared seconds later. I gulped at their smiling faces. Those two knew how precious they were to me!

"Worked fine, Lyam. Don't look so stricken. We're good. Give Kallan one of the pieces, he and Lisbeth can go together, and you come alone."

She cocked an eyebrow at Kallan and Lisbeth, who were standing by each other. "You were planning to come along, weren't you?"

"Of course!" Kallan spluttered. "I don't appreciate you suggesting otherwise, Deputy."

"I'm sure. Well, shall we?"

"Yes." I handed Kallan the brooch, and put the last piece around my neck. "Let's move."

Chapter 29. The Dreams of Gods
It was immense.

So MANY OTHER WORDS AND ADJECTIVES could have been used, and even they didn't cut it.

We stood on a ridge, looking down on a whole city of stone. The road led down half a mile to a façade that had to rise about a hundred feet or more to the sky. On each side of the entry were relief sculptures of one of the Egyptian Gods, probably Ra. Beyond the façade we could see, half as high as the façade, the brick wall that surrounded the entire complex, with paved walkways beyond the walls, just so someone could walk all the way around the whole damned thing in comfort. Within the walls, we could just make out hundreds of buildings, open court spaces, a massive column, or stela, or statue every twenty feet it seemed. Administrative buildings or living quarters, all in brick or shaved stone, rising twenty, in some cases thirty feet from the paved streets. None of it seemed to have been built on what could be considered 'human' scale.

"That's a lot of temple there," Kallan noted. "Looks like the pictures of some of those ruins the archeologists discovered, on either side of The Veil."

"They recreated those maps, made those models to give people the idea of what they would look like," Melene whispered. "But to see this? All of it?"

"What do we not see?" Della asked, bringing back to task. "There's nobody here. No animals either. Nothing."

"That's either major terrifying, because what happened to all the people, while this complex seems in such perfect condition," Lisbeth offered, "Or major terrifying because if whoever had this built wanted it just for themselves, then we're talking major Ego Issues!"

I quirked an eyebrow. "Possibly a God-like ego?"

Melene pointed. "I'm betting, if anyone of any kind is here, they're going to be in the temple in the back. It rises all the way as high as the front façade, and takes up the back quarter of the complex!"

"We'll check it out. Let's walk careful."

We made our way down the slope, keeping an eye out, though the surrounding terrain was full of nothing but dark, rich earth and low-lying ground cover, as if nature was specifically designed to not distract from people beholding the complex with proper awe. As we drew closer, I began to hear a sound, a whispering sound, like voices, hundreds, thousands of voices, all chattering away in languages I couldn't understand. The sound grew in volume as we drew closer to the entryway. Ever louder as we drew ever closer.

"Is anybody else hearing this?" Lisbeth asked irritably.

"Yes," Della replied, and we all nodded with her.

"Where is it coming from?" The Sorceress looked around her worriedly.

"I'm guessing from there." Della pointed towards the impossibly high entrance, with the base-relief gods staring down on us.

"But there's no one—" Lisbeth cut off her words as we passed through the entrance and saw a sea of beings before us.

Tall, short, wearing robes, long tunics or scaled armor, or rough furs that would be more fitting in colder climates, or diaphanous skirts and little else. There were children, running everywhere and playing with pets of every type and description.

We kept walking, speechless, as we watched customers haggling with vendors working from pushcarts or out of the nearby storefronts with their wares brightly displayed. We moved aside for palanquins carried by tall, beautifully muscled servants, ornately crafted chariots being drawn by matching pairs of finely muscled horses, and there were riders as well, carried by horses, bears, monstrous wolves and even massive cats.

We kept walking, watching the colorful, loud, energetic sea of humanity pass us by. After seconds, the truth of the matter was made clear.

"They don't see us." Della waved her hand before two shoppers disputing who had the right to buy a bolt of cloth. Neither paused in their debate, neither acknowledged the hand. Della finally gave into impulse and tapped one of the customers on the shoulder. Her hand passed through the shoulder, chest and arm of her target.

"Oh, well, damn." Kallan gasped. "I sure hope that means they aren't really here!"

"Yeah," Della agreed. "The alternative isn't appealing."

"They seem so real!" Lisbeth stuttered.

"Maybe they were," I replied. "Or are, in a different dimension. Let's keep moving to the Big House."

We continued on. I noted that there seemed to be a wide variety of cultures on display. I was assuming in a major way. Archaeology and Historical Cultures were not my strong points, but it just seemed to me that I was seeing differences. Dark, slim men in silken kirtles, tall, pale men in beards and metal rings around their arms. Dusky-hued women in light, shimmering gowns with their eyes heavily painted, blonde women in layers of robes of rich fabric. Countless children of many hues, wearing a multitude of clothing styles, from loincloths to leather shirts. Some wore headdresses, some went bald, some had their hair braided and some had a mare's nest of tangled locks. All treated each other as however they looked, whatever they said, all of it was perfectly natural and acceptable.

And the languages! I knew they had to be speaking in different languages to each other, but they seemed to understand each other perfectly. How could it be possible?

As two priestly-looking men walked through me in deep conversation, an answer came to me.

It isn't possible. My team was walking in two places. We were walking through an empty, desolate temple city in a pocket dimension.

And we were walking through someone's dreams. Or memories?

"We'll go to the big temple first, and then we'll look through the other buildings if necessary."

"What are we looking for, Lyam?"

"The dreamer, Aunt. Or dreamers. All this is coming from at least one mind. I'm not feeling any mystical energies coming from these people, and all living beings give off some energies, including those immune to The Mystic. Even spirits of the dead leave an echo a person with Talent can detect. They aren't here.

"Somebody, or somebodies, with great mental power is creating them. They might be strong enough to put suggestions to weakened minds. Suggestions of death and mayhem."

I caught my aunt staring at me strangely.

"Sometimes, I think your teachers and I have no idea what we did in our work with you, Maahes. The way your mind works at such an early age is disturbing, every once and a while. The way you constantly seek out strategies, tactics, motivations, pressure points in people's minds and bodies. Contemplating possible responses to situations that may never happen, simply for the sake of mental exercise." She shook her head. "When you started challenging the Masters in Go when you were not even fifteen, we should have paid attention."

"I love you, Melene, but it really isn't that complex. The Psychomancy Talents told us the trail led here, and we are in a place where a mind of great capacity is projecting images into existence. This is not that much more than following the breadcrumbs."

"But, Lee," Della interjected, waving a hand at Kallan and Lisbeth, who were still walking somewhat in a daze. "What if you're the only one who can see the breadcrumbs? Don't disparage your aunt's comments, my Lion. You have the Eye of the Hunter. It is a rare gift. Cherish it, and keep it keen!"

***

It took a couple of hours, but we finally hit the stairs that lead up to the temple. It was a struggle climbing stairs that seemed to be made for beings of a larger scale than us. The columns seemed to reach up into the sky. All of us holding hands could only reach halfway around one at the base. The courtyard was populated with a great number of statues depicting a wide variety of deities. One was a depiction I sort of expected—long kirtle, bare-chested, with the head of a hawk. A similar female one had the head of a cat. But there was another male with flowing robes, impossibly beautiful, and carrying a bow and arrows. Apollo? And not too far away, one angry-looking man with a heavy beard, dressed in furs, holding a hammer over his head?

And another, with what was clearly Afrocentric features with a long robe draping his slim, muscled frame, holding what looked like a complex spider's web in his hand. Was that Anansi? And that one there! Heavy set, long robes and complex headgear, Asian features with long, dangling mustaches, carrying in his hands a pillow with a treasure chest overflowing with coins and jewels. Was that supposed to be Caishen?

I looked to the others, who were just as confused as me. Okay. Whatever, we kept going, making it through the courtyard and into the Sanctuary space. There were more columns, with writing chiseled into them. Stairs leading to small chapels on a higher level. The walls were decorated with reliefs of scenes of battles, meetings of great import, panels telling tales of cunning, and treachery. Mythic beasts being hunted, impossible labors being accomplished. The panels depicting erotic art were very instructive, if not impossible for mortal beings. That alone told me that this was a further celebration of the different pantheons. But such a universal display, in what looked to be a mostly Egyptian setting? When did the different pantheons ever come together, hold hands and sing Kumbaya?

"I don't understand any of this," Lisbeth muttered. "This doesn't look like anything we've come to understand about the gods and goddesses! There was never a sense of community amongst them. Was there?"

"No," Melene stated flatly. "The Nemesene chroniclers write the facts; they do not skew them one way or another. They don't misquote, and they damn sure don't make stuff up. All the details from the 'Gods Crisis' point to the same thing. The Cadre didn't want to be bothered with going up against high-powered beings calling themselves gods and goddesses, but too many people were dying because of their stupidity. Which means to me, if these beings cooperated with each other just a little bit, it's likely The Cadre would have pretty much ignored them. Even if they weren't true immortal deities, who is The Cadre to tell people how and what to believe?"

"Then, what is all this?" Kallan asked as we continued further in. "This makes no sense! It's not, it's..." his voice sputtered and died off.

We had just entered the inner sanctuary.

It was more like the inner tomb.

A few hundred yards away, we saw a colossal, round table made of white marble. Around this table were fifty or so chairs, also made of marble. Behind the table, there was a short set of stairs leading up to a dais. On the dais was a massive throne of gold, intricately designed with golden vines and leaves as a background to the seat, with a huge sun disc suspended behind the throne.

And sitting on the throne, and in all the chairs around the marble table, were desiccated corpses. Dressed in faded finery, rings and bracelets and torques and crowns and circlets sitting on bones and skulls. Little wisps of hair not yet fallen away from mummified patches of skin.

From the size of the throne and the chairs, it looked to me that these dead beings had to have been at least seven feet tall, even eight feet, possibly even taller than that.

I didn't want to get any closer. I had to.

Even in their saddened state, the clothing of these beings seemed very well preserved. The colors were still brilliant, the styles unique and eye-catching. It was as if, even in death, the clothes seemed to flow to a rhythm of their own, wafting in a breeze that didn't exist.

Oops. My bad. The one to my left actually was moving.

The head slowly raised from the table. This particular head did have a head of healthy, raven black tresses, and the full-length robes with long sleeves covered the fact that her bones did indeed have flesh on them. She leaned back in the chair, sighed, and then slowly rose to her feet. Compared to the others at the table, she looked to be on the small side, only seven and a half feet tall. She was perfectly beautiful, with her heart-shaped face in smooth, olive-toned skin. The figure under the robes suggested a lithe, but voluptuous figure. Too bad she looked so put out.

"Thalmus?" Her voice resonated through my ears and bones. "Why do you come? I have to rebuild my energies." The female's voice was slightly slurred, but still strong, melodious. "You know how exhausting projecting myself can be! Or, could it be you wish to attack me while in this weakened state? It did not work out well for you last time, Thalmus! "

Thalmus? Who?

Oh.

I was wearing the vampire's cloak, with the hood up and everything. Play along? Or...

Um, no.

I pulled the hood back. "I am not Thalmus. Thalmus will not be coming here anymore."

"Who are you?" she hissed, her anger radiating through her voice. "What do you mean, Thalmus will not be coming?"

"I mean he's dead, as are all the vampires at Pilgrim's Cove."

"That voice! I have heard that voice. I have seen that face!" She took a step back. "You? You come here? How did you find this place? Why have you come?"

"To end this. Too many lives have been lost. Too many innocents have died because of you."

"Innocents?" she raged. "They are not innocents. They are nothing but sheep. You are all nothing but cattle!" She swept her hand toward the table. "You see them? My brothers and sisters? These are the innocents that have been taken before their time! These are the Divine Gods and Goddesses that were forced to abandon their flock, forced to watch their charges fall away from their devotion to my blessed brethren. How dare you compare the momentary pain of beasts to the centuries of torture and horror endured by these sacred souls?"

"I..." I paused, took a breath. "Look, I mean no disrespect, milady. Trading insults is a waste of everyone's time. My name is Maahes Seckett. May I know to whom I am addressing?"

"Maahes?" The woman took a moment to look me over. "No, you are not the Maahes I knew and loved like a brother. He is long past, and he was much taller. But you do remind me of him. There was something undeniable about him. He had no hesitation to take on a host of enemies alone, never waiting for Horus or Set to bring reinforcements. Headstrong, sometimes rash, but courageous."

"My people are descended from his Mother Sekhmet, milady."

She jerked. "Is this the truth?"

I nodded. "The descendants of her daughter Nosi made their way back to Lyrodrylle more than ten thousand years ago and created their own culture. We name ourselves Children of Sekhmet's Pride." I gestured to Della and Melene. "These two also have the blood of Sekhmet in their veins."

She peered at them, then sagged back into her chair. "Sekhmet has been dust for countless millennia, but her blood continues to flow in these lands. She has gained her immortality. We did not consider this. We considered her foolish for breeding with mere mortals. Now, she has a nation of her children honoring her, and we? We are forgotten. We are dust."

I moved to stand before her. "If you would honor me with your name, Milady, if you could explain so I could understand why you have done what you have done, I swear that you will not be forgotten."

She smiled. "One last true disciple?" she mocked.

"No, I cannot worship you. There has been too much blood, and I am a Child of The Pride, as well as an acolyte to Nemesis. But I will remember you, and will give you honor for who you were, not for who you have become."

She was silent for an eternity, which lasted ten seconds.

"So be it. I know you now, Maahes The Seckett. I know you are an agent of the Goddess Nemesis. I can feel her presence all over you. You know where I am, so others will know as well, sooner or later. Possibly the Goddess herself. None can withstand Nemesis, one of the few Celestials brought forth by The Creator's hand."

She straightened her posture, eye level with me while seated. "Know you then that you stand in the presence of Euterpe, The Muse, Goddess of Music and Poetry, The Giver of Delight to my devotees."

"Er," I cleared my throat. "So, um, all this never had anything to do, uh, with, Dionysus?"

"That misbegotten HACK!" she raged. "That fat drunken slob could not even hold his lyre correctly, much less play it! And singing? Strangling bullfrogs had more sweetness of tone than that inept abomination," Her eyes widened in realization. "By the Heavens! You all thought these attacks were by his band of idiot whores, the Maenads. This is the outside of enough. I strike a blow for the blessed music of the Eternals, and NOBODY KNOWS IT?!"

"But, Milady Euterpe," I tried to keep my tone calm. It was a struggle. She really deserved a good strangling. "When one sees a horde of wild-haired women dressed in rags, screaming incomprehensible chants and raving like lunatics, that seemed to be all the classic setup for Maenads on a rampage. Their targeting great Talents as victims further confused the issue."

"Great mortal Talents, Child of Sekhmet!" the Muse snarled. "They had no influence from me. They were not given that touch of perfection, that sublime suggestion to the heart that would set their music apart from anything ever heard before. They didn't have that Divine Spark. They were only pretenders! When these women were brought before me, I played that Divine music for them. I sang for them, played my harp, and they were so enthralled, so enraptured, they themselves demanded to be allowed to go forth and end the lives of those who pretended greatness, who gulled the masses with their false claim to the Divine!"

I waited her out, swallowed my bile, my rage, and when she was done, I leaned towards her.

"How do you know?"

"What do you mean? How do I know, what?"

"How do you know they weren't inspired by the Divine, Milady?"

There was a look of profound confusion on her perfect face. As if my question raised a whole new train of thought she never considered. Maybe she was so focused on music, she left deep thinking to someone else at the table. "What do you mean?" She whispered. "What are you saying?"

"I'm looking at this table, Milady. This is the merest fraction of all the deities that existed at one time or another. There were so many of you, multitudes of pantheons, of countless cultures. Some came here, it seems, when they were driven out of their divine positions. Some returned to Lyrodrylle. Some died. But did they all die? Perhaps some repackaged themselves and are still serving in the same capacity under a different name, or brand. Perhaps there were some gods and goddesses of music that found a place amongst mere mortals. Maybe they created schools, and are fondly remembered for inspiring hundreds of gifted performers who have shared exquisite music with millions."

I couldn't help but let some of my white-hot rage bleed through.

"Perhaps a few went the same route as Sekhmet, and had children with mortals. And perhaps those children, grandchildren, or great-grandchildren were given that divine spark from birth, maybe they were so full of that inheritance that they could not stop themselves from creating music. Maybe they couldn't do anything else with themselves but give in to that internal drive to reach for the perfect set of chords, that perfect phrase, that blessed joining of words, melody and voice that could make the angels weep for joy."

I leaned forward more, my face inches from hers.

"And maybe, with that otherworldly something lifting them beyond what should have been possible, maybe they were just about there, just on the edge of creating that song of true divine inspiration, then your fanatical worshippers crashed onto the scene, killed the artist, killed the song from ever being born, and doomed us all to another cycle of mediocre drivel! Maybe your sending out these bug-eyed crazy lunatics after newly emerging artists is the reason music sucks so scraggin' bad these days!

"So I ask again, milady, Muse of Music, How do you know they weren't touched by the Divine? All we can know for sure is that we will never know for sure, because you didn't give us the chance to find out!"

By the end of my rant, she was pressed back in her chair, and a look of perfect horror was etched on her face. I could see in her eyes that for the first time in eons, maybe, she saw the reality of her actions from another's perspective. And it sickened her.

Good. I hoped she choked on it.

"How did I become this, thing?" She whispered fearfully. Wannabe Divines get scared too. Nice. "How could I not see this? We had music competitions, my fellow deities of music and me. I had Orpheus, so of course I usually won, but we all shared and laughed, and played songs, and watched them grow. How did I come to this place?"

She hung her head, and wept.

"I was so alone. For so long. It was Ra's idea to come here. He had built this place, long and long before we were driven out. It was in one of our very rare harmonious moments. When the purging entered its this third century, he suggested we come here, as a sanctuary. No one would look for us here. And no one did. Century after century, then, a millennium. Just us. No followers, no worshippers. No one to remind us how important we were. Just us.

"Baldur was the first. He was the Beloved of the Gods, with no one to love him. He asked us to drain him of his energy; he couldn't bring himself to ending his own life. None of us could. Anansi was next. He said he would live on through his children, and the stories they would tell. The others didn't last much longer. You see, if we drain them of their vital energies, that means we all would live that much longer. None of them could face an extra four or five thousand years of this existence.

"Finally, it was just myself and Ra. He was so very sad. All his hopes for this sanctuary turned crypt. He no longer wanted anything. Didn't eat, didn't drink. It doesn't matter for us, you know. We spent so much time absorbing the energies of our foes while we were gods, we only ate and drank for taste, and to pass the time. He was sitting in his throne, weeping endlessly. I felt pity for him. So I drained him, and he died. And now here I am. A bitter, despicable hag who had others killed for being free to create joy without my permission!

"And even now, there is that in me that does not allow me to end my own life. If I could, I would have done it a thousand years ago."

I looked to my team. Melene looked strangely serene. Lisbeth looked like she was sucking a bag of lemons, and Kallan looked neutral, taking it all in.

Della, however, looked worryingly eager, and gave in to the moment.

"I have to ask, Muse," She snapped. "Minnie Riperton. Was her death your doing? A breast cancer that came out of nowhere and spread through her system at impossible speeds? Was that YOU?!"

The deity turned her head away. "Yes," she murmured. "Young, of African descent. I think I sent a minion to activate and accelerate the aberrant cells. Yes."

I held Della tightly as she leaned towards Euterpe, tears cascading down her face.

"You hateful Bitch! I've watched the old recordings, listened to her music! She was beautiful! Her voice, her music, it was so beautiful! So perfect! Oh, By The Divine! She filled so many with hope and joy after The Sundering! And you! You had to kill that joy! How could you?"

I held my lioness close, as she wept for a woman who died twenty years before she was born. I shared her sorrow. My parents and aunts shared the singer's music with me. Truly, she was a desperately needed voice of love and hope for people of both worlds.

"I was wrong," Euterpe whispered, head bowed. "So very wrong. I'm so tired. I want to end this. I want to die. I can't die. Not for a long, long time."

I turned back to Euterpe. "Not so long, if that's your wish."

"Eh? What are you saying?"

"I'm saying, you don't have to wait so very long to die, if that's what you want."

"Oh? And how will you arrange that, little Maahes?"

"That's my problem. Is that what you want?"

"What if it is? What then?"

"First, you'll explain to me how a Goddess of Music had the power to reach into the minds of others to force them to do their bidding, then after we make sure that can't happen anymore, we'll get to the Rest In Peace part."

"You truly are a Son of Sekhmet, aren't you?" The Goddess laughed. "Thank you for that, Maahes, namesake of my friend. It's been many centuries since I heard myself laugh. I'm almost tempted to keep you here to make me laugh again."

"Trust me, Milady, that wouldn't work out well for you."

"You think not?" She reached into her robes, and then pulled out an armlet of darkened, luminous metal with onyx stones decorating it. "With Hypnos' device, I've found it rather simple to enter the minds of mortals, as you might have noticed. She sighed, mournfully. "Simple, but so very draining. Maybe there's a blessing in that. If it wasn't for the need to replenish my strength, perhaps many more innocents might have perished."

"Well, if you'll remember, Milady, when you entered my mind, you got jammed up pretty tight, and had to run when reinforcements came. Do you think I wouldn't have increased my defenses even more since then? To the point where you might end up being the one trapped?"

She sighed, not ready to call my bluff.

(It wasn't a bluff, by the way. She might have won a mind battle with me, but the skank woulda been limpin' bad, and wide open for payback from any of the members of my team. Alistra and Delphine put some Hella-nasty memes and constructs in our noggins!)

"Alright, then. Hypnos would probably hate me for what I've done with it anyway. Here." She stood up, looking down on me as she reached out with the device. I took it, and basically had to snatch it away from Kallan.

"I think I should hold on to that, Deputy. If you're going to do what I think you're planning to do, it just might be lost forever!"

"Would that be all that bad a thing to happen, Companion?"

"Its loss to future research would be a crime against all sapient beings!"

"Yes. You might be right."

The smile that stretched his face turned to a brief snarl of rage before he wiped it away, as he watched me hand the armlet to Della. At that point, I don't think he cared whether I saw the look on his face.

"Take care of that for me, Dee?"

"Of course, My Lion," Della winked wickedly as she placed the jewelry into her PDP.

"Now." Euterpe briskly came to her feet and stood before me. "How will you be taking care of my issue?"

"By killing you, of course."

"Will you?" she grinned. "And I'll just be standing here, letting that happen?"

"I wouldn't think so. If you did that, then that would be too close to taking your own life. You're celestial batteries are basically drained at the moment, so it's just one native of Lyrodrylle going head-up with another. I like my odds. And if you take me out, then I've got two lionesses eagerly waiting to finish the job." I smiled up at the muse. "Of course, I'm not telling you anything you don't already know. A big part of you is counting on it. Instead of taking your own life, we arrange conditions that would make your imminent death the most likely outcome. The humans I know call this sort of thing 'Suicide by Police', amongst other like terms."

"I get the idea. So you are expecting me to defend myself, then? Wouldn't that be unfair to you? I mean, you are only mortal, after all."

"No kidding, milady. So are you, when it comes down to it. Longer living, true, but still, especially at this particular moment in time, quite mortal."

"Well, that is true, so I suppose I should—"

She was inhumanly fast. Her arm was nothing but a blur, and her fist hitting the back of her chair made the whole piece of marble furniture explode. But she telegraphed her punch. As blindingly fast as it was, I still saw it coming from a month away.

I didn't have her speed, or power, hoped I didn't need it. What I did have was my hand on her stomach, and a Chained Lightning spell that I unleashed full-out in her exposed abdomen. The blast blew her across the space and had her back smash a full-body dent into the marbled wall. She shook herself free of the wall, and kept shuddering from the effect of a billion volts of electricity, the equivalent of three lightning bolts, simultaneously coursing through her body. She shook herself, patted out the mini fires amongst her clothing, and pulled out a pretty damned big sword.

"It's been ages," She snarled with glee. She flew in for the attack.

I faced her, braced and ready, with my Staff out and fully extended in my left hand, and one of my 24" Bowie knives in the right.

Major disadvantage? Not quite. My Staff was made of Tellerind wood, from the Mystic woodlands of Atlantis itself, and was imbued with my blood and Mana as I shaped sigils runes, shapes, symbols, and myself, into the wood with my fingers and nails alone. That was the way you not only strengthened the bond between you and your Staff, but you also strengthened and already near-on unbreakable slab of wood to the point where it was truly indestructible. Besides that, my Bowies were pretty much short swords, great for close-in work, and I chose to keep her close, not give her room to maneuver. And it really didn't matter which weapon was in which hand. Did anyone really think, after twenty years of full-out, no-holds barred hammering by a legion of deadly Maestros, that I hadn't become comfortably ambidextrous by then?

Her sword came hammering down, and I angled the Staff so it screeched down its side. She leapt back, away from my counter, and then kept leaping when I kept on the attack. Whatever rust she might have accumulated was starting to slide off.

Her sword was a modified scimitar. Not quite so hooked, more elongated. More like a stylized falchion, really. I loved its looks, even as it hammered into my Staff and made me stagger over and numbed my arm for a moment. She followed the side sweep with a thrust of its wicked sharp point. I redirected the thrust with my Bowie while brought the fist-sized knob of my Staff in towards her head. She whipped back just in time, and it just grazed her chin.

We circled around each other, looking for cues, finding none. She was enveloped in layers, I was covered by the cloak. Then she smiled, and disappeared.

Dammit.

I pulled a massive body shield down, just in time to get mule-kicked from behind and sent a good twenty feet through the air. Thank the Creator for conditioned reflexes, and the cloak, or she would have split me in two!

I padded my shield so I landed gently, then kept rolling when I saw her waiting to bring the sword down. She missed, and I dropped my Bowie long enough to bring the Staff two-handed into her right leg. If she wasn't a wannabe deity, she'd no longer have a leg from the knee down. As it was, she fell pretty damn hard, and I scrambled back to my feet after picking up my Bowie. We were both wounded. My back was screaming, her blade didn't penetrate, but by the Goddess, it hurt! Meanwhile, she would recover from the damage in her leg, but she was slowed at that moment.

We reengaged.

She had to work her sword with her off hand on the blade. I was staying in close. I jammed my Bowie to her chest. She grabbed it pulled me in for a head, but Hells, no! I yanked back, pulled her with me, then sent her over me and launched her into the air with my feet in her waist. I hopped to my feet while she scrambled to her feet, my Bowie in her hand. She smiled and launched the blade at my face. Again, she telegraphed, so it wasn't the most spectacular move in the world for me to catch the blade, pivot around, and send it right back, sinking it into her left shoulder. She yanked it free, howled with pain, and then launched it all the way out of the sanctuary. She stalked forward with her sword, rage turning her olive skin red. I gripped my Staff and flowed into my Bo Staff forms. The gems embedded on the shaft glowed reassuringly to me.

She was a lower-case goddess, true enough. Lived thousands of years. She seen 'em come, seen 'em go. Plenty of experience, plenty of lessons learned, plenty of triumphs. There was no way I should have been a few minutes from ending her existence.

Thing is, with all those millennia of experience, she spent most of it inspiring others to create great art with music. She fought nearly all of her wars by proxy. She rarely got her own hands dirty.

I, on the other hand, was a Child of Sekhmet. Sekhmet's Son. The Atlanteans created our race to be so many levels above 'human' limits, my ancestors Sekhmet, Menchit, and Maahes rivaled, and even defeated these 'Celestials', who were, in the final analysis, no more than extremely powerful sapient beings that left Lyrodrylle to rule the weak, ignorant humans.

They left because, even ten or twenty thousand years ago, there were plenty of beings native to Lyrodrylle that would wipe these pretenders out of existence if they even thought about acting like gods and goddesses on their home planet.

Beings like me.

I knew even then that I was outclassed. She did have thousands of years of experience, and even if she didn't have all that hellacious energy siphoned from others like her to hand, she was still an ex-goddess! But I didn't hesitate, whirling my Staff into the attack. Her sword became the merest blur as she blocked one attack after another. The air around us was scorched with spells. Twice more, my back and chest were blasted with Fire Storm spells, with only the dead vampire's cloak and the Order's hauberk saving me. That and my high resistance to magic. A backhand slash from her sword slammed into my Staff so hard, it sent me across the chamber, slamming me into one of the massive stone chairs. Her triumphant scream as she leapt in to finish me was cut off as I picked up the chair and smashed it into her, destroying the piece and sending her tumbling across the floor. I retrieved my Staff as she slowly made her way back to her feet.

It was that moment when I saw it in her eyes, the realization that it was more than just my name that was similar to the Maahes she remembered. That the blood of the Lioness did not get watered down over the countless generations. The glance she sent towards Melene and Della, both of whom were leaning against nearby chairs and waiting, with a touch of impatience on their faces, likely informed her that her time had indeed come. The Lionesses were being polite in allowing Euterpe to have her duel. They would not be if she triumphed. I couldn't tell if the deep sigh she released was in resignation, or relief, but it didn't matter either way. We faced each other, nodded as one, and reengaged.

If there's anyone reading this journal, and thinking I was criminally egotistical and far beyond merely stupid in challenging even a lower-case goddess, you clearly weren't paying attention. I reiterate—the Atlanteans built my kind to rival these beings, and/or defeat them. From the few records that still exist regarding the times of the Atlanteans, the enemies our creators had to contend with could destroy continents, ravage the ocean depths, even travel to other planets. And for close to two thousand years, my ancestors succeeded in safeguarding their creators, until the folly of the fatally curious Atlanteans destroyed themselves. This was the blood that ran through my veins. Besides that, as powerful as she might have been, Euterpe was not a Warrior. I was. I might have only been around for less than twenty-four years, but twenty of them were spent, day in day out, hour after bone-breaking, blood-spilling hour, preparing for War. For Euterpe, she created music and fought battles only when she was forced to. For me, the sound of battle is my music!

That made all the difference.

I hoped.

With a stabbed shoulder and a still-recovering knee, she was slowed noticeably. She put up a helluva battle; she was a proud ex-goddess, still with plenty of juice. But with my Staff, I twirled around her, kept her on the defensive, learned to roll as soon as she disappeared, then began using my shield to trip her up, confuse her footing. I timed one hard blow, for when she was stumbling forward, and caught her flush on the side of her face. She was slow to get up, and I waited, my left hand on my back. She saw my position. I guess she thought that if she could tag me again from behind, it might change the momentum. She really needed to stop telegraphing her moves.

I whirled as she disappeared. When she reappeared, instead of facing my back, she was facing my front, and had 24 inches of blade from my other Bowie sticking in her chest. Before she could react, I pulled the blade upward, the razor-sharp blade slicing through her lungs, then punching into her heart.

She coughed up blood, slumped into me. I held her up.

"It is done. Thank you, Maahes, Son of Sekhmet."

"My honor, Lady Muse. Sleep well."

Chapter 30. Those Damned Wobbe-gongs!

I wiped my Bowie on her robes, sheathed it on my back, then picked up her sword.

MY HANDS WERE ABOUT AS BIG AS HERS, so the grips felt very good. It felt like perfect balance, a little forward for great cleaving action. No way I was lettin' it go.

Melene arched an eyebrow as I moved in her direction.

"I know, my blade is coming, I know. And when it comes, I'll go two-handed!"

"I said nothing, Maahes. It's only your guilty conscious that makes you speak so to one who loves you so deeply."

"Wow, you went there." I hugged my beloved aunt/mother with both arms.

"I'm so very proud, my cub."

"Thank you, Mother."

She sniffed back a tear, and slowly let go. I kept a hold on her hand as Della came forward, and I gave her a big hug too.

"Kallan asked for the device," she whispered in my ear. "Twice."

"Okay. Get ready."

"Lee! That was absolutely brilliant!" Lisbeth gushed as she rushed forward, arms out. She jammed herself into my arms, hugging me. As she moved back, I felt her grab my left wrist, then, without warning, I felt light-headed, weakened. I fell to my knees. My whole body felt impossibly heavy, and worse, my magic. It was gone. I couldn't feel it at all! It felt like losing my hearing. Sense of touch—that and more.

"There, that's done, finally," Lisbeth smirked. "Waited long enough for that."

Both Della and Melene pounced to the attack, then suddenly shuddered and fell to their knees, then to the ground, writhing in agony. No—from the looks on their faces, writhing in ecstasy. I was thoroughly confused, until I smelt the scent in the air. Pheromones! There were pheromones in the air. Scat that—male pheromones!

"Sure comes in handy amongst your kind,"

It was hard to turn my head, but I did, and saw Kallan holding an aerosol sprayer. "You'll never know how much effort it took to get this sample of male pheromones of your breed. But then, you will probably be on your way to finding out, won't you?"

He chuckled as Lisbeth sidled up next to him. "I wish I could take a picture. You defeated vampires, defeated a significant section of a whole continent. You even executed a Goddess!

"And now, here you are, on your knees, watching your women laid out in clueless ecstasy, and you, defeated by your own team! How very pathetic you are."

"Cat-Scat," I snapped back. "You two pieces of hog turds aren't on my team! Where are they? Where are Liz and Kal?"

"But, Lee, darling! It's us," Lisbeth teased. "Don't you recognize your dearest teammates?"

"Where. Are. They?" I grounded out. "Did you kill them? Leave 'em in a ditch at The Cove. Seems like the kind of low class job you two might pull!"

"You insult your betters, you pathetic Beast!" Kal snarled. "Have you a clue as to how painful these days have been? Watching you strutting around, giving orders, as if you had a clue as to the true meaning of leadership! How an ape like you ever emerged as a leader is the best reason to wipe your kind out of existence."

"Blah, blah, scraggin' blah!" I ranted. "You packed them off to the smarter members of whatever lightweight, low-budget crew you got oozing through the cracks. Bloody amateurs!"

"Lightweight he says!" Lisbeth screeched! "You dare!"

"Hells Yes!" I railed back. I lifted my left arm, saw the Nullifier on my wrist and waved it at them. "Yeah, I know what this is. It's an Arcana Nullifier. It disrupts the brainwaves from perceiving one's own pool of Mystic energy. You know what else it is? It's a clear sign to even a dead, wretched dog that you are such a big pair of losers that you had to get that clamped on my arm before you even thought of coming at me!" I shrugged. "But then, hey, that's how low-budget, back-stabbing, third-rate jock-crabs like you two do business, so why should I be surprised?"

"Third rate!" The female dug into her bag and pulled out a large collector's satchel, then reached in, and pulled out another. "How's that, you black-faced baboon? How do you like that for third rate?"

"You have two big bags. Nice. Laundry? No, wait, we're in December on Earth. It's Mr. and Mrs. Claus, celebratin' Christmas. Presents for me! Wheeee!"

"You, disgusting, slobbering moron!" Kal roared. He unsealed the satchels and pulled them back, showing Kal and Liz in the satchels with Eliondrian oxygen masks on their faces. They were pale, and unconscious, but they were still breathing. "See your precious teammates? Alive, even while in a PDP! No one thought it possible, but we knew it was. That's how we'll be transporting you and these whores back to our labs."

"When you say 'we,' I assume you're talking about the U.S. Postal? Or maybe Federal Express?"

"No, you burnt-faced worm." The two shimmered. When they were done, two wholly different beings stood before me. Tall, pale, lithe, muscled. Beautiful. With long, pale hair and long, pointed ears.

"Well, horse turds sunny-side up!" I forced a chuckle. "Scraggin' Elves. The lowest, filthiest, back-stabbing'-est bags of maggot dung that ever existed in life. Of course you low-life cockroaches had to crawl up from the cracks sooner or later."

"Bastard!" The female's hand flared out, and I was bathed in flames. Thank The Creator for my mostly immune body and my new war cloak. Still felt a bit toasty.

I took my time crawling my way to my feet. Rolled a bit to my left. "So, Pus-Plus Twins, the plan is, what? Spray my aunt and Della with the pheromones, get them so caught up in their loins they can't think straight, while putting the clamp on me, and then what? Taking it off when you got me all locked up?" I smirked. "That's sounds about stupid enough for you two to Scrag up!"

"No, fool." The male sniggered. "These Nullifiers don't come off. You'll be having that one on, even after we've removed that arm from the rest of your body. By that time we'll have another placed elsewhere—probably around your neck."

Once again, I felt tired all over, as I pulled my clothing back, exposing the Nullifier clearly, then bent down to pick up my new sword. "Well, damn, I was so hoping that wouldn't be the case. Not removable, huh?"

"That's right, scum, you belong to us now." The female was actually drooling! What a slag. "You all belong to The Clans!"

"Beg to differ, darlin'," I replied as I got a good grip on the sword.

"Oh! He's going to try to fight us!" She clapped gleefully. "Remember, we can't kill him, at least not permanently."

"Look at him. He can barely stand. He's like a rabid dog."

"Wrong comparison, Bruh," I replied. "More like a wolf with his leg in a trap."

"What do you... No! You wouldn't!"

Yep, I would, and did. I put whatever muscle I had into my slash.

And cut that hand clean off.

∗∗∗

Bad news: It hurt like sticking my face in a lava pool.

More bad news: I'm about to go into yet another throw-down, this time one-handed.

Not so bad news: My Pride genetics meant my blood was already clotting around the wound, so I didn't have to worry too much about bleeding out.

Pretty good news: Even through the agony, I could feel my magic flowing through me.

Even better news: I'll save that for a bit.

I'm such a tease.

The male raced forward. I assumed he had a spare Nullifier. So I wasn't gentle with the kick I sent into his face.

The female expected me to go on the attack. That seemed my first, second and third option, in most cases. She was caught flat-footed when I hunkered down under a real heavy shield.

Caught flat-footed by Della, that is, who plowed a rabbit punch into her neck, hard enough for me to hear the snap from fifteen feet away and under my shield. The male had slowly risen to his feet, his face mostly smashed in, coherent enough to recognize his partner not being about to get up. In this life, at least.

"What? How?" Then he shut up and tried to save himself from the onslaught. He mostly failed.

That thing that folks in the know say about Ellovysians; That they're so dangerous because they can wield Talent, and are almost as physically gifted as Children of The Pride? See, when you're up against an actual Warrior Lioness of The Pride, that almost is gonna bite you in the butt, every time.

"My Lion! Maahes!" Della raced over to me after she made sure the male elf was thoroughly done, but alive. I heard our Director of Operations liked surprise gifts. "What have they done?"

"I did it, Dee," I replied. Thankfully the pain receptors were dialing it down some. "Thank The Creator you were able to pull out of the pheromone frenzy."

"Oh, that was done after about a minute. I was playing possum again. But I waited too late! You cut your damned hand off!"

"We're still behind enemy lines, love. I need my Talent more than I need two hands!"

"But you'll only have one hand to molest me," She whined. "I like getting gripped with both hands."

"You're certainly big enough for four hands, but you'll just have to be patient. It'll grow back eventually."

"We are getting very close to TMI Zone," my aunt groaned as she slowly rolled into a kneeling position. "Please tell me those vile creatures are dead!"

"One's dead, the other's about to be bagged and tagged." Della moved to help Melene to her feet, then went to the satchels and began freeing our teammates.

Melene collapsed into my arms. "I'll never forgive them, Maahes! Whoever's done this, they will all die in agony."

"They were Elves, Melene."

"Of course they were! Scraggin blight on all existence." She sobbed into my shoulder. "It was him, Lee. I recognized it. Those demons from the lowest pits are using Lionel's scent to capture Lionesses."

"Oh, Gods, No!" We wept, then wept a bit more when Melene realized I was holding her with only one hand.

"Where is the hand?" When she saw where it lay, she ran to it, put it in a smaller, secure satchel and put it away. "As long as we can get to a specialist in a few days, a week at the most, they can reattach it, and the healing process will be that much faster."

"But it took us four days to get here, and five days on the sub."

"We were walking in a combat crawl, Mas! We'll figure it out later. Come!"

It took about an hour for Liz and Kal to revive. Liz's first words were, "Jupiter's bowels! My mouth tastes like a baboon's behind."

Eloquent, our Liz.

She looked up at us bleary-eyed. "So? What did I miss?"

I hugged the Hells out of her. Kal, too. I was so glad they would be okay.

We spent some time bagging up the various articles of clothing and belongings of the dead deities. Not to loot this time. The Cadre needed to know who they were, how they died, and have their stuff inspected, inventoried, then laid to rest with the honors they deserved. They were lower-case deities, after all.

After all that, we broke out.

When we left the temple grounds, we noted that the space was deserted. No people, no visions, nothing.

"Euterpe must have been sending the visions," Della noted.

"Visions?"

"We'll explain later, Kal. We gotta move."

"Okay, Della. Wait! Stop! Where's our necklaces? We need them now!"

Melene handed him one she was holding. "The other one's around the Elf's neck."

"We need it. Right damned now!"

"Why? Why do we need them right now?"

"Melene, you have to trust me on this. Everything will be clear soon. Very soon. But we need those necklaces around our necks every waking second! Please!"

So, yes, we pulled the Elves, alive and dead, out of storage, took the necklaces, put them back in storage, and Kal and Liz settled down.

"There, now I got my Sexy back!" Liz snickered. "Hey, Lee. These streets look pretty wide, and I'm tired. Pull out the RV."

"That's a good call there," Della agreed. "It's not like we'll run anyone down."

So what took a few hours coming in took a lot less time going out. We stored the vehicle, then made our way through the gate.

Then jumped back into the pocket dimension.

"Who the Unholy Hells was that?" Kal stammered.

"I suspect that's an Ellovysian reception committee," Melene replied. "I guess the tracking device worked well enough."

"Certainly seems to be a lot of them." Liz noted breathlessly. "Gonna be a bear getting passed them!"

"Nah," I replied. It'll be easy-peasy."

"Are you okay, Lee?" Della asked worriedly.

"I'm fine. Okay let's go back to the temple."

"Why, boss?"

"Come, I'll show you."

We raced back down, and I looked around some. "Yeah, that section of wall will do. Let's get it!"

"I'm starting to catch up," Melene noted with a grin.

Soon, we had collapsed a building for a section of stone wall. Six feet high, six feet wide, two feet thick. Once we got it shaped properly using our blades, it took a while, we began carving grooves into the wall, eventually creating grips that would allow us to carry the wall before us without exposing any fingers.

"This is a nice little wall, Lee," Kal noted. "But it won't last very long with all that firepower out there."

"It doesn't have to. With the wall, and Liz and my shields, all we need is about six seconds—seven at most."

"And then what?"

"And then, boom."

✳✳✳

As expected, the enemy was waiting anxiously for our return. We'd barely cleared the gate before the stone wall began to disintegrate under the barrage of bullets, shells and spells. The team held the wall in place, Liz laid down the heaviest shields she could, and I began shaping the spell.

It was another AOE. The AOE. I learned it even before I could actually use it, and never did when I could. I always said that I never hated that many people to use it. That condition had changed.

I chided Billie Grantham for using it in the completely wrong setting. And I was right in doing so. Thor's Hammer was crafted for exactly these conditions.

"Della, Melene, remember…when I say 'Blitz,' pull us back through the archway."

"Ready!"

"Ready, my Lion!"

"Gotta go, Lee!" Liz's shields were taking a serious pounding. Imminent collapse.

I was done. I raised the hand I hand left, gripped it into a fist, and yanked it down as I shouted, "Kommen der Blitz!"

Then I leapt backwards through the portal.

"Everyone here?"

"Yep."

"Here."

"You're sitting on my face!"

"Is that why I was so comfortable?"

"Liz!"

"You're no fun at all, Kal. Lee, can—"

"No, Liz."

"Poo!"

"Should we check it out?"

"Nah, give it a few minutes, Kal."

"Why?"

"Because Thor's Hammer's been known to start forest fires, Kal. If Lee's Hammer was as big as I suspect, we might be walking into a lot of fire, secondary explosions of ammo cooking off, all manner of insanity!"

Della shook her head. "Good thing this area seems immune to fires. You're sure leaving your mark on Decados, Lion."

So while we waited, we gave Kal and Liz a quick sketch of life without them.

Liz shook her head. "Lee, I have to tell you, none of the Nemesenes sent to take down the pseudo-deities ever took out one solo. If Della and Melene weren't backing you, I'd have to call you a liar!"

I smiled. "But I didn't fight her by myself, Liz. I had help."

Della snapped a look at me. "What are you talking about? No one helped you!"

I shook my head. "Euterpe did."

Kal shook his head. "But you fought her. I'm confused."

"Euterpe had the accumulated energies of fifty Gods! Even if her major Mojo was drained to nothing, there was still no way in all Seven Hells that even a Child of The Pride would be able to defeat her straight-up. Unless she chose not to use that energy, and fight the duel as my equal. When she said she wanted to die, she really wasn't kidding about that. She fought as hard as she could, but on my terms, not hers."

Liz's eyes glazed over. "You knew that she would do that?"

"I suspected, didn't know."

My aunt leaned forward, her amber eyes glowing. "Liz, please don't try. There have been countless forums throughout all of Lyrodrylle that have discussed what might be the potential of a male of The Pride fully embracing the role he was specifically, meticulously created for by The Atlanteans tens of thousands of years ago. As much as we lionesses choose not to admit it, it was always supposed to be the males of our kind that were supposed to be the ultimate, super-soldier Warriors and Protectors.

"What I'm saying, Liz, is that for you, what Maahes did was a completely hare-brained, impossibly stupid act, and he was obviously blessed by The Creator to be able to survive his temporary insanity. You would see it that way, We All Would, because we don't see what he sees, we don't have his instincts. We don't share his feel for the moment, his genetic ability to assess his opponent, the circumstances and the possible options available the same way we would choose to go with a soup or salad before the entrée.

"Like you said before, Della. It's The Eye of The Predator. And the mind, and instincts to go with it. Sadly, dear heart, it'll be up to you to make sure he stays in one piece long enough for him to continue developing it into an asset he can rely on always, instead of every once and a while."

I didn't argue the point. As is often the case, Melene, my beloved aunt, my other mother, my Maestra, she helped to make clear to me, as well as others, what before was a vague, hazy notion in my head. I simply had to accept and embrace the fact that there were times when I saw patterns that seemingly no one else had a clue existed. It was disquieting, but it was real. Before Melene laid it out, I couldn't explain how I knew Euterpe wouldn't use all the power available to her, but at some unconscious level in my internal being, I did know that she would fight with what she was from her beginning, and not with all she had accumulated. I knew it, and acted accordingly.

I sighed internally as I felt Della's hand on my shoulder. Yet another something to explore and harness, somehow. Ah, well.

Kal, may Nemesene bless him, simply looked at me, smiled minimally, and winked. Then completely switched the subject.

"What really chaps my crack is all the good loot they got that we can't get to because of those Elf scabs. A whole damned vampire coven's lair? By the Gods and Goddesses!"

"We got plenty for you in our storage, Kal. And the guy isn't dead. With the right drugs, he'll probably pull out all his stuff. In fact, it might be crucial to find out what the Elf put in there, not wannabe-Kal." I stood up, sore all over, still drained. Della came up, put her arm around my waist.

"Thanks. Dee."

"My pleasure."

"Alright, Melene, lead out?"

She didn't haul it back. So we went through, and walked into Hell.

In a ragged circle of at least four football fields all around, there was nothing but burning trees, blackened earth, and burnt, broken bodies. Vehicles were flipped on their sides or completely on their backs, melted tires dripping into the ground. The air was thick and hard to breathe. I guess the space enclosing the PD entrance wasn't as immune as we thought.

"Scrag me!" Kal whispered. "This is Thor's Hammer?"

"Yeah," Liz coughed. "Learned it. Never wanna use it. No offense, Lee."

"None taken, Liz. This was a first for me. Hope it's the last."

"Enough!" Melene snapped. "The clock is ticking! Get out the RV!"

I did, then the fun really began, because my aunt got behind the wheel. My aunt was a great driver. I based this on the fact that she drove with reckless abandon and still somehow survived every time. If there was anything still alive between us and the east coast of this continent, it never stood a chance.

"Get on the horn to Lettie, tell her were coming in hot, should be there in a day and change!"

Liz did the honors. "Calling Tsunami, this is Decados away team!"

"Liz! Where the Hells ya been? How's the team? What's mission status?"

"Mission completed, were coming in fast, got an emergency. How fast can you make it back to the Cove?"

"Balls to walls? Major refitting after? Two days."

"Tell her Lion's Inc. will buy her a whole new friggin' sub if we have to!" Melene roared. "And get her to send a message to whoever's at Pilgrim's Cove. We'll be at the pick-up in about thirty hours. We need a surgical team and a portable Regen unit for the arm ready as soon as we get there."

"Surgical team?" Lettie stuttered. "Regen unit? Neptune's nuts! What happened?"

"My nephew was shaving the hair on his arm," Melene cried out. "And he cut his hand off!"

"Oh, thanks, Melene. Thanks heaps."

Chapter 31. Putting it All Together, Mostly

Things moved quickly from that point.

Lettie noted the state of the team, looked at the stump that used to have a hand attached, and dropped the hammer. Della took me to bed, and kept me there for the two days we hauled to Pilgrim's Cove. That was pretty great. We didn't do much at all. I was pretty damned tired. Dropping the two most powerful AOE spells in the whole damned book in less than a week, going toe-to-toe with a lower-case goddess, and cutting your own hand off. It takes it out of you after a while. So I cuddled up with my Lioness, ate tons of food, and tried to replenish my Energies. And I learned more about my Della. We shared, we laughed. And we loved.

From what I was told, as soon as the sub broke the surface at Pilgrim's Cove, Director Ginley had translocated to the conning tower and was banging on the hatch to be let in. He hopped down the ladder, followed the directions to my cabin, hauled up close to four hundred pounds of semi-conscious body, and translocated me directly to the operating theater they set up in one of the surviving structures in the town.

Then the surgeons had to wait for the hand to show up.

A few hours later, I was coming out of sedation with the portable Regen Unit attached to my arm. A silver haired, striking woman was standing over me. I recognized her immediately.

"Hello, ma'am?"

"We never did properly meet, did we?" The Chief Director smiled. "Jadis Morgan, your uber-boss. I am very pleased to finally meet you face to face, Maahes. You've certainly had a time of it, haven't you?"

"I sure hope it's not always this exciting, ma'am."

"I can't say, Young Man. Some people just can't avoid the eye of the hurricane, no matter how hard they try."

"Well, that just fills me with the warm and fuzzies."

"I'm sure," She chuckled. "Well, the surgery went well. Your hand is back in place, and the medical team tells me you only need a month with the unit and you'll be fully healed. That should be enough time to get your affairs in order."

"My affairs, ma'am?"

"Yes. First, if you're wondering where everyone is at the moment, they are all sitting in debriefing. If you are further wondering, yes, I did make it mandatory that they all have their debriefing now." She smiled wickedly. "I wanted a little alone time with you,"

"I see. Okay, no, I don't."

"Excellent, Lyam. Stick with honesty, it's your strong suit. Now, your affairs. Tomorrow, you will be going through your debrief. It will be thorough. From the time you were hired as a bodyguard for Ms. Flores, all the way up to being taken off the sub for your surgery. You'll not only be asked what happened and what you did, you will be asked to explain your choices, how did you feel, before, during and after, an honest, thorough evaluation of your own performance and that of your team. Please know beforehand that everyone involved is there to help you continue in your growth as an agent.

"After that little stroll through Paradise, you'll be celebrating your 24th birthday in a couple days. From what I've been informed, that will entail you coming into your full inheritance, which will include certain items of information as well as some rather fundamental financial adjustments you'll have to deal with." She smiled again. "I don't think I've ever sat with someone who could actually buy a whole country, easily. Anyway, these changes are going to cause a significant amount of reevaluation on your part. With this in mind, I think it best for you to go on medical sabbatical for two months, then when you are ready, you will be reactivated, with a higher Deputy ranking."

"Milady! I'm not worthy of the same rank as my aunt. I've only been the field this once!"

She smiled, "That's up for debate, Lyam—but no, I did not say Deputy Premier. I said higher rank. It will be a specialized designation, Lyam. The specialization will be explained to you very soon.

"For now, simply rest and recover, Lyam. You have indeed served the cause of Justice well."

I remember being visited later that day, but it was pretty fuzzy. I needed the rest anyway.

The next day, I found out the art of handling your business with one arm in a big metal cocoon. Not easy. Della came in with breakfast and kisses, Melene came in with mail and hugs, and Kal and Liz came in and tried to eat my food. They met with an extraordinary lack of success.

Then came the beatdown. I spent the whole day and half the next going over Every. Damned. Thing.

"Deputy Alabato has more field experience. Why did you not choose her for point?"

"What were you thinking as the Werebear punched you through the brick wall?"

"Did buying this vehicle assist the efficiency of the mission? And do you have a receipt for it?"

"What was your rationale for allowing Mistress De Vore to survive her possession?"

"When did you suspect that Mr. Drenner and Ms. Ridder were actually Elves?"

"Was there no other option in dealing with the retired deity Euterpe?"

And so on, and on.

And on.

By the middle of the second day of debrief, I was wondering if I really was Lyam Seckett, and whether there was an unconscious, subliminal urge to disassociate myself with the name 'Maahes.' Or something. And if there was a little Goth-chick in me, since I wore black so often.

Yeah, it went that deep.

Finally informed that the debrief was over, and thanked for my cooperation and forthright answers, I jumped in the RV and just scraggin' left. The crew came with, and we spent a day blazing our way North, back to La Pleasaunce. When we got there, we stayed on the perimeter, passed all the fun and play, and booked it to the Veil Waypoint. There were Lionesses of the Garrison on duty. They couldn't be avoided, and I wasn't in the mood to hide anyway. My team got off our vehicle, I popped it into the PDP (One handed!), and we waited online to make our way through the Waypoint.

Of course, a squad of soldiers came to a stop before me.

"Excuse me, Sir. Would you happen to be Deputy Seckett of The Nemesene Cadre?" The Master Sergeant asked.

"Yes."

"Our commandant, Major Varella, wished me to ask you if it were possible for you to stop by her office before your departure?"

"If it is not required, I'd rather just proceed." I pulled back the cloak to show them my arm in the Regen unit and in a sling. "We completed our mission successfully, but there were complications."

"I see. You are expecting a full recovery, we hope?"

I shrugged. "I'm a Child of The Pride, Master Sergeant. And I'm not dead."

Her lips quirked. "The Major will be happy to hear that, sir. As will the rest of the garrison."

I stayed silent at that. There was a lot that could have been said. The soldier's lips tightened.

"I understand, Deputy. But there are more of us that honor your family than you might be led to believe. Like the Major. And myself."

I nodded. "Thank you for that, Master Sergeant. And I do hold in high esteem our Homeland, even if I'm not fully welcome there yet. I would ask you to have your Major contact Director Alons Ginley of The Cadre. He's presently in Pilgrim's Cove, and he may have very valuable information regarding the disappearance of females of The Pride."

The soldier gasped. "Sir, if I may ask, what could possibly be happening at Pilgrim's Cove?"

I shrugged. As far as I knew, it wasn't classified. Yet.

"That's the fastest way to Decados. We went there to deal with the attacks on emerging young musicians. It's been dealt with."

The commentary amongst the listening soldiers ranged from shock to awe.

"You went into Decados? Just you five?"

I smiled. "I have a helluva team, Master Sergeant. Have a good day."

Before I could turn away, the six snapped into attention and gave me a salute. I placed my palm on my breast and bowed in reply, and we left.

"Kinda different from last time?" Liz noted.

"Kinda different."

***

After we made it through Mexico, and cleared customs, we found ourselves, once again, surrounded on all sides, low on resources and without a clear path to safety. This time, it wasn't enemy forces. At least, I don't think they were.

They were fans.

It must have been the calls we made to Trini and Megan that we dealt with the threat and they were safe. There were a scrag-ton of her fans, and at least three camera crews, and the hovering cam-pods made it clear that agencies on the other side of The Veil were lurking as well.

Oh yeah, there's Trini and her family and friends jumping and shouting with the rest of them. They're all insane!

"C'mon, Lee!" Lisbeth was pulling at me for some reason, then I saw the reason. She was unfastening the cloak, while Melene was bringing my 'signature' duster for me to put on.

"Et tu, Mater?"

"You didn't think you'd just sneak in through the back door did you?" Melene chortled. "You're a hero, Maahes. A real one, not a manufactured construct of Madison Avenue."

It was a mess. Not awful, per se. But a mess.

The camera caught Trini and crew rushing forward as we descended the hatch's stairs. Saw her gently touching the device on my arm, and then wrapping her arms around my neck. The whole team got swamped by the family, while the cops valiantly tried to keep the fans at bay. The crew led us to a line of luxury transports, and we whisked off. Not to home, but to a celebration fete at Dante's Retreat. U.T.A. rented out the whole damned venue. We ate, we drank, we shared a sanitized version of events. They didn't need to know the horrible bits. I loved 'em, but they weren't soldiers.

When we finally made it back to the house, Trini and Megan kissed me warmly then made their way to other bedrooms in the house. They respected the new dynamic, bless their hearts.

Honestly, it was Della's suggestion to go find them and drag them back to my room. Well, when we found them, it was more like us running to keep up with them.

The frisky little kittens.

***

The next day, I woke in a tangle of perfect womanhood and realized I had just turned 24 years old. When you're that young, you can't tell me there's a better way for a young hetero male to start the day!

After a few hours of early birthday presents, already delightfully unwrapped, we made our way down the stairs and were confronted by a platoon of suits.

"Well, damn!" I groaned. "Have I been drafted?"

"No," Melene chuckled. "You are of age, according to Lyrodryllian standards, as your parents stipulated. Since that is the case, it is time for you to meet with your personal lawyers as a fully autonomous adult, and receive a comprehensive study of your portfolio."

"And I've said often enough this particular stipulation is wrong-headed and full of beans," snorted Noah Silverstein, a tall, heavyset man who walked with a limp and silver-headed mane of hair that he only 'trimmed' after his wife threatened him with divorce for the fourth time that week. The swarm of children at family outings and the certain twinkle in the elderly lady's eye informed all that that possibility was remote at best.

I greeted the elder warmly. He and his partners were as devoted to the family as my parents were to them when they chose Blake, Silverstein and Goldman, as their family lawyers. Even as young men, just starting their practices, the three had always combined integrity, business acumen, instincts, and the ferocity of sharks with blood in the water to best assist their clients. When they decided to hitch their stars to the Seckett Family, my parents repaid that devotion by making them the wealthiest, most prestigious private practice in most of Earth. (Only middle-of-the-pack amongst the lawyer types on Lyrodrylle, but most of those were vampires, reformed warlocks, revenants, and had been in the business a minimum of four hundred years.)

I had spoken with the gentlemen on many occasions, broke bread with the families a number of times, but this would be the first time we broke open the seal to my portfolio, so to speak, and got down to brass tacks.

"I see you've got one of those Regen thingies on you," Jethro Blake commented as he shook hands. "You're well enough?"

"I'll be fine, Mr. Jethro. Rough turn on a mission, but I'll be fine."

"I don't like it!" Mr. Noah rumbled. "Said it often enough, meant it every time! Don't like my people putting themselves in harm's way when there's plenty others not doing a damned thing!"

"Noah, he's a Seckett!" Ira Goldman shook his finger at his partner. "They see it as their duty to make the worlds safer! He'll do his part. We always knew that! We, in the meantime, do our part and make sure they can afford to keep giving to others!"

"Hmph, well, it's unnatural, I say. A little selfishness, here and there, hey? Duck the bullets instead of running at them, hey? What's the harm, I ask you!"

"Oh really?" I laughed. "This coming from the one still limping from the bullets he took in Indochina! Only reason you started your lawyer gig so early is they kicked you off the Marines' active duty roster!"

"You young scapegrace!" He swung his cane at me, which I of course ducked.

"Will you children settle down!" Melene roared, though she was trying not to laugh. "Yes, Noah, it took long enough to get to this business, so quit your playing and let's get to it!"

It took a minute, with all the assistants, clerks getting everything organized.

I won't bore you with the details, list all the holdings, managing interests, investments, controlling shares, all the divisions, subdivisions, stock options.

The bottom line was, I was one of those individuals (not companies, individuals) that required a new word in the dictionary to clearly illuminate just how impossibly wealthy I was, not only my personal estate, but with those I accrue with my families controlling interest in Lion's Share Inc. I could literally go into a room with a billion dollars sitting around, light the room on fire, burn it and the billion dollars to ashes, and miss the room more than the money. Especially if the couches were comfy.

It was a weird feeling, being that wealthy. I mean, look—I grew up in a whale of a house, I had private tutors for every blessed thing, until I enrolled in Cremon Eft on scholarship. My teachers and trainers sure weren't doing it for free. I didn't have a car or bike, mainly because I had nowhere to go for so long. But if I did, I'm sure it wouldn't have been a buck-and-a-quarter hooptie. I was never hurtin' for money, never felt without, financially, that is.

But after this? Well, damn, what do I do with all this?

I had some ideas.

"You want a WHAT!" screeched Mr. Noah.

"I want a submarine."

"Lyam," Mr. Ira sighed. (He was really good at filling his sighs with anguish and despair.) "I know we asked you what might be the first thing you would splurge on, but we were thinking maybe a car, or a penthouse or maybe even a yacht! But a submarine?"

"If I might ask, why, Lyam?" Mr. Jethro leaned forward, thoroughly intrigued.

I lifted up my arm. "You see this Regen machine on my arm? It's there to finish healing the surgery on my hand, Mr. Jethro. I had to chop my own hand off to get free of a weapon that cut me off from my Mana. Aunt Melene said we needed to get me off Decados, back to the southern coast of Aldemeron for emergency surgery to reattach my wrist to my arm, and we had to get there in less than a week. The submarine captain turned a five-day run into two days. Now, I get to take this off in a month, instead of three to five months to grow back the whole hand. Because of that, and because with regard to ridiculous missions that no one should survive, I'm just getting started." I looked around the table. "I know it seems frivolous and unnecessary. But I'd rather have equipment that gathers dust than be stuck in the warzone needing something I chose not to get because it didn't seem the smart thing to do when I had the chance."

"You make a compelling point," Mr. Ira nodded. "I didn't consider your being so focused on your present line of business. You do intend to take the time to enjoy yourself, occasionally?"

I thought about the way the morning started. "Yes, Mr. Ira. I do take the time to have fun, every once and a while."

Melene spluttered into her coffee. No idea why. Really.

"Well, dammit, if the man's heart is set on a submarine, let's look over the possibilities."

"Mr. Noah, another consideration? It might be good for secure transport of precious or perishable items. I wouldn't think a full military crew would be needed, so I was thinking something along the attack sub size, but with decent capacity, which could be increased with modifications, and a smaller-"

"You had me at precious, Boy! Don't gild the lily! That might not be a bad idea at all! Who has a fleet of available submarines that can move cargo, or people, without anyone noticing a thing?"

317

I saw the silent communication amongst the elders. If there was a way to make a healthy profit (And there was), those three will think it was their idea in another two or three years.

"Was there anything else on your wish list, Lyam?"

"Well, Mr. Jethro, I did consider the possibility of a surface vessel that could assist in missions as well, and…"

"So, you do want a yacht. I knew it!"

We kicked a few other items around. One that I brought up that they could understand and endorse was me beginning the process of owning majority shares in Blue Star Security, personally. I liked that company a lot. They had good people, good management, and I wanted them to have a bigger footprint, to make sure they didn't have to get caught up in politics again. Except from me, of course.

And, well, it was fuzzy in my head at that moment, but there were some ideas floating around in my brain, and I wanted that particular company available to me when they became clearer to me.

"Well that wraps up just about everything," Mr. Ira looked at his watch. "And in less than four hours. Good job, everyone! Now, all there is to review are the trusts for the Twins, and…uh, hm."

Everyone at the table was frozen, looks of worry and almost fear etched clearly. Everyone but me, that is. I looked at the frozen faces with growing anxiety.

Then I heard his words resounding in my head.

Twins? These men of high finance, these quiet titans of industry, have a trust fund for my imaginary friends?

I thought of Melene's words, only a month or so ago. I thought about the conversation I overheard when I was rambling on the astral plane.

"Mr. Ira, what do you mean? Who are the Twins?"

"And this is where I come in!"

All eyes turned to Dr. Delphine Mendenhall, leaning in the doorway to the formal dining room where we were meeting. "It's time, Melene. As far as I'm concerned, past time."

"Yes, it's time. Ira, I feel confident in saying, do what you gentlemen think is best. We will be content. Now, I must pull Maahes away, for a long overdue session with his doctor. Thank you all. Lee? Let's go."

Melene's march had me close to racing after her. We turned into the study, where Doc Delphine was waiting. Melene closed the door behind us, and then opened it again to let Della through. Then she closed it, and locked it. "Thank you for coming Della. This concerns you too. When you hear what will be discussed, you'll understand."

Della nodded, and murmured something I could barely hear, something 'More than you know,'", then sat next to me and held my hand, her head turned down, and away from me. I was, again, clueless of what was happening with her, but I appreciated her being there. I was suddenly full of anxiety, and I didn't know why.

"This will go much easier on us all if you can find your way to relaxing, Mas."

"Mas?" I gulped.

"Yes, Mas. That was the familiar name we called you from the time you were born. You don't remember that now. You will."

"I...I think I like that nickname." I stared at the calm doctor. "It's kind of cool, I think. Why did we stop using it? Why did I choose to call myself Lyam?"

"Well, for one, Lyam's a pretty cool name, too. But mainly, it was because you had to call yourself something, after Mas was no longer available and you didn't feel comfortable with Maahes yet."

"Why was Mas no longer available to me?"

"We'll get to that in a bit. We have to get to the guts of the issue now, Mas. Do you trust me?"

I looked at her, worried, but not a lot. "Of course I trust you, Doctor Del. You've always been there for me."

"And I always will be, Mas. Believe that. Hold on to that. Now, I want you to lean back, relax, and talk to me."

"About what, Doc?"

"About your dreams, Mas. Talk to me about your dreams. Tell me of all your dreams about your imaginary friends.

"Your friends, Maia and Camilla.

"The Twins."

Epilogue.
Three weeks before

"BUT I DON'T WANT TO LEAVE YOU!"

"I know, Hal. I don't want you to go. You've grown on me. And you're finally hittin' it right on purpose instead of accidentally. But you have to go. Belinda and Lionel are finally at a point where they can defend themselves if they have to, but they still got a way to go. And it's been too long. We've had it rough, but we've been together through the rough times. Can you imagine what it's been like for Melene? For Maahes? Not knowing anything, not getting any messages, any kind of sign? Just those two against everything? Not even knowing for sure who the potential enemies are?

"Hal, what do you think'll happen if Maahes runs into Elves and he ain't ready?"

"You're right. I'll go. I gathered everything already, but I guess… no. You're right. It's been too long. Oh, God! All this time, I completely forgot. We never got a chance to tell Maia and Camilla anything. Oh, my God. I've got to go. Oh, those poor babies!"

"You're right, Hal. By the Gods, you're right. I can't imagine how abandoned they must be feeling. Please, Hal, you've got to make it through. We all need you to make it!"

"I think you've noticed by now, My Love, very little stops me when I've made up my mind."

320

"I did indeed notice. Will you stop that? Okay, one more…um yes, one. Oh, yes, yes! You are so bad, Mr. Bergen!"

✳✳✳

The drivers and militia men were at first annoyed at having the pale-faced stranger foisted upon them at the last minute. The members of the caravan all knew each other well; they had a standard. The white man wouldn't be tough enough. He would complain, whine about missing comforts. He would slow them down, annoy them. But the monks of New Israel were insistent. If the caravan wanted to continue being the private sellers of the exceptional pottery and leather goods from the nearly unfindable island community, they would have to include the stranger on the run back to Gravisol, the large city 500 miles off the west coast of Pangea. It wasn't their longest leg, the traders reasoned. They would drop him there and move on.

This was their opinion, up to when the raiders came to attack. The desert tribes in the area don't often raid passersby, but if the rainy season was dryer than hoped, they were more desperate, and more likely to take what they couldn't provide for themselves. The watchers had weapons, and knew how to use them well.

Not as well as the stranger. Seconds after the first cry of warning, four raiders were stretched out in the sand and two others were slowly crawling away. The rest were easy to convince to leave them be. Sudden, merciless death tends to win most debates in the desert.

Three days later, another desperate tribe attempted a night-time raid. They were able to wound two of the drivers before a flare burst high in the night sky, illuminating all skulking enemies around the wagons. Before the space fell back into darkness, eight raiders were killed by the stranger, and the rest were fleeing away.

The leaders of the caravan had soon decided that it might be a good idea to ask the white man just where he was going, and hope that he was going their way?

✳✳✳

A week later, two tall men dressed in the flowing robes and face wrappings of the locals took note of a tall, lanky man walking through the middle of the main street in Masook, a small, unobtrusive town on the outskirts of the Panquin Desert, located toward the interior of the southern regions of Pangea. The only reason for Masook's existence was the Veil Waypoint that attached this part of Lyrodrylle to the outskirts of Phoenix, Arizona. One of the bigger cities that survived The Sundering, mostly intact, the trade between the two locations was decidedly one-sided, but there were advantages to using Masook as a pseudo-Gateway to the rest of Lyrodrylle.

The two men noted that the man looked thoroughly trail worn, with a face darkened by constant days in the sun, but he walked strong, determined, and unerringly towards the Waypoint. The two spoke quietly in their race's lilting language.

"He is not of The Pride."

"He is a white man in a land of brownskins. He looks to have been on the road for a time. He might have seen something interesting."

"You are bored and want something different to do. Do not dress it up in suspicious cant!"

"Well, why not? It's been a while since we went over to the human city."

"Yes, why not?"

They followed as the man made his way to, then through the Waypoint. They took their time. No need to rush. They were disturbed, however, when they crossed over to Earth.

"Where did he go? He was just in front of us!"

"I don't know! Perhaps-"

"His words cut off as his throat suddenly exploded into blood and fragments. His partner decided that it was time to go. He was able to take one step back to the Waypoint before his head erupted and his corpse dropped to the ground, nearly headless.

Hal was courteous enough to drag the bodies away from the Waypoint. Who would want to see two bloody corpses as soon as they exit into Phoenix? He didn't bury them, though. Desert creatures had to eat too.

This was not who he was eleven years ago. He was kinder, gentler, more caring of others. That man wasn't gone. He was simply allowing the other Hal to run things for a while. The one who shot first and didn't bother with questions. The one who negotiated at the end of a rifled barrel. The man who had twice now left family, to go find family. And this Hal Bergen was grim and determined to accomplish this task, then turn right around and return to his family of warriors.

He smiled as he made his way to Phoenix.

Knowing one particular Lioness as well as he did, he was quite sure he wouldn't be returning to New Israel alone.

Maahes was a Lion, now. Melene would have made sure of that. It was time for Melene to rejoin her Pride, and for Maahes to form a Pride of his own. He would find his Maia and Camilla, and his Pride would grow from there.

It was time for Maahes, a Son of Sekhmet, to let the worlds hear his Lion's Roar!

End